JO BUER

Unspoken Truths

First published by Jo Buer Publications, New Zealand 2021

Copyright © 2021 by Jo Buer

Paperback - ISBN 978-0-473-57849-7

Kindle - ISBN 978-0-473-57851-0

EPUB - ISBN 978-0-473-57850-3

First edition

ISBN: 978-0-473-57849-7

Editing by https://www.hannahsullivanediting.com/
Cover art by https://www.valuedcreations.com/

This book was professionally typeset on Reedsy.
Find out more at reedsy.com

For dream chasers everywhere...

Contents

Prologue

"You said I killed you – haunt me, then! The murdered do haunt their murderers, I believe. I know that ghosts have wandered on earth. Be with me always – take any form – drive me mad! Only do not leave me in this abyss, where I cannot find you! Oh God! It is unutterable! I cannot live without my life! I cannot live without my soul!"
- ***Wuthering Heights***

Chapter 1 – Riley

Riley glanced around. She was alone. Exhaling, she loosened the grip on her keys. The whole thing was ridiculous. Victoria Stone, the principal of Te Tapu Primary School and her new boss, had handed the keys to her a month prior, assuring her she could set up class anytime during the summer holidays. Yet she felt as if she were trespassing.

The day was beautiful with the sun out in full force. It hit the side of the building with a blinding glare, reflecting off the white weatherboards. The azure sky met a horizon of rolling green hills, dotted with grazing black-and-white cattle. Three silk trees stood like decorations along the front of the main building, greeting her with candy-floss pink blossoms. *Welcome*, they whispered, *it'll be our secret.*

Four weeks earlier, Riley had met with Victoria. Along with giving her a set of school keys hanging from a frayed fabric lanyard, she showed Riley how to disarm the alarm and allowed her a cursory glance at her new classroom. It all seemed so strange. Exciting too. This was her new life. Far away from the city, far away from the people she knew, and far away from Justin. With a new career to boot.

The main building was original to the school. Concrete steps led to a long deck running the length of the sun-facing building. The office and staffroom took up the left portion of the building. Her classroom took up the middle lot, with resource rooms and toilets next door.

Double doors and large windows, relics of the fashion for open-air classrooms during the tuberculosis epidemic, took up much of the outward facing walls.

Riley made her way towards the front steps, smiling as she caught herself bouncing on the ball of her toes. On the wall of the building, a small sign in faded green print read "Office". She didn't need the sign, as she remembered her way from the previous few times she had visited the school for her interview and orientation.

She paused on reaching the door and turned around, looking out past the silk trees, across the courts and field. A newly painted fence separated the school from the drop-off area and the main road running through Te Tapu. Beyond that, more hills and valleys speckled with stock and a few distant houses. Perfectly idyllic.

Despite the heat of the day, goosebumps rose on her arms, and she shivered. Without the kids, the school was eerily quiet. It felt different, as if the school itself were holding its breath, lying in wait to see what she would do. She rubbed her arms and almost jumped out of her skin when a milk tanker roared past the school, ignoring the reduced speed limit.

She was alone; she reminded herself. Though the thought was meant to be comforting, her skin prickled more.

With one last glance around her, Riley turned back to the door and twisted the key in the lock. Pushing open the door,

3

she searched along the wall for the alarm pad Victoria had shown her. Small green lights flashed on the screen. Riley swallowed. What if she put in the wrong code? She shook the thought from her mind. 1905. Easy. The year the school first opened.

She pressed the keys of the number pad, slow and hard, listening for the beep after each selection. Then, with an exhale of relief, she flicked on the light switches beside the alarm.

Done. She was in. The school was hers to explore.

The admin block was as she remembered it from her tour. A disjointed fusion of past and present, the bones of the room were identical to her classroom next door. High ceilings and one wall of large double doors that folded in upon themselves and opened to the concrete deck. Windows too high to reach spanned the length of the room. Too high to clean too, as shown by the thick cloak of spider webs covering their corners.

At some point, the room she stood in had been a classroom. Now, a partial wall, not quite reaching the ceiling, divided the room into two: an office and reception area, and a staffroom. A photocopier stood proud and intimidating against this wall. Further along, a double-doored, stainless-steel fridge and freezer stood stoic. Posters and notices littered every other wall – pedagogical prompts and motivational prints, faded and curling from the sun.

Riley moved closer to the space where a whiteboard and yearly calendar hung on the wall. The calendar was from the previous year. Graffitied with dates and events, term starts and term ends, it offered no clues yet as to the year ahead. A printed class list hung from the whiteboard by two mismatched magnets. Victoria had given her an identical copy on her previous visit. Riley would start the year with twenty-two students. Small class sizes – a perk of working in a country school.

A staff photo hung on the wall, half-hidden by what appeared to be meeting minutes. Riley had already met most of the staff in passing during her orientation. She took the moment now to study them. What were they really like, she wondered, behind those frozen faces? How many of those smiles were real? Next, her face would hang on the wall. She bit down on her own creeping smile, her insides prickling with excitement.

Enough time being nosy; she scolded herself. What she had really come to do was take inventory of her classroom and make a list of things she needed and wanted to start the year off right.

After closing the unlocked reception door, she moved along the deck to her classroom. The door opened easily with a twist of her key, and Riley crossed the threshold into her new life.

The previous occupants had stacked the classroom furniture around the outskirts of the room. For the carpet cleaners, Victoria had mentioned.

When Riley had first been shown around, school was in session. Now, without warm bodies at desks and artwork covering the walls, the room showed its age. And its dirt. A film of dust and grime covered every flat surface. Random odds and ends lay scattered on chairs and under tables: pens and rulers, miscellaneous maths equipment, and what appeared to be a few pages torn from a dictionary. Staples tattooed the walls, some still holding torn corners of artwork, and long thick threads of webbing hung across the corners of the room. The first things she needed to purchase were cleaning products.

Victoria had said they'd had quite the succession of teachers for her role. For some reason, they just never seemed to work out. Riley decided she'd be the one to break the curse. And she'd start by giving the room a thorough cleaning.

Using her phone, she snapped a few pictures of the room, the furniture, the inside of the cupboards.

She shivered again. Someone was definitely tap dancing on her grave today. She stole a glance out a window. The front of the school and main road were empty. Silent. Riley shook herself and put it down to nerves. She had every right to be there, she reminded herself for the umpteenth time, despite a growing desire to leave.

It didn't take long to set the alarm and lock up, and with quick steps she made her way to her car. As she got to the driver-side door, she felt the weight of someone's gaze resting on her. Her heart faltered for a moment as she turned and locked eyes with a stranger.

Her gut had been right. She hadn't been alone.

From her position, she could see down to the end of the back field where a wooden shed stood in the corner. A wheelbarrow leaned up against its side. He stood beside it, leaning on his shovel in front of its door, just watching. Riley pulled her hand up to shade her eyes from the sun's glare. He didn't move.

She couldn't see his face, in part because of the distance, but also because it was in shadows from the brim of his baseball cap. He was tall, standing solid and self-assured, as if he had sprung from the earth itself. Rolled-up shirt sleeves exposed bronzed arms.

Riley fluttered her fingers in a cautious wave and gave a smile she hoped hinted at confidence. If he had smiled back, she couldn't see it. Instead of a return wave, he picked up the shovel and turned his back to her, making his way to the other side of the field.

Feeling the whiplash of his snub, she hugged her arms to herself, then stilled. She hadn't seen the other man at first, hidden as he'd been by the taller man's form, but she was grateful when he gave the front of his hat a small tug in her direction. An old-fashioned greeting. Riley offered another smile and a finger wave in return. With fewer shadows on his face, she was sure she saw his lips quirk upwards in response.

After climbing in the car, she turned the key, an unexpected lightness filling her chest. Before reversing, she took a last peep out the window towards the shed. Both men had disappeared.

How long had they been standing there? Had they spied her nosing around the staffroom? She winced at the thought, then shook it off. She belonged here. She could feel it.

Following the driveway to the main road, Riley thought of the second man's smile. Sometimes all you needed was one friendly face to know you were in the right place.

Chapter 2 – Gwen

"I wish I were a girl again, half-savage and hardy,
and free."
*- **Wuthering Heights***

The drive had been long and arduous. The metal road had given out to gravel and then dirt, as they weaved their way through the bends and folds of brush-dotted hills. Although the windows were closed, the vehicle still seemed to fill with dust, making Gwen's eyes gritty and sore.

Another half hour to Te Tapu Village, the driver told Gwen. This knowledge was met with mixed emotions. For one, she had been over the drive almost an hour earlier. Moving to the back-blocks swamp country had never been part of Gwen's plan for becoming a teacher. She'd learnt later how naïve she had been.

As if God himself had been listening and sought to punish her further, the weighted clouds opened above them and released a down-pouring, which slowed their journey even more.

"Okay, back there, miss?" The driver turned slightly in his seat, making eye contact with her.

Mother's going away gift was paying for a driver to take her to her new home, then to leave her there, stranded. That, at least, was the way Gwen saw it now.

"I'm fine," she said, crossing her arms over her chest.

The driver's eyes never moved from the road after that. The single windscreen wiper barely made a difference to the ferocity of the deluge. Water pooled on the surface of the dried earth, and the driver struggled to keep the car on the lane.

Gwen gritted her teeth and tried to stop herself from sliding around too much in the back seat.

Saints preserve us, she thought. This is not how I want to die.

Her anger surprised her.

Teaching had sounded like a good choice at the time. She needed something to escape her family, her mother and the wretched Dr Gerald. And the thrill of shocking them definitely added to the appeal.

Only it *hadn't* shocked them. Despite the Davies women not working, her mother seemed relieved to see her go. Maybe her father's coffers were not nearly as full as they had led her to believe, or maybe her moments of passion were too intense for her mother's austereness.

She was thankful to be out from under the watchful eye of the doctor, whose visits had become more frequent of late. At first, Gwen had wondered if her mother had feelings for him. It wouldn't have surprised her. For a man in his fifties, he was still quite striking. Moustache oiled to within an inch of its life. Clothes immaculately laundered. Profuse flattery gushing forth whenever he was in her presence. Few widows, Gwen was sure, could resist such attention.

But his profession worried her the most. His fascination with studying diseases of the mind, not to mention his particular interest in Gwen's Aunty Jeanne, who resided in such an asylum. Gwen caught the doctor staring at her sometimes at the dinner table and wondered if this was also how he studied her aunt. With a tightening of her skin, her jaw clenched, and she'd have to excuse herself so as not to cause a scene.

Gwen's sisters were not so bothered by the doctor's presence. Hilda, the eldest, had married an accountant. With her first child on the way, she was the perfect daughter, always doing what was expected of her, and a bore if anyone asked Gwen.

Gwen's younger sister, Marianne – innocence, blonde curls and big blue eyes – was Mother's favourite. Ten years younger than Gwen, she was a change-of-life-baby and seemed to have the doctor, too, wrapped around her little finger.

It was Gwen who was the black sheep. Gwen, who made her mother cry. Gwen, who reminded her mother, and maybe the great doctor too, of Aunty Jeanne.

Had she known she'd be placed in a school in a small backward village in the middle of nowhere, she might have reconsidered her plan.

But it was too late now. Arrangements had been made.

The rain eased to a drizzle, and a building that might be a school passed by the left window. Was that her new employ?

They continued by a patch-worked handful of amenities: a general store, a garage, a community hall and a church with a smattering of houses squeezed in between. It was indeed a village, with barely a blink before arriving at the outskirts of town. Macrocarpa trees and brush rose on both sides of the vehicle, hiding from view the driveway on the left. The driver noticed his mistake almost immediately and made a series of manoeuvres to turn the car around on the narrow road.

The house itself was quaint, with sturdy weatherboards painted white and an iron roof. To the right, a shed sheltered a Ford pickup, and an apple tree grew almost as tall. All Gwen knew of the people inside was they were a young married couple, solid Christian folk, and relatives of the district's founder.

The rain, having stopped, made puddles on the ground, and Gwen tiptoed around them with her luggage in hand. The driver had offered to help her to the door, but she declined. From here on, she was an independent woman.

After three knocks, a young woman close in age to herself opened the door. She was slight of build, with bones forming sharp edges under her shapeless dress. A checked green apron wrapped around her waist, marked with what Gwen hoped was berry or beetroot juice and not blood. The woman wrung her hands in the fabric of her apron after opening the door and stared at Gwen as if she had seen nothing quite like her before.

And maybe she hadn't, Gwen thought. The two of them standing there must have looked worlds apart. Gwen's shoulder-length blonde hair was coiffed into gentle waves. She wore a knee-length skirt with a fashionable light blouse purchased prior to her leaving the city.

The other woman wore her hair pulled back at the base of

11

her neck, drawing the skin on her face taunt across a shallow bone structure. Dark, deep-set eyes peered out from the shadowy abyss, suggesting she had not slept in a very long time. Her thin lips, pressed together, formed a tight line.

Gwen, wondering if she was mute, gently cleared her throat, allowing the woman a final chance to greet her appropriately.

Nothing.

Gwen grew impatient and dropped her luggage on the ground with a scowl.

"I'm here to see the lady of the house or Mr O'Regan himself if he's here." She handed an envelope with her credentials to the woman in front of her, who, instead of taking them, continued wringing her hands.

"I'm she," whispered the strange spectre before her.

It took Gwen a moment to register she meant she was the lady of the house. How peculiar. It was as if the poor thing was battling with some strange inner conflict about voicing that out loud. Heaven forbid, she thought.

Not to be deterred, Gwen straightened her shoulders and stuck out her chin.

"My name is Gwendolyn Davies. I'm here for the room." Gwen paused, searching the face before her for any sign of having heard her. "Mrs Carey called ahead? She said you had agreed to a boarder? I'm the new teacher? I've bought references?" She didn't mean everything to sound like a question, but this woman unnerved her.

Without a hint of emotion, the woman, or Mrs O'Regan, as Gwen now understood her to be, whispered an invitation to come inside before turning her back to her.

Gwen gave a quick wave to dismiss her driver before following Mrs O'Regan down the dark, narrow hallway. The wallpaper was stained and scented with tobacco smoke. The house itself felt heavy with stale air, a harsh tang of liquor and a weighty melancholy.

A few photographs hung in frames on the wall. She glanced at them as she passed. Stern men with deep-set eyes and smoothly shaped moustaches, with the classic unsmiling poses common in the Victorian age. Not the late 1930s, Gwen thought.

One picture stood out in contrast to the others: a wedding photograph.

It took Gwen a startled second glance to realize the bride was Mrs O'Regan, walking only a few paces before her. The woman in the photo shared the same face shape and lithe figure as the woman before her, if not for a few healthy additional pounds. However, her whole being was transformed by the gentle smile on her face and the way her eyes crinkled at the corners. This was a woman in love, Gwen thought.

Gwen was sure she had been told the people she was to board with were newlyweds of a year, yet the woman walking down the hall seemed aged well beyond the photo on the wall.

The man in the photo stood gruff and unsmiling. He might have been handsome had he returned his new wife's smile.

Through a door on the right Gwen glimpsed an oversized sofa in front of a fireplace framed by ornate wooden pillars and mantle.

Mrs O'Regan stopped abruptly outside a door on the left. "This is your room. Rent is due on the tenth of every month. Our room is next to yours. I will serve breakfast at seven, dinner at twelve on the weekends, and tea at six. The bathroom is at the end of the hall and the kitchen and dining room can be accessed to the left. You'll find fresh towels on your dresser." The words fell from her mouth in quick succession. She took a deep breath and handed Gwen a house key she'd dug out of her apron pocket. Having avoided eye contact until now, Mrs O'Regan allowed her gaze to make a slow crawl up the length of Gwen's body. "Mr. O'Regan is not to be bothered for any purpose," she said, her voice paling further. "His office is down the hall." She pointed to one of the closed doors on the right. "My husband is a busy man… " The words hung in the air as she twisted her hands in the folds of her apron again, then turned and walked away.

It was not the introduction to Te Tapu aristocracy that Gwen had expected, nor the most hospitable. Opening the door to her new room, she was just as disappointed. A single bed took up the middle of the room, its headboard pressed against the wall marking the front of the house. Curtains were pulled across the windows on either side of it. A dresser stood along the same wall as the door, with a mirror propped on top, its edges faded to black. Small black spots marred its surface, distorting Gwen's image as she peered into it. A small handwoven oval rug provided minimal warmth on the cold wooden floorboards. The window on the opposite side of the room was at least a thing of promise. It opened by a latch on top, and slid upwards, high enough for a captive to make their escape if the need should ever arise.

For the first time that day, Gwen smiled. The O'Regans could be as fuddy-duddy as they pleased, it didn't mean Gwen had to succumb to such an existence. If this was to be her new life, she would make the most of it – think of it as an adventure even. Surely more lively people existed somewhere in this village. Since she was going to be stuck here for any length of time, it was in her best interest to find them. As soon as possible. Who knew what possibilities lay ahead of her?

She felt a bubbliness then. It tingled in her hands and radiated through her body. She settled her small suitcase on the ground. Oh yes. Gwen Davies was meant for big things, and maybe, just maybe, Te Tapu would surprise her.

Chapter 3 – Riley

The children arrived at the school in a flurry of excitement, and all of Riley's first-day nerves disappeared with the mayhem of the moment.

While the sound of the stampede drew closer, she turned on her laptop, prepping it to take attendance. Another half an hour had to pass before class officially started, but she was determined for today, the first day of her new life, to go smoothly.

Fingers on the keyboard, she noticed her chewed fingernails and let out a groan. They looked horrible. She gave them a shake. Nothing she could do about them now, and likely no one would notice or care, anyway. She stood and paced the room, checking one last time everything was as it should be. Without thinking, she twisted the silver bracelet on her left wrist and wanted to groan again. She should have put the anniversary gift away with the rest of Justin's things, but she wasn't ready yet to say goodbye to the bracelet's promise.

Hearing a noise, she spun, and her eyes landed on several young faces pressed against the windows, noses smushed. She broke into a smile and laughed. Show time!

Opening the door, she welcomed the students who greeted

her. She introduced herself as Miss Cooper, directed them to where they could put their bags and pencil cases, and let them descend on the classroom with curious fingers and copious questions. A warmth filled her chest as they did so.

Then they left again, impatient to see friends and hear of holiday adventures.

On the whiteboard, Riley had scrawled *Welcome Room 2* in bubble writing, filling it with different designs and colours to make it pop. While she had been doing it, the thought flitted through her mind that she wasn't the first teacher, nor likely the last, to be welcoming new students in this room. How many memories of first days did this room hold? The school was built in 1905, well over one hundred years of teachers and students coming and going. Some comfort was found in that. She wasn't alone. She was simply one of many.

A wail broke out outside and Riley moved to the windowed doors to see where it was coming from. Outside the junior room, Brittany May, the new-entrant teacher, was bent over a child who was wrapped around his mother's leg and amid a full meltdown. Colour flamed high on the mother's cheeks while Brittany rubbed the boy's back and said who-knew-what to calm him enough to pry him from his mother. The mother, free at last, made a hasty retreat towards the drop off area while Brittany gently took the child by his hand and led him towards the classroom.

Riley had met all the staff during the Teacher-Only Day prior to school beginning. The small team consisted of four teachers for four classes, two teacher aids and an office lady. She had liked Brittany, who was all bubbles and bounce, right away.

The morning flew by, and lunchtime was a welcome

reprieve. As she pulled out her packed lunch, the teacher of the year threes and year fours, Robert McCreery, popped his head through her doorway. "Hey, newbie. How's it going?" His easy smile filled his face, eyes sparkling.

Riley grinned back. "Piece of cake, but I am so ready for this lunch break."

"Now they've sussed you out, just wait until tomorrow." He gave a wink and a pat of his dad-bod tummy. "Well, I'm off to enjoy the chow. On lunch duty. Enjoy your break."

When the end-of-day bell rang, Riley couldn't believe it was over. The kids had been attentive and eager to please, and she had thoroughly enjoyed herself, finding her teaching voice easily. Mirroring their boisterous arrival, the kids vanished from the classroom in a chaotic flurry of activity. The laughter, teasing and goodbyes trickled to silence as the bus and parent pickups pulled away.

It was eerie being alone in her room again. The classroom, which had felt so alive with the students, now felt hollow.

Riley turned to her planning book and went about writing up the next day's timetable on the whiteboard. Pins and needles prickled her fingers as the marker moved across the board, and she paused to flex her fingers.

A knock on the door made her breath hitch in her throat. She turned.

"Hiya!" Brittany sang out, bounding into the room. "Thought I'd check in and see how your first day went." A smile radiating across her face, she pushed a stray curl out of her eyes. A red smudge decorated her top, and some blue paint marked one cheek.

"It went great, thanks," Riley said, matching her enthusiasm. "They're such a great bunch of kiddies." She realised right away she had spoken with a sense of surprise. Had she really expected them not to be?

Brittany chuckled. "Give them another day or two."

"How was your day?" Riley asked.

"Well, I survived." She twirled around, arms open wide. "My clothes may not have, but *I* did." A few more smudges of paint were on Brittany's back, and a glob of silver glitter sat prominently on the toe of her shoe. "Probably not a good idea doing art on the first day when you haven't set down rules."

For a moment, Riley envied Brittany. To be so happy, so carefree... She gave her bracelet another turn around her wrist.

Brittany went about exploring her room, and Riley finished writing her plan on the whiteboard, stealing glances at her.

"Wow, I like this." Brittany stopped by one of Riley's motivational posters.

Riley stifled a smile. Watching someone pore over her set up felt weird, but with every "Ooh," and "Ahh" from Brittany, Riley couldn't help feeling a sense of pride in her hard work.

Her bracelet slipped from her wrist and slid straight down the back of the solid wood bench below the whiteboard. Though Riley snatched her hand out to grab it, she was too slow. "No!" she exclaimed, louder than she intended.

"What's wrong?" Brittany asked, her eyes wide.

"My bracelet. The clasp must've come undone. It fell down the back..." Riley tugged at the bench, trying to pry it out from the wall. It didn't budge.

"Let me help." Brittany pulled and tugged with her.

Tears prickled behind Riley's eyes. Stupid, stupid, stupid. Why was she even wearing the stupid thing, and now being

19

such a baby about it?

She had worn it almost every day for three years. It was a part of her. No, a voice reminded her, it was a part of her and Justin. Time to move on.

Riley blinked back the moisture and found Brittany staring at her, eyes wide and head tilted slightly.

"Liam will be able to get it for you. I'm sure I saw him out the back only a moment ago. I can get him for you if you like?"

Riley bit her lip. Whoever Liam was, if Brittany thought he could help, it would be worth a try. She gave a nod.

Brittany beamed and almost danced out the room.

Riley waited, embarrassment settling in. To get so upset over a bracelet her ex gave her...

Sniffing, Riley paced around the room. She would get the bracelet back, and there would be no harm done. Then she could think about letting it go. For real.

She took a few deep breaths to centre herself, then grabbed a metre ruler and poked it down the back of the bench, feeling for her bracelet. Even for the ruler, the fit was tight. How the bracelet had slid so perfectly in the small space, Riley couldn't guess.

And how could a bench be so damn heavy?

It looked old. Shelves were built into its front, so it was more like a low-lying bookcase. Its solid wood exterior was graffitied with sticker residue, pencil scribbles, and carved marks. She climbed on top of the thing and was still fussing with the ruler when they entered the classroom.

She recognised Liam when he walked in front of the window. He was momentarily back-lit, and his silhouette was the same as the man who had ignored her when she waved.

20

Her cheeks burned as she slid off the bench and stepped away to give him room.

"I'm so sorry," she said. "It fell off my wrist and…"

He paid no interest. Instead, he squatted at one end of the bench and pulled his phone from his back pocket. Opening the torch app, he directed its beam down the slight gap between bench and wall.

"This is Liam," Brittany said, standing beside Riley. "He's the go-to guy for almost everything around here. And Liam, this is Riley," she said, gesturing to Riley even though Liam had yet to even turn in her direction.

He grunted in response while he continued checking around the edges of the bench with his phone light.

"I think we've kind of met," Riley ventured. "I saw you by the shed out the back when I was checking out my classroom. Someone was with you."

Liam stopped what he was doing and stood up. He was tall, with dark hair sticking out from under his baseball cap. His green eyes would have been mesmerising had they not been narrowed in on her so intently.

She shifted under his gaze.

"I waved out," Riley offered, in case he had thought her rude.

"It was just me," Liam said, shaking his head before turning back to his project at hand. Finally, he stood up, wiped his hands on his pants, anchored his feet and wrenched one edge of the bench away from the wall. It moved enough for a small hand to maybe reach behind. He grabbed the ruler from Riley and bent back down, using it to draw out the bracelet.

"Crap." Brittany broke the silence, glancing at her watch. "I have to get going. I promised I'd meet Nathan," she said. "My boyfriend." She lifted a shoulder.

"Oh," Riley said. "Thanks for your help."

"No problem! I'll see you tomorrow. Bye, Liam!" She bounced out the door, leaving the two of them alone.

Riley bit her lip and perched herself on the edge of a desk to stop herself shifting from foot to foot. Her hand, by habit, went to her wrist despite it being bare.

She contemplated Liam's denial. Another man had been with him that day. She'd seen him. He tipped his hat at her. Standing as close as he'd been, Liam couldn't have missed him. Why would he lie?

Liam stood up again, this time placing a handful of bric-a-brac on top of the bench: a pen lid, a yellowed piece of folded paper, chalk, her bracelet. He walked over and placed the latter in her palm. The engraving in cursive script was clear to see: *"Whatever our souls are made of, yours and mine are the same."* A quote from her favourite book, *Wuthering Heights,* by Emily Bronte. It had seemed truly beautiful at the time. Especially to have come from Justin. Only a few months had passed since she had learnt their souls were not the same. Not even a little.

She closed her fingers around it, hoping Liam hadn't seen her sentimentality. His eyes locked on hers, a hint of bewilderment staining his features, and she blushed again.

She mumbled a thank you and slipped the bracelet into her pocket, dragging her eyes away from the thin line of his lips amongst a day's unshaven shadow. To busy herself, she gathered up the miscellaneous treasures he had pulled out from behind the bench and moved them onto her desk to sort. He gave a quiet grunt as he pushed the bench back into place.

"Thanks again," she offered as he stuck his phone back into his pocket.

He shrugged, opening his mouth for a second as if to say something, and then thinking better of it, he shook his head and left the room.

A prickle formed between her shoulder blades from the snub. How rude. Once he was gone from view, she pulled her bracelet from her pocket and turned it over in her hands. Simple silver with a floral pattern engraved on one side, and the quote on the other. She slipped it back on her wrist, doing up the clasp. She wasn't ready to put it away just yet.

Holding her rubbish bin against her desk, she swept the debris he'd found into it. Except for the small piece of yellowing paper. The pins and needles were back in her hand as she carefully unfolded it. She turned the paper over. One sentence was written on it. The writing was barely visible; having faded with time. It took a second to decipher the cursive swirls, and then she froze, her blood fleeing her body.

Spots danced before her eyes.

Whatever our souls are made of, yours and mine are the same, it read.

Chapter 4 – Gwen

"He'll love and hate equally under cover, and
esteem it a species of impertinence to be loved or
hated again."
*- **Wuthering Heights***

G wen settled into her life with the O'Regans easier than she had expected to. Mornings, she would wake to fresh milk, eggs and toast laid out by Mrs O'Regan, or Sarah, as she acquiesced to be called. Mr O'Regan – Jake – had often already left for the day, or holed himself up in his study. Gwen wasn't certain what his job was. It seemed more bookwork than anything else, as he spent more time in his study than out on the farms or at the garage or tending to any of the many other local businesses his father,Thomas O'Regan, owned. Ol' Man Tom, as he was more affectionately known, owned most of the village and many of the farms in the area, including the land the school was built on. Jake, his oldest son, was in line to inherit the family businesses on Ol' Man Tom's death. The younger son would likely have a job for life, working on the family holdings. If ever a family was set to succeed in the present economy, Gwen felt sure it would be them.

But something sat uneasy with her. The name O'Regan was held in such high esteem in the community, yet what she had seen of Jake and Sarah seemed ill-fitted to the reputation.

Gwen had few interactions with Jake during her first two weeks boarding with them. Both times had been in the evening during teatime, when he came bowling into the room with the stench of liquor stripping the air of oxygen. She recognised him from the wedding photo and a few of the other portraits in the hallway, although at these times he had little show of aristocracy about him. The man before her was unshaven with stubble covering his chin and growing up the sides of his face. His moustache was unkempt, and spittle hung to it as he slobbered and spat each slurred word.

"Who the hell is this?" Jake scowled when first discovering Gwen sitting at the table in the kitchen eating dinner. Gwen almost dropped her fork. She was not accustomed to being sworn at. Poor Sarah, if she had been a nervous wreck without him in the house, she was worse with him there.

"This is Miss Davies. Remember?" Sarah wrung her hands in the front of her skirt, her voice shaky. "She's the new teacher. She's boarding with us." Her eyes darted around without making eye contact with anyone.

Twice, on separate occasions, he had asked, and twice, in being answered, he muttered something unintelligible, slammed his fist on the table, and walked back out of the room.

Gwen listened to him stumbling, bouncing from wall to wall as he made his way down the hallway, cursing and

25

puffing. At one time, the sound of breaking glass had Sarah nearly faint away in front of Gwen. Gwen made her a cup of tea to soothe her nerves, then went to investigate. A photo had fallen from the wall.

Gwen had never been easily frightened. She certainly would not be bullied by a drunkard, as she believed Jake was. Sarah, however, was of a much weaker temperament, Gwen noticed. When Jake was home, Gwen would often boil the kettle and make Sarah a tea. She would sit with her then, mostly in silence, and she would watch the other woman's hands until their shaking lessened.

It was an unusual environment, but it was a roof over her head, and Sarah was a good cook. Jake kept to himself, allowing Gwen to do the same. For the moment, Gwen was enjoying the adventure of living in Te Tapu. She purchased a second-hand bicycle from the local garage on one of her walks home from school and enjoyed the freedom it allowed her. People seemed nice enough, waving to her as she passed them by, and she was already two weeks into the job and finding the students somewhat delightful, to her surprise. She had only used the strap three times and found a quick rapping over the knuckles with a ruler brought the students' attention back on task.

Every morning the school would meet, all fifty-four students, outside her classroom block, to sing "God Save the Queen" and recite a prayer for the day. Though Gwen was not religious, despite her parents' best intentions, she still found the singing and morning prayer a pleasant way to centre herself for the day before the proper work of teaching begun.

Writing was her favourite subject to teach. Whether it was stealing a paragraph from a book for the students to copy or reading the stories they created from their own imaginations, it gave her a thrill to see how words could evoke such emotion. She imagined it as a dance, the way the chalk, on a good day, would glide across the dusty green blackboard, or her pen across the pages of her journal. Plus, writing was meditative – the way the letters followed on from each other with soft links and ending flicks.

The change in place, the change in routine, being independent from her family had been great, yet Gwen itched for more.

Every afternoon, Gwen cleaned the classroom and blackboard, put away and straightened books, art utensils, chairs and other classroom equipment and swept the floor. When the weather cooled, she would have to ensure ample wood and kindling was prepared for the fire, but for the moment the long summer days were so hot and stifling she couldn't imagine a time when it would be otherwise.

She craved a way to spend her evenings with others of her own age. Others who might be a little livelier, a little more adventurous, a little less depressing than Jake and Sarah. She didn't want to admit to being bored; being bored often bred drama. As a teacher, she had been warned gravely against any sort of breach of conduct.

On her first day at Te Tapu School, the formidable headmistress, Ms Flemming, coached Gwen on her dress attire. Her skirt was apparently shy of correct decorum for a teacher, her blouse had one too many buttons unbuttoned, the sway of her hips too provocative. With her overly Victorian austere clothes and countenance, Ms Flemming hardly seemed the person to give fashion tips to anyone of this modern age. But Gwen was not yet willing to forfeit her job over outdated rules. So she smiled innocently, wide eyed, and with hands clasped demurely in her lap, while the old woman prattled on. She hated this makeshift persona of hers. Prior to this career, she would have been attending dances, flirting with strangers and sucking on the end of a cigarette had the opportunity arisen. What a contrast to the life she had landed, all to spite her mother and get away from the dreadful doctor.

"As you may have already come to realise, Miss Davies, this community esteems itself on its morality." Ms Flemming leaned forward in her chair, glasses perched on the edge of a rather severe nose. "And as the moral cornerstone of the community, next to the church of course – I do hope you'll be attending Sunday's service…"

"Yes, ma'am," Gwen ventured, silently cursing herself for agreeing to what would lead to regular attendance.

Ms Flemming tilted her head as if trying to read her thoughts. "It is imperative the teachers at this school conduct themselves with the utmost decency and show a strength of restraint against giving into those sins against character and society."

Strength of restraint, Gwen thought, gritting her teeth together whilst forcing a demure smile and nodding her head in agreement.

"Because of the responsibility bestowed on our teachers here at Te Tapu School—"

Teachers? Gwen wondered. To her knowledge, it was just her and Ms Flemming.

"—I have elected a few guiding principles for behaviour both in and out of school. Be aware, Miss Davies, I will watch closely to ensure you adhere to them."

With the conclusion of her speech, Ms Flemming passed a

nicely typed piece of paper across the desk to her. To humour the silly lady, Gwen perused its contents: No consumption of alcohol, no smoking, no keeping company with men who were not your father or brother, no marriage, no this, no that… Gwen didn't need to read it in its entirety to know what it was really saying was "No Fun!" She stifled a scowl. She was not here to wither away into an oppressed crone. If fun was to be had in this village, it was her duty to find it. She would have to be careful, was all.

So she nodded and made noises of assent in all the right places until dismissed.

After school, Gwen biked or walked the short distance back to the O'Regans'. She took her time to enjoy the long afternoons and to avoid the dispiriting atmosphere she knew waited for her inside. On her way, she would pass the local garage and wonder how it was that a deplorable drunk like Jake O'Regan would one day come to inherit half the town. She also wondered if Te Tapu's patriarch, Ol' Man Tom, was anything like his son? She had only ever heard praise his way, yet she had never heard a bad word against Jake either.

She passed the small general store with its carts of fresh fruit and gardening tools standing against its side. Often, she would see a young woman pushing a child in a perambulator into the store depths, or a young gentleman leave the store with a brown paper bag holding his newly purchased wares.

Although not as busy as any store she had come across in Alberton, there was a steady enough patronage to people-watch and imagine their life as she walked past. Occasionally she would wave out to them, and they would wave back or share a greeting. Or she might see one of her own students, and they would call out to her, "Afternoon, Miss Davies!" as they continued on their way. One day, as she passed the town hall, her life took a sharp turn from the tedious.

Two ladies had set a stall up on the sidewalk. They were dressed in their best – not nice enough to have been formal wear but not the usual attire of a homemaker or farmer's wife, as Gwen had become familiar with. One woman noticed her and called out in greeting. Gwen approached, curious about their purpose.

A sign on the front of their table presented them as the Te Tapu Young Farmers Women's Committee, and in brackets TTYFWC. A social club at its foundation, and to Gwen's relief it seemed you didn't need to be a farmer or be married to one to be included.

Fortnightly social events allowed for mingling and fundraising for the community. The committee had only been in action since the middle of the previous year and were attempting to garner interest for their upcoming event at the local hall: a dance for all the young singles, preferably, with couples of course allowed. The women spoke of it in whispered voices and conspiring giggles as if it were a scandalous dating event. Though she was sure Ms Flemming would think it exactly that, to Gwen, it was perfect. Now Te Tapu was getting interesting!

Gwen took the flier from one lady, who squealed with delight. Since the village was tiny, Gwen doubted the turnout would be big, but it was a start.

In three days, her life would begin.

The hours dragged slowly. The students were as amicable as could be expected. The days were hot and the room stifling, even with the double doors pushed wide open. Gwen was as inclined to rest her head a moment after lunch as some of her students.

Her anticipation for the dance also kept her distracted, and while her students practised their cursive from the blackboard, her mind drifted to what she would wear. How long would it take, she wondered, before her attendance would get back to Ms Flemming? And more importantly, would there be any dashing young men for her to dance with?

Her living arrangements were of little comfort against the slow slog towards Saturday. Jake grew more rude, drunk and threatening than Gwen had ever dreamed possible. Sarah was a constant quivering mess. In fact, her anxiety was so bad she now seemed prone to dropping things, which set Jake off with even more verbal ferocity. Sometimes, late at night, Gwen would hear a dish break or the movement of pots and pans and kitchenware, or cupboards opening and closing. On one of those nights, Gwen crawled out of bed, throwing her dressing gown over her shoulders to investigate. Sarah was sitting on the floor, a pale lace nightie hanging limp on her delicate frame, with dishes, and cups, and bowls, and pans sitting in piles all around her as she methodically transferred them back and forth from one cupboard to the next.

Jake had not returned from his mid-day escapade, which Gwen suspected led him straight to the local tavern and not the garage or the farm as most would have supposed, so Gwen kneeled beside her and asked what she was attempting to achieve at one thirty in the morning. As if seeing her for the first time, Sarah's eyes grew large. Had anyone ever inquired of her before? Gwen doubted Sarah's husband ever had.

When Sarah's bottom lip trembled, Gwen placed her arm gently around her shoulders to sooth her, not knowing what else to do. Whatever Sarah's reasoning, organising dishware seemed a slim lifesaver holding together a very broken doll.

Comforting her close like that, Gwen saw purplish-blue skin peek out from beneath the short sleeve of her nightie. The colour of a ripening bruise, yellowing at the edges. Sarah was clumsy, Gwen knew, but she wondered what it was really like in this house when she was away. For not the first time, she thought herself lucky to have a job to escape to.

It was not the last time Sarah rearranged cupboards in the middle of the night. Nor was it the last bruise Gwen saw on Sarah's translucent skin.

Jake wasn't always drunk. It stunned Gwen to see him talking to another man on her walk home from school one day. He flashed a winning grin and slapped the man on the shoulder in good humour, and Gwen saw nothing in that moment of the man she boarded with. She quickly averted her eyes when he spotted her watching, and pretending to have not noticed him, she darted across the street and continued home.

He really was the most dangerous of men, she thought. The flicker of his charisma was as enticing as a bejewelled cobra.

A feeling of seasickness accompanied Gwen much of the time she was at the house. She swayed side to side, seeking equilibrium while dealing with the opposing personalities surrounding her. To further set her off-balance, she noticed a hint of flirtation by Jake during his sober moods, an appraising look as his eyes wandered over her body when she entered the room. Questions as to her whereabouts and whom she might have been in attendance with, comments on her safety as she walked home after school, all left her with unease in the pit of her stomach.

When Saturday arrived, it was without ceremony. A

normal day. A boiled egg and toast for breakfast. No sign, thankfully, of Jake.

Gwen spent the morning helping Sarah in the vegetable garden and tidying around the home. Sarah never said much to her. Gwen tried to pull her into conversation but was met with such reserve, she bit her tongue when the desire rose to do so again. So it was with relief when Gwen found an excuse to go into the village, to pick up a few toiletry items she was getting low on.

She took her time, forgoing her bike to walk, losing herself in the daydream of what the dance would be like. She had already chosen her outfit. She had brought it with her from Alberton, not really expecting an opportunity to wear it. Her favourite midnight blue number with a high neck, short, ruffled sleeves and a low back. The dress hugged her waist and flared a little at mid-calf, but most of all it drew attention to the greens of her eyes. A little risqué for a teacher, maybe, in a village like Te Tapu, but part of her hoped to make an entrance. She could deal with the fallout later.

Arriving back at the house with the few toiletries she needed in a brown paper bag, her stomach dropped on seeing Jake's green Ford pickup in the shed. He was home.

It was hard to know what mood he would be in or if they would even cross paths. Often, he would go straight to his study, and she wouldn't see him until tea. She said a silent prayer this was one of those times. She would miss tea anyway. Her plan was to have something to eat early and then spend the next while getting herself ready. Whatever Jake's mood, *she* was in no mood to have him mess it up for her.

The house was quiet, as it was often apt to be. Gwen headed

to her bedroom first to drop her shopping on the bed, then headed to the kitchen, listening as she did so for any sign of Jake's whereabouts.

She had hoped to sneak a piece of cheese and maybe a slice of bread from the pantry. It seemed Jake had a similar idea.

Jake was cutting into a block of cheese when she walked into the room. Without thinking, Gwen apologised for intruding and made to leave, her hunger all but forgotten.

"You can join me if you like." His voice rose, not in question but in request.

"Okay," she replied slowly, uncertain how to proceed. She mentally kicked herself for not being more confident, for leaving regardless. The man made her uncomfortable. She consoled herself that at least the air seemed to be free of its usual distinct whisky smell. She might have stumbled upon him in one of the few moments he hadn't been drinking. To busy herself, she headed for the cupboard and pulled out a couple of plates, placing them on the table.

"There's bread in the cupboard if you want it," he offered, as if having read her mind. She pulled it out and searched for a bread knife to slice it. He set a piece of cheese on each of the plates and took a seat at the table, patient while Gwen cut a slice of bread for each plate.

"Sit," he said, gesturing to the chair opposite him, as if predicting she would make an excuse to take her food and leave. Gwen took the seat, cut her slice of bread in half and went about laying the cheese on top, aware this was the first time she had been alone with him. Despite the circumstances, she was still hungry.

"I think we might have got off on the wrong foot," Jake stated.

Feeling his eyes on her face while she studied the sandwich in her hand, she said nothing but took a bite of her sandwich. He could say what he wanted. When she had finished eating, she would leave.

The aged cheese was delightful, and she devoured her food, struggling a little as the bread clung to the top of her mouth and she had to use her tongue to pry it off. She looked up to see he was still watching her intently.

"You think you know us, Miss Davies, but you don't."

The sentence hung in the air between them, and Gwen swallowed hard. Where was Sarah? She hadn't seen or heard from her since arriving home.

"My wife was a fiery little thing once. Pretty too. She got pregnant. We were going to have a child. But she lost it. A son, as it happened."

Gwen's jaw dropped. She hadn't expected such bluntness, the divulging of such personal details. She set the rest of her sandwich on her plate. Could he really be making excuses for his behaviour? She met his eyes, daring him to make excuses. She noticed again, cleaned up and sober like this, he was not too unfortunate looking. Which, she reminded herself, made him all the more dangerous.

"It changed us," he continued.

Gwen's skin itched, and she shifted uncomfortably in her seat. "Look, thank you for the snack, Mr O'Regan, but none of this is any of my business." She stood up, ready to leave. She had heard enough.

"Sit down, Miss Davies." His voice rose in volume. "You need to hear this. You need to know who you're living with."

His manner was so abrupt, Gwen paused for a moment, unsure what to do. Seeing the alarming expression on his

35

face, the flash of fire in his eyes, she lowered herself into her chair.

"Okay, Mr O'Regan," she protested again, "but I hardly see—"

"It has plenty to do with you, Miss Davies. It was my wife's idea to have you board with us. And now that you are here, privy to the lives we lead, it is only right you know who you are dealing with before you go about making judgement."

Heat rose high in her cheeks. Could he really accuse her of gossiping about them? For heaven's sake.

"Mr O'Regan!" She put a bite into her tone and again made to leave.

"Sit down, Miss Davies. I will not tell you again." His voice got deeper, colder.

She did as bid, her heart thumping unnaturally in her chest. Whatever he wanted to say, she would have to hear him out.

"She took a child once, you know. A little boy. She brought it home, claiming it was my son. It wasn't. Stupid bitch had taken it from a shearer's wife down the road. Thought I wouldn't know." He slammed his fist down on the table, making Gwen jump and the plates rattle. Any sense of calm and control he had shown before was gone. This was closer to what she expected from such a man.

"What do you say to that, eh? You're a teacher. You tell me. How is a husband supposed to react to that? She stole a bloody baby, a bloody farmhand's baby, and tried to pass it off as my own."

Gwen was speechless. Could Sarah have really done such a thing?

"I'm an O'Regan. I own half this bloody town, or I will do when the old man goes. Don't think I don't know what they say about me."

"I'm sorry, Mr O'Regan, but I'm a teacher. I don't indulge in the gossip of others."

"Do you think I'm bloody stupid?" Spittle flew with his words, and he grabbed Gwen's arm across the table. His fingers dug into her wrist. She tried to pull her arm away, attempting to shake him off her.

"You're hurting me! Let go!" she cried, her voice rising with panic and outrage.

Jake's eyes softened.

Gwen swallowed and willed away the tears of anger prickling behind her eyes.

Jake slowly released his grip on her wrist, moving his hand to rest lightly over hers instead. Gwen went to pull away, but he held it in place.

"I know what they say." His voice was now a whisper.

The skin on her back crawled. A new type of danger lurked in his eyes. The calm before the storm.

"I trust you, Miss Davies. I think you might be one of the good ones. But … you watch my wife, mind, keep her away from the babies. Do that, and you and I … well, we'll look after each other, eh?"

Gwen bit her lip, willing away the emotions and nodding in agreement. She just wanted him to stop.

He moved his hand away from hers. Small purple bruises had already risen to the surface where his fingers had been. She dragged her arm to her and cradled it against her chest. Jake apparently lost interest in her. He rose from his chair, turning his back to her.

"Good evening, Miss Davies," he said without sparing her a glance. He left the room. His plate sat empty save for a few crumbs.

What the hell had just happened? Gwen trembled. She understood nothing of what had transpired. The small little shivers grew, rippling through her, until little tremors wracked her body with sobs. Half her sandwich remained uneaten on her plate. She thought herself stronger than this, but something in his eyes had terrified her. An unnamed evil.

She stifled any noise with her fist to her mouth, hoping he wouldn't hear, wouldn't come back. And he didn't. She was alone in the kitchen, his chair empty opposite her. Besides her own quiet crying, the house was dead quiet. No noise. When her nerves calmed, she stood, took a deep breath to steady herself and carried the plates to the basin. She dropped the remaining piece of her sandwich into the food scraps bin for the pigs.

Poor Sarah, she thought.

Sarah! Where the heck had Sarah been while her husband was tormenting her? It wasn't like her to have left the house on a Saturday. She had no friends that Gwen knew of. Nowhere to go.

Where was she?

Chapter 5 – Sarah

Sarah leaned against the door, the solid oak cooling the bruise on her cheek and giving her strength to stay somewhat upright. She was dressed in her nightie. Her knees drawn to her chest, with only her toes peeping out.

Jake's arrival home so early had come as a surprise. The only blessing was Gwen being out.

She thought he'd be drunk, retiring to his study to pass out; instead, he had searched for her. Found her in the kitchen and ordered her to bed. She tried talking calmly to him, making light, offering to get him a drink. But he hadn't been drinking. Something else had gotten to him, and he slapped her for her insolence, dragging her by the hair down the hall to their bedroom. It wasn't like him. Not during the day.

He was more apt to arrive home in the early hours of the morning, passing out beside her in bed, and she would hold her breath and wait, relaxing only when he started snoring. Or else, he would fall into bed, climb on top of her and force himself upon her. His hand over her face so he didn't have to look at her. Struggling with his own drawers, fumbling with her body, alcohol having made him thick and bumbling in movement. And she would close her eyes against the tears. On a good night, he'd have his way, grunting and sweating, then collapsing beside her, spent, and she could breathe again. But not in the middle of the day. Gwen could have been home.

And he had brought up the subject of their baby, the baby she had lost. Something had to have set him off.

He dragged her to the bedroom, throwing her on the bed, and the more she struggled, the more he hit back. And she couldn't help struggling this time. She willed her body to stop, but it wouldn't. He tore her dress down the centre, clawing her chest as he did so, and on seeing her flat belly, he punched her, cursing her for killing his baby. She wanted to tell him it hadn't been her fault, but he was too far gone. She was too far gone. Something had snapped and bubbling hysteria made her giggle. And nothing had been funny. And yet everything was.

And pants round his knees, he couldn't get it up. He cursed and slapped at it in a fury as it refused to cooperate, and she laughed even harder despite knowing it would be the end of her.

He whaled on her, his fists raining down, hitting bone as she curled herself into a ball and covered her face.

He beat her until her ribs ached and she could no longer breathe deeply.

He had been so foolish this time. The bruises would show. Even with makeup, she could do little to disguise them. One day her excuses would fall flat. She suspected they already had. No one was as clumsy as her.

When she had heard the front door open, and the clicking of heels on the hardwood floor, she knew Gwen had arrived home. She had wanted to warn her, had wanted to meet her in the hallway and urge her to her room or, better yet, out of the house. Get out of the house. But she hadn't. She reached for her nightie under her pillow and pulled it over her head. She dragged herself to the door, biting her tongue against the pain, but she couldn't stand. Not yet. The best she could do was lean against the door, willing Gwen to leave, run far, far away.

She should have warned her, but her body, her tongue, refused to cooperate, frozen by fear.

Instead, she listened. She heard Gwen enter the kitchen. Heard the soft murmur of voices. Heard him tell her to stay. Sarah's mind screamed the whole time, willing Gwen to get up and leave, but she hadn't. Jake had that effect on people. It was nearly impossible to walk away from him. She had pressed her ear up against the door, harder. Listening, listening. Her teeth gritting together as she strained to hear what he said.

It had been a sharp shock to hear him talk about their son, to confide in Gwen about the boy. Sarah had thought she would faint then. Everything darkened except for small lights that danced in front of her eyes. A roaring filled her ears. She shook her head, trying to clear it, sending a sharp pain spiralling through her temple as she did so. Her eyes had long ago dried up. Salt had formed trails on her cheeks.

She could only hear snatches of conversation, all from him. His voice had risen. She heard Gwen cry out. He was hurting her.

"No, no, no," Sarah mouthed. Though she had long lost faith in prayer, she nevertheless willed whoever was listening to stop whatever was about to transpire.

Then things went eerily quiet. She strained to hear, cursing

41

the thickness of the door. Her breath came in rasping waves as her panic rose. After a moment, a chair squeaked, solid footsteps beat on a hardwood floor, and her husband wished Gwen a good evening. His footsteps drew closer, coming down the hall. Sarah glanced around, panic spreading. What to do? Should she make a line for the bed, throw herself in, hide under the covers? Impossible. It would take every ounce of energy to pull herself upright from the floor, let alone to cross the room.

The footsteps paused outside the door. Sarah drew in a breath and held it, waiting to meet her fate, her heart beating its way out of her ribcage.

Then the footsteps started up again, moving away from the bedroom door, further down the hallway. A door opened and slammed. Sarah exhaled and slumped onto the floor. She was safe. For the moment, at least.

He would have locked himself in his study now. He wouldn't be out again for hours if not until the next day. She listened, hoping to learn something of Gwen in the kitchen, begging to know she was alright. There was no sound. Two women. Only metres apart and yet unable to call out to comfort each other, all because of one man. No... One *monster*.

"I'm so sorry, Gwen," Sarah whispered, before her strength gave out and her eyelids closed.

Chapter 6 – Riley

Riley was finding her feet. Not that she had the faintest idea half the time of what she was doing, but she had the kids' names memorised, and she was learning the idiosyncrasies of a few of them, in particular those most disruptive to the class. Treading water or not, she was not drowning yet, which was a good sign. She was enjoying herself. Sleeping better. Smiling more easily. The knot at the base of her neck had eased a little. She felt … happy.

She liked this new life. She enjoyed being around children, being immersed in the teaching life. And it was immersion – a full, life-consuming immersion. Just what she needed.

Sometimes, on her forty-five-minute drive into work, her mind slipped back towards regret and the wistfulness of the broken-hearted. Yet all she had to do was turn her focus to one child in her class, one of their small difficulties or something that made her giggle aloud, or to the mass of marking or lesson planning awaiting her attention. Now she often dreamt of achievement objectives and curriculum competencies. Little thinking time remained to dwell on the life she had left behind.

Which didn't mean it didn't sometimes still sneak up on her.

The first day in her granny flat a cockroach had raced across her kitchen bench and startled her so badly, a floodgate of hysterical sobs broke free and left her second guessing every decision she had made since leaving.

But those moments were lessening. She was even growing to like her new residence and enjoying the freedom of living alone.

The sharp toll of the school bell and the shuffling in chairs of eager students waiting to be dismissed, brought Riley back to the present. With quick instructions for their return, Riley let them go. A chaotic swarm all wanting to be the first to get to their bags, their food, the prized piece of playground equipment.

Riley shuffled a few finished worksheets into a pile on her desk. Feeling the heaviness of being watched, she stole a glance out the window towards the front of the school.

He was here.

Her stomach took a nauseating tumble.

Why had he come?

He sat at a picnic table under one of the silk trees. One ankle resting on his knee, leaning back on an elbow like he owned the place. He stared right at her, a lopsided grin dissolving the calm and confidence she'd felt as she'd dismissed her class. Her heart tripped in her chest, and she stopped herself in time for reaching for her bracelet. Instead, she wiped her clammy hands on her thighs.

Riley noticed two girls from her class eyeing him and whispering behind their hands. She couldn't blame them. His dark hair framed a handsome face and dusted the collar of his jacket. Angular cheek bones, deep-set eyes. A dimple on his cheek where his mouth curved up in an almost permanent smirk. He was slim, accentuated by the tight jeans he wore. Sex on a stick was what she had first thought on seeing him all those years ago. The quintessential charismatic musician. To a ten-year-old, he would look like a rock star.

Heat flooded her cheeks. Embarrassment, surprise and horror battling against an infuriating weakness in her legs. He looked good. Damn him, she thought.

A moment passed before she could convince her legs to move. She was supposed to be on duty, patrolling the playground, making sure there were no fights or tumbles. Now, to even get outside, she had to face him. And she had to persuade him to leave before the other teachers noticed him and she had to explain who he was and what he was doing here. The last part, she would rightly like to know too.

Riley clenched her fists at her side, pleased for once that she bit her fingernails. The tips of her fingers were digging so deep into her palms they would have drawn blood otherwise.

Because of her bracelet, she grabbed the jacket she'd slung over her chair. Slipping it on, she made sure the bracelet remained unseen up her sleeve. She would not give him the satisfaction of seeing it. Sliding a muesli bar into her pocket, she readied herself. Let's get this over with, she thought as she took a deep breath and headed to the classroom door.

As she stepped outside the classroom, she was ambushed by a five-year-old begging her to open his pack of chips. Bending down to do just that, she saw from the corner of her eye amusement flash across Justin's face. A pang of anger hit her in the chest.

Holding the opened bag of chips out to the eager chubby

fingers before her, she conjured a warm teacher smile and sent the child on his way.

Watching as the child raced off to sit with his friends, Riley's eyes locked on someone else. Liam. Only a few metres from her, he was setting up a "Caution Wet" yellow A-frame sign outside the boys' toilets, mop in one hand. She guessed the toilet or urinals were leaking again, an unfortunate regular occurrence.

His eyes passed over hers, and he looked away. She hadn't seen him since he had rescued her bracelet, and if she were honest, she had been fine with that. He had made it clear he had little interest in getting to know her.

But now, knowing Liam was within eye and earshot of her meeting with Justin, she felt even more nervous. She would rather no one was around. His obvious dislike of her would make worse whatever form of degradation was about to take place.

Taking a deep breath, Riley drew herself up as confident as she could to face Justin.

"Riles," he said, making no move to get up to meet her. Riley took the few steps down to him at a pace, ready to do whatever she could to send him on his way fast and inconspicuously.

"What are you doing here?" she hissed out the side of her mouth, glancing around her, checking no one else was paying attention.

"You've still got it?" Justin said, pointing to her wrist.

She stopped. She had given herself away. Without thinking, her hand had sought the comfort of her bracelet and twisted it around her wrist. A few silent swearwords circled in her mind. She dropped her arms to her sides and glanced around again.

Liam was facing them.

She caught his eye for a moment. His brow narrowed, and he turned away, disappearing into the boys' toilets to deal with whatever had drawn him there.

Fingers clasped around her wrist, digging the bracelet into her skin.

"I miss you, Riles," Justin said, still sitting though pulling her towards him.

"Let. Me. Go." Riley growled under her breath, wrenching her arm out of his grasp. "You need to leave." She stared at him hard now, resisting the urge to rub her wrist where his fingers had been.

"Riles..." He stood up, shrugged his shoulders and sunk his hands into the pockets of his jeans.

Riley was becoming more and more aware of the surrounding children. They seemed oblivious to the situation, but the sounds of their laughing and chatter made her blood burn with how inappropriate he was being right now.

"I'm working, Justin. It's not a good time." Her voice was stern. A teacher's voice. No room for argument. "You need to leave," she repeated, this time turning her back on him sharply and walking away, heading towards the playground, as she should have all along. She waited to hear his footsteps behind her. None came. She stayed herself from glancing towards the toilets. So what if Liam had seen? She had handled it.

When the bell rang to signal the end of morning tea, Riley headed back to class, relieved to see Justin had gone. It hardly mattered. The damage was done. A million questions fought for space in her mind: Why the hell was he here? Why now? Did he want her back? Did she want him back? And how,

47

how had he tracked her down?

She had forgotten to eat, and her stomach let out a low grumble in protest.

The kids entered the class with varying degrees of noise, some having forgotten to leave their outside voices outside, a few still pestering and teasing each other, an extension of whatever game they had been playing outside. A few of the girls, eager to please, were seated ready for instruction.

"Ms Cooper," one of them said, hand in the air but forgetting to wait to be acknowledged. "What's that on your desk?" She pointed to a piece of folded legal paper resting on her laptop.

Riley blinked hard. It hadn't been there before.

Her mind instantly jumped to Justin. Flushing, she took the letter and stuffed it into her pocket alongside her uneaten muesli bar. With a deep breath, Riley steadied herself, then turned to face her students.

The rest of the school day went with little disruption. One child stubbed her toe during physical education, requiring a half hug and a plaster. Another had to be redirected back to his chair a few times, forgetting how to keep still. By the afternoon, Riley had almost forgotten her unwanted visitor.

Until, of course, the students went home.

Laden with a bag of books to mark, she headed for her car. She sunk a hand into her jacket pocket, feeling for her keys. Instead, her fingers caught the sharp edge of the muesli bar wrapper and something else, something softer. Recoiling with the memory, she pulled her hand out of her pocket as if burnt. When fingers lightly tapped her on the shoulder, she jumped.

"Are you okay?" Brittany asked, worry lines marring her

forehead. "I saw you talking to a guy earlier today and…" She paused, giving Riley a second to straighten out her thoughts. "You didn't look happy about it," Brittany finished, raising her shoulders in a half shrug.

"It was nothing," Riley said, not knowing what else to say. "An old friend. He shouldn't have been here." She hoped that was enough to quell her curiosity. Who knew … maybe Justin would be a topic for another day, when they knew each other a little better.

"You know you're doing a great job, right?" Brittany said, catching Riley by surprise again. "The kids really love you. Whatever's going on outside of school … don't let it steal that from you, okay?"

Riley's jaw dropped. "Thanks," she whispered.

"I have to get going. Nathan again. You going to be okay?" Brittany rocked on her toes, her usual bounciness coming back.

"Of course. I'm heading home now too," Riley said, gesturing towards her car as if it wasn't obvious.

"Okay," Brittany said. "We'll see you tomorrow, then." She stayed where she was, looking torn, like she wanted to go but felt she should stay.

Here it comes. Riley braced herself.

"If you ever need someone to talk to, I make a good listener." A real smile this time.

"Thanks," Riley said.

Brittany waved and almost skipped to her car, all serious-ness having passed.

Riley stood still for a moment, the beginnings of a smile playing on her lips. She liked Brittany.

Reaching the side of her own car, she sunk her hand back

into her pocket to retrieve her key fob. It was still there. The note. Or letter. The reason Justin had shown up was no doubt scribed in ink on that very piece of paper.

Unlocking her car and dumping her bag of books on the backseat, she gave herself up to the inevitable. With clammy hands, she gripped the paper, noticing two other vehicles remained. Natalie's, the year two teacher, and Victoria's. For the moment, however, she was alone. It couldn't wait. Whatever it was, she wanted to know now.

She unfolded the paper. Slowly. Deliberately. The thought flitted through her mind: why hadn't he just texted her, left her a voice message?

He might have. She hadn't checked her phone.

It didn't matter.

She opened it up, holding her breath, bracing herself for whatever flood of emotions his words would evoke.

With a sharp exhale, she stared at the paper. Two words glared back at her. It was not his writing. It was not from Justin.

The words were scribbled in fat cursive.

Help me, they said.

Chapter 7 – Gwen

"… and the whole world awake and wild with joy."
- Wuthering Heights

O nce Gwen had washed up and changed, the shaking had mostly stopped. A new sensation had replaced it: a clawing at her stomach. Excitement. She would let no one, especially some degenerate landlord, stifle what was *her* night.

Gwen laid her dress out on the bed. She touched its hem gingerly with her fingers. It was perfect.

She slipped it over her head and reached behind to do up its zip. High heels, pearl earrings, and another lick of lipstick and she was ready. From what she could make out in the mirror on her dresser, she looked good. She had spent ages getting her hair just right with gentle waves pinned close to her head. Her green eyes peered out from under dark eyelashes, and although she couldn't see the full length of her dress, even standing on the bed, she felt amazing, and that would be enough to carry her forward.

Gwen crept from the house without incident. She knew Jake was still home by his parked pickup. Possibly Sarah was too, but she heard neither of them.

One pleasant thing about summer was how the nights stayed warm and light until late. Walking was not much of an inconvenience, except she had not yet broken her shoes in, and blisters were beginning before she got to the end of the driveway.

Gazing around to ensure no one could see her, she slipped off her shoes, holding them by the straps in one hand. Keeping to the grassy verge, she set off in stockinged feet.

It wasn't a particularly long walk, not much further than the trip she made every day to school.

A loud rumble and sound of churning gravel approached behind her. Hovering in the air was the echo of raucous catcalling and yelling. Gwen scowled at having her peaceful walk interrupted. The catcalls grew louder as the truck drew up alongside her.

Boys. All boys!

The driver hung his head out the window, his elbow resting on the door. On seeing her he drew his palm to his lips and blew her a kiss, while the three boys on the truck's deck all called out to her: "Want a lift, doll?" One playfully punched another on the shoulder. The hooting and hollering made Gwen summon her teacher scowl; the withering look could dissolve a child and, she had found, often had a similar effect on those with the maturity of a child.

It didn't help. Gwen continued walking, ignoring them the best she could. Chin out, shoulders back, trying to hide her niggling embarrassment at walking without shoes on.

The men – boys, Gwen corrected herself – didn't give up.

They laughed harder and slowed the vehicle to a near stop beside her as if to enjoy her discomfort.

Gwen ground her teeth to quell her growing anger. Then, with a searing pain, a high-pitched yelp escaped her lips. Hopping now on one foot, she gazed down to see a knife-edged piece of metal lying exposed amongst the grass. Though only the size of her index finger, the damage was done. Blood stained her stockings and left droplets on the grass. She swore loudly, squealing again in both surprise and pain, trying to keep her balance as she took in the damage. Blood. So much blood. Her arms failed as she tried to remain upright, a cool stickiness dampening the back of her neck.

"No, no, no," she repeated, her voice pitching, and the boys trailing her all but forgotten. She took a few hops away from the bloodied grass and plonked herself down, her new dress also forgotten.

Gwen tucked her foot to the side to survey the damage more closely. Her stockings were ruined. She couldn't tell if the slice into her flesh was deep, but it was definitely bleeding indiscriminately. "For heaven's sake," she swore again, feeling another surge of dizziness.

One boy yelled at the driver to stop, slapping the side of the vehicle for emphasis. Looking up, she caught him as he swung himself over the side of the deck, landing on the road close to her. He reached her in a couple of strides.

"Let me see that, doll," he said. Without waiting for her response, he crouched beside her. He bent his head over her foot, his hand gently cradling her ankle.

He smelled good. The thought made her take a sharp intake of breath. Earthy. Clean. Her dizziness faded.

"You okay there? You're not going to faint on me, are you?"

he asked.

"No… I'm fine." She fumbled the words and dared a glance down at her foot again. Catcalls and ribbing were still coming from the truck, only now it seemed far away. Like radio static. She closed her eyes as she felt gentle fingers palpitate the fleshy part of her sole, close enough to the wound to make another wave of clamminess creep up the back of her neck, moist and threatening. Nausea crawled higher up her chest.

He was still talking to her in a soft gravelly tone, only she wasn't really listening, couldn't quite make out what he was saying. She focused all her attention on not fainting in front of the hoard of boys beside her. But, God, she wished they would shut up, their voices an indiscernible roar in her ears.

Calloused fingers wrapped a piece of fabric around her foot, tightening it as if it were knotted. With some cautiousness, a little afraid of what she would see, she opened her eyes, willing herself to not swoon, the nausea to go.

Her foot still rested in the palm of his hand. Cheers and laughter carried from the truck's deck. She ignored them, focused instead on the checked blue handkerchief, which wrapped her foot with a small knot tied at the top. It wouldn't do much to stem the blood, but for the moment it was enough.

"Thank you," she whispered, not fully finding her voice yet. She brought her eyes up to meet those of her rescuer. He had deep brown eyes with small flecks of amber, long dark eyelashes. Pale pink lips quirked at the edges in a soft smile. His hair hung slightly too long, brushing his shirt collar and peeking out from under his cheese-cutter cap. He touched the brim of his cap in acknowledgment, and something warmed in her chest.

"Billy MacKenzie, ma'am. At your service."

The flutter of a smile played on her lips. She noticed his accent. A hint of Irish. "Gwendolyn Davies," she replied. "Thank you again."

Two quick blasts of the pickup's horn startled her back to their surroundings.

"Here, let me help you up." He clasped one of her hands in his and pulling her upright.

"Are you two coming?" a voice from the cab called out.

Gwen used her rescuer's arm to balance with, self-conscious that she still held her slingbacks in her other hand.

"I'll … um, get this back to you as soon as I can," she said awkwardly, pointing at the blood-stained handkerchief and wondering why she hadn't said she'd buy him a new one.

He winked at her, making her skin tingle.

"Keep it," he said. "You're going to the mixer in the hall?" he asked, appraising her dress with his eyes.

"Well, I was," she said, holding up her shoes. The heat rose to her cheeks. This wasn't the entrance she had planned on making.

"We'll give you a lift," he said, gesturing for the guy in the passenger seat to get out.

She chewed her lip, deciding what to do. She had been looking forward to this dance all week, and who knew what state Jake would be in when she returned home. To avoid that alone, she thought she could bring herself to stomach the teasing of Mr MacKenzie's Neanderthal companions. And she had to admit, she wouldn't mind getting to know him better.

Despite her first impression of them, the passengers of the truck were surprisingly obliging. As soon as they realised

55

Gwen was coming on board, their banter softened. Not enough to be called gentlemanly, but enough in her eyes to be elevated from children to men again. It had helped that Billy, as he insisted she call him, lingered protectively close to her. He had even lifted her into the front cab.

"Don't know if you'll be doing much dancing with that one," he said, making small talk and gesturing towards her foot as they drove through the centre of Te Tapu.

"You're right. You don't know," she said, raising her eyebrows, enjoying the sudden attention and chance to flirt. "I'm sure I could surprise you with a lot."

Gwen tried to keep her eyes on the road ahead and not on the warm leg pressed up against hers. It was a tight fit, the two of them and the driver, Jared. Billy had insisted on joining Gwen in the cab, which meant she was just as tightly pressed against the driver as she was to him, but it was Billy whom she kept stealing glimpses of from the corner of her eye.

He was certainly attractive. As childish as he and his mates had first seemed, it appeared chivalry was not dead.

Gwen's foot throbbed. She would need something more than a handkerchief for it when she arrived.

What an entrance she would also make, wearing a handkerchief wrapped around one foot.

She thought about putting a shoe on her good foot. Maybe that would lend her a sense of decorum? Or not. She suspected she would need to remove her stockings too.

The drive took only a couple of minutes. Streamers hung around the open doorway, and music from the orchestra floated through the air. A few people milled around the front door. The usually empty road was lined with vehicles, some even parked on the grass. The men on the flatbed jumped off as the vehicle slowed. Too impatient, too male, to wait until they had come to a complete stop. Jared pulled the truck up beside a deep blue Nash.

"Ya need a hand?" he offered Billy, shooting a glance in Gwen's direction.

"Nah, Billy replied. "I think Miss Davies and I will cope." His cheeks flushed as he glanced quickly at Gwen.

Gwen stifled a smile. He amused her. Most men were so assured of themselves, but something was different about this one. As if his confidence were just for show.

He slipped his fingers under the brim of his cap as if to brush his fringe from his eyes, opened the door and stood there, offering Gwen his arm for support. She paused, but there was no way around it. It was hard enough shuffling across the seat with her slingbacks and purse in one hand, let alone negotiating the drop from the cab to the grass with one hand free and one foot uninjured. She took his arm, steadying herself for the awkward manoeuvre to the ground, but before she even had time to move, he swung his other arm around her waist and was lifting her down to the ground. She drew a sharp intake of breath. His fingers, sitting just above her hip, seemed to dissolve the fabric of her dress with their touch.

His hand didn't leave the curve of her waist. Instead, while she clung to his arm, he escorted her into the building. Her heart jumped a beat, this time with excited anticipation: this was it – her first taste of civilisation since Alberton.

The hall was as she had imagined it. A long, rectangular room, with windows up high, a hardwood floor, and a stage at the furthest end where the orchestra performed. Tables

57

were set up along the sides of the room near the front, some for people to sit, and others with punch and finger food. A couple of matronly women manned a table of assorted cream filled sponge cakes and icing-topped cupcakes adorned with small, freshly picked flowers. Cardboard signs in front of each edible masterpiece presented a local family's name. She mentally kicked herself for not knowing about the bake sale and bringing in an offering to add to the array. Not that her baking skills could match what she saw, even from the other side of the hall. The walls and front of the stage were decorated with Nikau palms, tree ferns and trails of lycopodium. Pastel blue and pink streamers and paper flowers added extra accents to the décor.

People mingled around the edges of the room, either around the food tables or in small social circles, ignoring the rest of their surroundings.

Oh, she hoped more people than this would show up. Thus far, she counted about twenty.

Disappointment swirled through Gwen's limbs, making her almost limp with exhaustion. They had stopped in the doorway. She was still holding Billy's arm but had not realised until now that Billy was in conversation with a pretty young blonde thing seated at the entry table next to them.

The table was laid out with a register, a money box, and a few newsletters on the most recent triumphs of the TTYFWC. She had forgotten she needed to pay for entry. Letting go of Billy's arm, she tiptoed on her bad foot and rummaged through her purse for admission.

Billy stayed her. "I've got this," he said, feeling around his pockets for the correct change. "Two, please." He dropped the coins into the cash box. "Is Peggy here?" he asked.

"Sure is." The blonde smiled. "I'll get her for you."

Gwen glanced back, confused. The young woman at the table stood, a hand cupped to her mouth as she called through a door behind her.

"Coming," a voice echoed back as the blonde woman re-seated herself behind the table.

She took Billy's arm again, and they moved away from the front of the desk, allowing space for the next in line.

A woman appeared in the doorway, and Gwen was taken aback.

She was beautiful. A pang of envy coursed through her chest. Was this Billy's girlfriend? Not that it should matter, she scolded herself. She'd couldn't very well go all doe-eyed at the first man she met.

She appeared to be close to Gwen's age. Her hair had been curled and pulled back in a loose chignon at the nape of her neck with a few loose strands framing her face.

"Billy," the woman cooed, sweeping in for a kiss on the cheek.

"How ya doin', Peggy?"

"I'm good." She gave him a wide smile. "And who is this you've brought with you?" she asked, turning her eyes on Gwen.

"This is Miss Davies. And this is Peggy."

"Gwen," she said, smiling despite feeling so awkward. "Pleased to make your acquaintance."

"You can see there was a bit of an accident." He pointed down at Gwen's foot, and she tried to prevent the heat from rushing to her face again. "I thought you might be the one to patch Miss Davies – Gwen – up." He paused over her name as if shy to use it. He pulled his cap off his head and wrung it in his hands.

"Of course," Peggy said in a sing-song voice. "Come with me." She threaded her arm through Gwen's. "Don't worry, she'll be in expert hands." Peggy winked at Billy.

Peggy, gliding, led Gwen to the door behind the admissions table. It led to a small kitchen. A bench ran the length of the furthest wall of the modest room, complete with sink and AGA. Two small windows sat above it. To the right, a wall of shelves housed mismatched mugs and containers holding various kitchen utensils. A white enamel table with two chairs stood in the middle of the room. Peggy pulled a chair out with one hand and led Gwen to sit down.

"You really don't need to do this," Gwen said, feeling strange that someone as striking as Peggy would soon see the horrors under the handkerchief tied to her foot.

"Nonsense," Peggy replied as she went over the sink, proceeding to lather her hands with soap. She dried them on a fresh tea towel she pulled out from a drawer built into the bench.

"It's not often someone comes to these things wearing a handkerchief around their foot, let alone on the arm of Billy MacKenzie."

Gwen squirmed at the sparkle in her eye.

After sitting in a chair opposite Gwen, Peggy unwrapped her foot.

"How did you do this, anyway?"

"I had blisters," Gwen said.

"So you took off your shoes?" Peggy's eyes sparkled again. "Oh, you and I are going to be good friends."

Gwen suspected they would be. Gwen was so used to attracting the attention of a room. She would have her work cut out for her against Peggy, though. She could see that already. Both admiration and envy fluttered in the pit of her stomach.

"Well, the damage doesn't look too bad," Peggy said. "Although you'll have to lose the stockings."

"Ouch." Gwen let out a sharp breath.

"Sorry," Peggy said with genuine sympathy. "I just want to make sure it's clean. I have some nurse training. One day, I hope I can go back and finish it. I hate to say it, but I kind of live for these types of injuries."

Gwen pulled a face. "Not me," she said. "I'm afraid I'm not very good with blood."

"Well, then. You can get your mind off it by telling me about yourself. You're obviously new. Everyone knows most everyone around here, and I don't believe I've seen you before. Do you mind taking those off?" She pointed at Gwen's stockings, and Gwen did as she was asked.

Peggy went over to the cupboard under the sink and returned with a white metal container with a red cross painted on the top. She placed it on the table and filled a small bowl with water, bringing that and a cloth back with her before again plopping herself into the chair opposite Gwen.

"I just moved here from the city," Gwen said, balling up her stockings. "I'm the new teacher at the school."

"Really?" Peggy's eyebrows shot up. "I'd heard they'd hired someone new. Nothing stays quiet around here. I should have put two and two together. I apologise, I kinda thought you'd come in with the boys."

"Well, I guess I did. They were the ones who found me on the side of the road. They were rather rude, in fact."

"I bet they were." Peggy chuckled. "With a pretty thing like you in town, the men will all be tripping over themselves. It'll be the women you'll need to mind."She used the damp cloth and went about cleaning off the blood before applying ointment from a tube.

Gwen smiled. She was flattered. Maybe life in Te Tapu would be a bit of fun.

"So the dashing Mr MacKenzie swooped in and saved you, then?" Peggy asked, eyebrow arched.

Gwen grimaced. Her foot was throbbing again.

"Oh, I meant nothing by it. Billy's one of the good ones," Peggy said, concern showing on her face.

"Oh, no, it's not that. It's just … my foot. It hurts!" She pulled a face.

Peggy flashed a sympathetic smile. "I won't be much longer; I want to make sure it is clear of infection. Then I'll give you something for the pain."

Holding a gauze pad over the wound, she wrapped a bandage around Gwen's foot.

"So what do you think of this place so far? Te Tapu, I mean. It's a bit different to living in the city."

Gwen snorted at the understatement. "Well, that's why I'm here, really. All I've seen is the school and the kids, and I have to admit I've been craving an excuse to meet people – let my hair down a little. Plus, I love dancing, although now…" She wiggled her foot and gave a little shrug of her shoulders.

"Oh, I wouldn't worry about that." Peggy secured the bandage with a safety pin and handed her a couple of white pills.

"Once I have you all patched up, I'll introduce you around. It takes a while before these things warm up, anyway. Everyone rummages around the edges of the dance floor, making small talk and saying their hellos. Then, when they've either run out of things to say or had a little too much punch, people dance. That's when the real fun begins. And even with your foot wrapped, I hardly doubt you'll be short a dance partner. I'm sure you won't have seen the last of Billy tonight either." She winked at Gwen and put away the first aid kit.

Gwen's cheeks heated. She decided she liked her, rare as it was for her to find camaraderie with another woman.

Peggy brought over a glass of water. "Bottoms up."

Gwen lifted the pills to her lips and did as ordered.

"Alright!" Peggy said. "Do you want to put your other shoe on? It might be difficult to walk, but at least you won't do any harm to your good foot." At Gwen's nod, she helped put her slingback on.

Gwen placed her other shoe in her bag. Though it stuck out a little, it would be easier to carry around.

"Here, I'll help you up." Peggy said.

Gwen found she could walk if she stood on her toes on her injured foot. Though a little uneven, it wouldn't be proper for her to walk around with two bare feet, no matter how much easier it might have been.

Together they made their way through the door and out towards what was now a crowded dance floor. The tempo of the music had increased, and Gwen's spirits rose. She made a quick scan of those around her. No Billy.

Frustrating.

"Come sit over here with me," Peggy interrupted her thoughts. "I have a table set up. You'll be able to sit down and rest until you feel steady on your feet."

Gwen followed her over to a small round table set up in

the room's corner, a perfect people-watching position. Peggy was helping her into the seat when she let out a sharp squeal and stood up straight, leaving Gwen to plonk down sharply onto the chair.

"You terror!" Peggy squealed, turning around.

A man stood there, his face stretched in a wide grin. Peggy squealed again and threw herself into his arms. To Gwen's surprise, she gave him a kiss on the lips before turning back to face Gwen.

He was a very good-looking man. Tall, with dark blonde hair, parted at the side and slicked back. His dark eyes carried a warmth matching Peggy's, and his jawline was strong. For a second, he appeared familiar, although she couldn't for the life of her place him.

"Gwen – is it okay if I call you that?" Peggy dimpled.

Gwen nodded.

"I want you to meet my husband." She turned to the man standing behind her, his large hands laced around her waist.

"Husband?" Gwen said, taken aback and trying to hide her disappointment. Sure enough, a small gold band encircled Peggy's ring finger. She hadn't noticed it before. Somehow, she had assumed Peggy was a kindred spirit, someone unmarried and unshackled like her.

"Nice to meet you, Gwen," he said. He took her hand and gently kissed it. "I'm Hugh O'Regan." He was a charmer, for sure. She could see why Peggy had fallen for him.

"I'm so sorry, you caught me by surprise. It's nice to meet you … Mr O'Regan." Even as she said it, the blood drained from her face.

"And my wife's taken a liking to you. You must call me Hugh. We worry little with last name's around here."

It was ironic because that was exactly what had her worried.

"I ran into Billy. Said he'd rescued a beautiful woman who was being sewn up by my gorgeous wife."

Peggy rolled her eyes.

"Not exactly sewn up, but Peggy was amazing." She nodded her head in appreciation in Peggy's direction.

"Ah, yes! She's a woman of many talents, this one." They snuggled into each other like a pair of newlyweds. Their eyes were wide with adoration for each other, and Gwen shifted uneasily in her seat.

"Gwen's the new teacher," Peggy said, as if noticing Gwen's discomfort.

"Are you just? Well, that explains it, then. We're basically family! You must be staying with my brother, Jake, and his wife, Sarah?"

Gwen was sure Peggy's smile dropped for a moment, but before she could reply, three boisterous man-boys ambushed their table. One had his arm slung around the shoulder of a redhead.

Gwen felt a surge of relief at being spared from talking about her living arrangements.

The man with the redhead gave Hugh a friendly punch on the arm.

"O'Regan! Long time. How ya been?" The two men made small talk. The redhead, still with a heavy arm around her, gave Gwen and Peggy a half smile. The two other men pushed their way into the circle forming around their table. One, Gwen recognised from the deck of the truck on her ride in. The other, much more subdued in seeing her, was Billy Mackenzie.

"Looks like Peggy got you all patched up then?" He nodded

towards her wrapped foot.

"Billy!" Hugh exclaimed, noticing the new arrival. "We were just talking about you! I've met this beautiful creature of yours." He gestured to Gwen.

"I am so sorry," Peggy whispered, bending over the table to Gwen and shaking her head. Gwen arched an eyebrow in Hugh's direction, while Billy took to massaging his forehead. He shot Gwen an apologetic look.

"Ahh, lay off O'Regan. We've only just met."

There he was again, coming to her rescue. The redhead remained dead quiet, eyeing Gwen up and down, pausing for a moment too long on Gwen's bandaged foot.

"Can I get you ladies a drink," Billy offered. "Peggy? Matilda? Miss Davies?"

"Gwen," she corrected him again, giving him a nod in response to the drink. Oh yes, she would welcome a drink right now.

The other two women followed suit.

"Alright, then. I'll be back in a jiffy." He slipped off towards the punch table. Hugh introduced Gwen to the other members of the party as Peggy slipped into the chair beside her.

"How's your foot?" she asked.

"Much better. Thank you." And she was sincere with it. Whether it was Peggy's magical nursing, the drugs kicking in, or the distraction of so many people all talking at once, her foot was feeling much better. Most of the throbbing had gone.

Billy returned with the drinks, placing them down in front of each of them.

"Where's ours?" the man with Matilda the redhead moaned,

his attention drawn away from his conversation with the other men.

"I figured you were big enough and ugly enough to get your own," Billy teased, gaining a big guffaw from the men and a twitter of giggles from the girls.

Gwen sipped at hers greedily. She hadn't realised how thirsty she was. Out of the corner of her eye she saw Billy watching her, amusement on his face. When she finally put her cup down, he turned to her, offering her his arm. She was ready to protest, aware of everyone's stares.

"I'm not sure I can," she argued.

"Don't worry about it. I'll take care of you. You won't even notice you've only one foot."

She took his arm and let him pull her to her feet. The chatter from her group died down as they moved away.

Billy walked her out to the corner of the dance floor. She had guessed he'd chosen the corner so they wouldn't be so conspicuous. Regardless, she still felt several eyes on her. The song faded out and a slow song played. Gwen wondered if he had maybe chosen his moment accordingly.

Billy placed her hands on his shoulders. He slipped his own around her waist and pulled her close to him. It caught her off guard, and her heart fluttered in her chest – this man, who seemed so shy, suddenly being so forward. She wasn't complaining though. She liked the feel of his body close to hers, even if it made her skin tingle.

His breath brushed the top of her head, and she imagined the feel of his heartbeat against her own. She barely had to move her feet. Instead, she swayed side to side, guided by his hands on her waist. She moved her head ever so slowly until it rested on his shoulder. For a moment, it felt like it was just the two of them in the room. She wanted to close her eyes, savour the moment. Slipping her hands further up his shoulders until they were loosely clasped behind his neck, she wondered what he was thinking right now. Had this been his plan all along, to take advantage of an injured girl?

And what was she thinking? They had only just met…

It dawned on her a little late that maybe it hadn't been her best move to slow dance with a man on her first night attending, especially with Ms Flemming on her case about proper teacher decorum.

The song ended and Billy pulled away from her and smiled.

"Not bad," he said, his eyes sparkling.

"Yes, you did okay," she said, returning the flirt.

"How is your foot?"

"It's fine," she said, hoping the returning pain wasn't showing in her face. It must have. He suggested they return to the table, have another drink.

They made their way around the edges of the dance floor. They passed the redhead – Matilda, Gwen scolded herself – her name was Matilda – and Hugh's friend, who were swinging back and forth in each other's arms as they danced it out to the fast number now playing.

Gwen leaned on Billy's arm until they made it to their table. He let her slide into her seat before pulling another chair over from the table beside them. Peggy and Hugh sat with them. It had seemed Hugh had been pestering Peggy to dance, with no luck. She seemed happy leaning into his shoulder, people watching.

"Well, you two looked very cosy out there," she teased.

Gwen blushed.

"Pretty good dancer this one, even with her foot out of

commission."

The conversation moved on to other things, like how Billy's mum was doing. She was sick and Billy was living with her, helping on the farm. His father had passed away a couple of years back, and now he oversaw the farm. They talked of Peggy's dream of being a nurse, how she'd married Hugh and found it was more important she help with the family business. It seemed to Gwen that all people did in Te Tapu was help with the family business. It made her sad. No one seemed free to pursue their own dreams. Although she had to admit Peggy looked no worse for it. She obviously worshipped Hugh, and it seemed her adoration was returned.

No one mentioned Hugh's responsibilities and his family. Gwen found it hard to believe that Hugh and Jake were brothers. She now saw the similar angle to their jaws, their almost-equal height. But where one made her skin crawl, the other seemed warm and friendly. She wondered what Peggy thought of her brother-in-law.

They asked about her work at the school. Specifically, how did she manage with Dahlia Flemming as principal? Then they shared horror stories. Peggy, Hugh and Billy had all attended school together. Where both boys succumbed to the strap at Ms Flemming's hands – on multiple occasions, if they were to be believed – Peggy had suffered it across her knuckles.

Gwen enjoyed the banter. It was fun and light-hearted. Nothing too serious. Everything she had imagined and hoped for in a new group of friends, which she sincerely hoped they now were.

Eventually Peggy gave in and let Hugh take her out for a dance. Gwen and Billy followed suit. Her foot ached, but being in Billy's arms helped to take her mind off it. At one point they swapped partners, and she found herself swung around by Hugh. His dancing style was more fast-paced and jerky in movement. He had her stand on his feet while he moved them around the dance floor. When the song ended, she felt like she had whiplash and understood why it took Peggy so long to give in to his requests to dance.

She was glad when she found herself back in Billy's arms. It felt right, despite having just met him. After a while, she had to beg him to sit, her foot becoming too much to bear.

Billy took her back to her seat, while Peggy endured being thrown around the dance floor by her husband. Sitting there, the two of them alone, made her nervous. She wasn't usually like this, but this day had thrown her, starting with her interaction with Jake in the kitchen. And now here she was, sitting beside a man she barely knew, and she couldn't seem to get enough of him.

"I'm glad I met you, Miss Davies." He shifted in his seat, colour high on his cheeks.

"Me too," she whispered in reply. She loved that he looked as nervous as she felt.

"Do you think I could—" Whatever he meant to say, he put it aside as Hugh threw himself heavily into the chair beside him. Peggy moved behind him, placing her arms casually around his neck.

"This minx has worn me out," he said, carrying a smile that very much said otherwise.

"We're going to head on home, if you'd like a lift?" Peggy offered.

It hadn't even crossed Gwen's mind; how was she going to get home? She had originally planned to walk. It was light out late these days, and she had no fear of the dark, but with her silly foot the way it was, she likely wouldn't make it far. She looked expectantly at Billy to rescue her again.

"I think that would be great. Much more fitting than riding on the back of a truck with that lot." He nodded towards the men they had arrived with, whose raucous laughter carried over top of the music. From the way they were falling all over each other, Gwen assumed they had had too much punch. Two scowling women stood nearby with arms crossed, obviously irritated by their behaviour. She had a hard time picturing Billy running in their circle.

"Well, there's plenty of room. I brought Lucy," Hugh offered.

"Lucy?" Gwen asked.

"His car." Peggy rolled her eyes again.

Gwen was grateful. She hated the thought of having to make her own way home and was in no mood for the teasing she had endured earlier.

"Alright, let's go then." Peggy put her arm around Gwen and helped her walk towards the exit.

"So what do you think?" she whispered in Gwen's ear. Hugh and Billy were a few feet in front of them, and Gwen knew exactly what she was alluding to.

"He's very nice," was all Gwen could think of to say. It was true; he was very nice. Yet that didn't explain the butterflies in her stomach.

"Nice from this angle, too," Peggy quipped, raising her eyebrows at the two young men, deep in conversation.

Gwen stifled a giggle.

When they reached Lucy, Hugh held the door open for Peggy and Gwen. Peggy slid into the backseat first, letting

Gwen get in beside her. Billy went around to the front passenger seat. It was later than Gwen had expected, day light already fading, and she was glad for the ride home. The car started up with a gentle rumble. Hugh reversed, then floored it off the grassy verge and onto the road, flicking his lights on as he did.

"Well, Gwen, I think you live the closest, so I'll drop you off first," said Hugh.

Billy glanced at Hugh, confusion darting across his face.

It didn't take long, and disappointment surged in her, seeing the house before her. She hadn't wanted the night to end.

No lights were on, which meant the occupants were asleep. At least, Gwen hoped they were.

"Wait! You live here?" Billy asked. Realisation hitting him, he turned in his seat to face her. "You're living with Jake?" His voice rose, and Gwen felt a shift in the air.

"I board with him and Sarah," Gwen said, avoiding his eyes in case she gave anything away.

"You're all right with this?" Billy turned to Hugh, an edge to his tone.

"Ahh, you'll be alright," Hugh said to Gwen, ignoring Billy. "Let him know you're a friend of mine."

Billy's mouth gaped slightly. He stared at Hugh with an expression of disbelief. Gwen turned to Peggy, who's lips were pressed together tightly. If she was reading things right, neither Billy nor Peggy were fans of Hugh's darling brother. A chill trickled down her spine. It was nice knowing she wasn't alone in her feelings towards Jake, but she couldn't very well allow herself to be a prisoner of fear because of him either.

She opened the car door.

"Thanks for the ride," she said. "I had a really nice time."

"It was so nice meeting you," Peggy and Hugh replied in unison.

"We'll see you again, okay?" Peggy leaned over and gave her a kiss on the cheek. Before she even had a moment to realise it, Billy was at her door, holding it open for her and offering her his arm. She took it and followed him up the few steps to the front door.

"Are you going to be alright?" he asked. Genuine concern showed in his eyes, and Gwen suspected he was talking about more than her lame foot.

"Of course," she said, forcing a smile. He went to say something else, but she interrupted him.

"Thank you for tonight. For coming to my rescue." The air seemed to fizz between them, and she had to stay herself from reaching out and touching him.

"It's nothing. Anyone would've done the same."

She wondered if anyone would have. "Of course," she replied, turning her back to him to fish for her key out of her purse.

He gently pulled her arm so she would turn to face him.

"I wanted to ask—" he started.

She looked up at him, holding her breath.

"—if you'd like to get together again sometime? If you're free of course."

Gwen's heart swelled. She kept her face stoic, not wanting to give too much away, but inside she thought she was going to burst. "That would be lovely."

"Great," he said, the corners of his mouth creeping up. "Then I'll see you again soon, Miss Davies."

"Gwen," she reminded him.

73

"Gwen," he repeated before heading back to the car, and she didn't think her name had ever sounded so sweet. She found her key and turned it in the lock, giving a quick wave to the car behind her before turning it.

She opened the door to a darkened hallway, the smell of tobacco and whiskey greeting her.

Give me courage, she thought, crossing the threshold.

Chapter 8 – Riley

She drove with minimal shaking, the note pressed deep down into the bottom of her purse. *Help me*, it had read, but she really had no idea what it meant. Help who? Justin? It wasn't Justin's handwriting. One of her kids, then? Maybe? Experimenting with cursive? But what was it she was supposed to help with?

Whoever had written it, and for whatever reason, it gave her goosebumps. While reading it, she'd had an unnerving feeling of being watched and had to remind herself that was nonsense. Still, the whole thing niggled at her all the way home.

She normally enjoyed the drive despite the nearly forty-five minutes it tagged onto the end of her workday. It gave her a chance to decompress, to re-evaluate the happenings of the day to a picturesque backdrop of rolling hills and cow-spotted paddocks. The winding roads were soothing. It gave her a chance to think about Justin too. What gave him the right to appear at her school, during school time, with her kids and her colleagues around? What nerve! Did he *want* to create a scene?

How much had Liam overheard? And then, of course, her

mind went off on the tangent of Liam. Why was he always around to see her at her worst? She grew agitated. Bloody men! Couldn't they all just leave her alone?

Her phone's screen lit up. It was sitting in her drink holder beside her seat, and still on silent from being in class.

The nerve! He was ringing her! Justin was ringing her!

She let the phone screen continue flashing, keeping her eyes on the road. She wasn't answering it. Not now. She tightened her grip on the steering wheel and gritted her teeth, then reached over to turn up the volume on her music to distract her from her growing annoyance. She would call him when she got home, or better yet, maybe she wouldn't call him at all.

She made it the rest of the way home, alternating between imaginary arguments with Justin and singing loudly to allay her anger.

A small part of her missed him. He had broken her heart. And what hurt the most was that he never tried to stop her from leaving, he just let her go. Until now.

The driveway was empty when she reached it. Riley's landlady was out. Housie, most likely. She grimaced at the thought of her on the road in her ancient Honda Civic. She was not a good driver. Riley had shared a car once with her before, a trip to the supermarket. She swore they had spent more time off the road than on it. Never again, she promised herself, and she wished Molly had taken her advice to use the bus or call a taxi.

Part of her had half-expected to see Justin's Mazda in the driveway. She hadn't told him where she was living, but someone could have.

Riley exhaled a breath she hadn't realised she'd been

holding. Now, she'd be able to spend a quiet night at home, have time to think and reflect. She parked her car in front of her granny flat, grabbed her teacher bag from the back seat and made for the door, keys in hand. A note stuck partway out of the door. Riley flexed her fingers to stop their sudden trembling. When was this going to stop?

He *had* found out where she lived. Written on the back of a receipt for petrol were the words, *Call me. Please. We need to talk. J.* That was all. Brief. To the point. She cursed under her breath.

What was it with all the notes? This was not how she wanted to spend her evening, digging up the past, reliving a love lost. No, it wasn't lost. It was worn out. She'd given her all and it wasn't returned, so she had left. Simple.

Riley stuffed this second note into her pocket, juggling her purse and bag filled with homework books to mark and lesson planning to go over. She jiggled the keys until the door unlocked and inched open. Using her foot, she nudged the door open, jumping back in surprise as a fluffy ginger cat yowled and darted through her legs. Her heart lodged in her throat.

Damn cat. He was forever sneaking into her house – like when she was readying herself for a run – finding somewhere to hide and then acting all disgruntled when he ended up locked in for the day. It was the third day this week alone. You would think Edgar, as Molly had called him, would have learnt by now.

Edgar had the fury of a demon when pissed off, which was more often than not. He was a bully to the rest of Molly's cats, and in the past, happily swiped at Riley's legs if she ever got between him and his food or an exit.

Riley shut the door and threw her bags down beside her couch. It wasn't much of a home. One bedroom, a small kitchenette with a built-in oven and stovetop, a second-hand sofa and coffee table and a few knick-knacks to brighten up the place. It was the best she could do with the money she had. She had been in such a hurry to leave Justin before she changed her mind, she hadn't bothered to have the talk about splitting their belongings.

Maybe that was why he wanted to chat, she thought. He was feeling generous. Wanting to settle up? She snorted. Not likely.

She looked around her. She was starving. If she was going to go through with this – call him, get it over with – she needed some sort of sustenance to see her through. She opened the pantry cupboards and felt around the cereal boxes where she kept her secret stash of pick-me-up chocolate biscuits.

Holding the carton, she plonked herself down on the sofa. Then she stared at the phone in her hand while devouring a cookie. Like ripping off a plaster, she told herself.

She picked up her phone, held her breath and dialled.

He picked up on the second ring. She paused for a moment, feeling her courage seep away. She felt her fingers shake again.

"Riles? Hello. Riles, are you there?"

Damn caller ID.

"I'm here," she said, hearing the tightness in her words. She was just calling to find out what he wanted, nothing else. She would not be pulled back in.

"Riles, I'm so glad you called. We need to talk, baby. Tell me you're home, and I'll be around in five."

"Wait. What? You're here?"

"I'm at the Best Western down the road. Your mother gave me your address. Look, I want to talk, is all."

"No, Justin. If you want to talk, you need to do it now." She found her voice again. She stood up and paced around the small living space. He would not bully her.

"Come home, Riles. I want you to come home. I miss you."

Conflicting emotions welled up. His pained tone made her wince, pursued by a flash of grief and anger, remembering what it had been like to find out he had cheated on her.

"No," she said. It sounded weaker than she had meant it to.

"But, Riles … what about us? We have a life together—"

"*Had* a life together," she interrupted.

"It doesn't have to be this way, you know. Remember your bracelet?"

She glanced down at her wrist where it slid out from under her jacket.

"It means something. We're soulmates. We can make this work."

She paused for a moment before finding her words again.

"Then why did it take you so long? I've been out here nearly a month, and nothing! I've heard nothing from you."

"Look, Riles," he said, ignoring her accusation. "You can't be staying out there alone. You're working in the middle of nowhere, surrounded by country hicks. You're living in some old lady's flat…"

A red-hot flash of fury seared her chest up to her neck and face. Country hicks? What the hell was he talking about?

"We're done, Justin," she growled through clenched teeth.

"Help me. Tell me, Riles, what I need to do to make things right. Help me out, okay?" His voice had dropped an octave. Behind the pleading lurked something else. Almost a warning.

Alarm bells crashed in the back of her mind. She swapped the phone over to her other hand, taking the moment to wipe her palm on her pants.

"It was you," she accused. "You left that bloody note. What the hell, Justin?"

"What are you talking about?" he asked indignantly.

"The note you left me… on my desk…"

"I didn't leave you any note, Riley, just the one at your flat. Look. Just come home, okay?"

"I *am* home. I live here now. I have a house and a job. I'm making new friends…"

"Goddam it, Riley…"

"No!" It took a lot for her to get this fiery, but he just wasn't getting it. He'd given her no good reason to go back to him. "We're over, Justin. Stay away from me." Her voice pitched with the last few words, her whole body alight with fury. She hung up before he could say another word and threw her cell onto the sofa.

God, he was infuriating. And what the hell had her mother been thinking?

She kept pacing, flexing her fingers, not sure what else to do with herself.

She was serious about what she had said. She had a home and a job now. This was what she had wanted. She owed it to herself to give it a chance to work. She wasn't going back.

As she calmed, something else niggled at her.

He had said those words: *Help me*. It had been an unusual turn of phrase for him. And yet he swore he never left the note. So, if he didn't leave it, who had?

Chapter 9 – Riley

The class was unsettled the next day. Riley put it down to a change in routine. She didn't normally teach on Fridays and here she was back in the classroom instead of on classroom release, covering for Victoria who was called away for an urgent meeting. Or else a scheduled meeting she had forgotten. Riley suspected it could be either.

Her argument with Justin the night before had left her drained. She hadn't slept well, replaying every word said, over and over in her mind. She was counting down the minutes until Victoria returned and relieved her.

After answering why she was teaching instead of Mrs Stone, Riley went about her normal morning routine. The class was fidgety and chatty, her patience dwindling early on. Though she had tried some maths, she found it hard to keep the attention of the groups she was working with.

Mindfulness, the thought came to her. What they all needed, including herself, was a bit of mindfulness right now. A way to calm and focus the mind.

"Alright, class." She clapped as a way of getting their attention. "I thought we might spend some time practising our handwriting; please go to your tote trays, get out your literacy books and head up the page with the date."

The class moved before she had completed her instructions.

Riley loved handwriting. For this year group it wasn't an essential part of the curriculum, but she remembered practising cursive during her own school days and how calming and meditative it was, making the pen float across the paper with artistic flare. It would buy her fifteen minutes at least of quiet to soothe the headache she felt stirring behind her left eye.

"Right! To warm up, let's start with the alphabet – all lower case, please, so they join nicely together." The students had already had instruction on each letter. Riley had taught them on an earlier date. Regardless, she modelled it on the whiteboard for the students to copy her wrist weaving across the white surface, blue marker in hand, fluid in her grasp, a dance between pen and whiteboard.

While the students completed the exercise, Riley walked around the room, checking they had ruled their books up correctly, written the date and were on task, redirecting them when they started chatting with their neighbour. One child was intent on tattooing his arm. With gentle authority, she took his pen from his hand and gave him a pencil.

Next, she wrote out a few of her favourite lines from *Wuthering Heights*. Not only was it her favourite book, but it lent itself well to cursive script.

"I have dreamt in my life dreams that have stayed with me ever after and changed my ideas; they have gone through and through me, like wine through water, and altered the colour of my mind."

She continued with quotes from other books and a few other phrases, disguising as she did another motive, to find out who wrote her the note that read *"Help me!"*

She could have just asked the class, but as no one had approached her of their own accord she didn't want to make a big deal about it.

"Help me," the mouse called to his friend as the cat got ready to pounce.

She wrote two more brief sentences under it, to distract from it, then worked her way around the room again, offering small insights for correction, praising, and refocusing her students as she went. She'd have a quick check through them at morning tea before Victoria took over the class again.

Most of the students were now finishing up. A murmur had grown amongst the students, with a few chuckles from some boys in the back. Riley glanced up at the clock on the wall, thankful it was almost morning tea. She had gotten a few minutes of quiet and concentration from them, at least. For today, she would count that as a win. One girl, Amy, had her hand up and was twitching in her chair trying to get Riley's attention.

"Miss Cooper? Why did you write that?" She pointed at the whiteboard where Riley had written out a few more sentences to be copied. It took her a moment to register what she had written, and she leaned on the edge of Amy's desk to steady herself. The last sentence – surely she hadn't written that? The thought pitched funny in her mind. Staring at the whiteboard, she gasped as the letters moved, slowly at first, haphazardly, and then crashing into each other with such violence they bled darkness.

Riley's legs buckled under her; voices called out like echoes she couldn't quite grasp. Then she was falling, and everything went quiet. Everything went dark.

Chapter 10 – Riley

Riley blinked a few times, focusing in on the blur of worried faces staring down at her. Finally, Victoria's face sharpened into view with deep lines etched between her brows. Her mouth a tight, thin line. She bent over Riley and held a damp cloth to her forehead.

Victoria's mouth moved, and it took a moment for the ringing in Riley's ears to recede for her to realize Victoria was barking orders to a person standing on the other side of her. Riley turned her head slightly, her head pounding as she did so. Her eyes met Liam's, confusion and wariness obvious on his features, and a twinge of panic and embarrassment fluttered beneath her disorientation. The only word her brain was capable of thinking was "Shit!" And a new flush of heat rose in her chest.

Despite Victoria's protests, Riley tried to sit up. Her forehead throbbed under the cool cloth. She must have hit her head on the way down, she surmised. She'd never completely fainted before, and she fought the wave of nausea dancing in her stomach. Cool beads of sweat trailed down the back of her neck.

Oh God, the kids would have seen, she thought as she found

her bearings again. Wait? Where were the kids? She moved her head cautiously, scanning the room for curious faces. Other than Liam and Victoria, the room was empty. She had been sure she had seen other faces peering down at her too.

"What happened?" she asked, finding her voice.

"You fainted," Victoria said matter-of-factly, pulling the cloth away from Riley's head. "A kid screamed and Liam here came running to find you on the floor."

Riley cringed and squeezed her eyes tight for a moment, less from pain than Victoria and Liam probably imagined.

"I've sent the kids out to join Robert's class for a game. You'll be the talk of the school for a while though, I'm afraid."

Riley fingers traced the egg already blooming above her left eye.

"How are you feeling? Are you alright?" Victoria placed her hand on Riley's arm as if to steady her from fainting again.

"I think so." Riley continued to trace the lump with her fingers.

"It seems you knocked the desk as you went down. Do you remember what happened?"

Her memory was a little fuzzy, and it didn't help that Liam, who had perched himself on the edge of a desk, was still staring at her. She glanced away self-consciously.

As if sensing the awkwardness, Victoria turned to Liam. "An icepack might be useful right about now, don't you think?"

It seemed to shake Liam from his reverie, and he stood up and headed for the door.

Riley watched him for a second, then let her gaze float around the room once more.

The whiteboard.

She had been doing handwriting.

Her eyes travelled over the cursive script she'd written there for her students to copy. She read down it until she got to the sentence about a mouse calling for help. *"Help me," the mouse called to his friend as the cat got ready to pounce.*

It hit her like an axe to the chest, leaving her almost breathless for a moment. The writing stared back at her, willing her to accept responsibility. How could she not? She remembered writing it. It was her writing. But then, how was it that the words *"Help me"* looked identical to those on the note from her desk? She couldn't have written the note herself. She would have remembered…

Riley staggered to her feet. She caught Victoria giving her a strange look.

"What is going on, Riley?" she said, cutting the air with her tone.

"I … I don't know," Riley replied. As if in a trance, she moved to the whiteboard.

Liam appeared in the doorway.

"Here," he said, approaching her.

She turned and he held out an icepack to her, a scowl forming on his face, as he tracked where her attention had been pulled.

Ignoring him, she turned back to the whiteboard and traced the words *"Help me"* in the air a few centimetres away from where it was written.

"I don't understand why you'd write such a thing." Victoria stood beside her.

"I'm sorry?" Riley said, turning to Victoria. "It was just a random sentence to see who had written me the note." The words spilled out without thinking, and she mentally kicked herself. Now she would have to explain the note.

Victoria's jaw slackened in horror. "Someone wrote you this?" Her voice pitched as she tapped the whiteboard with her finger.

Riley's eyes travelled to where Victoria pointed at the last sentence, below where she'd been looking. But she hadn't written that. She would remember if she had.

She twisted the bracelet around her wrist, trying to make sense of what was written in her own hand:

Murderer! Murderer! He killed Billy!

"Why would anyone write you this? And why would you share this with the class?"

"I didn't write this," she whispered. "I mean, I don't remember writing this," she said, this time to Victoria.

Victoria massaged a spot between her brows and closed her eyes for a second.

"I … I don't know what happened." Riley knew it was a weak excuse, but she couldn't think what else to say. It was her handwriting; no one else could have written it. *Why* she wrote it was a whole other mystery.

"I don't think I should have to tell you, it's not appropriate." Victoria let out an exasperated sigh and shook her head. "We'll just have to hope the kids don't go home telling their parents. You fainting is drama enough without them mentioning their teacher had them practise writing out the word 'murderer' for handwriting practice." A sternness lay in her tone, but her eyes held a hint of sympathy.

Riley blushed. "I'm so sorry," she said again.

"Look, none of this is my business," a gruff voice interrupted the moment. "If you don't need anything else, I have other things to take care of."

Both Riley and Victoria spun around. Riley had completely

forgotten about Liam. He had been so quiet, hovering in the doorway with the icepack. By the expression on Victoria's face, she had too. He placed the icepack wrapped in a muslin cloth on the nearest desk and turned tail. Heat flared in her cheeks. She couldn't imagine being any more mortified.

Victoria turned back to Riley. "We'll put it down to a momentary lapse of judgement, shall we? My biggest concern is that you fainted. Are you okay?" she asked with genuine concern.

"I'm fine," she said, picking up the icepack and cradling it to her head. She cringed for a moment at its coldness.

"No trip to the medical centre then?"

Riley gave a slow shake of her head. The pain was nothing a painkiller wouldn't fix; she was sure of it. Her fainting had been just one of those things.

"Okay, then. I think it best you spend the rest of the period in the staffroom. You can call out to Sandra in the office if you need anything. The kids will be back soon, so I'll do damage control the best I can."

"Thank you," Riley said. Kids' voices draw closer, and Riley turned to leave.

"Oh, Miss Cooper—"

Riley glanced over her shoulder.

"—it's okay, you know. We all have our moments. Most of us have done far worse, but we'll talk later this afternoon, okay? After school." A shadow of a smile played on Victoria's lips now. The knot in Riley's stomach eased. She gave Victoria a small nod and headed towards the staffroom.

Chapter 11 – Gwen

"The thing that irks me most is this shattered
prison, after all. I'm tired of being enclosed here.
I'm wearying to escape into that glorious world
and to be always there: not seeing it dimly through
tears and yearning for it through the walls of an
aching heart, but really with it and in it."
- ***Wuthering Heights***

I t had been Peggy's idea, and Gwen jumped at the chance.
They bumped into each other at the grocer on
Thursday.

It had been a long week, the summer heat stifling. Ms
Flemming's expectation that Gwen wear full tights, a long
woollen skirt, and long-sleeved blouse when at school meant
Gwen fought heat exhaustion for most of the day.

Though it would hardly have mattered if she had fainted
in class. By the time the students had their lunch, they were
half asleep themselves. Trying to get them to focus on their
work was a wasted use of energy. She had to prod a few with

a ruler as they succumbed to sleeping at their desks.

She couldn't blame them. The sky was such a rich blue, and even with the classroom doors folded wide open, there was little breeze to stimulate the senses. No one would have noticed had she melted away into a puddle of perspiration at their feet. It made her curse Ms Flemming even more. The school felt an even worse hell than her home at present.

Though Gwen hadn't seen Sarah for a couple of days after the dance, notes were left with her meals. On Tuesday afternoon, Gwen headed to the kitchen to see about dinner. Her stomach flip-flopped when she heard noises, but as she passed through the doorway, relief flooded her. Sarah stood at the sink, back to her, hair pulled into a low bun.

"Oh, hello, Sarah! Can I hel—"

Sarah jumped, turning on tiptoe to face her. A couple of wayward strands of hair had loosened themselves around her face. A purple bruise, caked with powder, marred the right side of her jaw.

Gwen recoiled at seeing it, her mouth dropping open.

Eyes wide, Sarah held up the tea towel in her hand, effectively hiding the injury, then dropped it to her side just as fast in realising what she was doing and turned back to the sink. Without saying a word, she returned to scrubbing a roasting dish.

The room smelled amazing. A casserole sat covered, cooling on the bench. A bowl of potatoes rested on the dining table with three placings set. Gwen's stomach somersaulted. Three placings…

Trying to regain her composure, she asked again. "Can I do anything to help?" Gwen grimaced at the double-edged turn of phrase.

"No, I'm fine," Sarah said, grabbing another tea towel and using one in each hand to carry the casserole to the table, keeping her gaze averted the whole time.

Gwen couldn't take her eyes off her. She knew it was rude, but that man – he had struck his own wife. She knew it was him. She had guessed early on things were not right between them. Anyway, had she not, Jake's comments about Sarah and a baby would easily have convinced her.

Gwen didn't need to ask where to sit. Whenever they ate together, they always had their set places.

She eased herself into her seat, pulling herself up close to the oak dining table. Despite her hunger and the comforting smell of the food, she had to hold back nausea that had settled in her stomach.

She watched while Sarah stood still, seemingly unsure what to do. She wrung her hands in her apron while Gwen shifted uneasily in her chair, aware of the unspoken heaviness in the room. And this, Gwen thought, was the quiet before the storm.

Slowly, Sarah slipped into the chair opposite Gwen.

"Eat," was all she said. Sarah went about dishing herself some of the food: casserole, peas, potatoes. Three small piles. Lifting her fork, she went about chasing the food around her plate. Not once did she look in Gwen's direction.

Gwen knew she should stop staring, but she couldn't. Part of her was furious that someone could do such a thing to their spouse; the other part of her felt such pity for the creature in front of her. And fear buzzed just beneath the surface of her own skin.

He had been drinking. Again. Even before the smell assaulted her senses, it was obvious from the way he hit the doorjamb trying to enter the room. His feet shuffled across the linoleum. Sarah instantly put down her fork. Without looking up, and in a shaky voice, she said, "Dinner is ready if you're joining us."

"Pish," he spat. "Can't even wait for your own husband?" His words slurred.

Gwen gripped her cutlery tighter. It dug into the palms of her hand. She held her breath. She suspected Sarah was as well.

Without sparing a glance in their direction, Jake went over to the far cupboard up high. Upon opening it, he pulled out a glass bottle of amber liquor. Though only half full, it was still of a significant volume. As if it were too heavy for him, he plonked it down loudly on the bench.

Neither Gwen nor Sarah moved. Frozen in time, Gwen waited to see if he would join them.

Instead, he picked up the bottle and stumbled out of the room again, not acknowledging either of them. Gwen listened as he stumbled down the hall.

Once she heard his office door shut; she let herself move her fork and contemplate eating again. In honesty, she no longer had an appetite but didn't want Sarah's cooking – her hard work – to go unappreciated. She forced herself a few deliberate mouthfuls.

"This is really nice," she said, hoping it would break her from her trance. It seemed to do the trick. Sarah picked up her fork and moved it around her plate again.

"Thanks," she said. She didn't once lift the fork to her mouth.

After a while, Sarah picked up her plate and took it to the sink and went about scraping it into the scrap bin. The pigs would do well from this meal, Gwen thought.

Feeling excused from clearing her own plate, Gwen got up to do the same.

"Sarah?" she said, her voice shaking a little, unsure what to say that wouldn't make it worse. She just wanted the poor woman to know she wasn't alone.

"No," Sarah said in reply. Her tone was so severe it made Gwen pull up fast.

"I just—"

"No," Sarah said again. "You need to leave."

Gwen was stunned. The room or the house? She placed her plate back on the table and left the room. What else could she have done? Sarah didn't want to talk about it. It wasn't like Gwen could make her, and maybe this was how some marriages were.

It was weak. Not for a moment did she believe this was what marriage was like. As far as she was aware, when her own father was alive, he never once raised his hand to her mama.

Gwen went to her room, feeling like a prisoner in her own home. No, this wasn't her home, it was simply somewhere to sleep at night.

Lying down on her bed, Gwen picked up her diary and the dip pen she kept on her bedside table. Her father was the one who had got her into journaling, buying her first journal and telling her how to use it. Not being much of an academic, it had surprised her how much she came to enjoy the little ritual of writing her feelings, the goings on of the day. Even the mundane could be brought alive on paper. Problems could be solved and hurts healed.

She opened her small ink pot and took a moment to think

about what to write. The bruise on Sarah's jaw was something new, but she wasn't ready to delve deep into that drama.

Her mind flitted back to Saturday's dance, and words came up without restraint. She let the dip pen glide across the paper as she remembered him. Billy. By the end, she was smiling. She felt lighter, even.

That's why when Peggy bumped into her at the local grocer and invited her to go swimming on Saturday, she didn't hesitate. She would have gone even if Billy wouldn't be there, but Peggy mentioned it first thing when convincing Gwen to join them.

Gwen was giddy with excitement the whole of Friday. The moodiness of her students couldn't stifle her excitement for the weekend.

Peggy had also offered to lend her a swimsuit if she didn't have her own. And she didn't. Why would she? She couldn't swim. Her mother had an ungodly fear of water, which kept her from allowing Gwen and her sisters to learn how to swim. Because she loved them; she said. Gwen rolled her eyes. It was because it was one more thing she couldn't control, she thought, shaking her head.

Now Saturday had arrived and Gwen sat in her room, keeping her hands busy scribbling in her journal. Her entire body vibrated with excitement. This was what she had imagined a new start would feel like, she'd written in her diary. New adventures with new friends. Not to mention one who was particularly handsome.

She would write a couple of lines, dreaming about what the day might hold ahead, and then pace around the room before throwing herself back on to her bed to write some more.

The problem was this house. It was so stifling. Nowhere to

move. Both Sarah and Jake were home. She had seen them at breakfast. Jake had asked what her plans were for the day. Though the question was innocuous, her blood ran cold when he asked it, as if by telling him he would somehow strip the day of some of its pleasure – like a dream-sucking vampire.

When he asked who her friends were, she panicked a little. Should she tell him they included his brother and sister-in-law? Would he want to invite himself?

Better to play dumb, she thought. She had already gathered that although he might not be Peggy and Billy's favourite person, there could still be some brotherly idolisation from Hugh.

If Sarah noticed Gwen's hesitation, she showed no signs. She had been pushing her porridge around her bowl with her spoon the entire time, eyes downcast. A skeletal phantom, in the world but not of the world. Gwen wondered if she ever actually ate anything.

"Some people I met at last Saturday's dance," Gwen mumbled, barely glancing in Jake's direction. Beyond the fact he repelled her, she was also a little fearful of him. Married or not, he had no right to raise a hand to his wife. Gwen ground her teeth between mouthfuls, trying to stymy the flash of anger washing over her at the thought.

She wasn't even hungry. It was amazing what someone like Jake could do to an otherwise healthy appetite. She sat there more out of obligation. She also loathed the thought of leaving Sarah alone with the monster opposite her.

Nothing for it this afternoon, though. If she invited her, Jake might take it as his own personal invitation, and today was hers, Gwen's alone.

The sound of gravel under tyres propelled Gwen from

95

the bed and to her feet. She wanted to get the door before either of the other two did. Peggy had promised the loan of a bathing suit, and she'd need to try it on before they left. She'd leave it on under her clothes – as fun as it might be, general small-town decorum wouldn't smile kindly on her being caught changing behind a tree.

It crossed her mind that she'd still have to change out of her clothes if she were to go into the water. If the temperatures were going to be half as hot as they had been, she had no doubt she might be one of the first in. Her mother might be afraid of water, but with two handsome men around to rescue her, even if one was unapologetically taken, she had no concerns, no matter what happened.

A knock on the front door came just as Gwen pulled down on the door handle.

"Gwenny, darling, you look gorgeous," Peggy said, drawing Gwen to her with an air kiss to each cheek. "For you," she said, holding a bag out for Gwen to take.

Peggy looked beautiful, as always, Gwen thought. A small stab of jealously shot through her. She was tall, taller than Gwen, and slim, more of an athletic build than curvaceous like Gwen's own form. Gwen stood on her tiptoes and took a quick peek at those behind Peggy. A quick glimpse at Hugh's form striding towards her made her realise she had little chance of escaping interaction with Jake. Hugh obviously planned to say hello to his brother.

But it was Billy whom she really wanted to see.

He stood leaning on the open back door of Lucy. His cheese-cutter cap was pulled low over his forehead, and he was chewing on something. He gave a crooked smile in her direction, and her heart flip-flopped in her chest.

96

"Is Jakey home, then?" Hugh asked, moving beside Peggy and effectively blocking out Gwen's view of Billy.

Jakey, Gwen thought. Oh God.

She needn't have said anything, Jake beat her to it.

"So these are your friends, then, are they?" A voice drew up behind her. She could feel the warmth of his voice on the back of her neck, and instantly she recoiled, stepping aside to let Jake step into the doorway she had otherwise been blocking.

Gwen was sure she spotted Peggy's lips curl with repulsion too.

Peggy stepped back, giving Hugh some space. Hugh grabbed Jake's hand in a sort of handshake before pulling him in for a quick hug.

"Sarah!" Jake bellowed, turning his attention behind him to the end of the hallway where the kitchen was.

Gwen instinctively followed his gaze. Sarah stood there like a deer locked in headlights. Her hands were bunched in the apron she wore around her waist. Not clenching as they normally did, but dead still, as if she were paralysed, unsure how to move.

"Don't be rude, woman. Put the kettle on."

"No, that's all right, brother. We're not staying long, anyway." Hugh sent Sarah a wide smile.

How were these two men before her brothers?

"We're heading down to the Willows. Why don't you and Sarah join us?"

Sarah started from her trance and hurriedly disappeared into the kitchen.

"Pfft," Jake replied.

Hugh stepped inside and put his hand on Jake's shoulder.

"Come on, Jakey. How long has it been since you've had some fun?"

Jake shook his brother's hand off. His lips curled in a sneer. "I don't need your pity, brother."

Gwen took another step back as Jake almost spat the last word. She pressed herself up against the wall, feeling as she guessed Sarah did, paralysed. Unsure. A shiver of tension rippled in the air around the small party, as if a whole other conversation were taking place beyond words.

"Looks like you've met your charity quota for today as it is."

Gwen followed his line of sight beyond Hugh to where Billy stood. No longer leaning on the car, Billy's jaw had tightened, his lips now a thin line, his hands pressed into fists.

"Try on the swimsuit, Gwenny, we'll be waiting by the car." Ignoring the men between them, Peggy spun on her heel and headed back towards Billy. Gwen did as she suggested, leaving the two brothers to their sparring. She headed to her room, bag in hand. She hoped Sarah would be okay home alone with the brute. Gwen pulled a swimsuit out of the bag. It was lovely.

The emerald-green colour matched her eyes. It was woollen with a small modesty skirt and black lace decoration along the neckline. It looked new. Gwen could only imagine what Peggy would be wearing.

Despite the difference in their height, it fit well enough. A little tight across the bosom, Gwen being better endowed than Peggy, but it made the suit, dare she say, sexier.

Gwen hurriedly pulled a sundress over top and slipped on her sandals. Her foot had healed well, and she barely even noticed it now.

Making use of the tote bag the swimsuit had come in, Gwen stuffed a towel and a change of clothes in it to take with her. Peggy said she'd take care of the food, so she had nothing further to do but face whatever was going on in the hallway and leave.

She opened her bedroom door to hear the stomping footsteps of Jake coming towards her down the hall. Her breath caught in her throat, and then almost as immediately exhaled in relief as he threw open the door to his office and slammed it behind himself.

Gwen gave herself a second to compose herself before stepping fully into the hallway. Hugh was still standing in the front doorway. She glimpsed a frown on his face before, on seeing her, he automatically replaced it with a wide smile.

"Well, kitten. Should we head off, then?"

Gwen followed Hugh out to Lucy. Billy and Peggy stood by the car in hushed conversation. Billy spotted Gwen first, and his face immediately lit up. Gwen was sure hers did the same. She had wanted to play it cool, but who was she kidding? She was giddy with excitement, both about seeing Billy and about escaping the house.

"Alright, my people, let's do this." Hugh gave Peggy a peck on the forehead before opening the front passenger door for her.

Billy was already holding a back door open, and he gestured for Gwen to get in before closing it and going around to the other side of the car.

With them all seated, Hugh started the car. As he sharply turned the steering wheel to do a U-turn in the drive, Gwen peered out the window towards the house. She could just make out the window to Jake's office down the side of the house. With pulled curtains, she could only guess what went on in there. What had Hugh said to have Jake storm off in such a way?

She thought of Sarah left there, trapped in the house with that man. Striking it from her mind with a casual flick of her hair, Gwen returned her thoughts to what was really important, the here and now. For this moment, at least, she was free.

Chapter 12 – Liam

The sun was out in full blast, and the clock had barely tipped ten o'clock. Without a morning breeze to take the edge off, the heat felt oppressive already. Victoria had called him in to fix a swing some kid had broken, a simple job, but he was thankful for an excuse to leave the house.

Liam's father was having a bad day. Not that many good days occurred anymore. Not since Liam's mother had died, anyway.

They argued over breakfast. Arthur wanted to hand over more responsibility to Liam, have him take over the running of the farms to allow Arthur to retire. Liam had turned him down flat. Again. His father was well known in Te Tapu for his need to micro-manage others, no matter the state of his health. It was also well known that Liam and his father didn't get along. A business partnership would not work. For anyone.

He wanted Liam to attend an agricultural expo in Germany to view a few expensive items of farm machinery he'd had his eye on, then spend a couple of weeks on a farm belonging to an acquaintance of his to see the equipment in action, to make sure they were making a sound investment.

Liam refused, reminding his father his being back here in Te Tapu was a temporary thing. His father needed to interview for a business manager, someone he could trust to keep the business running, attend those damn expos, and make decisions when he wasn't around. He needed someone who could put up with his crankiness, his outbursts and arrogance, but by hell it would not be him! The problem was, in his father's eyes, it was all about the O'Regan name, and Liam was the last.

Having barely touched his toast, Liam left – both the conversation and the house – slamming the door on his way out. He was thankful Victoria had called, asked him to pop in when he was free. For Liam, it was the perfect excuse to get out of the house and put some distance between him and his father.

He was walking past the main classroom block towards the playground when a dull thud and a high-pitched scream interrupted the quiet chatter of children at work. He raced inside Room 2 to see most of the children out of their seats talking excitedly and a few kids crying and consoling each other. He fought his way through the crowd. The new teacher, Miss Cooper, lay unconscious on the ground. He assumed she had hit the edge of the desk as she fell. An egg was rising on her forehead.

He turned to a boy he knew. "Alex, go get Mrs Stone from her office. Tell her there's a medical issue in your class."

Alex gave a nod and darted from the room, and Liam directed the other students to stand back. He moved over to Miss Cooper and tapped her shoulder, trying for a response. "Are you okay, Miss Cooper." Nothing. Though her chest rose and fell with shallow breaths, he checked for a pulse, which was strong despite being on the slow side.

The kids grew quiet in the back of the room, and Victoria hustled through the door. Miss Cooper moaned and moved her head slightly side to side. She'd be waking up soon.

Victoria clapped her hands twice. "Alright, children. Single file. I want you to go outside for a free period. Mr. McCreery and his class are waiting for you."

As the children exited, she wetted a cloth and placed it on Miss Cooper's forehead.

"What happened?" she asked.

"No idea. I was on my way to fix the swings and heard a noise." He looked down at Miss Cooper. She was pretty, though he also found something strange about her. Mostly, she made him uncomfortable. When it hit him, an ache filled his chest. She reminded him of his wife. Same auburn hair, same slim figure. That was it.

Liam backed away, leaving Victoria to play nurse. "Do we need to call an ambulance?" he asked.

Victoria shook her head. "Not yet. She's waking up. We'll know shortly enough what's needed."

His eyes caught on the whiteboard at the sentences scrawled across it. One made him pause. Made the skin on the back of his neck crawl. Why the hell had she written that? In the background, Victoria murmured, and Miss Cooper responded.

Murderer! Murderer! He killed Billy!

Like a school yard chant of the most macabre.

Or an accusation.

A shock jolted through him, as if the words were meant for

him. Not possible, he told himself, and he rubbed the back of his neck to massage away the prickling sensation.

Of course, it hadn't been written for him. He was no murderer. But someone else in his family was, and the name Billy or William or something rang an alarming bell.

Coincidence. It could only be a coincidence. He tried to calm his breathing.

He looked at her again. Their eyes met for a moment, and she turned away. She was trouble. He could sense it in his bones.

Her face was pale. Drawn. In shock, he bet. Tearing his eyes away, he caught Victoria watching him, eyes narrowed. She had seen the sentence too; he had no doubt.

"An icepack might be useful right about now, don't you think?"

Of course. He stood up from where he had been sitting on a desk, transfixed by the scene before him. And he swiftly left, cursing himself for not thinking of it himself, yet also wanting to stay to hear what her excuse was.

When he got back, she was nearing the whiteboard, and she ignored him when he offered the icepack.

She couldn't remember what had happened, she said. But who else would have written it?

The thought hit him: she was a liar. It made little sense otherwise. A person didn't go talking about murders in Te Tapu, let alone writing about them in front of a bunch of kids. In a village like theirs, that sort of thing might just raise the dead. And too many people in this community needed the dead to stay dead. In the past. Where they belonged. Him included. So, if she intended to cause trouble…

He made his excuses to go, aware that behind the dull ache

of grief, and a flicker of anger, something else lingered – an emptiness in his stomach where disappointment had settled in.

Chapter 13 – Liam

The morning tea bell sounded as Liam finished tearing down the swing. There was nothing for it; the whole thing needed replacing. He had used a stepladder to untangle a rope swing, so at least one thing was fixed. It had calmed his mood a little, stopped the shaking in his hands and taken the edge off his agitation, as often happened when he busied himself with his hands. Now he was starving.

Damn having missed breakfast.

A quick walk down to the gas station to pick up some snacks was in order. It was only a five-minute trip. He'd come back and catch up with Victoria then, see what her thoughts were about the whole situation, about her newest teacher. She confided in him sometimes about these kinds of things. Not that these kinds of things happened regularly, or ever, really. But she had known his family for a long time. Lived in Te Tapu most of her life. She had been born here. And her family before her. She knew the community's secrets, his family's secrets. If this was something to worry about, Victoria would know.

He hoped she would want him to stick around. He was sure he could find some small jobs around the place to keep him busy. He wasn't in the right frame of mind to run into his father again.

The day was still heating up, the sun almost searing. He pulled his hat down lower to shield his eyes. He had never been one for sunglasses, but one of these days he would have to give in and invest in a pair.

The school yard already buzzed with students. Most sat in little pods, lunch boxes in front of them as they devoured whatever tasty snack was packed for them today. The chatter was rather musical, like a symphony of birds all singing their own songs at the same time. Once they finished their snacks, the noise would increase – and noise it would be as they ran and chased each other, teased each other in sing-song play.

He had another reason he wanted to stay at the school today, though he loathed to admit it.

He wanted to see her. Miss Cooper. Riley.

He played the name around in his mind. Riley. It felt too familiar for now. He'd stay with Miss Cooper.

He didn't like getting involved in other people's troubles, and from what he'd witnessed the last few days, she had a few. But after this morning, if something more was going on – if she was intent on stirring up trouble for the community or even just for the kids – he wanted to know about it.

Though he might not like being in Te Tapu, this had once been his home. His great grandfather, Thomas O'Regan, had rescued the area from brush and swamp to make it what it was today: a somewhat affluent farming community with a small village and a school. A community, that for better or worse, was close-knit. He would not sit idly by if some outsider wanted to make trouble for the people who did like it.

Someone needed to mow the curb, he thought, as he left the school grounds, turning right to follow the footpath down to the garage. Everything was overgrown. Wild weeds with bright flowers were overtaking the concrete. The houses along this street were not in the best state of repair. Many needed their weather boards painted. He paused for a moment, watching a strip of paint curl and fall to the ground, dry from the heat of the sun.

He'd seen pictures of this street from when his grandfather was a boy. Though it was mostly devoid of houses back then, further down, the garage still sat in the same place, as did the town hall and church.

A large cattle truck rumbled past, shaking the sidewalk beneath him and leaving behind the warm smell of animal and manure. As he rounded a corner, the gas station came into view. It looked deserted, a little lonely, baking in the sun without customers. Liam went in through the main entrance, happy to avoid the office and anyone who might want to talk. He grabbed a drink from the fridge and a pre-wrapped ham sandwich. It was his lucky day; he didn't recognise the cashier, a young Indian chap, so there would be no need for small talk. Both parties grunted hello, and Liam pulled his wallet from his back pocket and handed over his EFTPOS card.

Seconds later, he was back in the stinking heat again, making his way back to the school. He had no idea what he would say to Miss Cooper if they got the chance to talk, or why he even wanted to talk to her.

Possibly, she wasn't even up to talking. She had hit her head, he reminded himself. And what had made her faint in the first place? Maybe she hadn't fainted, the cynic in him argued.

Maybe it had all been a ploy for attention. He'd known people like that before. Narcissistic. Everything needed to be about them.

Whatever the truth, this morning's events weren't a great way to be starting a teaching career.

He cracked open his can of drink and took a swig, enjoying the cool bubbles as they slipped down his throat. He could hear the kids enjoying their playtime before he even caught sight of the school.

He had hoped to see Victoria first, but Miss Cooper was just sitting there, long auburn hair in gentle waves down her back, facing away from him. She was at one of the picnic tables in the sun. Avoiding the gossip of the staffroom, he supposed.

Now and then a kid would approach her, bring her a dandelion they had picked from the lawn, or ask her to open a muesli bar wrapper. Most of the kids were already around the back of the school, playing on the field or the playground. Damn, he hated how nervous she made him, but if he wanted a chance to talk to her, now was the time.

Before he reached her table, a little girl came running up to him – Sharyn, he remembered. She held out a dandelion to him, as she had done for Miss Cooper moments before.

"Here, Mr O'Weegan, this one's for you." Her grin came complete with a gap where her front teeth should have been.

He gave her a small smile in return and thanked her. Lifting his eyes, he saw Miss Cooper had turned and was watching him.

She turned away, but not before he caught the surprise on her face.

Now or never, he thought again.

He moved over to her. "Can I sit?"

Colour rose to her cheeks and her mouth opened and closed before she found her voice. He guessed he couldn't blame her; he hadn't exactly been prince charming around her.

"Of course." She shuffled over a little, despite there being plenty of room. He took a seat on the bench opposite her.

"How's your head?" he asked, not sure where else to start.

She touched the lump on her forehead, giving a grimace.

"It's fine," she said.

Some of the swelling had gone down, but it still blushed pink and purple.

"What happened back there?" The bell was going to ring soon. Better to jump to the chase, he thought. His stomach let out an unsettling growl, and he remembered the unopened sandwich in his hand.

"Do you mind?" he asked, gesturing to it and unwrapping it before she had a chance to respond.

"I fainted, was all. Maybe the heat?"

He took another bite of his sandwich, thinking how to phase his next question. "You wrote something before you fainted ...?" He made it sound like a question. Liam studied her.

She bit her lip and remained silent.

He was asking a lot of her, to open up to him like this – a stranger, who until now had remained aloof.

He bit into his sandwich, giving her a chance to think about what to say. She was eyeing him now, probably wondering if she could trust him.

Could she? He wondered. A little bit ago, he had decided she was a liar.

"So what was it then? A quote from a book in class? Doesn't sound like quality reading material if you're asking me." He sounded like an ass, but he was growing impatient.

"I don't know," she whispered. Her jaw tightened.

He'd pissed her off. He knew the tells.

The bell rang, relieving them both from their silent stand-off.

"I have to get back to class," she said, getting to her feet.

Her lips moved as if she were battling not to say something more. Fire flared in her eyes. He had screwed up. Pushed too hard, too fast. He mentally cursed himself.

At least she knew he was on to her if she really was trying to stir up trouble.

She turned her back on him and headed towards the resource room. Her shoulders looked tight and her strides resolute. He had got to her all right.

Liam finished the last few bites of his sandwich, then threw the packaging in the bin, dodging children racing to get their last drink or toilet stop before heading back to class.

Navigating his way through the throng, he headed to Victoria's office, arriving as she approached from the staffroom.

"We need to talk," he said.

"I've got a few minutes before class. The kids will settle themselves, but we'll have to make it quick."

She led him to her office and closed the door to the prying eyes of the office lady and other teachers as they headed to their classrooms.

"What was that?" he asked.

"I'm assuming you're referring to Miss Cooper fainting?" She perched herself on the edge of her desk and gestured for him to take a seat on the nearest chair.

111

Folding his arms, Liam ignored it. "I'm more concerned with what she wrote on the whiteboard."

"Why are you so interested, Liam? She's a new teacher. She copied some passages from books, and I'm sure they were purposeful for her class."

"You don't believe that, do you?" Though it was none of his business, something about it irked him.

Victoria studied him, and he shuffled uncomfortably from foot to foot. They knew each other well enough not to beat around the bush like this.

"I just…" He was lost for words. What was he scared of?

"I know what you're thinking, Liam, and you need to stop. You'll go the way of your father if you keep believing everyone's out to get you and to sully your family's past."

Liam tensed. Family friends or not, his family's past was not up for discussion.

"I'm sure it's a simple misunderstanding, a naïve mistake on Miss Cooper's part, and nothing to do with you." Victoria glanced at her wristwatch.

"It's in the kids' books." He cringed. Now he just sounded whiny.

"I know. I'll fix that today. No need to worry about it. I don't believe Miss Cooper meant anything by it. It was an unfortunate choice of phrase and a coincidence on her part."

Liam started to protest, but Victoria shut him down with one steely glance.

"Liam!"

There it was. The reason you didn't mess with Victoria. She would passionately protect the ones she loved, and just as easily put them in their place if they overstepped the mark. And he had overstepped the mark. His shoulders sagged.

"It's not like you to be worrying about other people's business. This is a school matter, and I'll deal with it as such. Now, if you're interested, I have a few other things around the property that could do with a keen eye to, if you're up to it. I need to get back to class."

Liam closed his eyes for a second, willing away his sense of chagrin, then nodded his head. Victoria was right. Probably.

"Great." Victoria detailed the tasks she needed taking care of and they headed out, Liam in the lead.

"Oh, Liam," she called to him as he reached the door to the outside. "You just focus on keeping your nose clean, okay, my boy?" She tapped the side of her nose and smiled at him.

Liam rolled his eyes as he turned away. The woman could be maddening.

Chapter 14 – Riley

Riley had lost all track of time. If it hadn't been for the scrambling sound of kids packing their bags in the cloakroom, she'd have forgotten where she was altogether.

Focusing after the events of the morning had taken a while, but at least her head had stopped pounding. She was, however, fuming after her interaction with Liam. What was his problem?

He had been cold to her from day one, with no reason for it. Maybe he was like that with everyone, yet it annoyed her all the same.

What bothered her more was how she let him get under her skin. Having him retrieve her bracelet and witness her sentimentality towards it, and then having him see her interaction with Justin was mortifying enough. But for him to be the one to find her collapsed on the floor with those words written on the whiteboard… Riley's cheeks flamed up again.

Oh, God. Where had those words even come from?

Try as she might, she couldn't remember writing them. She remembered the others clearly enough, but why, why,

why would she write the word "murderer" repeatedly on the board, followed by some weird type of accusation? And in front of kids? She sighed heavily. Liam needn't waste his energy being angry with her, she was furious enough with herself as it was.

She had spent some time trying to remember every book she'd read, every movie she'd watched to find where her subconscious might have picked it up from. Nothing jumped out at her.

When Liam had asked to sit by her at morning tea, she had been surprised. For a moment, she thought maybe he was trying to get to know her. Check on her after fainting. Something friendly and decent. Not that he had come to interrogate her. Only a moment passed before she realised that was exactly what he had come to do.

Riley ground her teeth and had to remind herself to relax her jaw. She took a couple of deep breaths for good measure, forcing her body to unwind, her heart to stop stampeding.

And now she had to think of what to say to Victoria. Understandably, she had questions. A new teacher faints in front of her class after writing something about a murderer on the whiteboard for her students to copy down for handwriting. She'd be lucky to hold on to her job after this. She dearly wished she had a reason, any reason, as to why it had happened. But she had nothing.

After an hour of trying to lesson plan, she gave up. Her mind was too insistent on ruminating. She needed to busy herself. Not her mind, but her hands or something. Do anything to cut out the noise in her head.

She had been meaning to collect readers for the following week's reading program, anyway. Now would be as good of

115

a time as any. The resource room was right next door to the little office she had set herself up in for the rest of the day. She could collect the readers she needed for each reading group and then come back to the teachers' office and see if she could build a reading programme around them. Keeping busy was better than fretting over what Victoria might have to say to her after school.

The resource room was a small room, conveniently attached to her own classroom just off the cloakroom. Two large shelving racks stood in the centre of the room and could be pushed aside to get to the shelving around the outskirts of the room. Except for the neatly organised readers in the middle, the room was a dumping ground for what Riley suspected had been many, many years of resources. A lot of it untouched, too, going by the layers of dust, thick cobwebs and a mummified mouse skeleton she nearly stood on when she went about exploring one of the outer shelving units.

Someone had left the shelves pushed together in the centre of the room. When she tugged on the large steel handles to draw the shelves apart, their unwillingness to budge surprised her.

Riley anchored herself and pulled again. Nothing. They were stuck.

She peeked her head around each shelf, checking nothing had fallen and blocked the shelves from moving on their tracks.

Nothing, which made no sense.

She tugged again.

A slight movement. A couple of centimetres before they rebounded back.

"Shit," she swore under her breath. She stood there for a

second, surveying the shelves in front of her.

She could leave it for later in the afternoon. After school. After her chat with Victoria.

Maybe she could ask Brittany to help her. The two of them could probably get them to move. Worst case, she could ask Robert. But then she'd probably have to explain what had happened to her today, why he had to babysit her class for some time in the morning. She'd been avoiding the staffroom for that very reason. Strange stares and cautious questions were not something she was looking forward to.

One more tug then she'd give up, head back to the teachers' office, and she would try to refocus again. She could get Liam to help her… She swallowed the thought with a grimace.

Gripping the steel handle, she pulled once more, grunting as she did so. No way would she go to Liam! She leaned back. Nothing visible was stopping its movement. She had checked. Why … (breathe) wasn't … (breathe) it … (breathe)—

The force of release sent her flying as the shelf moved on its tracks towards her. Her feet, slipping on the linoleum floor, slid out from under her. A loud crash of something hitting the ground startled her into a muffled squeal. Her firm grasp on the shelf's handle prevented her from landing on her butt, but only just.

Her heart leapt into her throat and her entire body pulsed with adrenalin. What if someone had heard?

Quickly, she pulled her legs under her and propelled herself to her feet. She wiped her hands on her thighs, trying to rid herself of their moistness and dustiness. It was plausible the noise had carried to Victoria or one of the students in her class next door. God, that was all she needed.

Riley stood motionless for a moment, straining to hear the

first signs of someone moving towards the room.

Nothing.

Knowing her luck, it would be Liam anyway, with the way he kept showing up when she least wanted him to.

She waited a second longer. Still nothing.

Letting out a loud exhale, she pressed her hands to her face and closed her eyes for a moment. Could this day get any worse?

Letting her hands fall to her side, she steeled herself to assess the damage, praying whatever had fallen was still intact – no damage done.

She peered down the aisle of readers; a box lay on its side. It was large, the corners mushed and sides somewhat sagging. A cloud of dust rose from it, then settled on the shelves and ground around it. Somehow, in its fall, it had missed knocking any of the boxes of readers down with it.

Glancing upwards, she noticed an old suitcase half-peering over the edge of the top shelf. Despite its brass buckles being closed, fabric hung out from its side. Next to it, a box clearly labelled "Costumes" suggested the suitcase might hold something similar. By the sound of the box hitting the ground, Riley suspected its contents were going to be much heavier than costumes. They could be props, however.

Whatever it was, she couldn't leave it there. It had landed almost slap-dab between the two shelving units. People would have to walk over it to get down to the readers at the other end of the aisle, and if they dare needed any of the forgotten resources on the shelves around the outside of the room, there would be no moving the shelves to get to them.

The box was lying on its side. The corner closest to her was splitting.

Squatting down, Riley got ready to pick it up. She wouldn't be able to put it back where it came from without a ladder, and even then, she wasn't sure she'd have the strength to lift the box or the courage to climb a ladder to put it back. Without there being anywhere obvious to stash the box, she'd have to carry it out into the cloakroom, maybe take it with her to the teachers' office until she could find someone to help her.

With a sigh, she hefted the box, her fingers flinching against the chalkiness of the who-knew-how-many years of dust coating its surface.

The box nearly disintegrated in her hands when it left the ground. One side gave out, spewing its guts onto the floor.

Riley let out a moan and stifled a cuss word.

She tilted the box, placing it upright as even more of its contents fell onto the floor. Ledgers and papers, by the looks of it.

The top of the box hadn't even been taped. Someone had folded together the box's flaps to hold it shut. Whoever had packed it hadn't accounted for the wear-and-tear of time.

Wrinkling her nose at the mess, Riley lowered herself onto her knees. Though the box at this point would be useless, if she removed what remained inside, she could put its contents into a pile and maybe find some space to shelve it. It would save her the nuisance of having to lug it back to the teachers' office.

While extracting the rest of the contents, she further broke the box down and then threw it out into the cloakroom to dispose of later. On the shambled pile before her, a large green ledger grabbed her attention. Curiosity won out. She opened it to a random page. It appeared to be an attendance

119

book. Someone had tightly scrawled a list of names down the left side of the page. Columns filled the rest of the page with markings in each box beside the names. Riley wondered how old the ledger was and flipped through to the beginning. 1939.

A whisper of excitement bubbled in Riley's stomach. She had always enjoyed history, and here she was holding a piece. 1939 was the year World War II started.

She shuffled through the rest of the pile. More papers – handwritten notes, lesson plans, photos. She pulled one out. Its edges were wavy with age, and it had yellowed significantly. It was a class photo. It looked like it had been taken on the deck outside of her very classroom.

How fascinating, Riley thought. It was a class of about twenty pupils of varying ages. To the back right of the photo was a young woman. Pretty, petite, with wavy, shoulder-length blonde hair. But something was off.

An icy finger ran its way down Riley's spine. The woman, a teacher, Riley suspected, wasn't facing the camera, instead she gazed slightly off to her left. The photographer had somehow captured the millisecond between expressions as if she had been smiling. And then… Then what? Riley wondered. Her eyes were wide, her mouth slightly open. Fear, maybe?

Riley stifled a shiver. Overactive imagination, much? The photo was old, aged and grainy. Black and white. There was no telling what emotions the young teacher was feeling.

Unlike in present day's class photos, no names were typed below the photo to tell who was in it. Riley turned it over. The same script she'd seen written on most of the documents so far was there. 1939 was scrawled in the top left corner. Nothing else. Turning the photo over again, she took another glance and set it aside; it made her uneasy.

Rifling through some more of the pile – receipts, a cute picture of two stick figures standing under a tree obviously drawn by a child, an old newspaper – she noticed something else.

She wasn't sure how she had missed it. Buried amongst everything was an A5-sized notebook. She pulled it out and placed it on top of the pile. As if hit by a rogue wave, Riley reeled, falling backwards against the shelves behind her. A tsunami of emotions, fear, pain, sadness washed over her. Thick sweat warmed the back of her neck, while an iciness shot down her spine.

She leaned forward, pressing her palms onto the cold linoleum on either side of the pile before her. Turning her head sideways as nausea threatened to overwhelm her, she closed her eyes, counting slow breaths as she willed it to subside. It didn't take long. She sat upright, wiping her clammy hands on her pants. What the hell had happened? Shit, maybe she had a concussion from her fall earlier?

She eyed the notebook in front of her. Nothing appeared unusual about its navy-blue hardcover.

"Riley? Are you okay?"

The female voice startled her. Without thinking, Riley pushed the small notebook under the shelving unit whilst turning to face her visitor.

"Oh. Hi." Riley hoped she sounded normal.

Brittany stood in the doorway, her head tilted to one side, confusion etched between her eyes. "What are you doing down there? Are you okay? You don't look well."

The onslaught of questions gave Riley a moment to compose herself. "Oh, yeah. I'm fine." Riley teamed what she hoped sounded like a light-hearted perkiness with a smile. She pulled herself up to a standing position and set about dusting the dirt off the legs of her pants.

Brittany stared her down. "What were you doing on the ground?" She peered around Riley's shoulder.

Riley cleared her throat. Nothing to hide here, she thought. "I was trying to get some readers, but the shelves were stuck, and when they moved, a box of papers fell down. I'm trying to pick them up now."

Brittany took in the pile and gave Riley the once over. Had she heard she'd fainted earlier? Riley forced another smile. It must have done the trick because Brittany's face relaxed.

"Do you need a hand? I can help you pick them up if you like?" She made a move towards the pile as if to do so.

"No, it's fine. Honestly. Plus, there's no room for both of us." Riley indicated the tiny space.

Brittany chuckled, all sense of previous unease gone. "I can't argue with that. I actually came to get another copy of this." She held out a book. "I was one short and thought I'd shoot over. Would you mind?" Brittany handed it to her.

"Of course not." She took the reader, finding the coloured sticker on its cover that made it easy to locate its box. She had to lean over the pile of papers on the floor but found what was needed and passed it back to Brittany.

"Thanks," Brittany said, flashing a grin. "Oh, Riley? What are you doing after school today?"

Riley hid how much the question had startled her. She wasn't used to being asked out anywhere, which was where she suspected this was headed.

"I have a quick meeting with Victoria" – God, she hoped it was quick, and she'd still have a job afterwards – "but otherwise, I'm free." By habit, Riley twisted the bracelet on her wrist.

"Great!" Brittany said, bouncing a little on the balls of her feet. "A couple of us are heading down to the tavern after work, and I thought you might want to join us."

"Sure. That … that would be great." Socialising wasn't really her thing; she always felt so self-conscious and unsure of what to say around others. This had often been at the core of many of her arguments with Justin.

"Wonderful! You know where it is, right?"

Riley didn't, but considering how small the Te Tapu village was, she suspected it wouldn't be too hard to find. Brittany told her anyway, then bounded out of the room like a puppy who'd found her favourite toy. Though Riley wished she could feel a similar sort of cheerfulness, it just wasn't who she was. She'd always looked at life seriously, rationally, with no big shows of emotion.

No. No, she hadn't. She shook her head with the realisation. She'd become that way when she'd started dating Justin. He didn't like intense emotions. Everything had to be kept at surface level. Riley had felt, in order to keep Justin happy, she had to stifle those very things that made her *her*. She ground her teeth again. Bloody men!

She turned back to the pile on the floor. With a cursory glance at the clock hanging on the wall, she knew she would have to get moving if she was going to tidy things up before the end of the day.

Crouching over the pile, she shuffled the papers, finding more photos, old photos, photos with short descriptors scrawled on the back: the village, the hall, Lucy. She recognised the village; it was Te Tapu, she was sure of it.

123

And the hall hardly seemed to have changed at all. Lucy was a beautiful old car, the sort Riley sometimes saw out driving during classic car conventions.

Having assembled everything into a pile, she ran her hand under the shelf where she had pushed the notebook. Her fingers found it instantly. She shuddered. Someone's walking over my grave, she thought. Shaking off the feeling, she brought the book out into the daylight.

She didn't know why her automatic reaction had been to hide it. It made no sense, the inexplicable need to protect it. Absurd.

Placing it on top of the pile, she remained there for a moment just looking at the towering stack. She should find another box, something to put it all in; it wouldn't work to place it on the shelf as she'd planned. A glance around showed her nothing useful.

The shelves were packed top to bottom with thin, labelled book boxes holding journals and readers, but nothing big enough to hold the pile on the floor.

Maybe on the shelves around the outside of the room, she thought. She picked up the papers and, making several trips, carried them into the teachers' office next door, where she placed them on her desk by her laptop. Better than moving them from one place on the floor to another.

After returning to the resource room, she grabbed hold of the large steel handles and moved the middle shelves towards the right this time. They moved with ease, surprising her. She felt the gentle impact of one shelf hitting the suitcase on the top shelf.

Venturing down the left side of the room first, she scoured the shelves for something to transport – no, she meant *hold*

– the papers. Why would she want to transport them? She pushed the thought from her mind, which seemed to flit from one idea to the next with a strange fogginess, as if the ideas weren't even her own. A side effect of hitting her head?

Still nothing that would do the job. Just binders and books of resources standing side by side, a box overflowing with chimes, triangles, recorders and various percussion instruments, and an assortment of grubby stuffed animals crammed over a couple of shelves.

Riley pulled the shelves the other way so she could check out the last aisle on the right. At first glance, it was much the same, this time with lots of ice cream containers harbouring maths equipment. Finally, she found something that might work. A cardboard box like those that reams of printer paper often came in.

It sat on one of the lower shelves, covered in a thick layer of dust.

Please don't let there be too much in it, Riley thought.

It was light, and she pulled it out with ease. A good sign.

Biting her lip, she lifted the lid and peered inside. Maybe a dozen old wooden abacuses made of dowel lay jumbled together. She could easily stack them on the shelf where the box had been. Riley remembered using similar when she was a child but doubted they ever got used nowadays. The little wooden donuts that went with them were nowhere to be found. Maybe lost in an ice cream container, she thought.

Emptying the abacuses took no time, particularly as Riley rushed it, feeling an inexplicable need to hurry, to pack up the papers, almost as if she wanted to stop anyone from finding them.

Sounds came from the class next door, typical of the final

125

tidy before the kids were dismissed for the day.

Having placed the last abacus on the shelf, Riley took the box with her into the teacher hub, and went about moving the papers into it, placing the notebook in the middle of the pile, where it would not be easily found.

Riley noticed a hint of the queasiness that often accompanied guilt. A bit like on the first day when she had come exploring the school during the holidays. She wasn't doing anything she shouldn't, but she felt guilty anyway.

After placing the cardboard lid on top of the box, she moved it to the floor beside her desk and dropped her handbag on top. She had already decided to take the box home. The idea, she realised, had been percolating since she first found the papers. She wasn't stealing; it was for lesson planning. And that was what she had decided it would be. From her first browse through the papers and photos, it seemed very much a historical tribute to the past, which seemed like a perfect topic idea for her students – delving into the history of their locale, Te Tapu. She could make an entire unit out of it. Have the students talk with their parents and family, learn the histories of those around them, and the histories of Te Tapu and the school they now attended.

It made sense then for Riley to take the box home. Besides, they were in the resource room for teachers to use. She was doing nothing wrong, and it had nothing to do with the strange desire she felt to protect the notebook and its contents. None at all.

A burst of noise and scampering from the cloakroom brought her senses back to the present. The chatter of students as they rushed to be the first to grab their belongings and race out the door was in lieu of the traditional bell that would sound the end of the school day.

Riley packed up the last of her belongings from her desk. She'd made very little headway on her own planning. What with finding the box of papers, she hadn't even grabbed the journals she needed for her reading groups and lesson planning.

She had promised to meet with Victoria, but knowing she was on bus duty, Riley had a couple of minutes to burn. If she hurried, she could get the journals she needed for her reading groups.

She sighed and grabbed the Post-it note onto which she had jotted down the group's numbers and reading levels.

It really was only a five-minute task. In and out. The sliding shelves moved easily now. Riley found the journals she needed, and after a cursory glance at the contents page of each, she grabbed the quantities she thought she would need.

With a firm tug, she closed the resource room's door behind her, added one of each journal to the pile of work she was going to take home, then went through to her classroom. It looked much the same as she had left it in the morning. No trace of the handwriting lesson, and Victoria had done a great job of having the students tidy up. Other than Victoria's laptop, a few resource books and her planner in a tidy pile on the desk, little remained to say she had even been there.

She placed her pile of journals on the desk beside Victoria's belongings, then she stood for a moment, taking it all in. Everything was the same, except … it wasn't. Something had changed. A faint heaviness filled the room. A sadness, even.

Riley's fingers went to her bracelet. No. It wasn't just sadness, it was something more. Her eyes sought the whiteboard where, only a few hours earlier, Riley had written up the handwriting for the day. What had she been thinking?

And what had made her faint? Riley had never fainted before, though she had come close. In wood-shop class as a kid, their instructor decided it would be fun to talk about how he had lost his finger. But although the room had swayed and spots had darkened eleven-year-old Riley's vision, she had not fully fainted. She'd croaked out her need to leave and made it to the restroom. Sitting on the cold linoleum floor with her head between her knees, she averted the worst.

Something else struck her about the room now. She felt like she was being watched.

Riley wiped the palms of her hands on her thighs again.

Deep breath, deep breath, she told herself. The knot in her stomach was also back. Through the windows of the large French doors, Riley saw Victoria making her way back from the bus, heading towards the class.

God, what could she say? Having absolutely no excuse for her actions, she hoped Victoria would put it down to new teacher jitters and not a sign of something being mentally wrong with her. God, maybe something was wrong with her. Riley cringed, remembering Liam's accusatory tone.

Riley went to the door, thinking to meet Victoria and follow her into her office. Victoria hastened her pace. Riley forced a smile and relaxed her shoulders, which had crept up to her ears. Victoria beamed back.

"How's your head feeling?" Victoria asked as she reached the doorway.

Riley touched the tender bump on her forehead. She had all but forgotten about it. "Fine," she said, moving aside for Victoria to come into the classroom.

"Good, good," Victoria returned. "Let's take a seat over

there, shall we?" She indicated one of the student tables.

No office then, Riley noted. Was that a good or a bad thing? She took a seat at a desk, with Victoria sitting opposite her, clasping her hands on the table.

Riley squirmed as she waited for Victoria to say something. When she didn't, Riley went ahead. "About this morning—" Riley stopped, unsure what to say. "I'm so sorry. I don't know what happened, it's not—"

"Like you?" Victoria interjected.

Riley nodded, blushing. It *wasn't* like her, not the fainting and definitely not what she wrote on the board.

"Maybe you can talk through what you remember," Victoria said gently.

Riley saw only kindness in her eyes and let herself relax. "It was handwriting time, and I have to admit, I had a bit of an ulterior motive." She stared down at the table before her. She had nothing to lose in telling Victoria the whole story. Victoria would make of it what she would, regardless.

"Someone left a note on my desk yesterday. They'd written 'Help me' on the piece of paper but didn't leave a name or anything on it."

"'Help me'?" Victoria repeated. A line settled between her brows.

Riley nodded.

"It was in cursive, so I thought a handwriting lesson might show who had written it, that's why one of my sentences started with "'Help me," said a mouse…'"

"Ahh…" Victoria nodded.

"The other sentences were random ones to cover it up, I guess." Riley's voice wavered a bit.

"And this one…" Victoria pulled out her phone and pressed

some buttons before handing the phone over for Riley to see.

It was a photo of the whiteboard. The words "*Murderer! Murderer! He killed Billy!*" Stood out to Riley like a slap in the face. She had written it. Of course she had. The handwriting was the same as the sentences above.

"I don't remember writing that," Riley whispered. "It wasn't until Amy drew my attention to it... I didn't..." She didn't know what to say. How could someone not remember writing something?

Victoria's eyes were fixed on her.

She's trying to decide if I'm lying or not, Riley decided with an inward cringe.

"How are you settling in?"

"F- fine," Riley said, surprised.

"And you enjoy teaching? Not feeling overwhelmed?"

"No. No, not overwhelmed at all, and I love teaching." Riley had found her voice again. God, she hoped Victoria believed her. She loved her job. It had been a steep learning curve, but Riley loved learning. It kept things interesting.

"And everything's okay at home?" Victoria asked, still not taking her eyes from Riley.

"Yes, yes, of course." Riley shuffled in her seat. Warmth swept up her neck.

"I saw you had a visitor the other day. A young man."

Riley wanted to crawl under the table. It hadn't gone as unnoticed as she had hoped. Damn it!

"Oh God, I am so sorry, Victoria. He just turned up. I told him to leave as soon as I saw him." The words tripped over each other in their hurry to get out.

Victoria reached across the table and placed her hand over Riley's.

"It's okay. It really is. We all have our … pasts," she said, something flitting across her face and then disappearing.

"If you like, we can let Sandra in the office know you'd prefer your man friend didn't come on-site. As gate keeper to the school, she can make that happen." Victoria's mouth quirked into the hint of a smile.

Sandra had that power. She doubted anyone could get past her without her permission. Plus, all visitors to the school had to sign in, so it would be easy enough to turn someone away.

"Thank you," Riley said. "There's probably no need. He shouldn't be back, anyway."

"Well, just in case, we can make it happen." She gave Riley's hand a squeeze. "Teaching can be stressful, particularly in the first couple of years. Shall we put this all down to a creative unconscious outburst brought on by stress?"

She was talking about what Riley had written again. Creative, all right, she thought. It was as if she had been accusing someone of being a murderer. God. Riley nodded. What else could she do? It had obviously been a lapse in sanity. Maybe it *was* stress related. She had moved across the country after a breakup to start a new life for herself. A new home. A new career. Maybe it was all taking its toll, and this was how her unconscious reacted.

"Thank you," Riley whispered again as Victoria pulled her hand away.

"Good. Well, I'm glad that's all- oh, I almost forgot about the note. Would you like me to take a look at it?"

Riley stifled a grimace. "No, it's okay. I think I know what it was about." She didn't, but she wasn't going to admit that to Victoria. How could she? The note was in her own handwriting.

Victoria gave her a strange look, then nodded slowly. "You know, Riley, we're like a family here. You'll find most of us are great listeners if you ever need someone to talk to. You don't need to do everything on your own. Get to know the others. I think you'll come to like them."

Riley felt chagrined. Her keeping to herself had been noticed. Opening up to other people had never been her forte, but new life and all. Maybe it was time to change.

Victoria stood and picked up her belongings. "Enjoy your weekend," she said to Riley with a smile before leaving the room.

Riley remained sitting for a moment. She could swear she was still being watched.

Chapter 15 – Riley

The weathered-looking building was in a perfect rural setting. Riley pulled into the car park. Though still early – going on four in the afternoon – the gravel surface already hosted half a dozen cars. It was Friday, Riley reminded herself, the end of a work week for most.

After her conversation with Victoria, Riley had hung around school for a while. She had a lot of planning to complete, and she wanted to stash the box of papers she'd found in her car without being noticed. She wasn't stealing, however guilty she felt. She was as entitled as anyone to take resources home to help her with her planning. And that's what they were.

She didn't quite know why she was trying to avoid others asking questions about the box and its contents, but she was. She felt a sense of protectiveness for it. Especially the notebook.

When she went to leave, having locked up her classroom, bag over her shoulder and box in her arms, Victoria's car was again the only one remaining. The others, she supposed, were already at the pub. She was proved right upon arrival when she recognised some of the other vehicles in the car park already.

Riley followed the concrete path to the double doors leading inside.

It took her eyes a moment to adjust to the dimmed lighting. Three middle-aged men crowded a bar table near the entrance. They had checked shirts rolled to the elbows, exposing bronzed arms, khaki shorts and steel-toed boots. The rest of their appearance was in varying degrees of disarray, having, by the looks of it, come straight from working on the farm. A jug of beer and beer mugs sat in front of them. Their loud laughter and ribbing boomed through the room.

One man with small eyes and receding hairline looked up, and on seeing Riley gave her a slow, appreciative once over before nudging one of his mates with his elbow and nodding his head in her direction. Riley stifled a shiver. She was new to the area; it went without saying she might draw a little attention from the regulars, but feeling like an insect under a microscope creeped her out.

An older man and woman huddled over a table in a booth. They gave a cursory glance in her direction, then turned back to whatever deep conversation they were in.

Swivelling again, Riley found the bar. A young woman stood behind it, wiping the surface with a cloth. She was pretty, in her thirties maybe. Tanned and toned in a white singlet top and jeans, a little heavy on the makeup, long blonde hair pulled back into a tight ponytail. On seeing Riley, she gave a wide smile.

"What can I do you for?" she asked, her high-pitched voice friendly.

Riley approached the bar. "Hi," she said. "Just a lemon, lime and bitters for me, please."

"You're the new teacher, eh?" she asked, pulling a glass out and shovelling it full of ice, barely taking her eyes off her.

"Yeah," Riley said, hesitating.

"Oh, don't look so shocked. Everyone knows everyone here in Te Tapu. New meat's going to get noticed." A gentle nod and eye roll towards the men at the bar table told Riley they were ogling her again.

The bartender leaned forward. "Don't worry; they're harmless," she whispered before straightening up and facing the men again. "Put ya tongues away, you dogs, or I'll be getting your wives on the phone." She reached out for the phone sitting in its carrier on the wall. Riley felt heat rise in her cheeks.

With a humph of muffled laughter, the men turned their eyes back to their table.

"I'm Katrina," the woman said, plopping Riley's drink down in front of her.

"Riley," Riley replied, handing over her card for payment.

"The rest of your crew are out back in the garden. Through those doors," she continued, pointing to another set of double doors on the far wall.

"Thanks," Riley said, wanting nothing more than to be out from under the watchful eye of the other patrons. She gave Katrina a small smile, picked up her drink and headed to the doors.

It wasn't so much a garden as a fenced-in backyard with a pizza barbeque and tiled area to one side, with a couple of wooden tables and benches painted dark brown and a few trees for shelter. Relieved to be free of leering locals, Riley made her way to Brittany, Robert – or Rob, as she was learning to call him – and Natalie, sitting together at the table in the centre.

Natalie, who was facing the doors Riley came through, spotted her first but looked away almost immediately.

Oh God. Riley thought. So it's going to be like that. Riley took a deep breath and shook off her discomfort.

"Newbie!" Rob called out, waving her over. Brittany twisted in her seat and beamed. She patted the seat beside her.

Riley placed her drink down on the table and shuffled in beside Brittany.

"You made it!" Brittany said.

"Of course. I just had to finish some things at work first," Riley said.

"Good to see you. Whatcha drinking there?" Rob pointed to her drink.

"Lemon, lime and bitters," Riley replied.

Rob guffawed. "What kind of teacher drink is that? You know it's Friday, right?"

"I'm not much of a drinker," Riley replied, swirling her ice cubes with her straw.

"Oh, don't listen to him," Brittany said, passing a mock scowl in Rob's direction. "Not all of us need alcohol to survive teaching; some of us enjoy it."

"Ouch!" Rob put his hands in the air. "Gun's down, ma'am."

Riley relaxed. They were fun, these two. Natalie, on the other hand, barely glanced up from her drink.

Conversation continued for a while, sharing stories of classroom antics. Though Rob, by far, monopolised the conversation, Riley didn't mind; he was a born entertainer. She could see why the kids loved him. He even made Natalie's lips quirk a few times.

Riley wondered if Natalie had turned so sullen because of her presence, or if it was just who she was. She couldn't think of anything she could have done to upset Natalie, but niceties seemed to be lost on her.

Nothing was said about Riley fainting, and she was thankful. Maybe Victoria had kept it quiet, or at least told the others to hold their tongues about it.

After a while, the conversation shifted towards family and partners.

"When's your man gonna finally man up and buy the cow, eh?" Rob turned to Brittany, a smile stretched across his face.

Ouch, Riley thought, taking a sip of her drink. She needn't have worried. Brittany seemed nonplussed, eyes sparkling as they always did when her man made it into conversation.

A grunt of pain from Rob's direction suggested that in all the playfulness, Brittany had given him a sharp kick to the shin. Riley couldn't stifle her giggles, and even Natalie appeared to struggle with holding the disdain on her face. Rob bent down to rub his leg, while Brittany turned to Riley, glass held high, ready to cheers her.

"What's going on here then?" a falsetto voice interrupted them.

Katrina had approached, round tray in hand with four fresh drinks.

"Thought you guys could do with another round," she said, placing the drinks on the table. "Has he been hassling you again?" Katrina turned to Brittany, one hand on her hip.

"Nothing I can't handle," Brittany replied.

"She kicked me," Rob whined, making a show of rubbing his shin.

Dropping her tray to her side, Katrina gave Rob a clip around the head. "Well, I'm sure you deserved it, you goof," she said.

"Ouch!" Rob shifted to rubbing his head. "What was that for?"

"Well, we girls have to stick together, and I know more than most what you're like." Bending down, Katrina gave him a quick peck on the head. "But I still love you."

Something on Riley's face must have caught Brittany's attention. "This is Katrina—"

"—the poor sucker married to this brute," Katrina added before Brittany could finish her sentence.

Riley nodded, a little dumbstruck. At first glance, they seemed ill-matched, yet seeing them together, their eyes shining when they looked at each other, she believed it. In fact, she envied it. Even with two little ones at home, the spark was most definitely still there.

"Anyway, other than the drinks, I came over to see if I could get you guys anything else. Snacks?"

"No, thank you," Brittany said, with everyone else following suit.

"Thanks, for the drink," Riley said, as Katrina went to leave. "I'll settle up on my way out."

"Nonsense, these are on us. It's the least we can do with what you guys have to put up with." She nodded her head in her husband's direction again.

Rob shook his head and put his hand over his chest in mock hurt.

Natalie stifled a smile, then turned to Riley. "So what's your story, Riley? What's with the man who dropped in to see you the other day?" Natalie's eyes narrowed.

Riley's jaw dropped. Until now, Natalie had said nothing, and by her tone, this wasn't a friendly getting to know you question.

Brittany shot Natalie a warning glance. Oblivious to the chill at the table, Rob joined in.

"What man? What did I miss? You've got a secret beau, Riley?"

From the small jump following Rob's line of questioning, Riley assumed Brittany gave Rob another kick under the table.

Natalie smirked before taking a sip of her fresh drink.

"He certainly wasn't too bad to look at," Natalie goaded.

Riley focused on her drink, swirling the ice with her straw. Her hand shook, so she dropped it below the table, twisting her bracelet as a distraction.

"He's no one." Riley tried to hide any show of emotion.

"He didn't look like no one—"

"Natalie!" Brittany bit out, all good humour gone.

Rob sat up a little straighter, glancing between Natalie and Brittney.

"What?" Natalie replied, pretending to be hurt. "It's only natural we should want to know a little about our new colleague."

Rob shook his head at Natalie.

"It's okay," Riley said, letting out a sigh. "It's no big deal. We dated for a while; then I broke it off. He had no reason to turn up at school. It won't happen again."

"A while?" Natalie asked, batting her eyes. "Looked a little more serious than that."

She was deliberately baiting her for reasons Riley couldn't fathom. She was doing a good job of it too. Riley clenched her teeth.

It was Rob who came to her rescue. "Enough, Natalie. If Riley wants to talk about it, she will." His usual humour was gone.

"Okay, okay!" Natalie said, hands up in mock surrender, pouting a little. "I have better things to do than discuss other people's love lives, or lack thereof," she said pointedly to Riley. "I'll see you guys Monday." Taking a last sip of her drink, Natalie stood up. Wobbling slightly on her feet, she wove her way towards the door. The others sat quietly, following her with their gaze.

Was she drunk? Riley wondered in shock.

"Don't mind her." Rob was the first to break the silence. "She's tough on the exterior but a good egg underneath. Just takes her a while to warm up to strangers is all."

Brittany reached an arm around Riley's shoulder and gave her a quick hug and squeeze.

"It's okay," Riley whispered, uncomfortable with the attention.

"How's your bracelet?" Brittany threw a glance towards Riley's hands on her lap. She was still twisting it around her wrist. Riley pulled her sleeve down lower to cover the bracelet and went back to swirling her ice with her straw.

"It's fine. No more dropping behind heavy bookcases." Riley went with a light tone and a small shrug of her shoulders.

"Oh, good. So it's not a dodgy clasp or anything?"

"Not as far as I can tell."

"Well, ladies, I'm feeling a bit on the outs. Anyone want to fill me in, or have we just moved on to talking about jewellery now?" Rob asked, rising an eyebrow in time with lifting his drink to his lips.

"Oh, it's nothing," Riley was quick to reply. "My bracelet came off after school on my first day and fell behind the bookcase in my room."

"The heavy one under the whiteboard," Brittany elaborated.

"I thought that was built in?" Rob scratched his eyebrow.

"It felt like it," Brittany continued. "Fortunately, Liam was around to help."

"Ah well, the dashing Mr O'Regan to the rescue then, huh?"

"Something like that," Riley said. "Although I wouldn't call him dashing."

She must have said it with a little more edge than she had intended. Rob exchanged a raised eyebrow with Brittany.

"Am I missing something?" Riley asked, feeling like some silent conversation was going on between her two colleagues.

"No. You might be one of the first not to fall for Te Tapu's number one bachelor, is all."

Riley took a sip of her drink. By appearance alone she could see why he might be in hot demand, but personality-wise...

"He's actually one of the good ones," Brittany said softly, perhaps catching Riley's hesitation.

Riley lifted her eyes from her drink to see both Rob and Brittany watching her. "He's just not good with new people? Like Natalie, I suppose?" She shifted in her seat. An uncomfortable heaviness settled on their table again.

Fortunately, it was interrupted by Katrina joining them.

She immediately took Natalie's spot at the table and placed a glass of what Riley assumed was Jack and Coke in front of her.

"Wow, what have I interrupted?" Her eyes narrowed when no one responded. "Well, it looks like you scared off the wicked witch. Kudos for that."

"Kat!" Rob growled.

The slight curl of the corner of his mouth wasn't missed by Riley, and she found herself doing the same. She was glad she wasn't alone in thinking little of Natalie's attitude.

"Kat's not a fan." Rob shrugged at Riley.

"Oh, please," Katrina said with what Riley assumed was a fake scowl. "Who is? She's a piece of work, better you learn that now." She took another sip of her drink.

"They have history," Rob said.

Riley nodded, smiling on the inside. She liked Katrina. Open and honest.

Brittany, Riley noticed, had remained quiet the whole time. She didn't like speaking badly of others, Riley assumed.

"Anyway, what did I miss?" Katrina asked.

"We were telling Riley here, that Liam's actually one of the good ones," Rob said, pointing his chin in Riley's direction.

"Oh, he is," Katrina agreed. "Don't look so shocked. He may not be much of a people person, but if you're in trouble, he'll do anything for you, and then some. You have to give the man a lot of credit considering where he comes from."

Riley watched as Rob put his face in his hands and let out a moan. Brittany giggled beside her. Katrina eyed Rob and shrugged off his exaggerated reaction before turning back to Riley.

"You've had a run in with Te Tapu's bachelor already?" she asked.

"You could say so," Riley said, thinking back to their conversation at morning tea and how he insinuated she was a crazy incompetent teacher.

"He rescued Riley's bracelet when it came loose and got

lost behind a bookcase," Brittany offered.

"Well, that's Liam for you—"

"Isn't that his job?" Riley interrupted. All eyes at the table focused in on her.

A line etched between Katrina's eyebrows. "You know he doesn't work at the school, right?"

It was Riley's turn to look confused. She turned to Brittany, hoping for a clearer explanation.

"He volunteers, helps, I think as a favour for Victoria," she replied.

"Or to escape his father," Katrina offered.

Rob let out another moan. "She's been here two minutes." Rob gestured in Riley's direction. "You don't need to share all the local gossip."

"Oh, shush," she said, turning to him. "Riley's one of us now; she might as well learn about the locals." Facing Riley, she continued: "Liam's family pretty much own Te Tapu. Most of the land and farms in this area were or still are owned by his family, going back generations. Including the land they built the school on. Liam doesn't need to work—"

"You don't know for sure," Rob interrupted.

Katrina shushed him again and continued, while Brittany took another sip of her drink, her eyes flitting between Katrina and Riley, as if she were waiting to see Riley's reaction to the news.

"The O'Regans have always been held in pretty high esteem around here. I guess until Arthur. Anyway, Liam's father's a drunk. Natalie's a nasty piece of work, but she's got nothing on Arthur. And if it weren't for his old man having a heart attack, Liam probably would have stayed away; instead he came to his dad's rescue and moved back here."

143

Riley tried to understand what Katrina was getting at. This man who made her feel so small was actually a good guy come home to care for his drunken, ill father. And he was rich, and his family owned most of Te Tapu. She supposed then it probably did put him right up there as far as eligible bachelors went in Te Tapu. Brittany must have seen scepticism in Riley's face.

"He really *is* a good guy, Riley. Once you get to know him... It takes him longer to open to people, ever since the accident," Brittany said.

Rob let out another groan. "I hope you ladies don't dish all the dirt on me when I'm not around."

"Oh please, what dirt?" Katrina replied.

"Accident?" Riley asked. She couldn't help it, she was hooked. And who knew, maybe he had a legit excuse for his innate rudeness, something bigger than having a drunk for a father.

Katrina and Brittany shared a glance, like they'd realised they'd said too much.

In the end, Rob answered her question.

"His lost his wife two years ago," Rob said, clearing his throat.

Riley instantly regretted asking. She took in the small group of people around her, a silence settling over their table.

"It was a car accident," Brittany said in a small voice. "An accident..."

"Was it though?" Katrina asked, and the hairs on the back of Riley's neck prickled.

"Either way, it changed him," Katrina said.

"Anyway..." Rob said, clearing his throat again.

Riley shifted in her seat. It was obvious, whoever Liam's

wife was, these people held her, and Liam, in high regard. No one made eye contact. Rob massaged his throat, Katrina took another sip of her drink, and Brittany played with the straw in her glass. Riley did the same, unsure of what to say.

"Anyway," Rob repeated. "That's in the past, eh? Best left there. Just wanted you to know, Liam's a good egg."

She knew he hadn't meant it that way, but Riley felt chastised. Whatever coolness Liam showed her, it was not what the others saw in him.

"I think a change of subject might be needed," Katrina said. Reverting to a bouncier version of herself, she gave her shoulders a quick shake and stood up. "Who wants another?" she asked, holding up her empty glass.

"Sure," Rob said.

Brittany nodded, while Riley shook her head no.

"I better be off," she said, picking up her handbag. She had mixed feelings about learning about Liam's past. She felt sympathy for everything he had been through, but everyone had a story. It didn't give him an excuse to act so cold towards her. Plus, she had a box of stuff in the car she wanted to go through.

Riley stood up and swung her handbag over her shoulder.

"You sure?" Brittany asked.

Riley smiled. "Yeah. Thanks so much for inviting me."

"Good to chat with you, newbie, probably best you forget most of what we said." Rob followed his statement up with a loud guffaw.

"Let me walk with you," Katrina said, grabbing the emptied glasses, as Riley gave a slight wave.

They walked together to the door leading into the pub.

"Sorry, if that seemed heavy," Katrina said. "Since you're

145

one of us now, you should know a bit about the goings on here. We're a tight community, have each other's backs and all."

Riley bit her lip from bringing up Natalie. She was certainly curious why Katrina disliked her so much.

"It was a big deal when Anna died."

Riley supposed Anna was Liam's wife.

"It threw the community and … well, none of us are really the same. Then Liam went away. Hadn't seen him for two years until last October, when his old man had a turn. And as much as some people were happy to have him return, as many were not so happy, and so … it's just important, you know. He *is* one of the good ones. Don't let his mood swings fool you."

Riley nodded. She wasn't sure what had made her new-found friends so insistent on making sure she believed the best in Liam. She barely knew him.

"Sure," Riley said, giving a half-smile. "Anyway, thanks for the drink. Did you want me to settle up?"

"No, it's on me," Katrina said, placing the glasses on the bar. "It was good to meet you, Riley," she said, holding Riley's gaze for a second longer than Riley thought was necessary. Riley felt herself on high alert. Something was a little off.

"You too," Riley said, in a way of farewell before moving past the bar table of men she had seen on her way in. Their numbers had increased by two. Before heading to the double doors, she paused and followed the signs for a restroom down a hallway to her left.

The pub had remained pretty empty, but Riley was relieved to be alone again for a moment. She liked them. All of them. Except maybe for Natalie. That woman had an obvious dislike for her, and it was beginning to feel mutual.

The hall had framed photos lining the wall. Many in black and white. Riley took her time to look at a few of them, reading the captions written below. A couple were of the bar itself, one from the 1980s. Another was from 1940. There were lots of pictures of people too. Smiling. Drinking. One photo, slightly larger than the rest, was of an older man with a white moustache and a twinkle in his eye, so thought Riley anyway. The caption below read "Te Tapu Founding Father, Thomas O'Regan". An ancestor of Liam's, she guessed. Another photo was of a group of people, some holding up fish in a competition-like setting.

Further down the hall were some familiar faces. One was of a group of four people standing around the barbeque in the garden area. She recognised Katrina and Rob right away. Standing slightly behind them was Liam. It shocked Riley to see his smile. He was handsome, she thought. His arm was around a woman. Riley did a double take. At first glance, it was like seeing herself. The woman had a similar build, similar hair. Her face shape was different, though. Heart-shaped. And she looked happier than Riley ever imagined herself to be.

Riley made it to the restroom and went inside. Dirty, yellow-painted walls, two stalls and, much like the rest of the pub, in a desperate need of an upgrade.

After finishing up and washing her hands, Riley stood in front of the sink for a moment. The lighting in the room was horrible. In the mirror, it highlighted the dark shadows under her eyes and the faint purple of the bruise poking out from under her fringe. She was grateful, at least, that no one had brought it up in conversation earlier. Maybe Victoria had said something to them, and it would explain some of the weird looks she was getting. Tentatively, Riley touched it with her fingers. A little raw, but not too bad.

A piece of white fluff on her shirt caught her attention in the mirror. Looking down at her chest, she pinched it between two fingers. It wasn't fluff, she realised, but a tiny white feather. Strange. She let it fall from her fingers, where it floated gently to land over the plug hole.

When her eyes caught the mirror again, ice froze her veins.

It wasn't her face looking back at her. It was, but it wasn't.

The eyes staring back at her were crystalline green. Riley's eyes were hazel.

Then something happened to her face.

It changed.

Morphed before her into a face she had seen earlier in the resource room. The woman from the class photo looked back at her.

Wavy blonde hair. Blue, figure-hugging dress and green, green eyes.

Her arms reached out for Riley from the other side of the mirror.

Her mouth gently opening, trying to say something but without words. Frozen, Riley gripped the edge of the basin.

The woman's face changed again. Her eyes grew wide in fear, her mouth opened wide as if to scream, stretching, stretching until it was a gaping black hole.

And the scream that tore through the air seemed to come from somewhere hidden deep within Riley's own mind. She scrunched her eyes tight, willing the demon away, holding onto the basin for dear life as her legs threatened to dissolve under her.

It's not real; it's not real. It's not.

She gingerly opened one eye. But it was still there. The woman, as real as anything.

And now the large gaping hole was moving. "Help me, help me, help me," it mouthed until the world passed away, and Riley let her legs give out under her.

Chapter 16 – Gwen

"It was not the thorn bending to the honeysuckles,
but the honeysuckles embracing the thorn."
- *Wuthering Heights*

It was a twenty-minute drive on a winding gravel road that headed out of Te Tapu. Pampas and tall grass lined both sides of the road. Sometimes the road would drop off sharply as they followed the wave of up, down, up, down of rolling hills. Eventually, Hugh took a turn on the left and followed a path almost completely obscured from the main road by overgrown brush and low-hanging willow trees.

Gwen was struck by its beauty. Everything was so green, where before the grass had turned a burnt golden colour from the harsh summer sun, and the earth looked dry and cracked. Here, everything appeared so alive. Beyond the dust from the road, Gwen imagined she could almost smell the damp earth and promise of water nearby.

Slowing as they came to a fence with a closed gate, Hugh pulled the car over to the side, two wheels well into the long grass.

"Well, we're here," he said.

Peggy let out a squeal, turning in her seat and flashing Gwen a toothy grin. Hugh went around to the passenger side and held the door open for Peggy, while Billy gestured for Gwen to slide across the seat and exit his way. It was nice to feel Billy's hand in hers as he helped her out of the car, keeping her balance against the gentle slope of the parked car.

The warmth of his hand and his closeness gave Gwen a strange, unsettling sense of shyness. He held her hand for a moment longer than necessary, and Gwen willed away the warmth she could feel moving up her chest to her neck. What she wasn't expecting was the loss she felt when he let her hand go. It was as if a tightly wrung spring had snapped. Her hand fell to her side.

Hugh and Peggy were already around the back of the car, hauling out two tote bags and a picnic basket from the trunk.

"Heads up," Hugh called out as he threw a rolled-up picnic blanket at Billy's head. He caught it just in time. Gwen offered to take one of the tote bags from Peggy. Peggy carried the other, leaving Hugh to heft the bulkier picnic basket.

Loaded up with their supplies, they headed after Hugh, who opened the gate for the party to walk through. Gwen fell in step beside Peggy, who told her how the three of them had been coming to the Willows since they were teens. Gwen only half listened as Peggy chatted on about how a lot of the locals used to bring their kids down for summer picnics and such, but not anymore, all because of the Taniwha.

Peggy's words floated around Gwen's head. She tried to focus on them, yet found her attention taken by the sound of footsteps and quiet conversation from the men behind her.

The road narrowed, and they followed it downhill. At one point Gwen's foot slipped out from under her, and a thick hand grabbed her arm from behind, steadying her. How he had grabbed her in time, she had no idea.

"Are you okay?" Peggy asked, seeing her flail.

"Yes, of course," Gwen said, a small giggle escaping. "Thanks to Billy." She flashed him a gracious smile. He had saved her from landing on her fanny. Something about this man made her nerves turn to jelly. She was like a smitten little child.

Billy tilted the tip of his hat as the corner of his mouth curved into a smile.

Gwen caught Hugh raise an eyebrow at the two of them. Peggy took this moment to fall into step with her husband, leaving Gwen and Billy to walk together.

"Peggy told you about the Taniwha, eh?"

"Sort of," Gwen said, shrugging her shoulders.

"Oh, so you don't believe in it then?"

"Of course not. A water monster that owns the swimming spot... I might as well believe in ghosts too, I suppose?" Gwen caught a look of amusement in Billy's eyes. A sparkle of gold in his brown irises.

"Well, it's true alright," Hugh called out from ahead, turning one eighty to face the two of them. Peggy stopped beside him and swatted his arm.

"Don't tease," she said.

"No, no. It's only right, Gwenny should know what she's in for. We don't want a repeat of what happened ten years ago, do we?" He winked in Gwen's direction.

"What happened ten years ago?" Gwen asked, the question escaping unaided. They had all stopped now, the two pairs facing each other. Hugh's face lit up with a grin. She'd taken the bait..

"Don't listen to him," Peggy said, shaking his head and threading her free arm through Hugh's, trying to redirect him back to where Gwen suspected the water hole waited.

Hugh and Peggy continued down the path in silence. Gwen and Billy pulled up alongside them as the path widened to a rocky shoreline, behind which a sleepy river flowed past a few smooth rocks. The water looked cool and dark with shadows from the rocky outcroppings, while the willow trees gave way to blue sky directly above them. On the other side of the river rose a steep bank and more lush, green vegetation.

Peggy pulled away from Hugh, and finding a spot on the stony shore, she placed the tote bag she was holding on the ground. Billy threw the picnic blanket her way. Peggy caught it and lay it out for them to sit on.

Gwen moved to help Peggy set everything else up. Hugh and Billy joined them, plonking down the picnic basket and other tote bag before finding themselves a seat on the blanket.

"So?" Gwen repeated. "We're here now. Am I supposed to say some great prayer to ensure the river monster doesn't eat me, or what?"

"Aye. There's stranger things in this world than river monsters. Just because you can't see something doesn't mean it's not there," Billy said gently. He was leaning on one arm, his hand incredibly close to her own.

Gwen's fingers twitched, and she wondered what it would be like to touch him again.

"Don't listen to them," Peggy said. "They're local superstitions, is all."

"I bet Henry Walken would disagree with you. If he were

alive, that is." Hugh pulled a blade of grass from between two rocks and went about sticking it between his teeth.

Well, he had her attention now. The twit, Gwen thought. A sigh escaped before she gave in and asked.

"Okay. Who's going to spill? Who was Henry Walken?"

Gwen glanced from Billy, who's eyes were downcast, to Peggy, who shook her head slightly in meeting Gwen's eyes, as if she were apologising for what was about to come next. Hugh moved the blade of grass around his mouth. His eyes radiating amusement. He was enjoying himself, Gwen thought. Might as well humour him.

"Go on then," she said.

"Well, it was ten or so years ago, and he was much like you, little kitten. Wide eyed. Sceptical."

Peggy snorted.

"Henry Walken was new to the area, see. We were young 'uns at the time, maybe fifteen, sixteen or so. He was only a few years older. The son of one of our workers. Him and Jakey became friends. Kinda funny, really. You might've noticed Jakey likes to keep to himself a bit."

"Your brother?" Gwen asked. She couldn't assimilate the name Jakey with the brute she boarded with. But then, neither could she see any similarity between Hugh and Jake. Not in personality, anyway. The idea that Jake was his friend didn't really say much for this Henry Walken character.

Hugh nodded his head in answer to her question.

"I know my brother can be a bit—" He paused, rolling the grass around his mouth some more as if feeling for the right word.

Peggy shifted uncomfortably. Brother-in-law or not, Gwen could tell Peggy was no fan.

"He can be a bit hard to get to know," he finished.

"He's an ass," Peggy interjected matter-of-factly, making Gwen's jaw drop.

Her hand flew to her mouth to stifle a giggle. Beside her, Billy let out a humph as if choking back a snigger.

"Alright, alright." Hugh held his palms facing towards them in supplication. "My brother can be a bit of an ass."

Gwen and Peggy dissolved into giggles. Billy slid a little closer, his body heat competing against that of the sun.

It was going to be hard work keeping her feelings in check around this man if her body kept giving her away like this.

"Anyway, Jakey had already been seeing Sarah for a time. The three of them did much like we're doing now. Sarah's friend was supposed to come, like as a setup for Henry, but something must've happened at the last minute for her to cancel."

A plopping sound from the river diverted their attention for the moment, just as a flash of silver from the water ducked back beneath the surface.

"A fish," Billy said, as if to reassure her.

"Anyone want a drink?" Peggy asked, setting about pulling out a couple of glasses and a vacuum flask of lemonade.

She poured out a measure for each of them, while Gwen pondered why she couldn't imagine Sarah younger, in love, with friends, coming here to the swimming hole. When had things changed? Other than to do chores around the house, go into the village for groceries or errands, or to attend church, Sarah seemed to barely leave the house.

A spark of guilt shot through her in remembering how, right now, Sarah was home alone with that brute.

"Anyway," Hugh said, taking a sip of his lemonade, "everyone knows you have to ask permission of the Taniwha before you go swimming here. It's a tradition, passed on since God-knows-when. Henry … well, Henry, was a good chap, don't get me wrong, but he cared little for the local myths, eh? He had his own God and asking permission of anyone else's God … well, he frowned on that sort of thing, is all. He shoulda listened, though. Even Jakey knew better."

He took another sip of his drink, and Gwen did the same. It was sweet and refreshing.

"So how do you ask permission then?" Gwen asked. She saw no reason not to humour him. He was obviously working up to some humorous or horrible climax to his story.

"Well, it's pretty easy," Billy answered for him.

Gwen turned so she could look at him. Did he really believe in this stuff?

"You just ask. See, I'll show you." Surprising Gwen, he grabbed her hand and pulled her up with him till they were standing. Not letting go of his hand, she bent down to place her cup on the blanket, feeling she might need her hand free.

"Come on then," he said, leading her to the edge of the water. "So, ya got to be serious. You can't be foolin' around."

Gwen's mouth curved until she noticed Billy was staring intently at the water. He wasn't joking, then. He believed in this.

Peggy had dragged Hugh to his feet and joined them, so the four of them stood in a line facing the water.

This was ridiculous, Gwen thought.

"Taniwha. Taniwha." Peggy was the first, her gentle voice calling forward the spirit of the river.

"Taniwha. Taniwha," the two men mimicked her, solemn.

"We're here to swim with your permission." The three of

them said it in chorus.

"Your turn, now," Billy said, turning to Gwen.

Were they having a joke at her expense? She flicked a glance at Peggy, who smiled reassuringly at her. Hugh shrugged his shoulders. Turning back to Billy, she saw he was still watching her. She scanned his eyes, searching for a sense of teasing to follow.

"Don't be scared," he said.

Scared? Though she wanted to retort how ridiculous this was, she bit her tongue instead. Billy reached for her hand again.

"I'll say it with you. Taniwha, Taniwha."

What the heck? Gwen thought, and followed his lead. Together they called out: "We're here to swim with your permission."

They stood there for a moment.

"Now what?" she asked.

"Shh. We wait," Billy said.

Not wanting to offend for asking what it was they were waiting for, she let her eyes follow the shadows under the surface in the water, scouring the dark spots along the furthest bank for signs of this mythical Taniwha. She would humour them it if meant she could keep Billy's hand in hers for a little longer.

A sound of fluttering and wings in the brush made her jump and squeal. A thrush flew out from the grass on the other side of the bank and flew off. Peggy burst into giggles again.

"And there you have it, kitten. The Taniwha has accepted your request." Hugh picked up Peggy in his arms and swung her around. Peggy threw her head back and laughed while Hugh bent down to kiss her quickly on the lips and placed her back on the blanket. Gwen watched, mesmerised. This was what real love looked like, she thought, feeling a fleeting stab of jealously. She wanted that.

"Shall we?" Billy asked, indicating they should join them on the blanket. Gwen pulled her hand out of his and led the way the few paces before sitting back on the blanket.

"That was it?" Gwen asked.

"What were you expecting?" Hugh burst out laughing, elbowing Peggy, who smiled at Gwen with sparkling eyes.

"Oh, I don't know. Some booming voice from the heavens telling us we had permission or else should scram, I don't know," Gwen said, relaxing. Even if it was tradition, she didn't really believe the others believed it. Except for maybe Billy. With him, she wasn't sure.

Hugh hit the blanket with his fist as his laughter overwhelmed him.

"It's tradition," Peggy said. "Something everyone does. Part of the experience."

"Billy might tell you otherwise, though," Hugh said, reaching over to clap Billy on the shoulder.

"Yeah, well. Myth or no, I'm not gonna fool around with what I don't know, is all."

Peggy lifted her dress over her head, revealing her dusky rose-coloured satin swimsuit underneath. Then, stretching her legs out before her, she lay back, resting on her elbows. She was beautiful, Gwen thought again. Gwen had never worried too much about her appearance. She knew she was attractive; she could thank her mama for that. But right now, she envied Peggy's slim, long-legged elegance and her confidence, not caring at all for normal modesty.

Hugh placed his hand on one of Peggy's lean legs, obviously

enjoying his wife's form as she lounged.

Gwen stole a glance at Billy. He had averted his eyes, as if somewhat uncomfortable.

"So what happened to Jake's friend then? Harry?"

"Henry," Hugh corrected her, obviously pleased to have the conversation roll back around to him. "Well, like I was saying, it was just the three of them, Jakey, Sarah and Henry. Jakey and Sarah, well, they asked permission. Henry, though, he wasn't gonna have anything of it. Later, Jakey said Sarah had got upset about it, but what could they do?"

Gwen took another sip of her lemonade, already warm from the sun.

"Hugh, darling, do you really think you should tell this story?" Peggy piped in.

"Well, Gwenny asked, and she doesn't look like she scares easy," he said, sending Gwen a wink.

"Maybe you could leave it till after we've had a swim, eh, chap?" Billy asked of his friend.

Hugh shrugged one shoulder.

"It's fine. I want to know now," Gwen said. As tempted as she was to strip down to her swimsuit like Peggy, she wanted to hear the story first. There had already been too many interruptions. This story had better be worth the wait, she thought. A bead of sweat dripped down her neck. She flipped her hair away to cool herself.

"Well, it's what happens, eh? He didn't ask the Taniwha to go swimming, and he drowned."

Gwen flinched. The others were obviously well-versed in the story. Their reactions were nonchalant. Gwen had to admit, she wasn't expecting such finality to the story.

"He drowned?" she repeated.

"So says Jake," Billy muttered under his breath. A fine line appeared between Hugh's eyebrows.

"What reason would he have to lie, eh? Sarah gave the same story," Hugh said.

Sarah, Gwen thought, would have had no choice.

"Boys," Peggy said, sitting back up and tucking her legs under her. "It was obviously an accident," she said, turning to Gwen.

Gwen thought it sounded rehearsed. "How did he drown?" she asked, her curiosity piqued.

"Well, he swam out to the other side, apparently, and got into some trouble. Jakey had wandered off to do – well, man's business, you know."

To relieve himself, Gwen suspected.

"Sarah was on shore. On standing up, she thinks she must've slipped. Hit her head. When she came to, Jakey was back, but Henry was missing. They found his body washed up a few days later, further downstream."

"Awful, isn't it?" Peggy asked, shaking her head.

Gwen gave an involuntary shudder. A man had drowned. Here, where they were about to go swimming. But the worst of it was how uncanny it was that Sarah had hit her head and blanked out, and Jake had just happened to not be around. Sarah seemed to be awfully clumsy in and out of Jake's presence.

She suspected Billy might think something similar.

"So who's up for a swim then?" Hugh said, jumping up and tearing off his shirt, throwing it onto a nearby rock.

"You ghoul!" Peggy cried after him as he ran up to the edge and dove in, the water darkening the rocky shoreline where it splashed behind him.

Chapter 17 – Riley

Riley didn't know how long she'd been out. She woke slumped against the wall with the hand basin beside her. It took her a moment to remember what happened. A wave of nausea threatened, and she put her head between her legs, gulping deep breaths until the nausea and clamminess dissipated.

Footsteps down the hallway made her haul herself up to stand against the sink again. Running the cold water, she held her wrists under the steady stream, hoping it would cool her down and make her feel human again. The last thing she wanted was to be found on the ground for the third time that day.

The bathroom doors opened and a woman walked in. Riley didn't recognise her, and she only gave Riley a cursory glance before heading into a stall.

Drawing a deep breath, Riley willed herself to peer into the mirror, to prove to herself it was all a nightmare, a waking nightmare. Placing both hands on the rim of the sink again, she focused on the feel of the cool ceramic under her hands and lifted her eyes.

Her face, pale in front of a row of stall doors, peered back at her. No deformed figure with gaping mouth. No one begging her to help them.

Of course not.

God, what the hell was wrong with her? Riley grimaced. She had never fainted before, and here she was twice in a day.

Focusing on her reflection, she saw beads of sweat at her hairline. She pulled a paper towel from its dispenser and dabbed at her forehead, feeling the slightly bruised pain from her lump.

Her handbag had slipped to the floor. Riley picked it up. She needed to get to her car, preferably with no one seeing her.

The woman in the stall flushed. Riley headed to the door. Pulling it open, she scanned the hallway. Empty. Her worst fear would be bumping into Katrina, Rob or Brittany, and having to explain why she was still there.

Hurrying down the hallway, she made it to the two large exit doors. She pulled them open and fast walked to her car, glad it was hidden from view of the beer garden. Riley wasted no time starting the engine and hauling ass out of the car park. She'd wait until she was out of Te Tapu before thinking about the events of the day.

She felt like she'd been holding her breath right until the speed limits changed, indicating she was leaving the village behind.

The drive home felt familiar now, meditative as the car seemed to follow the curves and valleys of the road on its own. It was still light out. Would be for hours. In summer, it didn't even think about getting dark until nine o'clock.

Green hills dotted with black and white cattle rose and dipped around her. Now and then they'd be blanked out by trees lining both sides of the road. Traffic was very light. In the morning, she always ran the risk of getting stuck behind a tractor or someone on a four-wheeler taking up the narrow road, but other than a couple of vehicles travelling in the opposite direction, she had the road to herself.

She relaxed into the swells and bends of the road, clinging to her side of the road to prevent drifting across the centre line. With so many blind corners, it could be a fatal mistake.

Is that what happened to Liam's wife?

She couldn't completely forgo the film of unease clinging to her. The day had been a carousel of crazy – the things that had happened, the things she'd seen, and the things she'd been told...

But despite everything, the thing she found hardest to shake was the fact that Liam had been married before. Never mind the face she thought she'd seen in the mirror. That was something to deliberate about another time.

Learning Liam had a wife, and she had died, struck a nerve with her. The doubt in Katrina's voice regarding the "accident" status unsettled her even more. What had she meant by her words? If it hadn't been an accident, what had it been?

The skin on her arms prickled and her car drifted a little across the centre line as she took a sharp corner.

Nope. No more thinking. She could analyse to death the day's crazy when she was safe at home.

Her landlady wasn't home again when Riley pulled into the driveway. The cat, however, was.

Edgar sat on her doorstep as if he owned the place, which Riley supposed he did in a way.

Grabbing what she could from her car in one go, she

approached the door. Surprising even her, Edgar wound himself around her legs, giving her a gentle head-butt of affection now and then.

"Well, you've changed your mind, haven't you?" Riley said, unused to anything but attitude from the fluffy feline.

Gently pushing him out of the way with her foot, she juggled her bags while unlocking the door. Darting between her legs, the cat beat her inside.

Riley made her way into the main living area and dumped her belongings on the coffee table opposite the sofa, then went out to collect the full box.

Locking the car behind her with her key fob, she carried the box inside and plonked it on the sofa, pushing aside the niggling guilt. She could bring resources home. Although these weren't exactly curriculum resources.

Riley flicked on a couple of lights and poured herself a glass of sparkling water from the fridge. Normally she'd strip off her work clothes and get about cooking something for dinner, a frozen meal or a couple of pieces of toast, but the box was calling her. More specifically, she was curious about the journal. Everything else could wait.

She remembered the strange feeling that had come over her in the resource room. Had it been a side effect from the morning's weirdness? Low blood sugar maybe? Dehydration? She'd never been great at remembering to drink lots, particularly during summer, and especially not during the short time she'd been teaching. Everything was so go-go-go, it barely lent time to eat or use the restroom, let alone remember to drink.

What she did know was books didn't make people sick.

A flashback to the woman in the mirror made her heart

leap into her throat, and she swallowed hard, pushing the memory away. She could think about that later too.

The cat had curled up on the sofa beside the box.

Weird. He sure seemed friendlier than usual. If he thought she'd give him a free feed, he was mistaken.

Moving towards the sofa, she placed her glass on the side table and went to shove the cat off the sofa so she could sit down.

He growled and took a swipe at her arm.

"Shit!" she cried out as his claws tore three straight lines across her forearm. Crazed, Edgar went racing across the room and down the hall. Damn it, she thought. He'd be heading for the bedroom. That would be fun trying to get him out from under the bed when it came time to kick him out.

Beads of blood appeared on her skin. The scratches burned.

Back to the kitchen, Riley covered the scratches with a couple of paper towels to stop any blood trickling onto the floor while she searched for the first aid kit. It was in the second place she looked: the cupboard above the microwave.

She placed it next to the sink and gave her arm a quick clean. Who knew how much dirt she had accumulated from being in the resource room. After drying it off with another paper towel, she went about smearing a large plaster with antiseptic cream. She was no nurse, but surely that would be enough for such a wound.

Deciding to skip the cat hunting, Riley settled on the sofa and opened the box of goodies before her.

She began by pulling out the papers stacked on top and moving them to a pile on the coffee table. A receipt fell out. For board and food. Strange. Nothing said it was for the on-site schoolhouse, where past teachers had lived. It was dated to 1939. Riley wasn't even sure if the schoolhouse had been around then.

She placed it on the table and, digging further, found the solid form of the notebook she'd hidden there earlier. Hidden. No way to avoid that phrasing now; she couldn't deny she'd acted intentionally.

She pulled out the notebook and placed it on her lap, gently stroking it with her fingers. She imagined it vibrating under her touch, as if it were coming alive.

Nothing jumped out as particularly spectacular about it. A simple blue cardboard cover. No name or anything inscribed on it. Before even cracking it open, Riley knew it was a diary. The thought should have been presumptuous, as it could be any type of record book or ledger.

But she *did* know. Something stirred in her chest, and the hairs on the back of her neck prickled.

Odd that even here she felt like she was being watched.

A loud bang from the bedroom startled her heart into a stampede and made Riley jump. The notebook slid to the floor as Riley's attention turned towards the hallway.

It had come from the bedroom.

The cat.

Damn it!

A flash of fur flew down the hall, skidding to a stop at the front door. Riley's heart thumped against her ribcage. He sat there swivelling his head almost a complete three-sixty to stare at Riley with total disdain for her taking so long to let him out.

"Blasted cat," she swore again under her breath.

No doubt he had knocked over the bedside lamp.

As she walked to the door, the wretched creature let out a low growl. Riley sighed and unlocked the door to let it out into the yard. Without any hesitation, it beelined for Molly's house.

Riley headed back to the sofa. She should have gone to find out what the cat had destroyed in her bedroom, but the draw to get back to the journal was too strong.

Getting comfy, she took a sip of drink and picked up the notebook. With care, she ran her fingers over the worn and aged cover, then gently opened it. On the inside cover, faded though still readable, were a name and date written in old-fashioned cursive script: Gwendolyn (Gwen) Davies, and underneath it the date 1939.

Riley traced the words with her finger as pins and needles prickled in her fingertips.

She turned the page.

She had been right. It was a diary or journal of sorts.

Riley moved the box to the floor. She then brought her legs up, tucking them under her on the sofa, and pulled a throw over her bottom half as she again opened the book and read.

Chapter 18 – Gwen

"He's more myself than I am. Whatever our souls
are made of, his and mine are the same."
- ***Wuthering Heights***

It was a wonderful day. One of the best Gwen
remembered.

Ever the entertainer, Hugh amused them with story
after story of some of the Te Tapu village inhabitants. He
seemed to know everyone's business. A benefit, or not, to
being the son of a local hero, Ol' Tom, who even Hugh
referred to as such despite him being his father. And yet,
it sounded like it wasn't actually Hugh who was the apple of
Ol' Tom's eye.

Being the eldest, it set Jake to inherit the family businesses.
It made no sense, Gwen thought. Hugh talked of him with a
sense of brotherly love bordering on hero worship. To Gwen,
Jake was no more than an abusive drunk and bully.

Conversation was easy. Gwen learnt Peggy was the only
child of a couple from the city. They had both died when

Peggy was seven, leaving her to be brought up by her grandparents here in Te Tapu.

And Billy, the oldest of four and the only boy. His parents moved from Ireland when he was nine years old, his father passing when Billy was fourteen, leaving Billy the man of the house, working to provide for his family the best he could.

Hugh hadn't even bothered with swimming trunks, saying his pants would dry soon enough in the sun. Billy had disappeared for a while amongst the bush, reappearing in a one-piece swimsuit.

Much like Peggy, Hugh was lean and tall. His body pale from little exposure to the sun. It seemed to Gwen, Peggy and Hugh were the perfect couple, well suited in form and personality. But it was Billy who held her attention. He wasn't as daring as Hugh; in many ways, he was more genteel. Hugh had to tease him to even change into his swimwear. When he reappeared from the trees, he ran right past them, diving into the water, surfacing mid-way out. Gwen clapped and laughed and quietly explored his body with her eyes. Where he stood waist deep, she saw more clearly the muscles of his arms and shoulders. Billy was shorter than Hugh, more solid too. But he also had the body of someone used to physical labour, and Gwen found she liked it. It made her feel safe. His hair darkened by the water was plastered to his head and water trickled down his chest. Gwen hadn't realised she had been staring until she felt the gentle nudge of Peggy's foot against hers.

Gwen's cheeks warmed as Peggy raised an eyebrow in her direction, a grin playing on her lips. A ruckus from the water drew Gwen's attention away, and she watched Billy and Hugh roughhouse, taking turns to push each other under the water.

169

Billy gasped for air as he rose back up to pounce on the back of Hugh again.

The girls watched, chuckling and helping themselves to some of the egg and cucumber sandwiches Peggy had brought with them.

"Your turn, ladies," Hugh said, standing above them, dripping water over their feet. Billy stood a little behind, a crooked smile on his own face.

"No, no, no," Peggy squealed. "We'll go in when we're ready."

"I don't think so," Hugh said. "You can't very well go on sitting there in your suits without getting them wet." With one deft movement, he swooped down and picked up Peggy in his arms, carrying her to the water's edge. Peggy squealed again but did very little to free herself from her husband's arms.

"Your turn," Billy said, grinning down at Gwen, his hint of an accent setting her blood afire. Behind Billy, Hugh stood waist deep in the water before dropping Peggy in.

For a second, Gwen thought of protesting. For starters, she had never learnt to swim properly. But no. She would be safe with Billy. And this new Gwen was fearless.

She slipped off her sandals, and then kneeling, peeled her dress over her head, revealing the emerald swimsuit underneath, then reached up a hand for Billy to help her up. For a moment he did nothing, and Gwen was secretly thrilled to see him awestruck, eyes wide and mouth slightly open as he gazed down at her. She saw the heat rise up his neck, and he physically shook himself before holding out his hand for hers. Gwen took it, her pulse quickening as he pulled her to her feet.

"I'll race you," she called as she dropped his hand and ran

over the polished rocks to the water, not stopping until she had thrown herself in, keeping her head above water. A solid form followed on her tail, splashing beside her. Gwen wiped away the water that splashed her face. The river here was shallow, so Gwen crouched down so it sat comfortably up to her shoulders. It was cool, but soothing in a way she hadn't expected.

A few metres away, Hugh had picked up Peggy and was holding her in his arms in the water like a child. Her arms were wrapped around his neck, and they tittered and whispered, their foreheads almost touching, lost in each other.

Gwen turned to Billy, who was watching them too. His eyes tore away and settled on hers.

Electricity fizzed between them, and Gwen's heart beat harder against her rib cage. Small lines crinkled at the corner of his eyes. For a moment, time stood still until a movement beside them broke their trance. Hugh followed Peggy out of the water, flopping down on the blanket as Peggy wrapped herself in a towel. An aura of whispers and giggles hung over the pair.

Billy's fingers brushed against hers under the water, once, twice, and then, growing bolder, wove between her own.

Holding her hand, he led her out deeper. Gwen stood and followed until the water crept closer to her shoulders. Whatever his intentions, she pulled him to a halt. The gentle current wove around her, caressing her limbs. Gwen stood on her tiptoes, not wanting to go further. Billy stopped and turned to her, letting go of her hand.

Gwen let her hands move slowly through the water, enjoying their gentle dance as they moved.

"Afraid of Taniwha?" he asked.

She knew he meant it as a joke, but his eyes held hers with a feverish intensity.

"More afraid of what happens when I can't touch the bottom anymore," she whispered back.

"Can you swim?"

"Not yet," she said.

Billy arched his eyebrow. "I didn't know," he said. "We could go back." He tilted his head in the shore's direction where, out of earshot, Peggy and Hugh continued their flirting and chatter.

"Or you could teach me," Gwen said, buoyed by a fearlessness that seemed to come from being in Billy's presence.

Billy tipped his head. "Really?" he asked.

"Really," she said, her confidence growing.

"Alright. Well…" He stalled for a moment, obviously unsure what to do. "Maybe we could start with you showing me what you can do?" He waited a moment, and Gwen shrugged her shoulders to indicate she was showing him already.

Gwen watched, enjoying his moment of awkwardness as realisation dawned.

"Can you put your head under?" he asked.

Gwen smiled. That she could do.

"Here, I'll do it with ya," he said, reaching once more for her hands.

Together they counted to three, Gwen bouncing on her toes before taking a breath and ducking under the water. The cool water heightening her senses, she could feel her hair weightless around her face. She opened her eyes to see Billy's face close to hers. The water, dark but not so murky she couldn't make out the thin curvature of his lips, and his eyes locked on hers.

And she knew it then.

He was hers.

Chapter 19 – Riley

When Riley woke, it was already late morning. The sun had found a path through a gap in her curtains, blinding her as it struck her eyes. She blinked a few times to acclimatise.

Then panic hit. What time was it? Was she going to be late for school? Then it dawned on her. It was Saturday. Her time was her own.

Riley's head pounded, a deep-set hammering behind her eyes. As she moved her head, she noticed the crick in her neck from sleeping on the sofa.

She didn't even remember falling asleep. She had been reading, and the blue journal lay open on her chest. The throw still covered her legs, but she had no memory of lying down.

Her stomach gave a growl, and Riley remembered all too quickly. She had also missed dinner. With a groan, she moved the journal to the coffee table beside her. On the count of three, she swung her legs onto the ground and heaved herself into a sitting position. Leaning forward, she rested her head in her hands, willing away another onslaught of pounding. Maybe she was dehydrated, she thought.

A banging at the door made her jolt upright again, her heart jumping in her chest. She was still wearing yesterday's clothes and suspected a night on the sofa certainly wouldn't have done anything for her appearance.

Wiping the sleep from her eyes, she made her way to the front door, surprised to find she was a little wobbly on her feet. The pounding on the door continued. She steadied herself, hand on the doorknob for a second before taking a deep breath and opening it. A flash of ginger fur swiped past her legs. Edgar.

She blinked for a second, her eyes adjusting to the light. It took a moment to focus on the person standing before her.

Justin took a step forward, blocking the sun and giving her a moment to collect her senses.

"Whoa, Riles. Rough night?" he asked, his wide eyes affirming she looked as she felt.

"What are you doing here, Justin?"

"We didn't get to talk." He stuffed his hands in his pockets, and Riley's stomach fell. He looked hurt. Genuinely hurt.

She tried to will away the guilt growing in her chest.

"Can I come in?" he asked.

At least he was asking, she thought. Justin was known for doing whatever he wanted.

"I have things to do. I really can't—"

"I won't be long," he said, pushing past her into the flat.

Riley sighed. Here was the Justin she knew. She watched him taking in the small space. It was nothing compared to the two-bedroom apartment in the city where they had lived together, but it was hers. Still, she felt herself getting defensive, expecting criticism and judgement.

Instead, he made his way over to the sofa and plopped

himself down.

"What's all this?" he asked, gesturing to the box of papers and picking up the journal Riley had been reading.

"Nothing, just school stuff," she said, grabbing the diary out of his hand. She set it on top of the box and moved it over to the kitchen counter. She wasn't ready to share this with anyone yet.

While in the kitchen, Riley grabbed a glass from the cupboard, filled her glass in the sink and gulped down the water, purposely not offering Justin anything.

"What do you want, Justin?" she asked again, working hard to keep her voice steady, unemotional. Seeing him brought on a wave of emotions. She was done with him, she told herself. No going back. No matter what.

"Riley…" he started. "This isn't you." He eyed the small space again, and Riley's hackles rose on the back of her neck. "Look, I made a mistake. We both did." He stood up then, and walked towards her.

"No," Riley said, with more force than she expected. "I didn't make a mistake. I didn't cheat." She placed her hands behind her on the laminate counter, her back to the sink, hoping it might quell her shaking.

"Come on," he said. "It was a mistake, and it wasn't like things were all that … well, you know … with us." He shrugged and traced one hand along the top of the box on the counter.

Riley gritted her teeth, a fire flaring in her chest.

He's a murderer! A murderer!

The voice came from everywhere and nowhere all at once. A woman's voice. Riley's knees buckled, and she leaned harder on the counter to keep herself upright.

176

"You weren't exactly, little-miss-eager-to-see-me when I got home—"

"I was studying!" Riley cried out indignantly. "I had practicums and exams and – it doesn't even *matter*!"

"A man wants to feel wanted—"

"Are you serious? You cheated!" Every word tasted bitter with anger, and she swallowed hard, her throat feeling parched. Her fingertips dug into the counter; her entire body shook with indignation. "I left. And then what? You show up a month later—"

"It's not like that," he said, stepping closer, his hands facing her as if approaching a wild animal. "I missed you—"

Liar. Murderer.

The words rose unbidden again. Riley glanced around her, trying to pinpoint where they came from. Justin was still talking, unaware.

He's a murderer. Murderer! He killed Billy!

Her breath caught in her throat.

"Whoa! What the hell?!" Justin took a step backwards, this time his hands were up as if to protect himself.

"What the hell are you doing?" His voice pitched as he did so, his cheekbones more prominent as the colour drained from his face.

It took Riley a second to notice she was no longer leaning on the countertop; instead, she had taken a step towards him. Her eyes followed down her body, as if she were outside of herself. She held her arm out; a vegetable knife was gripped in her fist, its tip aimed at Justin.

"Fuck, Riley. Put the knife down!" It took her another moment to make sense of what she was doing. It was *her* hand holding the knife. What was she doing? Threatening him?

Her hand shook, her fingers loosened, and the knife clattered to the floor. The tears that had been prickling behind eyelids before made rivulets down her cheeks.

"You need to leave," she whispered, unable to look up from where the knife lay. "You need to leave," she whispered again.

"What the hell is wrong with you?" Justin replied, voice wavering.

She had scared him. Probably not as much as she was scaring herself, though.

"This is not cool, Riles," he said, making his way to the door. A screech sounded, and Justin swore, bending down to rub his leg where Edgar had slashed him. The cat sat there indignantly, licking his paw with flexed claws.

"When you come to your senses, you can call me," Justin said, his mood dramatically altered from when he'd arrived. He saw himself out, slamming the door behind him.

Riles stood there. Her entire body shaking. Where the hell had the knife come from? She didn't remember picking it up. She must have left it on the bench, but what had possessed her to pick it up? She wasn't scared of Justin. She had never wanted to physically hurt him, had never wanted to hurt anyone before. But she had felt it. Something within her had wanted to hurt him. A part of her was so angry she had wanted to inflict bodily harm on him.

She slumped to the ground, legs tucked up under her, silent tears making puddles on the floor.

Murderer! the voice said again. *He killed Billy!*

Chapter 20 – Gwen

"…your veins are full of ice-water; but mine are
boiling…"
- *Wuthering Heights*

The trip to the river had been the start of something wonderful. Gwen Davies was unabashedly head over heels in love with Billy MacKenzie. She must have written that a million times in her diary, enjoying the way the words laced together on the page. She drew little love hearts with their initials and imagined what it would be like to sign her name as Mrs Billy MacKenzie. It was childish, she knew, but love was known to make a person lose their senses.

Many more get-togethers followed. Never alone, always chaperoned by Hugh and Peggy, and Gwen didn't really mind. They were fun to be around. Eager to let loose, have fun, and roll their eyes at society's proprieties.

They invited Gwen and Billy over for dinner one night. Their house was smaller, quainter than Jake and Sarah's, and yet was so much more welcoming. It surprised Gwen to see how domesticated Peggy was. A real housewife, she delighted in cooking and hostessing for the four of them. Crocheted cushions rested on the chairs and scenic watercolours of rolling hills and fields of sheep hung on the walls. Gwen was even more shocked to learn the watercolours were of Hugh's doing.

While keeping Peggy company in the kitchen, Gwen noticed a couple of family photos on the hutch in the dining area.

Gwen ran her eyes over the various nick-knacks and wedding china, but the photos drew her interest the most. One showed Peggy perched on the bonnet of an old car, head tilted back, laughing, Hugh beside her. Another was of two young boys dressed in their Sunday best. One tall, solemn, the other shorter with a hint of a smile playing on his lips.

"Is this Hugh?" Gwen asked, picking up the silver frame and bringing it closer for Peggy to see.

Peggy paused, stirring the stew on the stove. She took a glance and nodded her head.

"Then this must be Jake?" Gwen asked, pointing to the other child.

A scowl darkened Peggy's face.

"How is it they are so different?" Gwen whispered, half to herself.

"I honestly don't know," Peggy said, shaking her head. "I don't understand it either."

She returned to her pot, gave it a quick stir, then took it off the stove. She held out her hand for the photo. Gwen passed it to her and watched Peggy study it, her forehead wrinkling.

"Hugh takes after his father, Ol' Man Tom."

"I've heard villagers talk about him," Gwen said. The talk

had always been good. From what Gwen knew, he not only owned much of Te Tapu, but he was also held in high esteem by many of Te Tapu's residents.

Peggy hummed and nodded her head.

"The boys' mother died when they were in their teens," she said, "but I think Jake always had a darkness to him. Some people are born that way, I guess." She flinched before placing the photograph back where it came from on the hutch. She shifted a photo of her and Hugh in front of it.

The end of the night was Gwen's favourite part of the visit.

After thanking Peggy and Hugh and saying goodnight, Billy offered to walk her home. It was their one opportunity to be alone.

Outside, the cicadas were in full serenade. The night sky was clear, the Big Dipper suspended above them. A sliver of the moon hung high in the sky, shining just enough light to see by. Somewhere in the distance a morepork called its name.

Gwen shivered and pulled her shawl tighter across her shoulders. Summer was fading into autumn, and a slight chill clung to the night. The tyres of her bike grumbled over the gravel as she pushed it. Billy walked close to her, his hands in his pockets. He had offered to push it for her, but she had declined. If Gwen was anything, she was independent, and she wanted Billy to know that.

A quiet hung between them. After the laughter and liveliness of being at Peggy and Hugh's, a contented contemplation had settled over Gwen. It grew a nervousness of anticipation, and Gwen suspected Billy felt it too.

From the corner of her eye, she saw Billy's mouth twitch as if he were about to say something and then changed his mind.

Gwen had to admit, she had so much she wanted to say too. But being in his presence, especially alone with him, her emotions seemed to pool into colours, blending and fading, and it was too hard to separate them. All she knew was that since the moment their eyes had locked underwater, she had felt this pull, drawn to him in an inexplicable way. It made her voice catch in her throat, her heart constrict, and her usual self-confidence disappear. She became as giggly as some of the students she taught.

Whatever our souls are made of, his and mine are the same. The line from *Wuthering Heights* played over and over in her mind.

Billy cleared his throat beside her, and her heart gave a flutter in her chest.

"Gwen." His voice caught and he came to a halt.

Gwen stopped, steadying the bike, and turned to him.

He took a step forward and placed one hand on the handlebars and one on the seat.

Her skin tingled, and her breath caught in her chest.

Being alone with him…

Having him this close…

Her lips twitched, wanting to smile while she searched his face in the weak light. He was handsome, her Billy.

She traced his features with her eyes while a silence stretched out between them. Would he kiss her?

Billy was a gentleman. A little old-fashioned. Even so, here he was, walking her home, acting as chaperone, with the night closing in… Gwen was sure she saw desire in his eyes.

It took a moment to realise his expression had changed. His jawline hardened, his lips thinning into a line while his eyes narrowed. Her own eyes widened in surprise, his seriousness catching her off guard.

"Gwen," he said again, this time with a loud exhale of breath. "I know you're your own woman and all…" He kicked at a stone on the ground. "And it's not my place to say anything… "

Gwen stiffened. This wasn't the direction she expected.

"It's just – I don't like him, eh? I don't like the idea of you being in his house." Billy let out another exhale of breath.

It took Gwen a moment to understand what he was saying.

"Well, I don't honestly like him myself," Gwen said, keeping her voice warm. "But what would you have me do, Mr MacKenzie?" she said, teasing, her lips curving upwards. She leaned his direction, the bike being the only thing between them.

"I don't know," he said with a shake of his head. "We could find you other lodgings."

Gwen's heart picked up its pace. Maybe he would ask her to move in with him? It would cause quite the scandal, but oh, how wonderful to be with him.

This side of Billy, his protectiveness, his concern for her safety, she felt her chest expand even more.

"I'm not scared of Jake," she said, watching Billy's features carefully. It was a lie. The man scared her more than anything.

"Well, maybe you should be," Billy said sharply.

His change in tone felt like a slap, and Gwen recoiled.

"Och, I'm sorry. I am. It's just I don't like the idea of you being alone in that house with him."

"I'm not alone," Gwen was quick to reply. "Sarah's there."

Billy shook his head and looked away. "And some help she'd

be," he said.

"And what do you mean by that?" Something sparked in her chest, a hint of anger growing under the surface. Didn't he know she was more than capable of taking care of herself?

"I mean, you need to leave, that's what." The beginnings of real anger flared in his eyes.

"Leave? And what? Go back to the city, Billy Mackenzie? Is that what you want." Oh, how fast her anger could catch light.

"No." He released his hand from the handlebars to lift his cap and wipe his forehead. "No, I don't want you to leave. I want you to stay," he said, clearly exasperated. "But if that man ever lays a hand on you, I swear, I'll—"

"You'll what?" Gwen took a step back, letting go of the bike entirely. Fire seared her skin, and her body shook. "You think I'm such a floozy as to allow another man, a married man, to touch me?!" Her voice had risen.

"No. *No!*" he said more forcefully. "He's a brute, he is." He swallowed and shoved his hat back, obviously struggling with his own anger. "And you ... you're..."

She waited, hands clenched at her sides, angry tears prickling behind her eyes.

He looked around him, then let go of the seat, allowing the bike to fall to the ground. In two quick strides he had crossed the distance between them, and he held her face between the palms of his hands.

She was paralysed. Her heart trying to burst from her chest as his body pressed up against hers. Her hands hung limp at her sides, his eyes burrowed into hers, and her skin felt close to combustion.

"And you're mine," he whispered before pressing his forehead to her own.

She closed her eyes, breathing in his scent. Her hand moved of its own accord, up his body to the base of his neck. Her fingers tentatively felt their way into his hair. He let out a slight moan, his warm breath brushing her lips.

"You'll be the end of me, Gwendolyn Davies," he whispered, and closed his eyes, moving his hands down her body and settling on top of her hips.

"And you'll be mine," she whispered back before brushing his lips with her own.

Chapter 21 – Riley

Families were arriving.

The school felt different in the evening. It was still light out, but the day was fast fading into dusk. The air rippled with excitement as parents and their kids mingled outside by the picnic tables under the silk trees. She was fast learning everyone knew everyone in Te Tapu, so conversation flowed easily as the children ran around chatting and laughing with their friends. She was sure many of them had headed straight for the playground around the corner of the building. That was the power of the night; it made everything fresh and exciting again. It changed the way people saw things.

Riley noticed Victoria through the large French doors, chatting to a woman holding a toddler in her arms. She took the moment to glance around her classroom. Everything looked good. She had stayed late to make sure the room was tidy; everything in its place. The students' self-portraits hung bright and abstract above the whiteboard, showcasing varying degrees of artistic talent. Tote trays were accessible for parents to peer through their offspring's books, although secretly Riley hoped they didn't. They were only five weeks into the term, so the books were still quite bare.

She'd spent a lot of time getting the classroom set up ready for the parents and her colleagues. One wall was her masterpiece. She was quietly proud of it and hoped it would show how much she wanted to be a part of the Te Tapu community.

Almost a week had passed since she had heard from Justin, and she was a little torn about it. She had yet to make sense of what had happened with the knife. She shook her head. She hadn't threatened him. But why had she even picked it up? And the voice...

No. There had been no voice.

I'm not crazy.

The words floated through her head.

I'm not my aunt!

She shook her head again. Not even her thoughts made sense. As far as she knew, she had no aunts.

Riley had spent the rest of the weekend sorting through more of the box and reading the journal. Too many hours, in fact, had she sat there on the sofa and studied it. In the end, she had to set the timer on her phone to remind her to do other things – lesson planning for one.

The journal was riveting. Something about reading the handwritten thoughts of a person from over seventy years ago was both unsettling and compelling. Even more so when that person had taught at the same school, maybe even in the same classroom as she did.

Riley glanced around again. If any ghosts from back then were still here, she couldn't see them.

From what she had learned, Gwen Davies had moved from the city for her first teaching job in Te Tapu. It had been rather a culture shock for her, a little like it had been for Riley. Riley noticed right away, Gwen was passionate, with her emotions acting as living entities on the page. And they could change swiftly, bouncing from manic to melancholic even within the same entry.

Much of her writing was about her disgust towards the man she boarded with, her envy of her beautiful friend, Peggy, but mostly her budding love for Billy.

Billy.

That name seemed to be popping up a lot lately, Riley thought, remembering the accusatory sentence during writing practice and the voice from when she had nearly attacked Justin.

No, she reminded herself. She never attacked him.

Gwen had written little about her actual time teaching except for grumblings about her headmistress. She suspected teaching wasn't half as exciting for Gwen as everything else going on in her life.

Would they have been friends, Riley wondered, if she and Gwen had lived at the same time? They both had a love for the novel *Wuthering Heights,* evidenced by how often Gwen would scribble quotes from the book throughout her journal. Maybe she was the one who had written the yellowed note Riley had found on her first day when she had lost her bracelet.

Coincidence.

She shook her head again. Time to focus on what was at hand.

For the past week, Riley had shared many of the artefacts from the box with her class.

Not the journal, though. That was for her alone.

The class had undertaken a week-long investigation into Te

Tapu School's past based around the finds. They had explored what it was like to be a student in the 1930s and what life was like in 1939, with the Great Depression and the country being on the cusp of war.

Riley assigned the kids' homework to interview an adult of their choosing about what school was like for them. She had hoped to create a timeline about being a student through the ages. Wanting to keep the project on the down low as much as possible, she told the kids to keep what they could as a surprise for when their families visited.

On the wall hung large laminated letters spelling out "Te Tapu School in the Past". She intermixed some of the written research and photos from her students with things she had pulled from Gwen's box. The class photo Riley assumed was of Gwen and her students had a prime place in the centre of the display. A student's crude drawing with "*I love you, Miss Davies*" written on it, yellowed with wavy edges, also found itself on the wall. Receipts for groceries from the time, a flier from the local Young Farmers Women's Committee, a handwritten receipt for a dress, and some pictures she had discovered on the internet and in the museum in the next town over also filled the wall.

On the bench below, Riley had carefully laid out a couple of old children's books from the 1930s she'd purchased at a thrift store. She had no way of knowing if past students had ever read them, but it helped set the mood. She had also displayed the roll register and an old newspaper dating to August 1939. Riley had only had time to skim read the newspaper – lots of advertisements for fashion, medicines, and food, along with a recipe for hot fish sandwiches, a long list of social notes of who was visiting whom in the area, and headlines about jobs awaiting school children in the textile industry.

On the whiteboard, Riley had shown off her cursive, copying the alphabet and a passage carefully from one book. She must have re-read what she wrote a hundred times, ensuring there were no slip-ups. Or accusations of murder.

Finally, to add to the ambience, Riley set up a playlist of 1930s music to play quietly in the background. She hoped the parents might get as excited by the project as the kids and she were, willingly sharing their own stories and knowledge. From Riley's experience, nostalgia was always great at bringing people together, and she hoped to impress Victoria by collaborating with the community in such a way.

She had kept it pretty quiet from the other teachers too. All classes were left to choose a topic focus of their choice as long as it related to the interests of the students.

When Brittany and Victoria had questioned her about it, she had glossed over it, dismissing it as looking at history and comparing it to the present. Now, with everyone arriving, she couldn't wait to share what she and her class had been working on.

More parents were entering through the school gates, heading towards Victoria, who had picked up a megaphone and was calling everyone together. Riley had to admit, she was nervous too. Meeting parents, wondering what their children had told them of her, had made her a little twitchy. And, oh, she hoped they hadn't mentioned her fainting or that one particular handwriting lesson. Her bracelet had been getting a good workout on her arm today.

The growing crowd of people pulled closer together to join Victoria under the silk trees.

Riley brushed her hands down the sides of her pencil skirt. Show time. Biting her bottom lip to quell her nerves, she stood a little straighter and headed out the room to join them.

After brief greetings, Victoria explained how the evening would roll out. Parents were welcome to visit their child's class, meet the teacher, have their child show some of their work, and of course, help themselves to sausages in bread and butter, and a salad and condiment table, courtesy of the O'Regans.

Victoria gestured behind her to an older man, maybe in his seventies, who sat in a wheelchair, hand raised, accepting the attention. Another man stood beside him, his back towards Riley, deep in conversation with someone else. The man turned around, and with a start Riley realised it was Liam. Of course, Riley thought. Katrina had said Liam was looking after his dad, the infamous Arthur. And as bigwigs in the community, of course they would sponsor the food.

She was still doubtful Liam was as wonderful as Katrina, Brittany and Rob had said. Liam shuffled his feet, visually uncomfortable at the attention as the crowd clapped. His lips barely broke a smile, and even then, Riley thought it forced. Arthur turned to him where he was sitting and said something. Liam's jaw tightened for Riley to see, even across the distance between them. It was obvious they were not each other's fan.

By the murmur of excitement from the kids who milled around, Riley suspected many of them would make a beeline for the food before they even considered heading her way.

Across the crowd, Riley spotted Brittany kneeling down chatting to a little one whose hand was clasped in that of his mother. A sibling to one of her students, maybe, as he appeared preschool age.

Natalie was chatting to a couple of parents over by the salad table. It amazed Riley how well Natalie could schmooze when she wanted to. By the way she was smiling and using animated hand gestures, no one would guess the woman wore an almost permanent scowl.

With no sign of Rob, Riley assumed he had already taken up his spot in his classroom.

The crowd dispersed in various directions. A chill flooded through her veins, and she tried to shake it off. It was still warm outside, but she rubbed her arms, anyway.

The feeling was back again. Like she was being watched. Stupid, she thought. Someone was probably looking at her. She was a new teacher and new to the community. It would be normal, natural, for people to take an interest. A faint breath of air, like a whisper against her cheek, made the hairs on the back of her neck prickle. She rubbed her arms for a second time, where now goosebumps had risen.

Riley waited at the entrance of her room and tried to appear as approachable and cheerful as she could. Within seconds, one of her students, Jessica, appeared before her with her mum in tow.

"Come on, Mum," she said impatiently, tugging at her hand.

Riley held out her hand to the poor woman and introduced herself.

She led Jessica and her mum inside, chatting a bit about what the class had been up to, then she turned it over to Jessica who excitedly took care of the rest, dragging her mother around the room, pointing out where she sat, her work on the walls, and eagerly showcasing the artefacts and items on the Te Tapu feature wall.

Riley was thrilled. She loved hearing how passionate her students were about something they were learning or did in class.

It wasn't long before other parents and children swarmed into the room. A couple of times, she noticed adult eyes focused on her rather than their progenies.

She mingled the best she could, smiling and introducing herself, and was met with half smiles in return.

A small group assembled in front of her display. Riley mentally gave herself a pat on the back. It seemed like her display was a success.

One woman, Margot Bailey, seemed frozen to the spot. Her son had moved on and was chatting with a friend on the other side of the room, while Margot stood there as if in a trance. Unmoving. Staring.

Riley approached her, willing to answer questions she might have about the display. Margot turned to her as she drew near.

"Does Victoria know about this?" Her voice was choked with emotion, her face drawn.

A cold fingernail scraped down Riley's backbone. No warmth showed in Margot's face.

"The school's focus for this term is 'Change' so we've been looking at the changes over time in the students' locality," she said by way of sidestepping the question.

"Yes," Margot said sharply, swinging her arm to encompass the display, "but does Victoria know about *this*?"

Her voice had risen, and Riley flicked her eyes around the room. A couple of adult faces were turned in Riley's direction, and a flush of discomfort warmed her cheeks. She opened her mouth to say something, but nothing came out.

193

"Marg?" Another parent approached. The father of one of her boys, Riley remembered. She couldn't remember his name though she'd seen him dropping his son off at the gate and picking him up after school a few times.

"Have you seen this, Richard?" Margot said.

Riley twisted her bracelet. What was happening? She thought it would please the community to see the class's interest in local history.

Holding her breath, she watched as Richard washed his eyes over the wall. Then he stepped forward, picked up the attendance register. When he got to the newspaper, Riley saw him give pause.

"What?" he exhaled under his breath.

"Fletch!" he called out for his boy, who, with shoulders slumped, dragged his feet over to his father. "You need to go get Mr O'Regan."

Fletcher opened his mouth as if to argue, but with one stern look from his father he bowed his head, defeated, and headed back outside.

"Is something wrong?" Riley asked, unsure she wanted to hear the answer to her question.

A small crowd circled them.

"What were you thinking?" Richard's eyes settled on hers, his accusatory tone making Riley's heart skip a beat.

Riley opened and closed her mouth, like a fish gasping for air as she struggled to find her voice. Swallowing hard, she tried again, going into her spiel about the importance of children learning about their local history so they can make connections to themselves, their families and their place in the world. She knew even as she said it, it sounded rehearsed.

Richard's eyes narrowed. A couple of murmurs from the

194

back of the room made Riley's anxiety rise.

It wasn't long before she heard the squeak of wheels in the cloak bay. She suspected her grimace was clear for everyone to see as Liam wheeled Arthur into the room. Of course. The kingpin of the village and his prodigal son had been called in to feast their eyes on whatever line the new teacher had crossed. Riley's stomach dropped.

She had avoided Liam as much as possible since their last interaction. The man had been so rude, and honestly, she was still embarrassed.

Liam's eyes briefly flicked to hers, unsmiling, then focused where Richard was now directing their attention. Riley stepped back to give them some room, speechless. She had no idea what she had done wrong. She watched the side of Liam's face for clues. His expression was pinched. He looked as uncomfortable to be there as she was.

"What is it, Richard?" a gruff voice said. Liam's father. Arthur. Thick, wrinkled hands clasped the sides of his chair. Dressed in khakis and a light blazer, with days' worth of grey whiskers across his jawline, and hair almost completely white. His skin was pallid, with a faint spiderweb of broken veins across his bulbous nose.

Riley noticed a disinterested Fletcher was already chatting with a friend and seemed ready to leave.

"Have you seen this, Art?" his voice, low and sharp.

Riley stood motionless, not knowing whether to intercede. Everyone had gone silent, their eyes shifting back and forth from the display and Arthur to her.

Liam's eyes scanned the display and widened. The muscles in his jaw clenched. Standing behind his father, his knuckles turned white as he tightened his grip on the wheelchair's handles.

Liam's reaction unsettled her the most, and she reached once more for her bracelet. What *had* she done?

"The date, Art. Look at the date!" Richard thrust the newspaper in the old man's face.

Riley caught herself before reaching out for it. She felt a protectiveness for it. She hated to see something of such historical interest treated so recklessly.

She steeled herself, clenching her fists to stop her hands from shaking.

Liam turned to her then. His eyes settled on hers, steely cold. But behind the freeze lurked something else.

Whatever taboo or line in the sand she had crossed, right now all she wanted was to disappear.

She opened her mouth to say something. To explain. Nothing came out.

"What is this about, Arthur?" Victoria's voice cut through the room, and Riley turned to see Victoria storming through the crowd towards Liam and his father.

Riley felt a hint of relief at seeing her. She looked from Arthur to Riley. A small lifting of Riley's hands at her sides showed her puzzlement. Then Victoria's eyes meet Liam's. Riley followed the silent communication between the two of them. Liam shifted his eyes to the display, and Victoria and Riley followed his gaze. Victoria's jaw slackened as if slapped, her eyes scanning the display before her.

Arthur turned in his chair to face Victoria.

"What the hell is going on here, Vicky?" he growled. His voice vibrating deep in his throat. He threw the newspaper at Victoria. Falling short, it landed on the ground. Riley stepped forward again, willing to pick it up, aware all eyes were on her, but Victoria beat her to it.

Finally finding her voice, Riley approached her. She'd understand, she was sure of it.

"I don't under—" she started before being shut down by Victoria's hand raised in a "stop" to silence her.

Riley obeyed as Victoria scanned over the front page of the newspaper. She saw the very moment Victoria noticed whatever had so upset Arthur and Liam. Her free hand flew to her chest, massaging the area where her heart was.

"I'll deal with it," Victoria whispered, only taking her eyes away to glance back over to the wall. A queer expression came over her as her eyes settled on the photo of who Riley assumed was Gwen.

"You had better," the old man growled. "Turn me around," he demanded of Liam, whose jaw tightened again though he obeyed. Arthur faced Riley now. He glared at her, fire blazing behind dark eyes.

"Whatever you are playing at, girl, you need to stop!" he said. "We have no tolerance for troublemakers in this town." His voice boomed and Riley shrank back. Tears prickled behind her eyelids. For a moment she caught Liam's eyes. No warmth lay there. Just horror.

What had she done so wrong?

"That's enough, Arthur," Victoria said before turning to Liam. "I think your father needs to leave."

"Don't you talk to me like that, Vic—"

"Now!" Victoria cut him off, pointing at Liam to leave.

Riley turned away, biting down on her lip to stop it from trembling. She couldn't look at anyone, yet she felt eyes on her. So many of them. Adults and children. She massaged her lip with her teeth, trying to stop the oncoming tears. She played with her fingers, clicking them to stop them from shaking. When that didn't work, she moved to her desk and busied her hands rearranging things on her desk.

"Okay, everyone, food's going to go cold if you don't go help yourselves now." It was an order rather than a suggestion.

Riley couldn't bring herself to lift her head, but she knew from the lack of sound and movement no one but Liam and his father had made any attempt to leave.

"You can come back later, but right now, this room is closed," Victoria said in her no-nonsense way. Amongst a couple of grumbles and humphs, Riley heard them leave. She batted back the tears. One escaped anyway and made a wet stain on her desk.

Riley sniffed, gathered what courage she could, aware Victoria was waiting for her to turn around and face her. Riley gradually lifted her eyes, facing the windows that looked out to the court area where the parents now all mingled. Some pointed in her direction while speaking to their friends; others moved on to the food area. A car backed out of the car park in the distance, its lights momentarily cutting across the school grounds, hitting her straight in the eyes.

She blinked, seeing black dots floating before her. As her vision cleared, she noticed a face pressed almost completely up to the glass pane, staring at her. It was the man again. The one she saw her first day, his hat pulled low. A kind face. His lips slightly curved in sympathy, and his eyes were warm. He nodded his head at her in acknowledgement before tilting his head in Victoria's direction, as if reminding her she was waiting. Taking a deep breath, Riley closed her eyes for a second.

The man was gone when she opened them.

She turned to face Victoria. Whatever she had unknowingly done, it was big.

And with that, she realised with surprise what the other emotion playing out on Liam's face was.

Fear.

He had been scared.

Chapter 22 – Gwen

"Terror made me cruel; and, finding it useless to
attempt shaking the creature off, I pulled its wrist
on to the broken pane, and rubbed it to and fro till
the blood ran down and soaked the bedclothes…"
- Wuthering Heights

The house was quiet when Gwen arrived home. The
lights were off, and night had closed in.

It had taken the two of them longer than expected
to get home, but she had no complaints. Her heart felt full,
her skin raw and tingly all over. Billy had taken hold of the
bike and pushed it for her while his other hand held Gwen's.
There was a gentle possessiveness with his hold too. His
fingers wrapped around hers like she belonged to him. She
had to keep biting her lip to stop the stupid smile trying to
take over.

Conversation had stalled. Both content in the silence. They
walked slower. She suspected he was as reluctant as she was
to end the night and say goodbye.

With relief, she saw the house was darkened and quiet, its inhabitants likely asleep. Little could disguise Billy's animosity towards Jake, and she felt certain Jake reciprocated the feeling.

"Are you sure?" Billy asked as they arrived at the front of the house. He let go of her hand and gently leaned the bike up against the house siding under a window.

"I live here," Gwen said teasingly. "Honestly, what else would you have me do?"

"We could go back to Hugh and Peggy's. Peggy would understand. They would put you up."

Gwen shook her head. Jake was a bully and a pig. But it wasn't forever. She was an independent woman; she could fend for herself. Taking his hand, she gently pulled him closer.

"I don't think it's right, leaving you here like this…" he said.

She leaned forward and, before he could protest, found his lips with her own once more. Savouring the moment for a few seconds, she felt her body sink into his. Billy let out a soft moan. Summoning the last of her reserve, she pulled away and bolted the last few steps to the front door. With her hand on the door handle, she turned, blowing him a kiss before twisting the handle and diving inside. With her back against the door, facing down the darkened hallway, and a hand pressed tightly to her mouth, she stifled a giggle. His expression had nearly undone her. His mouth slightly agape, surprised by her teasing.

Her heart hammered in her chest, and she wondered if he had any idea how hard it had been for her to let him go just then, when the world seemed to be so entirely about the two of them.

Relaxing her hand to her side, she took a moment, calming

her breathing. A noise came from Jake's office, a shuffling sound, and her hand flew back to her chest. Her body tensed.

Dammit. He was still awake. The prickling of the skin on the back of her neck reminded her that pretending she wasn't afraid of Jake was a lie.

She waited a few counts for the room to fall silent again. The clock in the kitchen mercilessly counted down the beats of her heart as she tiptoed down the hall to her room, every sense heightened for more sounds from Jake's office.

A wave of relief hit her again when she got to her room. Praying no one noticed as her door squeaked open, she held her breath and gently closed it behind her before pulling on the light switch beside her.

The single light hanging from the ceiling came alive, illuminating the shadows.

On seeing him, Gwen stumbled backwards against the door. The heady smell of alcohol attacking her senses simultaneously.

He'd been waiting for her. In the dark.

Jake sat on the end of the bed, bent over, his elbows leaning on his knees. A bottle of whiskey sat on the ground between his feet. He hung his head, staring at the floorboards. Gwen fought to regain her composure and hide her shaking.

She wanted to ask him what he was doing here but words escaped her; her tongue felt thick, unwilling to do her bidding.

Slowly, Jake's eyes rose to meet hers. A few days of stubble shadowed his jawline. He might have been handsome once, she thought, then shook it from her mind. The coldness in his eyes had been there since he'd been a child, she'd seen as much in Peggy's photo. And *that* was what made him ugly.

"I don't abide by whores in my house," he said, his voice a low rumble. Despite the stench of whiskey, his words were sure.

Gwen swallowed hard. If she yelled, would Billy hear her? Could she yell? Her mouth still felt full of cotton.

"What are you doing here?" she whispered back, cursing the way her voice trembled. Summoning courage, she stood straighter, lifted her chin and took a step away from the door, hoping to portray some confidence.

He picked up the bottle and took a swig.

Didn't even use a glass, she thought. He was a drunkard through and through.

He gulped it down and, still holding the bottle by the neck, wiped his mouth with the back of his other hand. Then he stood up, wobbling for a moment before finding his balance.

"I don't abide by whores in my house, Miss Davies," he repeated.

Gwen felt a spark of anger. He might speak to his wife like this, but she would not let him speak to her in this way.

"I'll kindly ask you to leave, Mr O'Regan. It has been a long night and I wish to retire." Her voice didn't waver this time.

His eyes narrowed in on hers, dark empty pits that they were.

"We can talk in the morning when you have … recovered." She almost spat the last word. He'd be no better in the morning, she knew.

She instantly regretted her comment.

He took a staggered step towards her, and Gwen moved along the wall to give him space to leave.

Instead, he approached her. With her back now pressed up against her dresser, she had nowhere to go. He towered over her.

One of his suspenders hung loose at his side, his shirt sleeves rolled up to his elbows. He rested the bottle on the top of the dresser behind her head, the other hand he placed on the dresser close to her shoulder.

He leaned in close, his breath warm and sickly. Gwen willed herself not to turn away, but to show this man she was no coward. She would face the devil, show him she was not to be pushed around.

"My brother might find you tolerable, Miss Davies, but he is weak. He cares nothing for what others think of him, and that is why he'll amount to nothing."

Spittle sprayed her, and she turned away involuntarily, closing her eyes. The handles of the dresser pressed into her back.

He leaned closer, his breath moist in her ear. She recoiled, her body no longer obeying her will to hide her fear.

"If you wish to whore yourself out to such people as the MacKenzie's, you will not be doing so under my roof." His eyes flashed with anger.

Gwen spiralled through a torrent of emotions.

"Te Tapu is a good community, Miss Davies. It is my father's weakness for the underdog that allows the likes of the MacKenzie's to live here. Irish scum." He swore, turned and spat onto the floorboards and their feet. "You continue your little…" He pulled away slightly, overcome with a coughing fit.

Gwen scrunched her eyes. Her legs felt weak. She needed him to leave.

Recovering, he pressed his body up against hers, his mouth almost touching her ear.

"You are mine, Miss Davies. As long as you are under this roof, you are mine. You disobey me, and I'll be going to Ms Flemming and the school board. It's only right they should know what kind of harlot they have under their employ, tutoring their children."

He spat again, a hawk that sunk into the crack between the floorboards.

Gwen's blood froze. Was he really threatening her job, her position here in Te Tapu, for spending time with Billy? Losing her job would mean having to leave Te Tapu, and although she would have never thought to believe it, she loathed to do so.

She did her best to keep her emotions void from her face. How dare he? She straightened again, turning her face towards him, their noses almost touching. She would not be bullied.

With her last reserves of courage, she glared at him.

"And what would your wife say to find her husband in another woman's bedroom?" she asked, her voice controlled; cool. This man would not intimidate her. Stand up to bullies, her father had always said.

"My wife would no doubt celebrate," he said, barely missing a beat, "to be spared performing her wifely duties." Disgust crossed his face before his eyes settled again on her. He took a step back to appraise her, his eyes wolfishly scanning her body.

Gwen stifled a shiver under his gaze, panic sending her nerves into overdrive. She swallowed down the bile rising in her throat.

"You need to leave, Mr O'Regan," Gwen said, her voice quavering.

205

"I wonder what he sees in you?" Jake said, almost as if to himself, his demeanour somehow changing. With his free hand he reached out for the side of her face and Gwen flinched, pulling back further.

"What? Is it because my hands are not as calloused as MacKenzie's, my blood not as lowbrow? Do you only pleasure farmhands then? I thought you of better class than that, Miss Davies."

Gwen swiped at his hand and he grabbed her wrist, his fingers digging deep, making her want to cry out in pain, but she bit her tongue, not wanting to give him the satisfaction.

She should scream, she told herself. Do it! Yet her throat remained constricted. Jake stepped closer again, this time pressing one leg tight between her thighs. His body pressed against hers. She pushed against him, but he was too heavy, and the way he moved against her made her think he was enjoying it.

"Whore," he whispered.

She closed her eyes, her body shaking. Don't cry, don't cry. Someone help me! Help me! She screamed, only no sound came.

He dropped the bottle on the floor then. A thud without a shatter. It rolled across the floorboards.

Gwen found her voice then.

"Get away from me," she screamed, all her instincts on fire to fight and escape.

She pushed against his weight, her hands hitting against the sides of his body. She tried to kick out, but his knee held her skirt pinned to the wall. His other hand rose, and he grabbed her by the throat, pressing tightly into her vocal cords. She choked and clawed at his hand with her fingernails.

Even intoxicated, his strength well out did hers. He swore at her, told her to stop fighting. Red dots danced before her eyes. For a second, he relaxed his grip, and Gwen tried to move out from under him, away from the dresser. He slammed her hard against the wall, her head taking the impact. Pain radiating through her skull. Her legs buckled, but she could not fall, pinned as she was by him. A roaring in her ears brought with it a blackness that seemed to cover her eyes. Help! The one word screamed in her mind, round and around. She sagged against him, and she felt him half drag, half lift her before throwing her down on the bed. Her neck whipped backwards, and a fresh burst of pain threatened to split her head open. Help, she tried to scream, aware of the word's silence. Rough hands fought to lift her skirt. Then he was on top of her.

Crazy whore were the last words she heard before she slipped into unconsciousness.

Chapter 23 – Riley

Victoria waited with her back to Riley. With the newspaper in hand, she stood, eyes glued to the wall before her, carefully scanning Riley's display.

Riley took a couple of deep breaths. She didn't even know where to begin. She couldn't think what she'd done wrong or why an inquiry into Te Tapu's past would illicit such a strong response.

"Where did you get all this?" Victoria asked without turning around, her voice calm.

Was that it? Riley wondered. Was this box put away for a reason and she was in trouble for going through it?

"It was in a box in the resource room," Riley explained. "It fell down and when I was repacking it, I thought it would make a great topic focus for the kids: The history of Te Tapu prior to World War II." Her voice wavered.

Victoria turned then, her face drawn and pale. Her eyes, void of their usual warmth, held a tiredness Riley hadn't remembered seeing before.

"And this newspaper?" she asked, holding it out for Riley.

Riley nodded.

"What do you know about this date, Riley?"

"August 31st, 1939" ran just under the header – *Te Tapu Tribune*.

"It's a few days prior to New Zealand announcing its involvement in the war," Riley answered. She hadn't had time to browse the newspaper closely enough to know if anything else was significant about the date. She had thought the kids might find the pictures interesting.

She wasn't sure if Victoria believed her; she seemed to search her face for something. Riley bit down on her lip again and willed herself not to look away in case it made her seem guilty. Guilty of what, though? If the contents of the box had been so controversial, why had it been stored in the resource room?

"And this photo?" Victoria asked, pointing to the class photo.

Riley shrugged her shoulders. "It was taken the same year," Riley said, "and my guess was this teacher had taught in this room."

An uneasiness crept across Riley's shoulders. It sounded like things had returned to normal outside. Vague twitters of laughter and conversation came from outside of her class, but she resisted the temptation to turn around and see. In the classroom, though, the pregnant silences between questions weighed heavily.

"You're saying you know nothing of this woman, then?" Victoria asked. The chill crept further down Riley's back. She thought of the diary she kept in her purse and resisted the urge to look over at where she kept it in a cupboard.

"No." Riley tried to keep her expression blank, praying Victoria wouldn't be able to tell that she was lying.

Why was she lying, though? Who was she protecting?

Victoria held her gaze for a second more and then let out a small exhale. She rubbed a hand over her eyes before talking again.

"I don't know her either ... she just looks so ... so familiar... " Victoria's voice trailed off. She exhaled sharply and then resumed her usual direct tone.

"Te Tapu is not a place to be digging into the past," she said. "A lot of the families here have lived here for a very long time, and there's a loyalty between them, and some will not take kindly to outsiders prying into their history. The past is best left in the past."

Riley recoiled slightly, like someone had slapped her, and felt the tell-tale prickling behind her eyes again.

Outsider, that was what she was.

"I wasn't prying," she tried to argue. "I thought the kids would enjoy learning about Te Tapu – having conversations about the past."

"You should have passed it by me," Victoria said. "There cannot be secrets in this school, Riley, particularly when it comes to this community. Now, is there anything else you think you should share with me?"

Was there?

She wanted to ask why the box had been in the resource room in the first place, if it was off limits, but thought better of it.

"No." She shook her head, pushing aside the bubbling guilt that sat heavy in her stomach.

"Good. Then let's see if we can do a bit of damage control. We'll start by taking this stuff down, and I can help you come up with a new topic focus next week." Victoria pulled things from the wall as she talked and made a pile on the table.

Riley's mouth dropped. "I don't understand," she said, her voice a whisper of disbelief.

Victoria turned again to study her. "Good," she said. "The less you understand, the better. Just know this: the man you met in the wheelchair, Liam's father, is not someone you want on your bad side. So if we can find a way to appease him, the better for all of us," she said, surprising Riley.

If Victoria was intimidated by Arthur, she had sure done a good job disguising it.

"Come on then, we'll get it down and invite people back in. I'm sure there are still a lot of parents who want to meet the new teacher, and I'll make sure the conversations stay on track."

Riley gulped. The last thing she felt up to now was facing any of the parents, or even the kids, for that matter. All she wanted was to get in her car, get home and hibernate for at least the weekend ahead.

Instead, she forced her leaden legs over to where Victoria was standing and helped her pull down the display, pausing a moment to peer at the class photo once more. She was sure the woman was looking beyond the photographer, off to his right, just as she was sure it was fear that pinched her features beyond the fuzziness of the photo.

Help me, a voice echoed in her head. *He killed Billy.*

Chapter 24 – Gwen

"A wild, wicked slip she was…"
- *Wuthering Heights*

A sliver of daylight broke through the gap in the curtains, painting the inside of Gwen's eyelids red. She scrunched her eyes tight, fighting off the threat of consciousness. A low groan slipped out as her senses came alive. Her body throbbed, raw and achy. Dark, twisted images flashed through her mind like a slide show. She pushed them away as best she could, willing her mind to succumb to darkness.

But it wouldn't.

She twisted onto her side, aware she was lying on her bed. Curling her knees up to her chest, she covered her face with one arm while hugging her waist with the other.

Goosepimples rose on her bare legs, the fabric of her skirt high above her hips. Stifling a guttural wail, she clenched her thighs against the throbbing and stickiness between her legs.

Wetness painted her cheeks.

God. Was he still here? In this room, watching her? She stiffened and held her breath, straining for any sound of movement, any sixth sense of being watched.

She waited a few moments more. Nothing. Maybe she was alone.

Tentatively, she pushed herself into a sitting position, her swollen eyes watering in the light as she forced them open. Her head pounded with pressure stemming from the back of her neck and forming a thick band across her forehead. But she was alive. Only she wasn't sure if she felt regret or gratitude.

The dresser looked so innocuous now, the mirror still balanced on top, leaning against the wall. Because of its angle, she could not see her reflection from the bed. The lingering smell of whiskey, was the only clue he had even been there. But he had.

Gwen swallowed the bile that rose in her throat.

If he was somewhere in the house, she needed to protect herself. A spike of adrenaline set her trembling. She needed to do something. She couldn't just wait until he returned.

With senses heightened, Gwen slipped her legs over the side of the bed and pulled the front of her skirt down to cover her knees. Her underwear lay discarded on the floor, and she clasped her hand to her mouth to stifle a sob. Her eyes welled.

Focus, she told herself, blinking back tears. Right now, she needed to protect herself until she could make sense of what to do.

She eased herself onto her feet. Her legs felt heavy, no longer connected to her, unwilling to do as she meant, and it took an immense amount of willpower for them to carry her the few paces to the dresser.

On reaching it, she steadied herself, hands clasping the top of the dresser. Her entire body shook. Refusing to meet her reflection, she felt out blindly for the mirror, then gently pulled it until it lay flat on the dresser's top.

A distant sound made her pause. A clanging of metal against metal, maybe coming from the kitchen. With her heart pulsing in her throat, she waited, paralysed. He was still here. Oh God.

She needed to barricade the door, stop him from coming back. The dresser was tall. Solid oak. Even without her body feeling so beaten, it would be a beast to move. But what choice did she have? She had to block the door.

On the side of the dresser, she pressed her shoulder into its bulk, took a deep breath and pushed. It slid ten centimetres or so across the wooden floorboards. Gwen straightened, hands held to her chest, waiting to see if he had noticed the scuffing noises.

No one came.

On an exhale, she braced her shoulder against the dresser and pushed again, biting her tongue to stifle a cry of pain and exertion. This time she covered more distance.

She paused once more.

Still no sound. Her heart tripped in her chest, panic building. Any moment he could return, making his way down the hallway. The distance between her and the door felt like a chasm of unfathomable proportions. She shook herself; this time, she'd push until it was there. To hell with the noise if it meant she'd be somewhat safe from him...

Summoning the last of her reserves, she shoved, her feet

fighting for grip on the floorboards. She grunted until it found momentum and slid across the floor, blocking the bedroom door. Her legs gave out, and she slumped to the ground.

She let herself cry then, really cry. Holding her forehead against the cool oak wood of the dresser, she let the sobs come. Her body convulsed, wracked with emotion.

He had raped her.

The words swirled around her head. She tried to make sense of them, but couldn't. How? How had she allowed this to happen? She had just been with Billy… Everything had been going so well…

Heavy footsteps in the hallway made Gwen inhale sharply and her jaw clamp. Her body tensed as they neared her room. When they paused outside her door, panic sent her scuttling backwards on her bottom, across the room.

Please let the dresser hold, she prayed.

The door lurched open an inch before hitting the dresser, and Jake cursed from the hallway. Her breath hitched in her throat. With nowhere to go, she pressed her back hard against the wall.

"I'm going out," Jake announced. "I expect you to be here when I get back. Remember who I am, Miss Davies." He jiggled the door. "And remember who you are."

The words hit Gwen with icy force. She swallowed back bile.

"You say anything to anyone, and you're done. You'll be out on your ass – no house, no job – and don't think for a second anyone, including MacKenzie, will think you're anything but a common whore when I'm done telling them how you threw yourself at me."

215

A fresh wave of horror set her skin alight. A coughing fit gave way to more cursing from the hallway.

"No one would believe any different. So, you tell anyone…
"

The threat hung heavy in the air. The sound of a fist hitting the wall made Gwen jump, a small, startled squeal escaping her lips. His footsteps thudded down the hall and away from her, and the front door creaked open and banged close. The sound of boots on gravel was followed by the rumble of an engine she'd heard many times before. When she could no longer hear the hum of his pickup, she allowed herself to breathe again. A million thoughts, a million fears, crashed together in her mind, until she felt powerless to do anything but succumb to the deluge of emotions.

Some time passed before she exhausted herself into such a state that her tears dried. She sat there for a while, huddled on the floor, almost welcoming the numbness descending on her mind and body. She stared blankly at the knots in the floorboards and the dust that had settled between the cracks. Then she dragged them away, etching to memory every join of wallpaper, every curling edge, every speck of fly dust. Anything to stop the onslaught of memories.

The sun had moved in the sky, away from the gap in the curtains, and the room had darkened. The growing need to relieve herself shook her from her trance.

She had no way of telling when Jake would be back. She should run, leave, get as far away as possible. But to what end?

Where would she go? Back home? Back to her mother and the doctor? Returning as a failure? And what if they learnt of what had happened to her? Would they believe her, or would the doctor see it as a sign of something wrong with her; a wanton woman on a slippery slope to join Aunt Jeanne in an asylum?

She couldn't seek refuge with Peggy and Hugh. She knew no matter how much Peggy might dislike Jake, Hugh would protect him. They were brothers. They were *O'Regans*. His name shielded him. He was untouchable, and she … she was a nobody.

But what about Billy? The voice pleaded with her. Surely he would believe her? He hated Jake. He had warned her. Oh God … he had warned her. She choked back another sob, her heart breaking apart.

Jake had ruined her. Would Billy really want to be with someone so defiled? Wouldn't it ruin him, too?

No!

Jake was right. She needed to keep quiet. Tell no one. She would do what she could to protect herself. Keep a low profile until she could find other accommodation. Pretend it had never happened. And Sarah would be home soon … five more days and his attention would be off her…

The uncharitable thought caught her off guard. Gwen covered her mouth with her hand, thinking she was going to be sick.

Right now, she had to look after herself.

She pulled at the corner of the dresser until it made a gap large enough for her to squeeze through, panting with exertion. She hurried on leaden legs to the bathroom, her ears on high alert for any sound of his return.

She left the door ajar while she relieved herself, listening. Her pulse was fast, her hands shaky as she wiped herself. The inside of her thighs felt bruised, and she noticed a small

217

amount of dried blood.

An onslaught of nausea made her drop to her knees, and she emptied her stomach in the toilet bowl.

Closing her eyes for a second to steady herself, she willed herself to get up. After heaving herself to her feet, she pulled the toilet chain and grabbed a folded facecloth from the shelf nearby. Gwen filled the sink with water and set about cleaning herself. Gingerly at first, wet facecloth in hand, her skin tender to the touch under the rough cloth. Then harder, scrubbing herself raw while fresh tears streamed down her cheeks. She emptied and refilled the basin again and again. What would it take to make her feel clean?

Hurry, the thought interrupted, he could be back anytime.

She emptied the basin one last time. She couldn't let him find her outside of her room.

From the bathroom, she moved to the kitchen and pulled open the pantry, where her eyes scanned the shelves. Soon, she'd wrapped an apple, crust of bread and slab of cheese in a tea towel. Though she had no appetite, she realised that could change and didn't know when she would be able to escape again before Sarah got back.

With a growing sense of urgency to retreat to her room, she glanced around. What else did she need? She scoured the cupboards below the sink and pulled out an old bowl and jug. Jake would miss neither. She filled the jug with water and placed it and her food in the bowl. The bowl would have to suffice as a chamber pot should she need it. Her stomach dropped at the thought. What was she doing?

A final scan of the kitchen and her eyes landed on a butcher knife lying on the bench. Her heart hammered in her ears. Body shaking, she gripped its handle. She took a deep breath, slid the knife in beside the jug, and made her way as fast as she could back to her room. Her arms strained under the weight of everything.

When she was back in her room, dresser firmly barricading the door, she took stock of her situation. She ached with a tiredness and soreness she had never known before. Not only were her eyes swollen and limbs bruised, but the back of her skull had a lump. She wanted to crawl into bed. To disappear. To erase everything from memory. After slipping out of her clothes, she pulled back the covers, placed the butcher knife under her pillow, then lay down on the mattress. Knees to chest, she closed her eyes and willed away every thought, every memory, until exhaustion did the job for her.

But it was a temporary fix. When she woke, her mind flitted between a shrieking demon of disgust, shame and anger, and a complete vacuum of emotion. She tried to tell herself it had never actually happened; she'd imagined the whole thing, but her bruises said otherwise.

The memories replayed themselves over and over, and she could still smell Jake's warm, sour breath and the stench of alcohol, making her stomach curdle. The worst was when the memories got jumbled and Billy's face transposed itself over Jake's. She gripped the butcher knife tighter, her anger a palpable, living entity. She'd use the knife if she had to. She would not let him take Billy from her! Not let him dirty their time together.

A loud pounding on her door woke her from a fitful sleep. She had lost all sense of time. It could have been a day or two, or even a lifetime, for all Gwen knew.

Jake's voice pierced through her grogginess and jolted her upright. She huddled closer to the headboard, clutching the bedclothes to her chest in one hand. Her other arm outstretched with the tip of the knife pointing to the door.

"I've talked to Ms Flemming." The gruff timbre of his voice sent ice through Gwen's veins. "She has agreed to relieve you of your duties this week. I have explained how I need you to look after the house until Sarah's return."

No. There was no way Ms Flemming would have acquiesced to Jake's request. Except, the little voice of doubt reminded her, Jake was an O'Regan. What choice would she have had?

"I suggest you use this time to consider your next step, Miss Davies. You cannot hide in your room forever, and I am not someone you want to cross."

The knife wavered in Gwen's hand. He was right. She couldn't hide in there forever. Jake had bought her a week from her school duties, and time for her bruises to fade enough for makeup, but as soon as Sarah was home, things had to change.

Fresh tears filled her eyes as his footsteps disappeared down the hall again. What was she going to do? Could she really pretend nothing had happened?

Billy's face flashed in her mind. And a new wave of grief and shame threatened to overwhelm her. If he found out…

No. He couldn't. She couldn't lose him.

Jake wouldn't let it slip. Admitting to his crime could lose him his family business. Ol' Man Tom wouldn't stand for such a thing.

So that left her to keep the secret.

And she could pretend. She would have to. Billy would never need to know. And she would get out, find somewhere else to live. Somehow. It might take time, but she would do it.

She looked down at the knife lying across her lap.

As much as anyone could hate a person, she hated Jake O'Regan.

So much so, she would happily see him dead.

Chapter 25 – Riley

The book shook in Riley's trembling hands. She couldn't believe it! The bastard! He raped her! It made her furious and feel ill at the same time.

She stood up from the sofa, letting the diary fall onto the seat cushion. Her entire body prickled with pins and needles. Shaking out her arms and hands, she paced around her small living room, not sure what to do with herself.

Was that it, then? She wondered. Was the rape the reason Liam and his father had reacted so poorly to her display? What did they know about it?

She headed to the kitchen and filled a glass with cold tap water before letting the cool liquid soothe her parched throat. Something about her display must have reminded them of the skeletons in their family closet. So why were some of the parents upset too? What else had happened? It was a small community, and the O'Regans had owned most of Te Tapu for generations. Liam was an O'Regan.

Which meant Liam and the brute Jake were related somehow.

She slammed the glass on the bench, surprising herself when it didn't shatter, and let out an exasperated growl.

Regardless of what the others said, if he was so willing to keep hidden the crimes of his family at the expense of a young girl, well … well … he was an ass!

She stamped her foot, unsure what to do with her agitation.

That must have been why the box of Gwen's stuff had been hidden away. Why not just destroy it, though, if they didn't want anyone to know of the crime committed?

So many questions remained. The only clear thing was her display and the date of the newspaper had struck a chord. They must have recognised the photo of Gwen.

Was Victoria in on it, too? The thought made tears spring to her eyes. Who would condone such a thing? O'Regan or not, Jake was a monster!

The evening before had been a disaster. Few parents had entered her classroom after she and Victoria had pulled down the display. Instead, it was Riley who felt on display. Most of the parents kept their distance, shielding their mouths with their hands and whispering, glaring or shaking her head at her. A few parents, either new to the area or knowing no better, Riley suspected, introduced themselves and asked about their child's progress in class. Victoria remained close the entire night, ever ready to intercept if the conversation went in an unsuitable direction, Riley supposed.

She never saw the kind man in the cap again, but nor did she search for him. Her mind had been preoccupied with praying for the night to end. She avoided Brittany, who tried a couple of times to catch her attention; Riley just wasn't up to it as she fought back tears.

The one person she saw again was Liam. He seemed to watch her almost as eagle-eyed as Victoria, although she thankfully kept a much more acceptable distance.

As awful as the evening had been, she realised now she hadn't done anything wrong – unless, of course, you were of the mind that inadvertently exposing a seventy-year-old crime was wrong.

Riley couldn't remember ever being so angry before. She needed to do something. Needed to get out of the house. Needed to make things right somehow.

There had to be more to the story, of course. And the part confusing her was the date on the newspaper Victoria had questioned her about. Gwen's diary entry had been the end of March. The newspaper date was August.

Yes, there was more to it. No doubt, much of which was in the diary, but she cursed herself all the same for not having properly scrutinised the newspaper before adding it to the display.

What she should do, she knew, was sit her butt back down on the sofa and continue reading. Look for the answers in Gwen's diary, but her outrage for this woman she didn't know was so strong. As was her outrage for a school community who were so willing to cover it up.

So her next step was clear. She was going back to school.

If the newspaper and other items from her display were still there, she was going to find them and photograph them. She would find out what else she was missing. Thus far, she knew the two events – the reaction to her display and Gwen's trauma – were related.

She crossed her fingers Victoria hadn't taken anything home with her or seen fit to destroy anything. Gwen's diary would have to wait because the feeling that Te Tapu was hiding something else, something tied to the newspaper, was too strong. She only hoped she wasn't too late.

After grabbing her purse and throwing in her phone, keys, wallet and sunglasses from the kitchen island, Riley headed to her door. Just as she reached for the door handle, she paused, then quickly turned around. She headed back to the sofa, scooped up the diary and shoved it in her purse. Gwen was coming with her.

Chapter 26 – Gwen

"You fight against that devil for love as long as you may; when the time comes, not all the angels in heaven shall save him!"
- Wuthering Heights

T his time it was the raised voices that woke her. She must have finally fallen into a deep sleep, for she hadn't heard any vehicle or knock on the door, just two male voices arguing.

Then her name. She heard it. The sweet timbre of his voice calling her name, and for a second, she wanted to call out. It was Billy. Her Billy had come for her. But just as quickly she remembered – she was in no state to be seen.

She still had not looked in the mirror and could only guess what state she was in. The lump on the back of her skull had diminished slightly and would be hidden by her hair anyway. However, her eyes felt swollen from crying, and she couldn't bear the thought of Billy seeing her.

Biting her lip, she sat up in bed and put her ear to the wall, closer to the voices. She pulled the covers up to her chin, straining to hear. The words were muffled, but she could decipher them.

"Where is she, Jake?"

"Go home, MacKenzie. What concern is she to you, anyway?"

"She's a friend, eh? And I'm tired of you sending me away. Now you tell me where she is, or I'll be letting myself in."

"Just you try, and I'll be claiming self-defence when I fill you with holes," Jake growled.

Gwen swallowed hard. Jake kept a .22 in his office. Surely he didn't have it with him now. Her heart danced in her chest. Go home, Billy, go home, she willed him.

"Gwen!" Billy called out for her again. "If you lay a finger on her—"

"Ever stop to think maybe she doesn't want to see you, Paddy?"

Gwen could imagine Jake hawking and spitting at Billy's feet to punctuate his slur.

Bastard! she thought, a flare of anger dissolving some of her fear.

"I swear Jake, if I find out you've done anything to her—"

"You need to leave," Jake growled again.

She could imagine Jake pointing his rifle at Billy. She clenched the bedspread tighter in her palms. So much of her wanted to rush from the room and throw herself at Billy, but she couldn't, she just couldn't. She needed more time. More time to hide the shame Jake had done to her.

"Leave, Billy. Please leave," she whispered.

"Next time I'll have Hugh with me. You can explain to him where Gwen is and why you're touting a gun at me."

Gwen held her breath. Would he do that? Would he really bring Hugh back, and would that make Jake back down?

She heard the start of a motorbike engine then, recognising it as Billy's. Tears welled as she listened to it disappear down the gravel path, and then after what felt like forever, a door slammed and heavy steps tromped down the hallway, pausing for a second outside of her door.

"I'm going out," his gruff voice said. "Sarah will be back by end of day. Make sure you've put yourself together by then."

Gwen said nothing; listening as his footsteps continued down the hall and disappeared into what Gwen suspected was his office. Not long after, they came back, and a door opened and slammed again. Finally came the rumble of the motor as he started his truck and ambled it down the drive. Only then did she feel she could breathe again.

She did not know how long he'd be gone, but he was right. She needed to pull herself together, clean herself up. With Sarah back, she hoped the attention would be off her. Ugh, poor, poor Sarah...

No, she couldn't think along those lines. Survival of the fittest. She needed to get out of this house, and if she was going to do that, some serious acting would have to come into play.

Slowly, she pulled back the bedcovers and gingerly touched her feet down on the oak floorboards.

Somehow, she would make him pay. She'd make him pay for what he did to her, what he stole from her, and she'd do it for Sarah too, and maybe even Henry Walken, the boy who'd supposedly drowned.

Who else had Jake hurt? She was certain there were others.

Chapter 27 – Riley

T he last time Riley had felt this much fury was when she had found out Justin was cheating on her.

Her little Swift hugged the corners as she followed the country terrain. Her knuckles were white on the steering wheel, and she had to remind herself to slow down.

What would her excuse be if anyone else was at the school? Since it was Saturday, she thought it unlikely anyone else would be there, but she wanted to be prepared all the same.

The newspaper, the photo and the other items might very well have been hidden away or destroyed, even if the items meant a lot to the community. However, if the newspaper was there, she needed to find it. Needed to see it for herself. Even if she had to let herself into Victoria's office to do so.

She shuddered. Was she really going to risk her job, her new life, for something that happened seventy-odd years ago?

Yet she couldn't put from her mind the indignation Liam and his father had met her with. And knowing a little more of Gwen's story…

If it had been her, she would want her story told, to have her rapist be held accountable regardless of his last name and his family lineage.

She felt a fresh wave of anger remembering the fear she saw flit across Liam's face. Was he really so scared people would find out his family were not as saintlike as they were made out to be? She had a hard time believing he was one of the good ones.

Her fingers tightened on the steering wheel. It wasn't often she got so worked up and mad like this. Her emotions could have belonged to someone else.

Green hills and paddocks rolled out towards the horizon on either side of her. Tall tussocks and pampas grass grew on the road's shoulders. At one point she slowed for a pheasant and its young ones to move off her side of the road into the grass. However picturesque the drive might be, all she wanted was to be at school, find her evidence and leave.

As often happened nearing Te Tapu school in the morning, a heavy fog appeared out of nowhere, blanketing the otherwise blue sky with a pale grey wash. She flicked her lights on and slowed her speed a little. You never knew when a cow might escape from its paddock and meander back and forth across the road. Sometimes, too, other vehicles were not so vigilant with turning their lights on in these conditions. Better to be safe, she thought.

Typical of country roads in this region, this one weaved around hills and dipped and rose through valleys. Occasionally, rows of trees signposted long gravel driveways shooting off to the left or right. She had slowed to about eighty kilometres to be safe. Hidden driveways were a hazard, particularly in the fog.

Behind her came the dull glow of two headlights, fast approaching. Riley hoped they weren't the impatient sort. Her Swift wasn't strong on guts, and some inclines allowed for little run up.

No such luck.

The driver behind her either knew the roads better than she did or else didn't care for the change in visibility.

Well, they'd just have to wait. She knew this part of the road well enough now to know there would be no room for passing for a while yet, and she certainly would not allow herself to be bullied. But her nerves amped up, anyway.

The vehicle behind her drew closer, and Riley's own speed increased almost automatically. Be sensible, a small voice inside her head said. Don't go getting yourself in trouble because someone else wants to drive like an idiot.

She slowed down for a sharp corner, a million worst-case scenarios running through her head – what if a cow was on the road ahead or a vehicle had broken down? She'd have no time or visibility to stop in time.

She didn't want to die here. Shaking her head, she gave herself a stern mental telling off for being so melodramatic.

The vehicle had closed the distance even more. Riley spared a glance in the rear-view mirror. She couldn't quite see who was driving. A man with a baseball cap in a silver ute. The ute looked familiar, but the road needed her attention, and she couldn't stare long enough to work out where she'd seen it before.

She dipped down into another valley, her heart lodged in her throat.

Her entire body felt on edge now, her nervousness smothering her anger. The other vehicle was so close. She hated when people did that. If she were to brake, she doubted he would have time to stop. Why did people have to be in such a hurry? she thought, before recognising her own hypocrisy.

Riley slowed down some more to make a corner at the bottom of a dip, then pushed her foot down on the accelerator, hoping her car would have enough oomph to make it back out of the valley without upsetting whoever was behind her too much.

Another quick glance in the rear-view mirror. God, she couldn't even see the driver now, just the bonnet of the ute. They were that close. Riley gulped. What were they doing?

Not long now, she told herself. One more corner and then came a straightaway. He could pass then, and good riddance to him.

Out of the valley, the fog lifted, and Riley was met with blue sky and sun rays streaming from fluffy clouds in the distance. She exhaled loudly.

Pass, she urged the other vehicle, pass now. She slowed and pulled closer to the shoulder of the road, allowing even more room for the person to jot around her. She waited what felt like an eternity before the silver ute pulled out towards the centre line. Nothing was coming. It had plenty of room. But instead of speeding past her, it slowed down to be beside her.

What are you doing? She thought, her panic rising. Pass, already!

Their windows were side by side and she was sure eyes were watching her, but she kept hers focused on the road ahead. She didn't want to look, didn't really want to know what cretin was trying to scare her. A parent from last night who recognised her car? She shuddered at the thought.

Up ahead, the road took another dip. It would be impossible to know if another vehicle was coming at them from there.

"Pass already," she said again under her breath, her teeth

gnashing together. She tensed, the steering wheel tight within her grip. Out of the corner of her eye, she saw the vehicle pull ahead slightly.

Hurry, she thought, slowing her Swift further to allow the ute more room to slide ahead of her.

Please, don't let there be any oncoming traffic.

The ute zipped back into the lane ahead of her with very little room between them. Riley slammed on her brakes, scared she was going to rear-end it. The brakes shuddered underneath her, and Gwen's diary flew from her purse. Both items hit the glove compartment and dropped to the floor, and Riley twisted the steering wheel to avoid hitting the deck of the vehicle in front of her that seemed to have slowed down further.

In her panic, she over-steered and felt two of the tyres hit the grass verge. She struggled to straighten the vehicle before it went too far off into the ditch on the side of the road. The Swift bounced a little. With her foot on the brake, she wrestled the steering wheel back and forth, trying to gain some control as the vehicle ahead of her stepped on the gas and disappeared ahead.

Finally, she came to a stop. Two wheels on the road and two wheels buried deep in the tall grass, but not yet in the trench separating the road from the wire fence.

"Shit!" She thumped the steering wheel with the palms of her hands. What the hell had just happened? Her heart was in her throat and she felt a prickle of tears. Why hadn't the other vehicle stopped? Surely, they would have seen her go off the road. Riley shook.

They could have killed her. Her hands tingled, and she tried to steady her breath. Three deep breaths, she told herself, like she'd learnt on a meditation course once.

She choked back a sob. They had run her off the road; the thought settled over her. Someone had actually tried to run her off the road.

As the first tear ran down her cheek, she gave a sniffle. And what was worse, the vehicle had looked so familiar, though she couldn't quite place it.

That meant it was someone she knew.

Chapter 28 – Gwen

"I have to remind myself to breathe – almost to
remind my heart to beat!"
- Wuthering Heights

"Miss Davies!" His voice rang out across the front field, startling Gwen. She finished tying the shoelace on little Rebecca's boot. She really needed new ones. The sole was pulling away from the rest of the shoe. It had no doubt already done the rounds of the three older siblings, but this was the way it was. With four mouths to feed during a depression, for some, shoes were more a luxury than a need.

She had recognised his voice right away and felt the flush of colour rise to her cheeks. It had been a week since she'd been back at school. He'd called at the house a couple of times, and it had surprised even her when she could not bring herself to see him. But she still felt dirty. Tainted. And not worthy of Billy Mackenzie.

Taking her time, she pulled the lace taut then straightened

up, pulling her cardigan tight around her body.

"There we are, Rebecca." She gave the young girl a pat on the head. "Remember your bag. Off you go now."

The little girl with ginger plaits grabbed her bag in one hand and ran awkwardly off to the front gate. It was a wonder she didn't fall, Gwen thought, what with those stupid boots.

He was waiting by the front fence, sitting on his motorbike. Even from across the school she could see he wore his usual cap and a white long-sleeved shirt rolled at the arms and suspenders. For a second, bile rose in her throat. Jake had worn similar that night. She pushed the thought away. The past was the past. Never to be thought of again, she reminded herself. And if she was brave enough, there was a chance this man could be her future.

"Miss Davies," he called again before dismounting from his motorbike and waving out to her.

Gwen looked around her surreptitiously. All she needed was the headmistress to hear, and she would be reprimanded again with another lecture on decorum and what was and wasn't acceptable for a young teacher in this community.

A couple of young boys crowded around Billy, in awe of his bike. Most of the other children seemed unaffected by his arrival. Those on horses ensured they kept a wide berth to prevent their ride being spooked. The old school bus had already picked up many of the students. Others were setting off on foot.

Gwen soothed her skirt with her hands. Now or never, she thought. Just smile. Remember, nothing happened. This is Billy. You are safe. The words repeated themselves around her head as she walked across the field separating her classroom from the pickup and drop-off area.

As she called out a few goodbyes to students rushing past, she begged her heart to stop racing in her chest. When she got closer, he pulled his hat off his head and wrung it in his hands. He said nothing until she reached the fence.

She couldn't help but smile at seeing him. He was beautiful, as far as a man could be. His blond hair shone in the sunshine, his arms a deep brown from working outside. The muscles of his shoulders were visible through the fabric of his shirt, and she was sure the colour on her cheeks would give away how good it felt to see him again. Somehow, he made her feel lighter.

"Gwen," he whispered on seeing her. A small smile played on his lips, though his eyes reflected nothing but worry.

"Hello, Billy," Gwen said. Oh God, she hated this distance between them, both literally and figuratively. She wanted to dissolve the fence between them, delete the last few weeks.

"I went to your house—"

"I know," Gwen said.

"Jake wouldn't tell me where you were."

Gwen flinched unwillingly at his name.

"I was fine. Just unwell," she said, words she'd rehearsed repeatedly for this moment, except for the headmistress. For her she'd kept to the story Jake had told; she'd been needed to help at home with Sarah away.

"I… I…" He stumbled over his words, and she hated the awkwardness between them.

Part of her, the most alive part, wanted to climb over the fence, to hell with decorum, and throw herself at the man, demanding he marry her and they move away together to some place where despicable men like Jake did not exist. A smáller part of her wanted to run, to hide, to forget about

237

Billy.

"We've been worried about you. Peggy's been asking about you and—"

"I'm fine," Gwen said again, aware of how false it sounded even to her own ears.

He paused for a moment, his eyes studying every part of her face. It had surprised Gwen when she'd first looked in the mirror. Other than a puffiness around her eyes, her face was unchanged. Her throat had some bruising and redness, but a little makeup and high-necked blouses had hidden the worst of it. For someone who didn't know better, she appeared fine. Just like she told everyone she was. Sarah had been the only one who looked at her differently.

Gwen suspected she knew why too. Sarah saw something others couldn't, something that until now, only she had experienced. Between the two of them they shared an unspoken secret, a bond, an unspoken truth. In that way, Sarah had given her strength.

"I was thinking, maybe … if you wanted to…" he wrung his hat in his hands again, and Gwen's heart opened again. "Well, there's this nice picnic spot I've been told about, and I thought you might like to…"

She made him nervous. Because he loved her. She knew it, and the thought warmed her further.

"I'd love to," Gwen said, meaning it.

Billy visibly relaxed. His shoulders fell a little, and he beamed unabashedly. "Really?" he asked.

Gwen nodded.

"Miss Davies!" a voice shrilled from behind.

Turning, Gwen saw Ms Flemming storming towards them. Gwen scowled and spun back to Billy.

"I'm sorry, I have to go." She rolled her eyes.

"Of course," he said, pulling his cap back onto his head. "I'll pick you up Saturday, then. Eleven a.m."

With a smile, Gwen gave a small wave while Billy threw a leg back over his bike, lucky to get away from the black storm cloud striding their way.

Gwen felt herself lighten. She continued to stand there as Billy used his legs to roll his bike around, kicked down on the kick start, opened throttle and took off.

Things were going to be alright, she told herself.

As long as she had Billy, how could they not be?

Chapter 29 – Riley

Riley sat there for a few minutes, slowing her breathing and calming her nerves before pulling the car back onto the road, grateful the ground was hard and dry and the autumn's wet weather hadn't yet taken hold.

It had been intentional.

No, it couldn't have been.

Yes, it was.

The argument went back and forth in her mind.

After a couple more kilometres, over a rise, the school came into view.

How quaint and idyllic it looked, she thought. The old building with white cladding and concrete grey roofing, with a background of green fields and a variety of trees.

Ahead, signs warned her of a change of speed limit and school zone. It made little difference. She was still driving at a crawl.

Welcome to Te Tapu, the large green sign said. Riley turned on her indicators to turn up the school driveway, letting out a sigh as she did. For the moment at least, the place was deserted of any other vehicles or human presence. She parked slightly behind the main classroom block. Her car was small enough to do so, and no one could see her from the road and wonder what she was doing.

She killed the engine and took a moment just sitting in her car. Peering out the side window, she saw the shed where Liam and the other man had stood when she had first come to check out her classroom.

How strange, she thought. It seemed so long ago, and yet really it wasn't. Stranger still for Liam to refuse to admit anyone had been with him that day. She'd seen the other man clear as day and had seen him again only the night previous. He would have to have been a parent, surely. She wondered whose.

Okay, game plan, she tried to pep talk herself. It made her nervous to be at school all alone. Nervous to be seen, questioned. She had never been a good liar. Never been able to pull it off. And where did that leave her if someone asked what she was doing there?

She'd be quick. Victoria had taken the pile of papers from her display out of her room. Riley hadn't thought to wonder where she'd taken them, but the first place to look would be her office.

She bent over and picked up her purse, its contents, and the diary off the car floor. The diary she put in the glove box. In case anyone arrived, they wouldn't see it sitting there. It seemed important somehow. Everything else, she stuffed back into her purse, which she threw over her shoulder.

Keys in hand, she exited the car, pressed the fob to lock the door and headed towards the main building: the staffroom. Once there, she spared a glance around her. The road past the school was quiet. She was alone. It was both a comforting and horrifying thought.

After unlocking the door into the office and staffroom, Riley unset the alarm and closed the door behind her. Though the sun wasn't yet high enough in the sky to bring full sunlight into the building, she would not risk turning on any lights, in case passers-by saw them.

She made a beeline for Victoria's office right away. The door was closed though not locked. Opening it, she found it much like it had been the last time she'd been there. Everything was neat and tidy. Pens and pencils in a pencil holder beside the computer monitor. A photo of Victoria and her three young grandkids smiling beside that. A mouse pad, cordless mouse and keypad. Along one wall was a bookcase lined with books and folders, all speaking of teaching pedagogy, inquiry, literacy in the classroom and the likes, and a folder with *Minutes* written on the side, but nothing, nothing that spoke of a strange Te Tapu cover-up.

The waste basket was empty; the cleaner had obviously already been in. The grey, three-drawer filing cabinet had a small gold key hanging from its lock. If she was hiding something, she wasn't overly concerned about it being found. She twisted the key and pulled it open anyway, all her senses on high alert. What she was doing was illegal or, at the very least, enough to get her fired. She scrolled through the brown swing files, knowing what she wanted to find. A newspaper would stand out, but she wasn't a snoop, wasn't going to lower herself to being nosey about anything else, including the personal files she came across in the second draw down.

Now and then she would pause, listening with her entire body for any sound that would suggest anyone else was there. Nothing. The school was deserted.

How eerie a school was without the sounds of children.

Finding nothing, she next went through the cupboards along the bottom of the bookcase. Still, nothing. Riley's heart plummeted. The whole thing had been a waste of time. Victoria could just as likely have taken the artefacts home or destroyed them. Riley might never know what the newspaper hid or why the photo and ledger and all the other artefacts had turned so many faces pale.

Next place she could look was the reception area. She didn't want to. It was more visible through the windows to the road outside. Plus, if Sandra, the office lady, ever found out, she suspected she would meet with a fate worse than being fired. Besides, it wasn't like Victoria would hide it in the reception area, unless of course Sandra was in on it.

Riley gave a cursory glance over the desk and its surroundings, her courage fading.

It had been a waste of time, she decided. Wherever Victoria had put it all, it wasn't here.

She leaned for a second on the wall, being careful not to disturb the children's artwork hanging there. Utterly defeated and suddenly exhausted, she rubbed her eyes.

What had she been thinking? Maybe the whole thing had been a colossal mistake. Not just the coming back to school to look for the papers, but the display, taking the position, everything. What was wrong with her? In the few months she had been teaching, she had not exactly broken into the school – she had a key to use anytime – yet she'd snooped through the principal's office, started an inquiry and created a display that seemed to have turned the locals against her, fainted in class after writing some inappropriate nonsense on the board for the kids to copy, and unrelated, but still just as nuts, pulled a knife on her ex.

243

What the hell was going on with her? she wondered for the millionth time.

Moving her fists away from her eyes, she felt that uncanny sensation again, as if someone were watching her. The hairs on the back of her neck rose, and her temperature plummeted. She crept closer to the window and peered out. Still no signs of vehicles – out the front at least. If it were another teacher, they would have had to come into the main building to turn off the alarm before entering their class. No one was there, and yet…

A noise from behind the school made her start. Footsteps, maybe. Running.

Oh, shit! Maybe she wasn't alone.

Think fast, think fast, she told herself, scouting around the room. She needed an excuse for being there. After moving into the staffroom, she grabbed a couple of the math resource books from the bookshelf. She could pretend she needed them for planning. She was a new teacher, surely no one would think it strange she had travelled all the way into school to pick them up on a Saturday. She also grabbed a handful of discarded worksheets from the paper recycling bin by the photocopier and stuck them half inside the books so it looked like she'd been photocopying. Trying to steady her breathing, she crept towards the door.

She could do this. Plenty of people lied. If need be, she could too.

She typed the code into the alarm pad and quickly stepped outside. Locking the door behind her. She glanced around her. Nothing. And yet…

Her heart was racing, and she swore she could hear heavy breathing as if it were right beside her ear.

No one is there, she told herself, frozen to the spot. She closed her eyes for a moment, trying to make the sudden dizziness abate.

"You need to run," a women's voice whispered in her ear.

No one is there, no one is there, Riley chanted.

"RUN!" the voice screamed, splitting Riley's skull open. She dropped the books she was holding, and her purse slid off her shoulder.

"NOW!" the voice shouted again.

And she did, heading away from her car, towards the other end of the classroom block, then around towards the back field. She ran like the devil himself was after her.

Chapter 30 – Gwen

"I lingered round them, under that benign sky;
watched the moths fluttering among the heath and
hare-bells; listened to the soft wind breathing
through the grass, and wondered how anyone
could ever imagine unquiet slumbers for the
sleepers in that quiet earth."
- ***Wuthering Heights***

I t was Gwen who insisted Peggy and Hugh join them for the picnic. She had been a bundle of nerves about the picnic for the rest of the week, barely able to concentrate in class but going through the motions.

The problem was, she kept flipping between how she felt about things. She would go from wanting nothing more than to spend some alone time with Billy, just the two of them. She wanted to lose herself in his arms, his kisses… But then she'd remember. She would remember Jake's breath on her face, his body pressing down on hers, the way he leered at her. One saving grace had been blacking out. But the next morning, the ache in her body, the bruises from his touch and the stickiness between her legs … it all served to make their own memories of that night.

Why? If it had to happen, why on the same night?

She had been so happy kissing Billy goodnight, as if the entire universe had conspired in the perfect happily ever after.

And then there was Jake.

She hated him. *Hated* him. He had ruined everything.

So she invited Peggy and Hugh. Safety in numbers. Just until the memories faded.

Then she remembered Hugh was Jake's brother. Despite how different they were in personality, could she really handle being in the presence of an O'Regan so soon?

And so it was that she bounced back and forth. Maybe she really was as crazy as Aunty Jeanne, she thought, then quickly shrugged away the thought. She would not give her mother or the doctor that kind of satisfaction.

The invite had already been given, so there really was no backing out now. It would have to be the four of them.

Jake had made himself scarce around the home since Sarah had been back, and Gwen had been thankful for it. Gwen had done her best to act as if nothing was different, although maybe sending a little more attention Sarah's way, like helping with the meals. Suddenly she felt a great deal of protectiveness for the woman. What else did she have to deal with, married to this brute?

Gwen was sure Sarah had noticed something different about her. From the corner of Gwen's eye, she caught her looking at her strangely. Maybe she saw Gwen tremble sometimes when Jake was nearby. Or heard the stammer in her voice. Maybe she noticed how Gwen almost tiptoed from room to room and tried to make herself smaller in his presence. She understood why she had thought Sarah a mouse and wondered who she had been prior to meeting Jake.

Hugh pulled up in Lucy with Peggy and Billy inside.

The churn of the tyres on the gravel drew Gwen's attention, and having already packed, she raced out to meet them before Hugh had even brought the car to a complete stop. She wanted to avoid any interaction with Jake if she could.

Billy was the first one out of the vehicle. Her heart fluttered on seeing him. No words could describe the look he gave her, but the heat rose in her cheeks, anyway. He held the back door open for her to join Peggy, who immediately wrapped her in her arms as Gwen slid across the seat.

"It's been so long," Peggy cooed. "Are you feeling better?"

"Yes. Much," Gwen replied, and for the moment she meant it. She was safe here, with friends. A small part of her though, was impatient to leave.

"Hey, kitten." Hugh turned around in his seat, and Gwen found she had to swallow hard and force a smile. They had the same angular jawline.

"Is Jakey home then? I should go say hello." Hugh made to open his own door.

"N-no," Gwen said, frustrated by the wobbliness in her voice. "I think he's out. Won't be back until later."

It was a lie. He was in his office. She'd heard the radio in there when the car pulled up, but she wasn't sure she would have it in her to face him now. By the narrowing of his eyes, she very much doubted Billy wanted to see him either. Peggy reached over and gave her hand a squeeze as if she could see into her soul.

"Oh," Hugh said, sounding disheartened. "Maybe he'll be home when we get back."

Gwen truly hoped not.

It was easy to slip back into the way things were. Hugh and Peggy had such an uncomplicated way about them. No one asked about her mysterious sickness, and she was thankful for it. Billy didn't bring up visiting her and being turned away by Jake. It was always possible he'd told the others about it when she wasn't around, but for the moment, she was glad she was in the dark.

They decided against returning to the Willows swimming hole and the place Billy had heard of. It was way too cold to swim now. The leaves were already changing colours. Hugh had another place in mind. Gwen paid no attention to the drive, instead listening to Peggy chatter on about this piece of gossip and that. As a member of Te Tapu's Young Farmers Women's Committee, she seemed to know almost everything going on in Te Tapu and its neighbouring towns too.

"You know, you should really join us," she said to Gwen. "We're always looking for fresh blood, and it's a great way to be meeting new people."

"Oh, what does Gwenny need with new people?" Hugh asked, flashing a toothy grin their way. "When she has us?" He gave Billy a nudge.

He'd remained quiet most of the trip, and Gwen wondered why this time he hadn't joined her in the back seat. Had she done something wrong? Had he changed the way he felt about her?

After following the bumpy gravel road for some time, Hugh pulled off to his left and brought the car up to a halt before a gate. "Be a champ," he said, turning to Billy.

With quiet acknowledgement, Billy got out of the car and pushed the gate open for Hugh to drive through. Gwen studied him. She could almost make out the lines of his shoulders and the muscles of his back through his shirt, and she remembered again what it felt like to run her hands over his arms, up his back to play with the hair at the nape of his neck. She felt a prickling under her skin. A good one this time.

Hugh drove the vehicle through, then stopped to wait for Billy to close the gate and join them again in the car.

It was a small drive up the hill, the gravel turning to dirt ruts before Hugh pulled off to the side in the grass. They were on top of a hill. Ahead of them, a large weeping willow stood proud, its leaves still held to its branches. Gwen remembered from some trivia learnt in her own school days that they were often the last to lose their leaves in autumn.

After getting out of the car, she helped Peggy carry the blankets while the men carried the picnic basket and drinks.

It was steeper than Gwen anticipated, and she was panting by the time they reached the top. The crisp autumn breeze made goosebumps on her arms and legs, but the breath-taking view was worth it a million times over.

They stood at the top of the hill, where Gwen felt she could see most of Te Tapu. Peggy laid a blanket on the ground and Hugh put down the picnic basket. Finished adding the wine and glasses to the ground, Billy came and stood beside her.

"See over there?" He pointed off in the distance to where a small white speck stood out amongst a few trees. "There's your school. And over there, with the other cluster of trees, is where you live."

Gwen followed his fingers. She saw the dark cluster, deciduous and evergreen, and gave an involuntary shudder.

"Are you cold?" he asked softly. Without waiting for her response, he took a blanket from her arms, flicked it in the air and wrapped it around her shoulders. She went to protest, but he was quick to silence her. "It's what they're meant for," he said.

"And where do you live?" she whispered. He considered her for a second, searching her eyes, before making a quarter turn and pointing towards a valley.

"Over there," he said, "though you can't really see it from here."

What would it be like, she wondered, to live so far from the school?

"Can we have some blankets over here, please? My wife is near freezing to death."

"Oh shush," Peggy said, gently swatting at him.

Gwen and Billy joined them, passing a blanket to Peggy, who did indeed look like she was freezing. Her lips were tinged a gentle shade of blue beneath her pale lipstick.

The banter between the four of them fell into instant comfort. Hugh and Peggy seemed to compete with story after story. Gwen was content to listen, although sometimes she ventured in with a story of something ridiculous a child did in class or of a memory about fooling around at teaching college. A bit of fun was also had at the headmistress's expense as she mimicked her lectures on what was and wasn't appropriate for teachers.

Billy stayed mostly quiet, though he smiled and laughed with the rest of them, and Gwen caught him watching her a few times with an intensity that made her blush.

251

They enjoyed a glass of wine Hugh had brought, and they ate the delicious sandwiches and cake Peggy had made. After some time, when the conversation had quietened, Peggy suggested she and Gwen have a little girl time away from the men.

Wrapped in a blanket each, they walked further away so the willow was behind them, leaving the men to their conversation.

"And you're all recovered?" Peggy asked, as the two of them sat huddled together looking out across the hills and valleys.

"Oh, yes," Gwen said. "All better."

"You know, Billy was so worried about you. He told me he even went to your house to check on you, but Jake wouldn't let him in."

Gwen's stomach fell as she remembered that day. Had he mentioned Jake pulled a gun on him? Gwen attempted a giggle and a smile to hide the racing of her heart. "Good thing he didn't," she said, hoping it sounded light-hearted enough. "I was hardly in any state I would want Billy to see me in." It was as close to the truth as she could get.

"So," Peggy said, drawing it out. "You and Billy then…" She gave Gwen's shoulder a gentle nudge with her own.

Gwen found herself giggle this time for real.

"Well … do tell!"

"There's nothing to tell, really."

"Oh, come off it," Peggy replied. "You two can barely keep your eyes off each other."

Gwen was glad for the chill air because it cooled the heat on her chest and cheeks.

What harm was it, she wondered, in telling Peggy how she felt?

"Have you ever read the book *Wuthering Heights?*" Gwen asked.

"Maybe, I'm not sure." Confusion marked her features.

"Well," Gwen said, "there's this part where the main character Catherine is talking to her nanny Nelly Dean about her feelings for her adopted brother Heathcliff. She says, 'Whatever our souls are made of, his and mine are the same.'"

Gwen bit her lip, waiting for a response, while Peggy eyed her quizzically for a moment.

"You really feel that way," Peggy breathed.

Gwen nodded.

"Because, Billy … he's been through a lot, you know. He has his ma and sisters to look after now his dad has gone…"

Gwen felt an uneasiness settle across her shoulders. Was she not good enough?

"He's special, you know…" Peggy's eyes held Gwen's as if searching them for any scrap of doubt.

Gwen held her gaze steady, refusing to acknowledge the niggling wonder. Did she really mean what she had said?

Peggy broke out into roaring laughter. She nudged Gwen with her shoulder affectionately, and Gwen followed suit, all intensity of the moment evaporating all most instantly.

"I'm so happy for you," Peggy said, giving her a one-armed hug. "Does he know? Have you told him?"

"No!" Her cheeks flushed again. Her voice had come out shriller than she had expected. "I couldn't, possibly. Not until I knew he felt the same."

"Oh, I'm sure he does," Peggy said, pressing the sides of their heads together. "This is so wonderful," she said. "I'll be helping you plan your wedding soon, I'm sure of it."

They dissolved in another burst of laughter.

"We should get back," Peggy said, making a move to stand up. "The boys will miss us."

"Peggy?" Gwen said, finding courage she didn't know she had. She paused, unsure how to phrase what she wanted to ask.

Peggy stopped and must have noticed the seriousness on Gwen's face as her eyes filled with compassion.

"I was wondering…" She pulled at some of the grass, not wanting to give too much away.

"Yes?" Peggy tipped her head to the side.

"No, never mind," she said quickly, shaking her head. She had wanted to ask if she knew of other places for board, but it was a whole can of worms she wasn't sure how to tackle just yet. How could she explain to Peggy she needed out of that house, that she couldn't bear to be around Peggy's brother-in-law for one more second? Peggy was no fan of Jake's, but Hugh was his brother, after all. She didn't want to risk their friendship hinting something was wrong, nor risk Billy confronting Jake again.

She bit her lip, her heart plummeting. She was stuck. The only way out was to either return home or … maybe…

It would be a long shot, but maybe she could move things along with Billy. They could marry, move in together…

Depending, of course, on whether he returned her feelings. She forced a smile in Peggy's direction.

"Honestly, it's nothing. We should return to the boys," she said, standing up, gripping the blanket around her shoulders with one hand. She reached out for Peggy's free hand and pulled her along, giving her no opportunity to argue.

Hugh and Billy were deep in conversation when Gwen and Peggy returned to the picnic spot. From the bits and pieces

Gwen heard as they drew closer, it sounded like they were discussing wool exports, textiles and the impact of the war overseas.

As they drew closer, the two stopped talking, and Hugh jumped up from his spot. "You've been gone too long, my wife, let's go for a walk."

"But I've just been for a walk," Peggy protested.

Hugh gave her a wink.

"You know, that sounds great," she corrected. They headed off in the direction she and Gwen had come from.

"Not very subtle, are they?" Billy said, sitting up from his lounging position. He patted the spot on the picnic blanket beside him. Gwen plonked herself down. Every fibre of her being on fire being so close to him, lust and fear both competing for her attention. She tried her best to push away the dark shadow of fear.

Billy was no Jake, she reminded herself.

"Do you want another drink?" he asked, picking up the wine bottle.

"Sure," she said.

"You know…" he paused, the hint of a blush colouring his cheeks as he poured them both a little more wine.

"I haven't seen you since that night…"

Gwen tensed. That night! When she thought of *that* night, it was no longer Billy's face first in her mind. She pulled the blanket even tighter around her.

"Are you still cold?"

Gwen nodded. She was, and she wasn't. Competing temperatures like competing emotions swayed for her attention.

He shuffled a little closer. Gwen focused on her lap and swallowed hard. She smelled his cologne, like cinnamon –

warming, inviting.

Silence hung between them, and Gwen struggled to think of what to say. To hell with it, she thought. She was tired of being at the whims of others.

She looked up and saw him watching her. His dark eyes tracing her face as if trying to work out what she was thinking. She was thinking of kissing him, was what she was thinking.

"I want to move out." The words seemed to come from nowhere. She was shocked at herself for saying them aloud.

Billy's brows drew together. "Has he hurt you?" he asked, his jawline tightening.

"No, no, it's nothing like that." She tried to calm him, while a part of her screamed inside, yes, yes, I want to kill the bastard!

"It's just … I want to be with you." The words fell out of her mouth unaided. It was true, she realised. Life seemed too short to squander it on wasting time. It was what she wanted, and it would solve all her problems. Surely it was what he wanted too.

Billy's jaw dropped.

She had surprised him.

"Gwen," he said, his voice almost breathy. "I… I—"

"Say nothing," she said, quickly realising her mistake. She couldn't bear to hear him turn her down, so she did the only thing she could think of. She leaned forward and sought his lips with her own.

Electricity was the only way she could describe it. She melted into him. As his lips returned the fever, his tongue sought hers, tentatively at first; teasing. His arms slipped around her waist.

And then, just as suddenly, she saw him. She saw Jake. She tasted the sour taste of whiskey as he smothered her mouth with his own, and she pushed him back suddenly, sobbing as she did so, needing to be as far away as possible. Tears sprung to her eyes, and she almost fell backwards. She slid her body across the blanket and away from him, covering her mouth with her hand.

The face before her flashed a million different emotions: lust, surprise, hurt, fear, and it took her a moment to realise it was Billy's face looking back at her, not Jake's.

She realised it too late.

"I'm so sorry," she whispered. The horror of the moment coming to full realisation. She felt paralysed.

"What…?" Wide eyed and stunned, he shuffled away slightly, widening the gap between them.

"No, I'm sorry," he said, confusion still marring his features. "I shouldn't have—" He closed his mouth and shrugged.

She knew why; he had done nothing wrong. It was all her. First her suggesting they move in together, then her throwing herself at him. What was wrong with her? She blinked back tears.

She shook, mortification and the crisp breeze chilling her.

Billy swallowed hard, clenching his fists. "I want to be with you too," he whispered, watching her intently, keeping his eyes on her face. "But it's got to be done properly, eh? When the time's right. There's no rush."

Oh, but there was, she thought. There was. She would lose her mind if she had to stay in that house with that man for much longer. She cursed Jake again for ruining another perfect moment. Her bottom lip trembled. She bit down hard, hoping Billy hadn't seen.

She felt a deep-seated ache for the hurt and fear blurring his features.

257

"You know I'll never hurt you, right?" he whispered. Something else crossed his face then, a realisation, as if pieces of a puzzle had somehow slipped together in his mind, and a coldness settled on his features.

He knew, she thought.

Somehow, he'd pieced it together.

What had she done?

Chapter 31 – Riley

I t was like stepping into someone else's body; into someone else's world.

The day had suddenly grown so dark. Riley pressed her back against the cladding of the old school building. Her heart thundered in her chest. She was not alone. She didn't know how she knew it, but she did. Thoughts kept flitting through her mind. Thoughts she was having difficulty hanging on to, difficulty understanding.

He's here...

He knows...

Bile rose in her throat and she swallowed hard. She was grateful for the cool night air. Because it was night – it had to be; she could see the crescent moon... It cooled the sweat on the back of her neck.

She pressed her hands against the wall of the building, trying to make herself as inconspicuous as possible.

It was slightly damp under her fingers, and the moisture from the grass beneath her sneakers seeped through their fabric.

Grass? But there was a concrete path here...

Why? Why would he come here? The thought whirred

through her mind.

Who is "he"? Riley silently screamed at the voice. Justin? She wasn't scared of Justin.

He might fear her, though?

Saints preserve us! The knife! I don't have the knife!

Knife? Riley pressed her hands to her face. No, no, no, she whispered, shaking her head from side to side. Why would she need a knife? Why was it dark? Tremors of panic pulsed through her limbs. A strange pain, movement, made her hands fly to her stomach, and she doubled over. Nothing made sense.

Footsteps made her stand upright again, clasping one hand over her mouth to quieten her breathing. Padded footsteps on grass. They were coming around the building. They were going to find her.

JAKE! The thought came so strong it shot arrows through Riley's head.

It made no sense. But it was Jake! He was here, and he was coming for her.

Why? Had he found out? No, no, no. The panic was all-engulfing now; it made her thoughts crash together like cymbals. Nonsense words.

Whore! Crazy whore! I don't abide by whores in my house, Miss Davies.

Help me! He knows! Find something! Anything! Rapist! Bastard! He can't have me!

Then clearer, cutting through the chaos of thoughts, she saw an image of an axe on a chopping block. By the shed, the caretaker's shed.

Get to the shed! The voice pitched in her mind. *The shed! RUN!*

260

And Riley did. There was no explaining what propelled her forward. Her feet were no longer her own, they moved of their own accord. And it was dark. So dark. And shadowed. Everything was shadowed.

She broke loose of the safety of the building and sprinted across the field. So exposed. All she could do was run towards where she thought the shed was, the chopping block. But he was after her, she could tell, and another voice came, someone yelling her name, but it couldn't break through the white noise of the other voices.

She stumbled once, her arms flailing.

Noooo! A voice screamed. *You're nearly there. Get the axe. Save yourself. He'll kill you if he catches you!*

The other voice, a deeper voice, raged at her, shouting her name, but there was too much noise. Maybe it wasn't her name – it sounded different, foreign.

Stop. Stop. It's here. The chopping block. The axe is always here. Find it!

Riley slowed down, scared of what she might trip over, but also scared of whoever was chasing her. She could hear breathing, panting.

No! No! No! The voice tore at her head. *Protect yourself! You can't let him get you.*

She bent down. There were only shadows. Feeling with her hands, her feet. Where was the chopping block? She knew it was around here somewhere.

The voice again. Yelling her name. Trying to get her attention.

She hit the block with her shin and stifled a yelp of pain. Bending down, she found the smooth wooden neck of what she knew was the axe. It was lodged in the chopping block

261

Riley wiggled it back and forth until it finally let go of its hold, making her stumble backwards.

Hide! the voice implored her. And she moved to where a darker silhouette suggested the shed. Pressing her back against its wooden walls, she slid around its side, hoping the moon would stay hidden so she could stay lost in the shadows. She kept her hands wrapped around the handle of the axe. It wasn't too heavy. Could she do it? She knew what the voice wanted her to do; she could feel it poking at her, in her stomach, in her head.

You must! He'll kill you if you don't! He'll kill you and the baby!

The baby?

The footsteps slowed; they were mere metres away. He was looking for her, deep breaths punctuating her name.

Her name.

The voice was gentle now, trying to lull her out.

Her name? Was it, though?

Riley tried to push through the confusion. She needed the voices to stop. She couldn't hear properly with so many people talking at once.

It was someone's name; she just wasn't sure if it was her own.

When the fingers grabbed her shoulder, it was with a supernatural sense of terror that she tore around to face her stalker. The axe was still clenched in her hands; for a moment she forgot it was there, then she brought it down in a panic, feeling the impact reverberate through her hands and arms up to her shoulder. A wet cracking. A muffled gargle. She released her grip on the smooth wood and felt it fall with its victim. And she leapt backwards, avoiding the monster who was falling on her.

There was wailing then. Oh God, she wanted it to stop. Why wouldn't it stop?

She put her hands to her head, covering her ears. Make the crying stop! But it was even louder in her head. She pressed her palms to her eyes. They came back wet.

Murderer. You killed him! Oh God, what have you done?

The ground seemed to shift, and Riley with it. And she fell, like Alice down the rabbit hole. Such a funny thing, she thought, to be such a wild, wicked slip of a girl.

Chapter 32 – Gwen

"It was a strange way of killing: not by inches, but
by fractions of hairbreadths, to beguile me with
the spectre of a hope…"
- *Wuthering Heights*

The nausea came in waves. One minute Gwen would be rehearsing multiplication facts with her class, the next, a wave of queasiness and dizziness disarmed her. She'd have to wave for the class to continue without her, while she turned her back, leaned on her desk and willed the sickness to abate.

She had already thrown up twice on waking this morning, and this had been the third day in a row. One boy, Marcus, had been off sick some of the week before with a tummy bug, so she was sure she was suffering the same affliction.

She closed her eyes and willed the feeling away. Sweat cooled on the back of her neck.

The recitation ended.

Taking a deep breath, she turned back to her class. A glance at the clock on the wall showed she still had a good ten minutes before she could let the students out for recess.

Flipping through her copy of their maths textbook, she found a practise page of long form addition and subtraction facts.

"Please turn to page forty-nine and complete exercises one A and one B in your maths book." With a low murmur of activity, the students opened their desks and pulled out their text and exercise books, their dip pens and inkpots at the ready. They dutifully set about their work, although with a little more talking than she would normally allow. Another wave of nausea had hit. Turning her back to the class, Gwen put her hand over her mouth, closed her eyes and swallowed. Oh, for the bell to ring.

It was Sarah who put the pieces together two days later.

Gwen had spent the morning, as discreetly as possible, going back and forth to the water closet. She had vomited three times already. If it kept up like this, she was going to be late to school.

This was day five. She was sure her student's tummy upset had only lasted a couple of days. She was thankful it would soon be the weekend. She was even more thankful that Jake was away with his father, Old Man Tom, whom she'd still not met, down south somewhere to purchase farm equipment. It was one less thing to deal with when she already felt so horrid.

The hunger that hit her immediately after vomiting was almost as intense. Gwen headed to the kitchen for a piece of toasted bread or whatever she could find to fill the hole without upsetting her stomach any further.

Sarah was already in the kitchen, her back to Gwen as she

entered. She was busying herself at the sink. Gwen headed to the pantry.

"Morning," she said in a way of greeting.

Sarah turned around slowly, wiping her hands on her apron, her eyes narrowed in on Gwen.

"I'm making toast for you," she said, glancing in the direction of the toaster sitting on the corner of the bench.

"Oh," Gwen said, surprised by how easily Sarah had read her mind. Most weekday mornings, Gwen was left to sort a breakfast before she headed into work.

"Sit."

Gwen did as she was told. She had hoped to leave with the toast in hand; she had a lot to do to prepare before school began, but she'd never seen Sarah so assertive before, and an icy trickle of warning told her to do as the woman said.

Gwen took a seat closest to the door, all the same.

Sarah turned to the toaster. She already had a small plate set aside; Gwen noticed. She placed the toast on the plate with a butter knife and set it before Gwen. Then she returned to the pantry to pull out butter and a small paper bag, which she added to the table. Finally, Sarah took a seat opposite Gwen.

Sarah didn't normally make her nervous like this. But her eyes seemed to scrutinise every movement Gwen made as she set about buttering her bread and then taking a tentative bite.

"You're pregnant," Sarah said matter-of-factly, wringing her hands in her apron.

Gwen coughed, a small morsel of toast having gone down her throat funny. Her heart sped up.

Sarah's eyes were shiny. She bit her lip and waited for Gwen to stop coughing.

"No, of course not," Gwen said, pushing her chair back, ready to flee. There was absolutely no way. "Thank you for the toast," she said, remembering her manners, "but I need to be leaving for school."

"You've been throwing up every morning. I can hear you. And you pushed your chicken around your plate last night like the very smell was toxic. I know the signs." Sarah breathed.

In shock, Gwen dropped her toast onto her plate. The blood drained from her face.

Sarah had been pregnant once, she remembered. She would know.

No, no, no, her mind screamed. She scraped her chair back in a hurry on the linoleum and lunged towards the kitchen sink, when she emptied her stomach once more, before sinking to the floor, resting her head on the cupboards.

Sarah was by her side instantly, her hand rubbing Gwen's back. Gwen took a couple of gulps of air before turning to face Sarah, surprised to see tears running unabated down Sarah's cheeks.

"He did this to you, didn't he?" she whispered.

Gwen shut her eyes, the question like a slap.

"The bastard did this to you…"

Gwen bit down hard on her lip to keep the tears welling behind her lids from escaping. Instead, she gave the slightest of nods. She hadn't known. It hadn't crossed her mind. It had been five… no, six weeks ago. And now? It made sense, and it utterly, tragically ruined everything. How could she hide it from Billy? Peggy and Hugh? From the headmistress? How could she keep living here and hide it from Jake?

Sarah sat down beside her, pulling Gwen to her until

Gwen's head rested on her chest. A motherly embrace, Gwen thought, as she felt the other woman's sobs. Gentle, cathartic sobs. Enough for the two of them.

"You cannot tell anyone," Gwen said after a while. "Promise me you won't tell anyone." She pushed Sarah away and locked eyes with her.

Sarah, pale, nodded. "What will you do?" she asked. "You can't stay here. Jake cannot know." She sniffled and wiped her eyes with the back of her hand.

The way she said it sent ice through Gwen's veins. She knew that too.

"I don't know." She bit hard again on her lip to stop it from trembling. A million thoughts raced through her mind. She couldn't think. Not right now.

"I have to get to school," she said again.

Sarah pulled herself up to standing and held out a hand to help Gwen do the same. Then she crossed the room to the table, picked up the paper bag and held it out for Gwen.

"These will help," she said. Gwen opened the paper bag to see small yellow cubes.

"Crystallised ginger. For the nausea."

Gwen looked at her, wide eyed. This wasn't a tummy bug then. A million curse words cycled through her mind, and she took a deep breath to quell the building panic. She nodded. It was the only "thanks" she could give.

"Jake will be back tomorrow," Sarah told her. "He can't know."

No. Other than Sarah, no one could know.

Chapter 33 – Riley

"Damn it, Riley! Wake up!"

She lay there for a moment, trying to pull herself back into her body. Taking a mental inventory, she noticed she was lying down. A light ache pounded above her eyes, across her forehead, but no pain anywhere else. She was obviously alive, and by the red glow from the inside of her eyelids, it was sunny out. Like a film being rewound, she unspooled the events she guessed had led to her being here with a figure bent over her, his voice all too familiar and all too unwelcome.

Liam swore under his breath, and she risked opening her eyes, blinking them a few times to get used to the light.

"What the hell?" he asked.

Riley dragged herself up to a sitting position. "What the hell" was right.

Liam crouched beside her, a thin red line above his left eye. A small trickle of congealed blood ran to his eyebrow.

Thank God! She thought she'd killed someone. She quickly glanced around her for the axe. She was sure she'd been holding an axe.

"It's over there," he said, reading her mind, and gesturing a couple of feet away from them. A plank of wood, no bigger than fifty or so centimetres, lay discarded on the ground.

It didn't make sense. She was by the shed, like she had thought she was. But the ground was dirt and dry. And worse, it was midday or close to it. The sun was high in the sky. No dew dampened the ground.

"Well? Can you talk? Do you want to tell me why you attacked me with a plank of wood?" Liam's eyes were hard. He didn't trust her. She could hardly blame him.

She gaped at him. She really had attacked someone, then. It hadn't been a dream.

"I'm so sorry," she said, bringing her hands to her cheeks. "I thought you were someone else…"

"Really? Just who was it you were planning on attacking on a Saturday morning at school?"

There was no humour in his voice. She felt like she was being scolded. And she hated it. She was already confused as hell, and his anger did nothing but get her own hackles up. She bristled at his tone.

"I don't know!" she said, indignation coming to the fore. She scrambled to stand up so he wouldn't be hovering over her.

He stood up too, running a hand through his hair in exasperation and wincing a little as his fingers touched the wound on his head.

"We should clean that up," she said. It went without saying – angry or not, if she saw a need she wanted to help.

"It's fine," he said coolly. "I want to know what you're doing here, why you were running around like the devil himself were after you, why you were screaming like a banshee," – he took a breath – "and why the hell you attacked me?"

270

"Look, I told you. I. Don't. *Know*!" She was losing grip on her self-control, and she stamped her foot like a child. More than anyone, she wanted to know what was going on. And it infuriated her that he was always the one catching her out.

They stood there for a moment, both glaring at each other, him a head taller than her. Right now, she was kind of wishing she had hit him harder with the wood.

She broke the spell. Throwing her hands in the air and turning on her heel. "If you want me to look at your head wound, I'm heading to the sick bay, otherwise, stand here and be angry at the world," she said.

She wasn't sure why she had said that, but it seemed apt. Every time she had seen him, he had seemed angry. If what the others had said was true, he might have a right to be, but it was no excuse for being an ass to her all the time.

She headed back to the office. The sick bay would have pain killers, and she needed something to kill her headache before driving home again.

The trip had been a colossal waste of time. And bordering on mental. First, she had been driven off the road, and then she fainted again after a nice little vacation from reality. Might be time for a check-up, she thought. And then shivered. God, what if she really was going crazy?

She was surprised to hear footsteps behind her. She didn't dare turn around. If he came with her back into the reception area, she'd do her due diligence and patch him up in the sick bay. That was it. She owed him nothing else.

Riley picked up the books and her bag, which still lay sprawled on the steps to the office area. Her school keys were thankfully in her back pocket. She pulled them out and went about unlocking the door again. Her hands shook, making it nearly impossible.

"Here," Liam said from behind her. "Let me do it." He took the keys from her hand, and she stepped aside. He was tall with a strong build. If he wasn't so arrogant, she might have found him attractive. His eyes in particular – she'd never seen eyes like his.

Then a memory flashed before her of someone else with emerald-green eyes, and she shook it away.

Despite being attacked by her, he seemed no worse for wear. He deftly turned the key and disarmed the alarm before fully opening the door for her.

She walked past him, dumped her belongings on the reception desk and headed straight for the sickbay off the office. From the medicine cabinet and drawers, she pulled out a few items she thought she might need: antiseptic cream, butterfly plasters, and painkillers for herself. She grabbed a small disposable cup from the dispenser and filled it with water from the sink, dropped two painkillers onto her tongue and took a swallow of water.

Liam stood in the doorway. He said nothing.

"Sit," she ordered, pointing to the cot along one wall of the room, refusing to meet his eyes. It surprised her to see him do as he was told. He looked ridiculous. The cot was low to the ground, meant for kids. He sat there awkwardly with his knees up to his chin.

It certainly wasn't a big wound. No need for a doctor, although the first blushing of a bruise suggested she should get him an icepack after.

She cleaned his wound the best she could with a little water and a cotton pad and used a cotton bud to apply some cream, then affixed the butterfly plasters. As she was finishing up, he spoke.

"Why are you at school?" he asked, his tone gentler this time. Riley turned her back to throw the plaster papers in the rubbish bin. Her defences rose again as if she were on trial, so she took a deep breath. She wasn't on trial. She had a right to come into school whenever she wanted.

After washing her hands in the basin, and still avoiding his eyes, she pulled a paper towel from the dispenser and dried her hands. "I had some books to collect," she said.

Out of the corner of her eye she saw his forehead crinkle, then he grimaced. She threw the paper towel in the bin. He made no move to get up from where he was sitting.

"And the real reason?" he said, his voice steady, unwavering.

She gritted her teeth and sought the bracelet with her fingers.

"Shit!" she said, startled. "It's gone!" Her wrist was bare. She had it on this morning, she knew she had; she wore it every day. It must have fallen off. She went to race out the room, but a hand on her arm stayed her. She turned on her toes, her nose almost hitting Liam on the chest as he towered over her. He rummaged in his pocket with his spare hand and pulled out her bracelet.

"Here," he said. "You dropped it when you attacked me." He let go of her wrist and went about securing it where it belonged.

"Thank you," she whispered, tears flickering behind her lids. Even if it had been given by Justin, the bracelet was a promise of something better, and she loathed the idea of losing it.

"What does it mean?" he asked.

She wrinkled her nose, confused for a second.

"The inscription?"

273

"Oh. It's a quote from *Wuthering Heights*," she answered, feeling the threat of a blush on her cheeks. "Whatever our souls are made of, yours and mine are the same." Her heart tripped in her chest, and she turned away. It seemed silly, saying it aloud like that. Especially to Liam.

She headed towards the fridge in the staffroom. "You need an icepack."

"I'm fine," he said.

Preferring to be busy, she ignored him. He put her on edge. Though she had a million questions she wanted to ask him, she wasn't sure where to start.

She pulled an icepack out of the mini freezer beneath the fridge and a clean cloth to wrap around it. Then held it out to him. He paused before taking it and pressing it to his head. He winced and plopped down on the small two-seater.

"Why are you really here?" he asked again.

Riley sighed. She should just tell him. He probably already thought her nuts, so where was the harm? Plus, maybe he'd tell her why the community was so protective of covering up a rape.

She pursed her lips, remembering.

"I wanted Gwen's things," she said, watching him closely to gauge his reaction.

"Who's Gwen?" he asked, his face giving nothing away.

"Gwendolyn Davies, the woman who used to teach in my class." Though it was purely a guess, she liked to think she had inherited Gwen's classroom.

He still gave no sense of recognition. He was either a fantastic poker player or really didn't know the name of the woman his relative had brutalised.

Riley took a deep breath, pulled out a chair from the kitchen table and sat down.

"The woman Jake O'Regan raped," she said, letting the words hang heavy between them.

Liam's jaw dropped.

"A family member of yours?" She hadn't meant it to sound so accusatory, yet she couldn't help it. She didn't know this woman, but for all women out there, she was pissed her name had been forgotten.

"Whoa!" Liam said, sliding forward on his seat "What do you mean rape? And who the hell is this Gwen person?"

He really didn't know? Riley dug her fingers into the palms of her hands, wishing she didn't bite her fingernails. Right now, she would welcome the pain to stifle her growing frustration.

However, if he didn't know Gwen, why had he got so angry at seeing her display the night before? And why had he looked so scared?

"Those photos, the newspaper, those items for my display last night that you and your father and everyone reacted so horribly too, they were Gwen's," she said.

The colour slid from Liam's face. He pulled the icepack away from his forehead and placed it on the sofa cushion beside him.

"I have her journal," she said, unsure if she was baiting him or telling him because she wanted to tell someone. "She says the man she boarded with, Jake O'Regan, raped her."

Liam closed his eyes for a moment and Riley watched him.

"Rape," he whispered, opening his eyes again. It surprised her to see they looked glassy.

"You didn't know?" she asked, confused.

He shook his head.

275

"Then why—" She paused, unsure how to go on. A barb of guilt shot through her. Who was she to pull skeletons out of someone else's closet?

"What else did he do?" she asked, half to herself.

"Sometimes," Liam said, finding his voice, "the past is better left in the past." He opened his eyes and fixed them on Riley's. He looked different. Defeated.

"So we just forget this woman, a woman who worked here, was raped seventy-odd years ago and probably never got the justice she deserved?" It hurt her, physically hurt her like a clawing in her stomach that Jake – whoever he was – got away with such a heinous act.

She felt the threatening onslaught of tears again, empathy and anger vying for release. Yet she hadn't actually finished reading Gwen's journal. Maybe Jake hadn't got away with it. "Who was Jake O'Regan?" she asked, trying hard to steady her voice and keep her emotions in check.

"You know what?" Liam said, appearing to regain his own composure. "I think it's my turn to ask a question."

Riley crossed her arms. To hell with it. If this was the game she had to play, so be it.

"Why were you running around like a crazy person before, and why did you attack me?"

"I wasn't running around like a crazy person." She couldn't keep the indignation from her voice. She clenched her teeth and dropped her hand to the bracelet around her wrist. She hated being called crazy. "I thought someone was after me, and it was dark—"

"How could it have been dark?" he asked, his eyebrows shooting up in surprise. "What time did you get here?"

"Nine. Ten…" she traced the wood veins in the table with

her finger.

"At night?" he asked, horror marring his face.

"This morning."

She'd left him speechless.

"But it wasn't dark—"

"She thought it was Jake." It made sense to her now. The other voice. It hadn't been some part of her subconscious; it had been Gwen's voice, she was sure of it.

"What the fuck?" Liam said, standing up and pacing in front of the sofa. He swept his hand through his hair again and then threw his hands up in the air.

"You hear yourself, right? You thought what? You were being chased by my great uncle who's been dead for the last seventy years? Shit!" he swore. The colour had come back to his cheeks, and his eyes flashed.

Riley stood up too, leaning on the table. "Well, I'm sorry. But that's what happened. Only it wasn't me, it was Gwen, and she was scared because your great whoever was an abusive rapist who terrorised his wife and his boarder. And if this community wants to keep that hidden because of some stupid hierarchy of name around here, well then – then…" She didn't know what to say. It all sounded crazy. *She* sounded crazy.

Pain killers or not, her head was back to pounding, and her whole body trembled with anger. Liam's seemed to do the same.

"My great uncle was a murderer, Riley. And yes, the community is pretty damn protective of my family name. My great grandfather founded this village – this was his town. This school, the church. Most of the things you see around here are thanks to him. Loyalties run deep. And for you

277

to come here and stir up trouble, getting your kicks from pulling apart the past—"

"Hold up!" Riley said, holding her palm face-out in a "stop" gesture. "He was a *murderer*? Are you kidding me? I got run off the road today because this community sees fit to protect a murderer!?"

Tears escaped, and she wiped them away with the back of her hand, frustrated that her default for anger was to cry.

Liam put his hands to his head again, clutching at his hair as he continued to pace back and forth.

Riley took a few deep breaths to steady herself. She suspected he was doing the same. She sniffed and wiped her eyes again.

After a while he put his hands down, plonked back on the sofa, and bent over, resting his head in his hands.

She wanted to leave. That's what she wanted. Whatever weird family and community drama she'd got herself involved in, she'd had enough. And here she was, thinking she'd left drama behind when she'd left Justin. This was supposed to be her new start. Her new life.

"What do you mean you got run off the road?" Liam mumbled from the sofa.

Riley said nothing.

He looked up at her then. The green of his eyes rimmed red, and something pulled sharply in her chest. Riley slumped backwards into the chair behind her. She'd broken him. Somehow, she'd broken him. It took her a second to make the connection. Brittany had told her he'd lost his wife that way. A car accident. Except there were doubts.

"I'm so sorry," she whispered.

"Tell me what happened."

278

She told him, calmer now. "It could have been anyone."

He shook his head, as if he already knew who it had been.
"What kind of vehicle was it?" He sounded defeated.

She had really dumped a lot on him this morning, right after
hitting him with a plank of wood. She grimaced inwardly and
cleared her throat. "A silver ute." Other than that she couldn't
really say. Makes and models of cars were not something she
was very attuned to.

His shoulders slumped even more. He knew. She could
read it on his face, and she pitied him. Maybe it was like the
others had said: he was one of the good ones. You couldn't
choose the family you were born into. She knew that. So
why had she been holding it against him?

After a minute he got up again. "Lock up," he said gruffly,
"and come with me."

As he headed out the door, he turned. "And don't forget
your books." He gestured to the math books sitting at
reception by her bag. He already knew they were a farce.
What was the point? She left them where they were, set
the alarm for the second time that day, and locked the door
behind her.

She followed Liam out to the car park, coming to a standstill
as her eyes locked on the vehicle parked there.

Her jaw dropped. How was this even possible? Chills ran
through her body.

Liam must have noticed the shiver. His eyes pleaded with
sympathy. "I'm so sorry," he said.

"It was you," she whispered.

He shook his head. "No. But I know who it was."

279

Chapter 34 – Gwen

"Well, we must be for ourselves in the long run;
the mild and generous are only more justly selfish
than the domineering…"
- Wuthering Heights

"Marry me," Gwen said, hoping he didn't catch the desperation behind the words.

Billy held her gaze. The streetlights and the coloured lights from the shops across the road lit up the side of his face. She shouldn't have asked. It wasn't the done thing, and Billy liked to do things by the book.

She hadn't planned it either. Yes, she'd been thinking about it more and more. Who wouldn't in her circumstance? She had wracked her brain for every possible out, short of returning home. But her belly was showing; she wouldn't be able to hide things for much longer. And what then?

She reached up and drew her finger down the side of his face. Things had been going so well between them. Hugh had loaned Lucy to them for the night, and Billy had driven them into the city to catch the screening of Wuthering Heights. It was Gwen's favourite book, and so seeing it on the big screen, with a man she adored beside her … there were no words. She even forgave the fact half of the original story had been removed from the film.

It had been a big splurge on both of their parts. More so for Billy, who insisted on paying for both of them for everything.

And she didn't want the night to end, not without some promise of something better than what she was returning to.

"Marry me?" she said again, this time her voice pitching slightly higher. She kept her eyes locked on his and shuffled across the seat to be even closer to him.

"Gwen," he said. And she couldn't tell if he was blushing or if it was the lights from across the street reflecting on his face.

"You know I love you," he started, the timbre of his voice, his accent making her heart leap into her throat. Please don't say no, please don't say no, she prayed, waiting.

"But I want to do things the proper way. I want to give you a ring and a house. Nothing less. A few more years, and I should have what I need. My sisters should be married off, and it'll just be my ma to look after – "

"I don't care about the ring or the house," she said. It was a lie. Part of her did care. She cared a lot what other people thought, but there wasn't time.

"I want to do right by you, you know that."

She did. She blinked away the threatening tears. Of course he wanted to do right by her. Yet, if things didn't change, what use would any of it be?

A few times over the last month, she had thought she might get her way. Things had got heavy between them. Kissing

281

had led to other things, hands exploring … and she'd found, with time and with focus, all thoughts from that night could be pushed away. Occasionally a memory, a sensory response, would trigger, and she'd freeze; then, she'd remember whose arms she was in, and she'd remember how much she loved Billy, and the devil, the devil would fade away again.

But things never went too far. Even when she tried to push him to it. Even when her fingers slid beneath the waist of his pants, as she kissed along his jawline up to his ear, until he let out a soft moan, even when she felt his hardness pushing up against her through her skirts, he would find restraint and push her away. Because it wasn't proper. And every time it nearly killed her.

She wanted him. Oh, she wanted him for so many reasons. To cleanse herself of the other, to claim Billy for her unborn child, but largely because she just wanted him. Her entire body ached for him, and she wanted to feel him in a way she hadn't yet. To explore his soul with her own. And if they did it, then he may never need know how tainted she was, how ruined. It would be her secret to bear.

Gwen pulled away, shuffling back to her side of the car, she looked out the window. They had parked a good two blocks from the theatre. A couple walked arm in arm down the footpath, and she felt the stirrings of jealousy.

Did he ever push her away? What was so wrong with her? Had Billy not learnt anything from the tragedy of Heathcliff and Catherine? Love was not to be pushed aside for such trivialities like what was proper.

Tears slid down her cheeks. She no longer cared. One could only take so much rejection.

"Take me home," she said. For a moment, she glimpsed her

reflection in the window beside her. Her very image was like the ghost of Catherine Linton knocking at the window, "Let me in, let me in." She was a wraith of herself.

"Gwen," a hurting voice said from beside her. "Don't be like that. You know I love you."

She turned to him, feeling a fury mount beneath her sadness. "And yet you push me away!"

"It's not proper. We wait until marriage. We do things right. And I will marry you, I promise."

She hated his expression right now. His eyes pleading; fearful.

"A year or two is all I'm asking."

"So I am not *proper*, then?" she asked, the edge to her voice making her cringe. "Because I want to be with the one I love, now, I am not *proper*?" She knew she sounded like a whiny child, but she was running out of options. Those left to her were few and filled her with dread.

He sighed, wiping his hand across his mouth. "What if you were to get with child? What then? Could you really live with that? I would love it regardless, of course I would, but the poor thing would always be a bastard in the eyes of the church, in the eyes of our neighbours."

Gwen's stomach dropped. Though she had wanted to say there were ways to prevent accidental pregnancies, she knew how that would make her sound, how it had already made her sound. And it wouldn't have mattered, anyway. If they were to be together, she needed him to believe the child was his. But if he could not love her enough to be with her now in body or marriage, to hell with his church and the neighbours, then their future together had already been writ.

How cruel, your veins are full of ice-water and mine are boiling...

283

Catherine's words circled around her head.

"Take me home," she said again, utterly defeated. She closed her eyes and rested her forehead on the cool glass window.

Billy did nothing for a while, then he shuffled in his seat and turned the engine.

Oh God, but what was she to do?

Chapter 35 – Gwen

"Oh, I'm burning! I wish I were out of doors! I wish I were a girl again, half savage and hardy, and free, and laughing at injuries, not maddening under them! Why am I so changed? Why does my blood rush into a hell of tumult at a few words? I'm sure I should be myself were I once among the heather on those hills. Open the window again wide: fasten it open!"
- Wuthering Heights

"Billy's been asking about you," Peggy said, pouring tea into a dainty teacup Gwen was sure had been brought out of the cabinet just for this occasion.

Gwen took it from her, blowing softly to cool it before drinking any.

"Has something happened?" Peggy asked, sitting down opposite Gwen at the table. "You had been spending so much time together, I had thought things were going well?"

She was not letting up, and Gwen took a sip to stall for

285

time, burning her tongue. She loved Peggy, she did, but when she had a bone, she was loath to give it up. "They have been," Gwen said. "We've decided to take some time, is all."

"Does Billy know this?" Peggy asked. She hadn't yet taken a sip of her tea; instead, she continued to stir the cube of sugar she placed in it carefully with the teaspoon. Surely it had dissolved by now.

Gwen put her cup down on the saucer. "How long had you been seeing each other before Hugh proposed to you?" Gwen asked, making Peggy break into a wide smile.

"Is this what it's about, then?" she said, her voice slightly teasing. "He is completely, utterly in love with you Gwendolyn Davies, and if you doubt him for any reason, you're an absolute ninny." Peggy reached across the table for Gwen's hand and took it in her own.

"Billy's different from Hugh," she continued. "He has more responsibilities. He has his mama and younger sisters to take care of, and he – well he, likes to do things the right way. Don't think for a moment he wouldn't marry you today if the stars weren't better aligned."

Though her words were meant to be soothing, nothing could soothe Gwen now. She shifted uncomfortably in her chair, needing to relieve herself again, but feeling like only moments ago she had left to do just that.

"I know, I know," was all Gwen could say. Tears welled up again, and she turned away so Peggy wouldn't see.

"Gwenny? Are you okay?"

Though she wanted to say yes, to pretend as if nothing was the matter, her body betrayed her, and the floodgates opened without her say. Tears rolled down her cheeks, and her head shook from side to side, betraying her further.

Peggy was up in an instant and around to her side of the table, arm around Gwen's shoulders, trying to calm her with words a mother might use. "Now, now, it'll be alright, I promise."

Gwen shook her head a second time. It wouldn't be all right. Not now, not ever.

"What is it, Gwenny? You can tell me. Has he hurt you? Oh, if that man has hurt you—"

"I'm pregnant," Gwen blurted out, then, realising her mistake, dissolved into sobs.

Beside her, Peggy froze. It was cruel. For so many reasons, Gwen had wanted to say nothing. But oh, to have a friend, someone to understand, to go through this with her, to not be alone. How cruel it was that this was the secret, the drama she had to share, when only a few weeks previous, Gwen had comforted Peggy over the loss of her own unborn. It had been the second one for them, and Gwen had seen how it had broken her heart. They had been trying for so long, and fate seemed so cruel. And now here Gwen was, with a child of her own that she neither planned nor wanted. Peggy had gone on with life as if nothing had happened, but Gwen could guess how many tears had been cried in private.

"You're pregnant?" Peggy echoed in a whisper.

Gwen nodded.

A myriad of emotions flitted across Peggy's face. Shock, fear, sadness, quickly replaced by hope and sympathy.

"Does Billy know?"

"No, and you cannot tell him!" Gwen whirled in her seat, grabbing both of Peggy's hands in hers. "Promise me!" she said, not even caring any more for the tears rolling down her face. "You cannot tell him! You cannot tell anyone, not even

Hugh."

She let go and wiped the tears from her face with the palms of her hand. What had she done? What had she done? The question rolled around and around in her mind.

"Oh, Gwenny." Peggy sighed, her lips pulled down in a frown. She stood and paced back and forth.

Gwen shifted uncomfortably in her chair.

"But he has to know. He'll want to do the right thing, I'm sure of it." Peggy rubbed her forehead, squeezing her eyes closed for a minute.

Maybe, Gwen thought. Had the baby been his. "I'm so sorry, Peggy. I should never have unloaded this on you." Her voice caught in her throat, and she swallowed hard.

"We'll fix this, Gwenny, we will." Peggy came back over to Gwen, this time picking up her hands. "We'll tell Billy. And Hugh and I, we'll help the two of you the best we can. No one else need know. We can have a small wedding, here in the yard. You're still not showing, so we have time. It'll be our little secret, the four of us."

Gwen's head spun. Peggy's mind worked so fast; she had it all mapped out, and oh, if only it would be so easy. But it wouldn't. It couldn't. She had so much love for this woman. If things had been different, she knew Peggy would have fixed everything. However, Jake had ruined any chance of happily ever after. Unless Gwen could convince Billy to sleep with her, they were out of luck, and for that, Gwen already feared they were far too late. Not even Billy would want a woman so defiled as her.

"Please, Peggy," she whispered, squeezing her hands. "You cannot tell. Give me time. Please. Promise you'll tell no one, not Hugh and not Billy. I need time."

Peggy's eyes darted away, her brow furrowed.

"Please," she said again. She tugged at Peggy's hands. She needed to know the secret would stay safe.

"Okay," Peggy whispered, her own eyes shining with tears. "But you must promise me, you will do nothing silly, and you will tell him. When you're ready, but you will tell."

Gwen mentally crossed her fingers and slowly nodded her head. "I will," she said.

Chapter 36 – Liam

L iam pulled up outside the Victorian-style cottage. Gravel spat up from under his tyres as he skidded to a halt. He sat for a second, collecting his thoughts, his knuckles white on the steering wheel. A yapping from outside notified him Chester the retriever was on duty.

What the hell was he going to say? Ripples of anger pulsed through his veins, and he had to remind himself to cool it. There had already been enough yelling for one morning. But his father had crossed a line. No matter what harm to the O'Regan name, you didn't go chasing women off the road.

He took another deep breath and clenched his fists before opening the door and heading to the porch.

A pair of dirty gumboots stood upright by the welcome mat. Liam grimaced. Chester bounded up and down at his side, and he bent down and gave him a pat on the head. The dog's tail slapped against Liam's leg in frenzied excitement. In the background came the barking of the work dogs in their kennels, cottoning on to the fact there was a visitor.

It was a nice house. Or it had been. When Liam moved back eight months ago, the grounds and garden were overgrown, and it had taken him weeks to get things back to what would have passed as acceptable to his mum. He would have to prune the roses soon. It had been a while, and they had become so stalky they had almost surpassed the windows. The house had been in their family for generations, fresh additions built onto it as the family grew.

Liam paused for another moment at the front entrance. What a can of worms this woman had opened. Unintentionally, if she was to be believed. The past would always come back to haunt them, he guessed. But what was it with this woman, with her uncanny knack of bringing drama? Drama that affected him.

He resisted the temptation to knock. He'd been staying there for eight months, and yet he still felt like a visitor – or an unwelcomed guest, to be more precise. "Keep ya, cool," he whispered before opening the door. It wouldn't do any good to give his father a heart attack on top of everything else.

He walked down the hallway. Not a lot had changed since his mother had been alive. Old photographs in dusty frames lined the walls. One was of him and his sister; he must have been seven, Suzanne, five. Further down was a picture of the four of them in happier days. His mum with her arms embracing him and his sister, while his father stood behind. A proud man. Handsome in his time. It was one of the few Liam had seen where his father was smiling.

Older photos hung there as well. His grandma and grandfather on their wedding day. His grandfather looking especially dapper – he was sure that was the word for it – leaning back on the bonnet of a Ford saloon from the 1930s, with his blushing bride gazing up at him with adoring eyes.

He'd heard about his grandparents. They were said to be both a little ahead of their time with their mannerisms, drinking, partying. A little risqué with showing their affection in public. He had to smile. Even as a little boy, he recognised how they were easy to smile and joke and still looked at each other affectionately. His grandmother was treasurer of the Te Tapu Young Farmers Women's Committee until her death. His grandfather took over the family business from his father not long after … not long after the incident.

And then there was the man who started it all. Liam's great-grandfather, affectionately known by the village folk as Ol' Man Tom. He made a small fortune at a young age in the textile industry, before immigrating from England and purchasing land here in what was to become Te Tapu. Born under a lucky star, and with sound business savvy, everything he touched seemed to turn to gold, and he was able to buy up more and more land. Despite the stern expression on his face as he stood outside the first Te Tapu garage, Liam had only ever heard good things about him. His generosity had made him something of a hero in these parts, and his legacy continued through to present day.

His grandparents and Ol' Man Tom were the reasons people stuck by the O'Regan name, Liam thought. Loyalties ran deep. He wondered, if his mother had still been alive, if his dad would have been worthy of the name too.

The only photo missing was of his great uncle, Jacob, oldest son to Ol' Man Tom. The man whose life and death were almost scrubbed from history. The black sheep of the family. Taboo to speak of.

Liam knew bits and pieces, though he'd learnt at an early age to not ask questions. He had tried once with his grandfather; the old man's eyes had filled with tears and Liam quickly changed the subject.

But no more secrecy. Not today.

He knew where he'd find his father. He'd be in the drawing room, where he spent most of his time nowadays. And it surprised Liam not at all when he walked in to find the curtains pulled, the room bathed in darkness and the heady scent of whisky heavy in the air. His father sat with his back to the door in his favourite recliner.

Liam ignored him and walked over to the windows, pulling back the curtains and letting the light throw dust mites around the room. He then pushed open a window to let some fresh air in.

"What the hell are you doing?" A grumbling came from the chair behind him.

Liam willed himself to keep his cool before turning around to face his father.

The wheelchair sat discarded in the room's corner. He didn't really need it. His dad could still walk. He relied on it more when he was inebriated than for any physical deficit, and that had been increasing more and more as of late.

His father sagged in his chair, a glass in his hand. An old-fashioned decanter of whiskey rested on the side table. On the floor lay a newspaper.

The newspaper.

With two quick strides Liam reached the newspaper, turning away again from his father, ignoring his curses and protests as he scanned the front page. There it was, as he knew it would be. The small article that had stirred up this mess.

"Murder on school grounds implicates Te Tapu's founding family."

It was surprising how short the article was. Liam had heard

293

rumours that despite his family's insistence on pulling the article, the best they could do was make it as small and as inconspicuous as an article could be on the front page. It hadn't worked. The scandal had been massive. Te Tapu was divided, half the community throwing accusations of a coverup, the other half declaring injustice and using their resources to protect the O'Regans' good name.

Liam skimmed the article, confirming what little he already knew. The bludgeoned body of a local farmer had been found at the school. After a couple of days of no leads, and interviews with friends and family, it was his own great-aunt and a boarder who lived with her – Riley's Gwen, he suspected – who came forward, pointing the finger at his great-uncle Jacob. It had nearly given Ol' Man Tom a heart attack, and when Jacob couldn't be found, the village turned into a war zone as neighbour turned upon neighbour, family member upon family member.

Some accused his great aunt of backstabbing her own husband, others turned on Ol' Man Tom and Liam's grandmother and grandfather. People accused them of harbouring a murderer or aiding in his escape. Fights broke out. If the rumours were to be believed, his family were nearly run out of town, his great-aunt in fact, Jacob's wife, disappeared not long after. Jacob's body was found about two weeks later, washed up on the riverbank. Some thought he'd killed himself. The local church turned their back on the family. It took an almost complete eradication of Jacob and the farmer he supposedly killed from town gossip and news reports before things somewhat settled again. Liam had even heard rumours that his grandfather had gone about having as many printed publications as possible about the murder destroyed.

Jacob the murderer, the suicide, the insult to the O'Regan name and Te Tapu's heritage disappeared – but for those with a long memory.

Liam turned back to his father. "Where did you get this?" he thrust the newspaper at his father, who scowled back at him. Liam narrowed his eyes. This. This was the family name they were trying to protect.

"None of your business, boy. If you've come back early to cause trouble, you're wasting your time." He took a swig of his drink before plonking it down on the side table, wiping his mouth with the back of his hand.

"A little early, don't you think, Dad?"

"Piss off." Arthur shuffled in his seat, picked up the decanter and poured himself another one.

"You went to Victoria's, didn't you? That's where you got this?"

Arthur shrugged, reached for the TV remote on the arm of his chair and switched on the TV beside Liam. An antique show was on.

"Turn it off, Dad. We need to talk."

His father ignored him.

Liam clenched his fists. He was so close to losing his temper again, a common occurrence where his father was concerned. They'd never been close, but now the division between them had become a chasm. Liam doubted they'd ever see eye to eye.

Exhaling loudly, he marched across the room, grabbed the remote from the side table just before his father went to pick it up, and deftly turned off the TV, throwing the remote onto the sofa on the other side of the room.

"We're talking about this now," he said, fighting to keep

his voice steady. "You took my ute? You took my ute to get this stupid newspaper and then tried to run someone off the road?!"

Liam closed his eyes and tried to calm his breathing. He didn't want to believe his father could really do something so heinous. He'd run Riley off the road, and over what? A stupid display that drew attention to skeletons in their family closet? After what had happened to his wife, he couldn't go much lower.

"I didn't know she was going to be on the road, but I'd seen her car about before. I just wanted to scare the nosey little whore. I've given Vicky the hard word. That woman needs to go. It's no concern of yours."

It was Liam's turn to swear. "Anna died from some idiot drunk running her off the road, and you thought this was a good idea?!" His voice rose. His fingers bit into his palms.

"Piss off! It's not any of your business, but I hadn't started drinking till I got back. And the woman was fine. 'Twas just a scare. Sending a message. Pfft."

Liam paced, his body pulsing with anger. "You *ever*, do something as stupid as that again, old man, and I will kill you." His voice came out as a growl. He felt the stirring of satisfaction when the smugness on his father's face slid a little. "Now, you tell me what the hell this is all about. What are you so bloody scared of everyone knowing? Your uncle was a murderer. We wouldn't be the first family with an ass in the family."

"Jacob never killed no one!" Liam's father spat at him. "It was a witch hunt against our family started by the two whores he lived with. He didn't kill himself either! Your great-grandfather made this town, bled for it, and I won't have our

296

name undone by some spiteful attack on our family. Grudges run deep, and this community depends on the farms around here supporting each other, looking out for each other. We don't need no Little Miss City coming here, putting trenches in these relationships and bringing up the past when it's best left buried. The boy who was killed – he was well liked, eh? He still has family here. I won't go risking our name or our business because a little whore wants to stir up shit."

"Watch who you go calling a whore." Liam folded his arms to restrain himself. He'd had enough. There was no talking to his father. All their conversations ended like this, with him leaving the room. He'd learnt nothing more than he already knew.

Liam stormed over to the door, then paused. A new thought entering his mind. He turned slowly to face his father. "Who's Gwendolyn Davies, Dad?"

The old man's visage wilted. The tumbler slipped from his hand and rolled across the floor, the amber liquid soaking the carpet.

Chapter 37 – Riley

Riley sat in her car for a while after Liam had peeled out of the car park. Nothing made sense anymore. Her shock on seeing his vehicle had left her shakier than anything else that morning.

She could tell Liam had been working hard to stifle his own anger at the discovery. He was up front, telling her he hadn't known his father had taken his ute while his own vehicle was in the shop. When Liam had left the house to come to school, his ute had been where it usually was, and he thought nothing of it.

She'd been sceptical at first. Only the night before, Arthur O'Regan was being pushed around in a wheelchair by his son. And now he was driving?

Liam had explained that too. He wasn't supposed to be driving. Not yet. He had six more weeks to go before being given the all-clear. His being in a wheelchair was for the loss of feeling he often got in his left leg. Not an issue for driving an automatic, but an issue when it came to walking or standing for periods of time. He obviously hadn't planned on doing either.

What most convinced her he was telling the truth was the

anger flaring under the surface. His green eyes flamed, and he clenched and unclenched his fists. Katrina had said their relationship was strained, and in seeing him now, she could believe it. He had gone speeding out of the car park with an almost uncontrolled fury after checking she would be alright to get home. It had taken some convincing, but he eventually had left, leaving Riley glad she wasn't Arthur O'Regan.

Everything else that had happened needed more explaining.

She'd attacked him with a plank of wood. Or else Gwen had. Did that mean she believed in ghosts now?

This beautiful little village, this quaint little country school where she'd hoped to start a new life, had fast become something out of a horror story. Now, on top of suffering from weird fainting spells and hallucinations, she had the community against her and was on thin ice with the principal. She let out a groan and fought the urge to beat her head against the steering wheel. It wouldn't do her headache any good.

Everything around her looked so peaceful. The sun was high in the too-perfect blue sky. The trees overhanging the car park were lush green and filtered the light, dappling the side of the whitewashed building with dancing shadows. A flash of wings and a magpie shot across from one tree to the next. Here she was, potentially losing her job and her mind, and yet life went on.

She needed to get home, where she could continue reading Gwen's journal. With that thought, she opened the glove compartment. The book was still there, untouched. She exhaled heavily, unsure what she had expected.

She also wanted to hook into the internet and do some research. Surely there would be something online about what happened in Te Tapu back in 1939. Maybe she would even find the same newspaper archived because she was getting the stronger and stronger sense that something in that paper was crucial to what was going on.

Feeling the unsettling sensation of eyes on her again, she glanced around. Her eyes landed on the caretaker's shed down the back of the school grounds. She expected the man with kind eyes and a low-browed cap to be staring back at her.

But no one was there. As far as she could tell, she was alone. She turned on the car, steeling herself for the drive back to her flat. Hopefully, the trip would be uneventful, and she'd have the roads to herself.

She drove slowly, more cautiously than usual, checking the rear-view mirror more frequently than it warranted to ensure no one was behind her. It put her on edge knowing someone wanted to run her off the road for an innocent classroom display.

It put her more on edge that it was Liam's dad. What was wrong with that family?

She parked outside her flat and got out of the car.

"Hi," a voice called out, and Riley turned to see Molly hanging washing on the line between their houses.

"Hi," Riley called back, giving a small wave. Molly seemed none too interested in making conversation either, it seemed, as she went back to pegging up towels and humming under her breath. Edgar weaved through Molly's feet, giving Riley a look like, *See, I can be nice*.

With her bag over her shoulder and Gwen's journal under her arm, Riley jiggled the key in the lock, feeling a gentle head butt on her shin. How had he got there so fast? she wondered, as Edgar pawed at her door.

"Shoo. Go away," she whispered, trying not to draw Molly's attention while gently pushing the cat away with her leg. Edgar was having none of it, and as soon as the door was open the cat raced inside and down the hallway.

Sighing, Riley went through to the living room, plonking her keys and purse on the coffee table and dropping the journal on the sofa. She went to the kitchen to get herself a drink. With the day she was having, a cider could be excused. She rarely drank, but today she would make an exception.

She found a bottle pushed right to the back of her fridge. For emergencies.

After grabbing a glass, she settled herself on the sofa, poured a drink and flicked through Gwen's journal until she arrived where she had left off. She skimmed for a while, scanning her eyes down the page for anything that might allude to why Riley's display was confiscated. And why Arthur O'Regan would run her off the road.

Chapter 38 – Gwen

"I have no pity! I have no pity! The more worms
writhe, the more I yearn to crush out their entrails!
It is a moral teething, and I grind with greater
energy in proportion to the increase of pain."
- ***Wuthering Heights***

The room was cold. Winter had seeped in through the walls, the ceiling, the floor, bringing with it a frost. Gwen was sure of it. As soon as she built up the courage to swing her legs out from under the bedclothes, she was certain her feet would touch ice on the floorboards.

She had woken with a start, the room still dark and shadowy, as it often was now. The days were shorter, and Gwen was rarely home during daylight hours.

She didn't know what had woken her. Her heart raced as she listened, senses alert for any hint of a threat, but the house lay silent. Her hand sought the handle of the knife under her pillow anyway, and she held it until her heart stopped racing.

Gradually her mind wandered to the day ahead of her and

the lessons she had planned for her students. Saints preserve us! She'd forgotten to get firewood for the burner in her classroom. The thought propelled her out of bed.

She almost never forgot, but lately her mind seemed to wander of its own accord, and a fogginess would sometimes take over, making simple things slip away from her. Like making sure there was firewood and kindling in the classroom ready for the fire in the morning. A job she would normally send a couple of students out to do the evening before.

She cursed again. She would have to go in early to spare the admonishment from Ms Flemming.

She fumbled her way towards the light switch, pulled it on, and then set about getting dressed as fast and quietly as possible. The house was silent, and she wanted to keep it that way. Creeping past Sarah and Jake's room to the bathroom, she avoided the familiar squeaky floorboards as best as she could, while listening for any hint of stirrings behind the closed doors. After finishing in the bathroom, she headed to the kitchen. The clock on the wall showed she was up an entire hour earlier than normal. Plenty of time to collect the wood and set up her lessons for the day.

After plopping a couple of apples from the fruit bowl into her shoulder bag, she edged open the pantry and grabbed a thick slice of bread. Something to nibble on to ease her stomach.

As a last thought, she pulled open a drawer and searched for a flashlight she had seen there before. Though it wasn't hers to take, one glance out the kitchen window told her she'd need it to find her way to school. She'd remember to slip it back into the drawer when she arrived home. No one needed to know she had taken it.

303

Gwen crept back down the hallway, holding her breath until she slipped out the front door.

The air was crisp. She pulled her cardigan tighter around her body to fend off the chill biting at her bones. Her bicycle leaned against her bedroom window. After setting her bag into the front basket, she wheeled it down the driveway, keeping to the grass verge to avoid the churning of gravel. Despite the passage of months, she was still scared of drawing Jake's attention.

On reaching the gate, Gwen mounted the bike, doing her best to juggle the flashlight in one hand so she could see where she was going. The distance to school was short, and as she had suspected, she was the first one there.

The school had a strange air to it in the dark. A palpable loneliness or sadness, Gwen thought. Though the moon was high in the sky, dark clouds shielded it. The deep shadows behind the glass windows combined with the hollow echo of her footsteps made her shiver. The walls of the school seemed alive when filled with children's laughter and little bodies running around. Now the silence was as solemn as death.

At her classroom, Gwen turned on the lights and checked if an angel had refilled the logs and kindling for the wood burner, which, of course, they hadn't. She cursed her forgetfulness and rubbed her hands together to warm her fingers, already stiff from the cold.

Her torch illuminating the ground before her, she retraced her steps and cut across the lawn. Frosted grass crunched beneath her feet and the dampness seeped through her shoes. Her torch light flicked across the backfield where the small shed stood lonely in the corner.

It was then she heard the footsteps. Her heart leapt into her throat and paralysed, she waited for a second, in case she had been imagining things. No. She was sure of it. The deep sound of heavy footsteps around the side of the building echoed in the otherwise mute night. She took a step backwards and pressed against the side of the building. Turning off her torch, she waited. Surely Ms Flemming wasn't already here? No. The headmistress had a lighter, fast-paced determination to her gait.

She was right beneath her classroom. Because she'd left her light on, it glowed through the high windows above, illuminating some of the ground before her.

Maybe someone had seen her light from the road and stopped to investigate since it was unusual for anyone to be at school so early. A farmer maybe, or a good Samaritan? Oh, she wanted to believe that, but the whirlwind of thoughts she fought to keep at bay rose to the surface. What if it was him? Jake? What if he had followed her, thinking he could catch her alone? She tried so hard to put distance between them. The very thought of being alone with him made her legs tremble, and she stifled a sob of fear.

It had been months since … since … but that didn't mean he hadn't thought of attacking her again.

Her heart pounded behind her ribs, and despite the cold, perspiration warmed the back of her neck. Oh God, no. Do not let it be Jake.

Everything fell silent. No footsteps, just the sound of blood rushing in her ears. Gwen's hand flew to her stomach as a flutter from within drew more dread. A warning. Surely. The baby was warning her.

Then she heard it. Closer. Feet nearing the corner of the

building.

The hairs on her arms rose. He was here. For whatever reason, he *had* followed her here. Maybe he knew. Maybe Sarah had given in and told him she was with child. One dark thought followed another.

She must protect herself. Oh God! What would he do to her? She had to protect herself!

Adrenalin kicked in and she lunged forward, eager to put distance between her and her pursuer. She dropped the torch as she tore across the field, trying not to slide on the icy grass as she did so.

"Gwen!" a voice called. A man's voice, muffled by the distance between them and the screaming in her own head. It *was* him! He was coming! She could think of nothing but getting to the shed. Get there and find something to protect herself with. Why hadn't she brought the knife?

The moon lent a sliver of light from between clouds to illuminate her way. From memory, she moved towards what she thought was the shed, a darker shadow than the rest.

Her name rang out again as she reached her destination. Banging her shin into the chopping block, she yelped and fought to steady herself from falling. Her breath came in gasps as her senses struggled for equilibrium. For a second, she had thought the voice belonged to someone else, and hope flared, but she pushed it aside. No. It was Jake. No one else would wish to harm her. The heavy padding of footsteps crunched across the field towards her. A weapon. She needed a weapon.

The axe. Of course!

A few tugs released it from its jail. Feeling her way around the side of the shed, she closed her ears to her name being called. No, no, no, her mind screamed.

He was closer now. She flattened her back to the side of the shed. Hugging the axe close to her chest, she tried her best to still her heart and quieten her breathing.

He was here. She could feel him, all her senses alert and ready to fight if he found her.

Why had he come?

His breathing grew louder, his footsteps mere metres away. And a fury boiled within her. How *dare* he? How could he ruin everything? Her life? Her reputation? How could he take away her one chance at happiness with Billy? He was the devil. She would not submit to his brutality.

A fire tore at her chest. A wave of anger flooded her veins. She stepped out from the shadows of the shed, axe raised. With an animalistic growl, she brought it down. It hit its target; the impact reverberating up her arms. A scream burned in her ears along with the sickening thud of her attacker's body hitting the ground, stripping the axe from her hands. And she ran, her only goal to put as much distance as she could between herself and the demon on the ground. The glow from the window at the back of her class was her sole light source.

She sped across the field, slipping on the wet grass. She scrambled onto all fours, desperate to get away in case he was still chasing her. She pushed herself back up onto her feet.

Rounding the corner of the school building, she headed towards her classroom. She'd be safe there.

No, her mind argued. How could she be? With such large glass windows, she would be a sitting duck.

What else to do?

She pulled at the light switch, slammed the door shut, and

left.

The sky was lightening, making it easier to see as she ran for her bike. After mounting it, she cycled home the best she could, squinting in the dreary morning light. Her body shook and sobs came in waves.

But beneath all that was a clarity of knowing. She knew what she had to do. She had to change. She had to clean up. And she had to go back. To school. To pretend as if nothing had happened.

Bile rose in her throat. She had killed him. Oh God! She was a murderer. Would she go to jail for this? Hang?

She stumbled off her bike into the grass on the side of the road and emptied her stomach.

What had she done?

Oh God. What had she done?

Chapter 39 – Riley

R iley sat for a moment, processing what she had read. Her hands shaking, it surprised her when a drop of water plopped onto the open page, smearing the ink. She hadn't realised she was crying.

That poor woman. She had acted in self-defence; she was sure of it. But knowing the time she was living in, who could have blamed her? Jake had ruined her. In so many ways. And now he had done it again with his own deserved demise.

Riley quickly flicked ahead. That was it. The entries had ended. She didn't know if Gwen got found out or what happened to her or the baby or her relationship with Billy. It was all too much. Too many unanswered questions. Her disappointment hit hard.

"Oh, Gwen," Riley said, wiping the tears from her eyes.

Gwen had killed Jake. Accidental or not, here was the proof. Gwen had said she would burn this book, but she never had, and now Riley held the evidence of Jake's demise. She picked up her glass of cider, not knowing what else to do, and took a sip. Her hand was shaking so much she hit the glass against her tooth as she put it to her lips.

Shit. Something just wasn't adding up. Why had Liam

called his great uncle a murderer? Gwen made no mention of him killing anyone. Nor had Liam heard Gwen's name before. Did that mean she got away with it? And why was the community so angry with her display? She would understand if they had seen it as immortalising Jake's killer.

Her head had stopped pounding from her faint, but now it acted differently.

So many questions. Too many.

Riley stood. She needed her laptop. Whatever her drive to find answers, it was clear she needed to go beyond Gwen's diary. She walked down the short hallway to her bedroom where she had taken her laptop to do some work the night before. She hadn't, of course; she'd been too upset and instead spent the night on the sofa.

It did not surprise her to find Edgar curled on the end of the bed. A growing layer of cat hair had been piling there for some time. She sighed, and he opened one eye to glare at her before closing it again, deciding apparently she was not worth his attention.

After grabbing the laptop from her nightstand, she settled on the bed with a pillow behind her as she leaned back on the wall. With her legs outstretched, her feet were within centimetres of the cat. She set the laptop on her lap.

Oh, for the love of the internet.

Her first search was for online archives of the *Te Tapu Tribune* from August 1939. No luck. It seemed other communities had sought to savour their past by donating their newspapers to museums and the likes, but she couldn't for the life of her find any from mid-August 1939.

She tried other searches. The name Gwendolyn Davies turned up in the society pages of the Alberton Guardian

310

prior to the August date, and Riley pieced together Gwen was brought up in high society, her father being a well-known banker. His obituary, a few years prior to when Gwen started teaching, made it to the front page of one edition of the paper.

Riley spent another few hours browsing all the search entries for O'Regans in Te Tapu. There were lots, from present day all the way back to the 1920s. The family certainly had made an impact not just in their area but in farming in general. It seemed Te Tapu had also won its share of awards in different arenas too, from kitsch ones like safest rural community, to the O'Regans' farm winning an award for most enterprising irrigation. Yet nothing spoke of the drama that had occurred back in 1939 and the scars it kept today.

Exhausted, Riley gave up. It was no use. When it came to Te Tapu's secrets, someone had done a good job of keeping them buried. All she had was Gwen's diary to go on. She closed the lid to the laptop and shut her eyes, startling them open again when she heard the voice.

Murderer! it screamed, making Riley's hand fly to her temples. *Murderer! He killed Billy!*

The last was said with such force and ferocity she jumped, sending the cat straight up in the air. With raised hackles, arched back, and puffed tail, Edgar let out a bloodcurdling yowl and ran from the room, leaving Riley's heart hammering in her chest.

Oh God, she thought. How was that possible?

Ask Sarah. A whisper in her ear made Riley whip her head around. Her heart felt like it would burst from her chest.

This voice had been different. She hadn't heard it before. A man's voice.

Sarah. Sarah, of course. The one name she hadn't researched. With shaky fingers, she opened her laptop again and typed in Sarah O'Regan. A long list of entries came up, so she narrowed it down by adding Te Tapu to the end.

An archived newspaper appeared, dating to 1937. Following the link, she found the announcement of the marriage of Jacob Thomas O'Regan to Sarah Elizabeth Brighton.

But what about now? Was there any chance she could still be alive? From the way Gwen had described her in her journal, if she were alive she'd be in her mid to late nineties. It was a slim shot.

Again, Riley skimmed down the list of entries for the name Sarah O'Regan. She dismissed them one by one; the person was either too young or had already passed. Her heart sank lower in her chest. Too much was stacked against her finding Sarah. For all Riley knew, she could have moved to another country, taken another name…

Sarah Brighton, she typed into the search bar. Riley scanned down the list of hits again, pausing for a second when she got to one. Rosewood Retirement Village. Two hours away, in the city. It was a possibility. Stronger than any of the others. One hundred to one, if Sarah were alive, she'd be in a retirement village or the like.

The link took her to a webpage advertising Rosewood Retirement Village, settled amongst lush native bush with independent living quarters, villas, apartments and a hospice on-site. The list of amenities the residents had access to made Riley spare a quick, disappointed glance around her own living quarters.

Scrolling through the pages, she came across an article, an interview really, where the author asked residents what they enjoyed about living at Rosewood. It was in this article she stumbled across Sarah's name. Nearing ninety-six at the time the article was written, Sarah talked about enjoying the freedom and quiet of her residence. She lived alone with on-site help and care available to her and enjoyed spending her days partaking in some of the craft classes offered in the communal area. A picture showed an old woman with papery skin and clear blue eyes, her white hair pulled back in a tight low bun, smiling amongst a background of hedges and roses. Underneath was the name Sarah Brighton. Could it be? Could this woman have known Gwen and be Liam's great aunt?

She couldn't believe she hadn't thought of that before. She could have saved herself a lot of time by asking Liam if his great aunt were still alive and if he knew where to find her. True, she wasn't convinced she'd be met with anything less than another yelling match and derision towards her nosiness into his family history.

Riley's hackles bristled. Well, who else was looking into Gwen's history, or was she just an unfortunate side note in the whole thing? Someone to be damaged and thrown away in the O'Regan family saga.

No.

Gwen had come to her. Sought her out for God knows what reason.

And now there was a new voice.

She needed to see this thing through to the end.

Chapter 40 – Riley

Riley was napping when the phone rang. It jarred her from shadowy dreams and muddled thoughts, and it took her a moment to realise where she was.

Her laptop was closed beside her on the bed. A furry lump had cushioned itself up against her legs. She guessed the cat had come back. Even with the curtains open, the light outside had dulled, and the corners of the room were already becoming dusky. She had to search for her phone, finding it on the bed. Number unknown. Normally, she wouldn't have bothered to answer but, in her half-asleep haze, she did so without thinking.

"Hello," she said, realising how groggy her voice sounded.

Silence filled the other end of the line, then finally, "Riley? It's Liam."

She sat upright, alert. She switched on the lamp on her side table and checked the time on her alarm clock. Just past five in the afternoon.

"Are you there?" his deep voice said again.

"How did you get my number?" she asked, genuinely surprised. He was the last person she expected to be hearing from.

"Victoria," he said. "And before you say anything, she's not in the habit of giving out teacher numbers, I had to tell her it was important and—"

Riley waited. Whatever he wanted to say, he was obviously wrestling with it.

"—and promise to keep my attitude in check," he said, sounding defeated.

The corners of her mouth twisted a little at his admission. Thank you, Victoria.

"I was hoping we could meet up. I want to apologise, and I think there're some things we need to talk about."

Riley froze. Why the change? she wondered. She knew it had upset him learning his father had tried to run her off the road but … to meet up?

"I'm in Riccarston," she said, not completely sure if he knew she lived out of Te Tapu.

"I know. I'm here now. I had some things to do, and I was hoping you could meet me."

Edgar was looking at her with one eye. Judging.

What was the worst that could happen? Maybe she could learn more about Gwen and what happened; she was certain a big chunk of the story was missing.

She agreed, and Liam named a place not too far from where she lived. A newly opened little cafe bar. They'd meet in half an hour.

As soon as she hung up, Riley's stomach flipped with nervousness. It seemed so important suddenly that she look good and was calm and prepared for any eventuality. Oh, hell, she thought. She really didn't think she could deal with any more drama. And what if Liam wanted to meet her to warn her off again, to tell her to mind her own business?

315

She ran a comb through her hair and tied it back into a ponytail with an elastic, added a little concealer to the dark shadows under her eyes and gave her teeth a quick brush. After changing into a clean pair of jeans and one of her favourite flowy blouses, she grabbed her jacket from a hook behind the closet door. If she was going to meet him on time, she had little time to do much else. But she gave herself a cursory glance-over in the full-length mirror, anyway. He had already seen her far too many times at her worst, often prone after fainting, so this had to be an improvement.

Oh God, she thought. What am I getting myself into?

It was a nice little bar and bistro. Ambient coffee-house music and warmth from an open fire met her on entering. This was not the type of bar people came to for getting drunk and causing a ruckus. From the exposed brick walls and abstract paintings, low hanging lights and copper fittings, it had an air about it of somewhere artists and authors and up-and-coming avant-gardes would come to get inspired or meet up with other creatives.

There were only a few patrons. As if to affirm her judgement, a young man with a goatee and hair pulled back in a bun worked away on his laptop at one table, a couple snuggled together in a booth near the back of the room, and some bar staff hovered behind the bar.

The only other person, impossible to miss, was Liam. He had claimed another booth, sitting so his back was to the door. His height and broad shoulders gave him away instantly, and Riley cursed as her nonchalance was betrayed by a gentle fluttering in her chest. One of the bartenders caught her eye and gave her a nod of his head, and she countered by gesturing towards Liam's booth.

"Hi," she said awkwardly, standing in front of him, not knowing what else to do but to give him a small smile.

"Hi," he said back, looking sheepish. He shuffled across his seat and stood, as gentlemanly as Riley had ever seen, gesturing for her to take the seat opposite him, which she did. "Can I get you a drink?" he offered.

"A lemon, lime and bitters, please." She needed to keep her head around him.

He left for the bar, and she took a moment to take a few deep breaths. God, she felt like she was on a first date, and she scolded herself. This was for Gwen, she reminded herself.

He came back with a glass in one hand for her, and a tall glass of something else for himself.

"Rum and coke?" she asked.

"Just coke," he said. "I don't drink."

For whatever reason, his response surprised her. Beyond that, she didn't know what to say. She sipped her drink, waiting for him to break the ice.

"I need to apologise for today," he said.

Riley put her glass down, and with her hands under the table began twisting her bracelet.

"You already have," she reminded him.

"For all of it, though. My father has … issues…"

She would not argue with that.

"He was trying to scare you – which he shouldn't have done – and took it too far. He should never have been so reckless. If there's any damage to your car, let me know and I'll get it dealt with."

"It's fine," she said. There had been no damage, and other than scaring the bejesus out of her, no harm done.

"And I want to apologise for my attitude towards you." His

eyes shifted uncomfortably.

Riley guessed he rarely found himself in a situation where he needed to apologise. Dismissing it with a nod, she asked about his head.

He reached his fingers up, touching where the butterfly plasters still held. "It's fine," he said.

"Good. Then, I think we're even."

After a second, he smiled a wide smile. It made his entire face light up, and Riley's pulse sped up, her eyes mesmerised by the way the light danced in his eyes. She'd never seen him smile like that before.

Trying to regain her composure, she picked up her glass and took another sip.

"I went and saw my father after I left you at school."

His expression grew serious, and Riley watched him intently, trying to work out what was coming next.

"He had the newspaper from your display."

The hairs on her arms prickled.

"He paid a visit to Victoria that morning. She'd taken it all home with her, and I guess my father thought to take it on himself to get it back. Meeting you on the road, I guess, was serendipitous on his part."

Not so much for her, she thought.

"You said he was trying to scare me. Why?"

Liam swallowed. "Have you actually looked at the newspaper?" he asked.

"I skimmed it," she said honestly. "I would never have included it in the display if I had thought anything sensitive was in there."

It was his turn to watch her closely now, and she wondered for a second if he believed her. He twisted in his seat and opened a satchel she hadn't noticed lying on the seat beside him. He pulled out a folded newspaper and handed it to her.

Te Tapu Tribune, it read. Dated August 31, 1939.

She examined the front page again. Taking her time. There were articles about the exportation of textiles, celebration of the Te Tapu Young Farmers Women's Committee turning twenty years old, and then in the bottom corner – as if an after-thought – was an article headed: "Murder on school grounds implicates Te Tapu's founding family".

Oh Christ, she thought. How had she missed that? "God, I'm so sorry, I didn't even notice…" Heat rose to her cheeks.

"Read it," he said.

"Police were called to Te Tapu School early yesterday morning to investigate the suspected murder of a local farmer. Master Harris and Master McLaughlin were collecting wood and kindling for their classroom's wood burner on arrival at school when they came across the body of local farmer William MacKenzie. Few details have yet to be made public, including why Mr MacKenzie was at the school at this time. Police are examining all evidence and leads. One source close to the case has shared that Jacob O'Regan, son of Te Tapu's founding father, Thomas O'Regan, and heir to the O'Regan empire, has been named on the suspect list. As this goes to print, he has not yet been located.

"The O'Regan family have declined all comments."

Riley gasped. No, it wasn't possible. Had they got the name wrong?

She met Liam's eyes and gently shook her head. "I didn't know."

"This murder," Liam started, "near tore Te Tapu apart. My great grandfather was well loved in the community, with many deeply loyal to him. People were furious the O'Regan name was being pulled through the mud, regardless of what they thought of my great uncle Jacob. People went as far as leaving death threats for the reporters and the newspaper printers if they continued printing about this story.

"This newspaper became really hard to find, as most copies were destroyed. Police were said to be paid off to keep things quiet, but in the end, they named Jacob the murderer, and my family's standing in the community fell considerably. It took a long time for us to build up our reputation again. My father's a loyalist to our family name. It's no excuse, but this community ... it doesn't forget easily." His shoulders slumped slightly.

Who would she be to hold his family name against him?

"I don't understand," she said. "This says it was William MacKenzie who was killed?"

It hit her then, seconds before the voice screamed in her head: *Murderer! He killed Billy!*

This time it was punctuated with a sob. Riley squeezed her eyes shut, waiting for the pain to subside. And it did. But still in the background she could hear the echo of sobbing, and it chilled her.

"Billy..." she whispered.

She raised her eyes and saw Liam looking at her, head to the side. Riley poked the paper with her finger, tears welling again.

"This name – William MacKenzie – this is Billy. But ... I don't think Jake killed him. I think it was Gwen..."

A scream tore through her body: *No, no, no!*

Riley placed her hands over her temples to hold herself together until the screaming ceased. After the longest few seconds of her life, the voice left completely and with it all her energy.

Liam's hand reached across the table, touching her lightly on the arm.

"Riley? Riley? Are you okay?"

She pulled her hands away from her head and could feel tears sliding down her cheeks. She nodded, and he passed her the napkin that came with his drink.

"What is going on, and who is Gwen? Who is Billy?"

She told him about the journal then, what she knew about Gwen and her relationship with Liam's relatives, and her relationship with Billy.

"I don't know what's happening," she said. "It's like, sometimes I can feel her here, with me, in my head even. I really don't think it was me attacking you. I think it was her, and only because she thought you were Jake." She held up a hand. "I know, I know, it sounds ridiculous."

Liam waited patiently. If he thought she was crazy, he didn't let on.

"Gwen thinks she killed Jake, and yet everyone else thinks Jake killed Billy, and what I don't know is what happened to Jake?" She wiped at another tear that had escaped and sniffed.

Liam put his glass down. "He washed up from the river two weeks later," he said. "With rocks in his pockets."

Riley's jaw dropped.

"If my father had his way, Jake would be scrubbed from the family tree. It was bad enough he was known as a drunk in his own time and then add to it a murderer who committed suicide to escape being caught. And now, you're saying he was a rapist too. Well, it certainly dims the light on the O'Regan legacy."

"Your legacy too," Riley whispered.

He narrowed his eyes. "I'm not my past or that of my family's, just as I'm sure you wouldn't want to be remembered for your past either," he said coolly.

Justin sprung to mind, and Riley instantly regretted having misspoken. She cursed silently. It wasn't entirely what she had meant, either; she had hoped to get him on side to talk with his great aunt, if in fact she was still alive.

"I'm sorry, I didn't mean it like that," she said. "I want to know what happened to Gwen. It sounds like she was more entangled with the O'Regans than anyone will admit, but for good or bad, no one is telling her story. So much of the truth seems unspoken," she said, and took a deep breath. She felt weird asking, yet the feeling she needed to do it for Gwen was too strong. "Is your great-aunt still alive?"

Liam's forehead furrowed again.

"Sarah. Jake's wife? Do you know what happened to her? Is she still alive?"

Liam's eyes widened and he shook his head. "After what happened with Jake, she vanished from the family record. They had no children. Rumours say she was the first to point the finger at Jake being the murderer. No one talks about her. I guess I had always assumed somewhere along the line she had died."

"I did some research," Riley said.

Liam raised an eyebrow and took another sip of his drink.

"It could be really far-fetched, but if she's alive, I want to talk to her. I think she'll know what happened, for real. To both Jake and Gwen. Gwen boarded with them, so it makes sense."

"I don't even know if she's alive," Liam said, massaging his forehead.

"I know. I searched the net, and there's a woman who goes by Sarah Brighton - which was her maiden name – who would be roughly her age, in a retirement village a couple of hours from here."

Liam said nothing.

"I want to go visit her. Tomorrow." Riley bit her tongue. She knew it was a long shot, but it felt right.

When she didn't get a reaction right away, she jumped in again. "I know it's not my business, not my family, but Gwen means something to me. There must have been a reason I found her diary and—"

"I'm coming with you," he said, stunning Riley into silence. "If she's really my great-aunt, I want to meet her. I'm tired of my family's secrets."

Riley nodded her head slightly, the corners of her mouth quirking upward. Maybe, just maybe, she had the enigmatic Liam O'Regan on-side.

She lifted her glass to her lips, a silent salute to Gwen.

They left early the next morning. Liam picked her up since her house was on the way. She was thankful it was Sunday and the traffic wasn't too heavy.

It had surprised Riley when Liam had told her he wanted to go with her. But now as she sat passenger in his ute with him humming along quietly to a tune on the radio, she was thankful. The last few days had taken their toll, and the gentle purr of the engine made her drowsy. She found her eyes closing of their own accord and then fluttering open, hoping he hadn't noticed.

"I can turn the radio off, you know. If you want to sleep." He said it without turning to her.

Her cheeks heated. "It's okay," she said. "I wasn't really

323

sleeping…"

They said little until they had arrived in Alberton. Riley hadn't really known what to say. Part of her was nervous this was a colossal waste of time; they'd get there, and the woman before them would be a stranger.

"How are we going to do this?" Liam asked as he turned off the motorway on the instructions of the GPS.

"I guess the first thing is to find out if it is our Sarah," Riley replied

"Our Sarah?"

"Well … Gwen's Sarah. Your great-aunt. And then, maybe we just be upfront and ask for the truth."

Liam shrugged his shoulders. "Could work, I guess."

It was another ten minutes traversing side streets and roundabouts before they came to a billboard on the side of the road announcing Rosewood Retirement Village.

Liam slowed and pulled up the driveway.

It was beautiful with its immaculately kept gardens and a prevailing feeling of peace. Cute white villas with dusky pink roofs and white picket fences spread out, true to the pictures she had seen on the website. A couple sat on a park bench under a tree nearby, and roses of different colours and varieties saluted their entrance on both sides. The driveway ended at a large two-storey building with a mostly brick exterior and Greek columns leading to the front entrance, where two automatic glass sliding doors stood. A car park was visible off to the right, so Liam veered the vehicle in that direction and squeezed it between two smaller vehicles that hadn't done well to stay between their lines.

God, she hoped this was worth it.

Riley's nerves felt raw.

Liam killed the engine. He sat there for a moment, saying nothing, his hands still on the steering wheel and thought lines on his forehead.

"Are you ready?" she asked, remembering Liam could be potentially meeting a family member for the first time today.

"Yeah," he said, giving his shoulders a shake before climbing out of the ute. Whatever he was thinking, he obviously wasn't ready to share it, not with her anyway.

They made their way back to the front entrance, entering through the glass doors into a large foyer, where pastel landscape paintings dotted the walls and two-seater sofas sat on either side of the room.

A few people walked past, many likely residents. Some smiled in their direction; others walked with purpose as if they didn't exist. At the end of the room resided a counter area. A young man sat, eyes glued to his computer, while a woman clasped her hands on the countertop and greeted them with a wide smile.

Riley couldn't help thinking this place appeared more like a hotel reception than what she had expected of an assisted living and retirement facility.

"Welcome to Rosewood. How may I help you?" the woman asked. She wore a pink pinstriped blouse. Her mousey brown hair was styled in a short perm, which added years to a face that looked surprisingly youthful.

"Hi," Liam said, taking charge. "I'm actually here to visit my aunt, Sarah Brighton."

Riley's eyes widened with surprise, and she fought to regain her composure. She hadn't known what he was going to say, but she hadn't expected that.

"Oh," the woman said, also clearly surprised. "I didn't know

Sarah had any relatives. Is she expecting you?"

Riley and Liam exchanged a glance.

Honesty, Riley thought. Right now, they needed honesty, or the closest to it.

"Well, to be honest…" Riley said, watching the pinched expression on Liam's face. "We didn't know Sarah was alive until recently. Maybe if you call ahead, you can let her know that her great-nephew Liam O'Regan is here and his friend Gwen Davies."

Okay, so the last bit had been a lie. But if it was the right Sarah, then hearing the name would hopefully spark her interest, or else Riley had just cost them a two-hour drive for nothing.

"Oh," the woman said. Then, picking up the receiver of her phone, she dialled through.

"Hi Sarah, this is Matilda at the front desk. We have a couple of visitors for you. Mmm, yes, I know. They said their names were—" She held her hand over the receiver for a second, waiting to be told again.

"Liam O'Regan and Gwen Davies," Riley repeated.

Matilda shared this over the phone. "Sarah? Sarah? Are you there?"

There was a pause, and Riley's hand clasped her bracelet. Please, please, please let it be the right Sarah, she silently pleaded.

"Oh good," Matilda finally said. "Yes. Liam says he is your nephew?"

Riley spared a glance at Liam. If he was nervous, he was disguising it really well. Riley wished she could do the same.

After a few more mmm's and ah's on the phone, Matilda hung up the receiver.

"Okay then," she said, turning back towards them. "Let me get you a map." She pulled out a brochure from under the counter and opened it before them so they could see a map of the complex.

After a few short instructions, with map in hand, they were on their way. The map had been unnecessary. Despite the large complex, everything was well signposted, and it didn't take them long to find Sarah's apartment, 24B.

Riley and Liam paused at the door. Riley patted her handbag at her side. Inside she had placed Gwen's journal, not sure if it would be useful or not.

"Ready?" Liam asked, turning to her.

Riley nodded, and Liam pressed the buzzer on the door.

A woman somewhere in her sixties opened the door. Right away, Riley recognised her as a nurse. She wore floral patterned scrubs, and the name tag on her chest read Bridget.

"You must be Liam and Gwen," the woman said. "Come in, come in. I'm just leaving, but Sarah knows I'm a button press away if she needs anything."

Before they replied, the woman hurried away down the corridor.

Liam held the door open for Riley to enter first. It was a small space. They had walked straight into a small kitchen opening to a sitting area. A door off to the left and a door off to the right suggested one must be a bedroom and the other a bathroom. Riley noticed the old woman right away. She sat in an armchair, staring out of the window overlooking a beautiful rose garden. A familiar theme for the residence, Riley thought. Her wispy white hair had been pulled back at the nape of her neck. A soft grey throw lay over her lap, covering her legs, and a cup of coffee steamed from the side table beside her. Liam closed the door behind them and came to stand beside Riley.

Slowly, the woman's attention turned to them. She took a moment to study them both. First Riley; she seemed to take in every bit of her, then her attention landed on Liam. With a sharp intake of breath, her hand flew to her mouth.

"Hi, Miss Brighton—"

"You look just like him," she said, studying Liam some more. "Except your eyes, your eyes belong to someone else."

Liam and Riley glanced at each other again. Riley was unsure what to say, but this could be a good sign.

Shaking herself from her reverie, and with sharp analysis she continued, "You, however, *you* are nothing like Gwen," she said to Riley before cackling as if she had made a joke.

Pins and needles crossed her back. She knew Gwen! Oh, thank God.

"A pot of coffee is on the bench, and cups are above the stove. You can help yourself if you want, then join me." She pointed to the two-seater opposite her. Riley nervously went to sit down while Liam went into the kitchen to make himself a cup as if he were completely at home.

"Do you want one?" he asked Riley, and she shook her head, sitting on the edge of the sofa, twisting the bracelet on her wrist.

"Who are you really?" Sarah asked, regarding Riley.

Despite her age, she seemed very in charge of her mental faculties.

"My name is Riley Cooper. I'm sorry for lying to you, I just needed to know if you were Gwen's Sarah."

The old woman's forehead crinkled some more.

"And this really is Liam O'Regan. We think he is your great

nephew," Riley said, aware her nerves were showing.

Liam came and plonked himself down beside Riley, and she shuffled over slightly. The whole situation had made her nervous, and Liam's leg pressing against hers didn't make it any easier.

"You really do look like him, you know," Sarah said scrutinising, Liam again. "He was handsome in his own way."

"Do you mean Jake?" Riley asked.

"Um-hmm." Sarah picked up her mug of coffee, blew on it a few times and took a sip.She placed it back down, her hand shaking a little as she did so. "Why are you here?" Sarah asked, past wasting time.

Riley took a deep breath and opened her handbag, pulling out Gwen's journal. She rested it on her knee. "Because of this," she said.

Sarah's brow crinkled some more, and a wateriness showed in her eyes.

"Gwen's journal," the old woman breathed. "I'd forgotten all about it."

"Gwen thought she'd killed Jake," Riley said, noticing how quiet Liam was beside her, "but the newspaper said it was Billy who was killed."

"I was brought up to believe Jake was a murderer," Liam said, finally finding his voice, "and that he killed himself. It was taboo to talk about it. I didn't even know you were still alive. And then, thanks to Riley, Gwen's name kept coming up and – some things aren't adding up."

A stream of emotions played across Sarah's face. "It was so long ago…" Her voice cracked.

"Yes, but I don't think anyone's really moved on, and … and—" Riley didn't know how to say the next part, not without sounding crazy, "-and ... I think Gwen can't move on until the truth is told."

The old woman's eyes grew large. "Gwen?" she repeated. "The truth was what killed Gwen in the end. There is no doubt about it. And it was Jake who set her on that path. He at least got what he deserved."

Chapter 41 – Sarah

S arah woke with a start. Her face ached, and she could feel with her tongue that a tooth was wiggly. She had fallen asleep on the ground, leaning up against the desk, the rifle laid across her lap. As far as she could tell, Jake hadn't come home yet from the tavern, which at least was a blessing.

She wasn't sure when she had passed out. From the faint light coming through the crack in the curtains, however, she could tell it was already a new day. God, please don't let him have gotten to Gwen yet, she prayed.

The house was silent. She tiptoed down the hall to listen at the door of their bedroom. There was still a chance he was here, and she didn't want to do anything to draw his attention before she had seen to Gwen and they'd come up with a plan. Pressing her ear gently to the door, she held her breath.

Nothing.

If Jake were home, she would at least have heard snoring, she was sure of it. But to be safe, she crept to Gwen's door. Quietly turning the knob, she opened the door and snuck in.

"Gwen. It's me, Sarah," she said, hoping it wouldn't startle Gwen into making too much noise. But no response came. In fact, from what she could make of the bed in the dim light, it was empty. Sarah reached for the light switch and surveyed the room. She had already left. Sarah spared a glance at the alarm clock that sat on the bedside table. Gwen didn't normally leave so early.

Oh, please don't let Jake have gotten to her, she thought. She plonked herself down on the end of bed. Things were bad. They needed a plan, and for the life of her, Sarah couldn't think of one. She gingerly reached her hand up to the side of her face and winced. It was bruised. How bad, she wasn't sure, but it was a tribute to how angry Jake had been that he'd hit her where others might see.

Gwen had still been at school when Billy had turned up on the doorstep the day before. Sarah suspected Billy had purposefully chosen the time. Seeing his face then, jaw clenched, face pale and eyes rimmed red, she had known right away something was wrong. The intensity of anger coming from him had made her momentarily sway on her feet. Billy had always seemed such a calm man and to see him turn up bristling with anger could mean only one thing.

Without even thinking, she had shaken her head. "You need to leave," she had tried to say as she attempted to close the door on him, but he'd been quicker and the door caught on his boot, which he'd lodged in the doorway.

"Where is he, Sarah?" he'd demanded.

And she couldn't tell him. Words escaped her, and it was taking all her effort to stay upright. Somehow, he must have found out.

Jake had heard, though. He stormed out of his study with a loud, "Who is it, Sarah?"

On seeing Billy, he immediately ducked back into his room

and came out with his .22, pointed straight at Billy, marching down the hallway.

Not knowing what to do, Sarah stepped in front of Billy and put her hands on his chest. "You have to leave," she whispered, finding her voice. She shook all over. "Please."

She tried pushing him towards the door, but he stood his ground. One look in his eyes, and she could tell he was going nowhere. He was like a wounded animal with nothing to live for but to fight or die. Sarah's heart thumped in her chest.

"Get out of the way, woman. If he wants to barge into my house uninvited, then I can shoot him for trespassing."

Sarah spun on her feet to face Jake. Pleading had never worked with him before when he'd been drinking or was in one of his moods, yet she couldn't think what other choice she had.

"Please, Jake. Put the gun down. Billy was just leaving." She spun back to Billy, begging with her eyes, but with a certain restraint he pushed her gently aside and strode down the hall to meet Jake undeterred by the rifle pointed at him.

Sarah tried to flatten herself against the wall. Oh, God, please don't let this be about what I think it is, she thought.

"I'm warning you, you Irish prick," Jake growled.

Billy stood only a foot away from the gun's barrel. His fists clenched and unclenched in fury. He swore then and spat at Jake's feet.

Jake's eyes blazed red, and Sarah started praying. One of them would end up dead if this continued. The air rippled with tension, and her heart thundered in her chest.

"I told you," Billy said, his voice choking up, "I told you … if you ever laid a finger on Gwen…" his own finger stretched in the air in front of Jake's face before clenching again into a fist.

"You … you…"

Through her own moist eyes, Sarah, who was now huddled on the floor as close to the wall as she could get, could see Billy's form shaking, anger and devastation playing out in waves, and Sarah knew. Somehow, he had found out Gwen was pregnant.

Oh, Gwen, if you told him… she thought, you stupid, stupid girl!

She had been focusing so strongly on the shaking of Billy's shoulders she wasn't sure how she'd missed it, but Billy pulled back his arm and lunged forward, swinging his fist at Jake's face, making Jake stumble and drop the gun. Though it hadn't looked to be a hard hit, Sarah could see the surprise on Jake's face as he spat out a mouthful of blood.

Billy didn't let up. He hit him again and again, until for the first time, Sarah had felt something lighten in her. Her husband was curled in a ball on the ground, his arms up, trying to protect his face, his knees curled into his chest. Part of Sarah wanted to turn away, part of her wanted to yell out – "Kill him, Billy! Kill him!" She did neither, but watched as the man who beat and raped her – who'd raped Gwen – lay a blithering coward on the ground. Billy took aim with his foot over and over into the small of his back, then the softness of his belly, until suddenly he stopped and fell to his knees, his back to her, his body heaving with sobs. And her heart broke for this man. On wobbly legs she pulled herself up, willing down the nausea from the blood splattering the floorboards. She used the wall to steady herself as she made her way to Billy.

Tentatively she crouched beside him, refusing to look at

334

her husband, who at some point must have passed out from pain – oh, please let him be dead, she prayed – and placed her hands on Billy's shoulders. At first, he recoiled, but then spent, his shoulders slumped, and the sobs came harder.

"Leave, Billy. You have to leave now," she whispered in his ear. Whatever the repercussions, she would deal with them; it was enough that she'd seen her bully turn into a whimpering mess, but no matter the circumstance, she did not want Gwen to see Billy so broken.

"Please, Billy." She swung his arm over her shoulder and tried what she could to make him stand. He obliged her and rubbed his face with a calloused hand.

"I'm so sorry, Sarah," he said, and Sarah could tell he meant it. "Did you know?" He asked her, slowly hobbling down the hallway. "Did you?"

She gave a short nod and saw something else break in his face.

"Don't tell Gwen," he said. "I'll tell her. But you and her, do you have somewhere to stay? You need to leave." They had reached the door now, and Sarah could hear unintelligible mutterings from further down the hall.

"I'll be fine," she said. "And I'll look after Gwen, but you, you need to leave. If he calls the police, you'll be no use to Gwen, anyway."

It worked. He swayed back and forth for a moment, obviously weighing his options, and then left, throwing his leg over his bike, and skidding on the gravel in his hurry to get away.

Down the other end of the hall came the sound of movement. She needed to hide the gun.

Adrenalin kicked in. Jake was still writhing on the floor,

335

the gun lying up against the skirting board a foot or so away.

She ran down the hall, kicking at it with her foot so it slid further away from him. She jumped, missing his outstretched hand that went to grab her ankle as he hissed and swore at her. Quickly, she bent down and picked it up – just as his foot swung out at her, hitting her in the jaw. She fell to her hands and knees while he tried to lever himself up onto his. The gun was heavier than she expected, but using it almost like a walking stick, she leaned on it to get to her feet before sprinting back down the hall towards the only room she knew that had a lock on the inside: Jake's study.

As she reached the door, she looked over her shoulder. He had pulled himself upright, and leaning heavily on the wall, was staggering towards her. She slammed the door shut and pushed across the deadbolt. She then went around securing the windows. It was possible he would smash them in, but she wondered if he'd find the effort worth it in the state he was in. More likely, he'd take off to the tavern to dull his beaten pride with liquor.

Sarah stood vigilant. She had learnt from her daddy how to shoot a rifle, though it didn't mean she'd ever wanted to. Yet she held it at the ready anyway, perched against his desk.

Once the banging of his fists and his swearing died down, she allowed herself to breathe more fully. Her mind swirled. Prayers came thick and fast. Please, God, don't let Gwen come home early. Please don't let her cross paths with Jake. Why, oh, why couldn't he have died? She would have come up with an excuse to protect Billy. He had deserved none of this.

When the door slammed and the engine of his pickup truck rumbled, she allowed herself to relax. The squeal of his tyres signalled he had left. Her hands still shook, and she found herself Jake's opened bottle of whiskey sitting on the desk. Skipping using a glass, she took a few mouthfuls, hoping it would give her courage and clear her mind. A few more to dull the ache of her jaw. More to dull the ache in her head and heart. Until eventually she fell into a deep, dreamless sleep.

She missed Gwen coming home completely.

Chapter 42 – Gwen

"By this curious turn of disposition I have gained
the reputation of deliberate heartlessness; how
undeserved, I alone can appreciate."
- Wuthering Heights

J ake's pickup had gone, which of course she knew it
would be. She'd missed seeing it at the school, but it
had been dark, and her mind had been so focused on
fleeing…

No lights were on in the house, though the sun was now
steadily rising from behind it. Oh God. Oh God. She had to
get back to school. It wouldn't look good to be late.

Her thoughts crashed together, each bringing a tidal wave
of emotion and overwhelm. Yet if the house was dark, Sarah
must not yet be awake. Sarah was usually the first one up.

Gwen needed to get inside, tidy up and leave again.

She dumped her bike at the end of the driveway in the long
grass. It would be quieter for her to proceed on foot. She
crept through the grass, her toes cold from the damp, her

legs shaking. On reaching the doorstep, she studied herself properly. She would need to take her shoes off; not only were they wet, but they were also muddy from where she had slipped.

There were other dark stains too on her skirt. She tentatively touched a mark with her fingertips, wondering if it was mud, and then seeing the same splatters on her hands and a few up her arms the realisation hit her with pure horror, making her legs almost crumple under her.

Oh, good God; it was blood!

Blood.

She turned her hands over, squinting in the dawning light. Blood. His blood. She had killed him. Or else she hadn't, and he was on his way right this second to exact his revenge. Shaking, she tried to calm her breath and gently turned the door handle. The door squeaked on its hinges, and Gwen winced. Please don't wake up, please don't wake up, she thought.

The hall was dark, the house quiet. Gingerly, she crept along the hallway, thankful her room was the first on the left. She turned the doorknob, holding her breath as she did so, and stepped into the room. With a sharp intake of breath, she stifled a scream. A wraith of a figure sat on the end of the bed, waiting for her. At first, she thought it a ghost. And then, as her eyes adjusted to the dim light, she saw the pale figure of Sarah staring back at her with wide eyes, mirroring her but with two hands pressed to her mouth.

Like a deer in headlights, Gwen didn't know what to do. She stood paralysed until Sarah's hands fell to her lap and she stood up.

"Did he hurt you?" she whispered, her eyes following up

339

and down Gwen's figure.

Gwen nodded, then shook her head, unsure of the question, before an onslaught of sobs erupted and she threw herself onto the bed, trying to stifle the sound.

A moment passed before Gwen felt Sarah move to her side, gently stroking her back, trying to calm her.

"He's not back yet," she said, "but we'll need to do something. You won't be safe here."

Confused, Gwen tried to sit up, hiccoughing whilst swallowing her sobs. "He's dead," she whispered.

Sarah pulled her hand back, staring at her intently, confusion marring her features.

"He's dead," Gwen choked out again. "I killed Jake." Then she bent in two and spilled her stomach onto the cold floorboards.

Sarah grabbed her by the shoulders, making her face her while Gwen tried to glance away, wiping her mouth with the back of her hand.

"What do you mean you killed him?"

To the best of her ability, Gwen tried to fill her in. She wasn't sure; she didn't know if he was dead. Oh God, what if he wasn't? What if he was just injured and came back for her, or told the police what she had done? A fresh wave of sobs erupted.

"Stop it!" Sarah said sternly. "Stop crying, we need a plan."

Gwen felt the short, sharp slap as Sarah's fingers swiped her cheek, stunning Gwen to attention.

"I need to get back to work," Gwen said, clarity coming back in a hurry. "I need to be there to meet the children. Oh God, we have photos today. Look at mc!" Her voice rose in panic.

"Okay," said Sarah, taking charge in a way Gwen had never seen before.

What had happened to the meek woman-child she was so used to?

"We're going to clean you up. You're going to pretend nothing happened, do you understand?" She waited for Gwen to nod before proceeding. "Did anyone see you at school?"

"I don't think so…" Gwen replied. Everything was such a blur, she didn't remember.

Sarah had her explain again where the body was. Content it might go undiscovered for a while, Sarah told her it was crucial she acted as if she knew nothing about it; she must act surprised, shocked even, when it is found. And she, Sarah, would be her alibi if she were questioned. She would say she had been home with her the entire morning.

Oh God, there'd be a manhunt, Gwen thought. She could lie, yes. But she'd slip up, she knew it.

The reality of the situation hit her. She needed to get back to school, to pretend nothing had happened. She had a job to do.

Then Sarah said the one thing Gwen had not expected but longed to hear.

"We're safe now," she said. "If he really is dead, then we're free."

And amongst the shock and fear, she felt a speck of lightness growing inside.

Maybe Sarah was right, and they were free.

Chapter 43 – Riley

"Do you want another cuppa?" Liam asked, getting up from the love seat.

Riley shook her head again; she was riveted by what Sarah had told them so far.

"No thank you, dear," Sarah said, holding her cup out for Liam to take to the kitchen.

It wasn't so much what she heard that had Riley enthralled; she knew about the murder from Gwen's diary entry, but hearing it – in person – in such a calm manner how he had attacked Billy and threatened Sarah … it left her speechless. She had to remind herself even though she was hearing Sarah's side for the first time now, it had happened such a very long time ago.

She bristled with impatience, waiting for Liam to make himself another drink.

"So she really went back to school and pretended nothing had happened?" Riley asked, wondering how a person could do such a thing.

"Yes," Sarah said, nodding her head. "Although I'm sure it wasn't easy for her. Gwen had this talent, you see. When she needed to, she could totally dismiss something right in front of her, lock it up in her mind and pretend it hadn't happened. To such a degree, in fact, I think she came to believe it.

"We hurried to clean her up, and I sent her on her way. I suspect she was late, though if Ms Flemming gave her a hard time about it, she never said.

"I set about tidying the house then. When they found his body, I suspected it would only be a matter of time before the police were knocking on the door. It worried me too, what the implication would be for Billy if they found out about their squabble.

"I remember little of that day other than waiting on tenterhooks for a knock on the door, which in the end never came."

Liam plonked himself back down on the sofa, another steaming cup of coffee in his hand.

Riley tried to read his face. He had said little the whole time. This was his family history they were talking about, and his expression had largely remained unchanged. She wondered what it would be like to hear such things about her own family.

Finally, he spoke. "It wasn't Jake who Gwen had killed, was it?" Liam placed his mug on the coffee table and, with hands clasped together on his knees, he waited.

"No, Gwen didn't kill Jake," Sarah said, a flash of regret flitting across her face.

"Gwen told me later of when she'd first noticed our mistake. Ms Flemming had organised a photographer to come to school that morning to photograph the two classes of students. It was as she was standing with her class, outside her classroom, that everything came crashing down.

"The camera man stood with his back to the road. Gwen

343

had been focused on him when she saw Jake's pickup pull up by the school gates. At first, she was confused, thinking maybe it was me. Then Jake, worse for wear from his altercation with Billy the day before and a hard night drinking, came stomping towards them. She said it was like seeing a ghost. In fact, at first she thought she *was* looking at a ghost."

Riley shivered. She knew the photograph; it was the one in her display, and Sarah's description aptly described the expression she'd seen on Gwen's face.

Sarah picked up her story. "He was limping and stumbling, yelling and cursing, and it took her a moment to realise what he was saying. The headmistress tried to intervene and started yelling, trying to get all the students to return to the classroom, but Gwen felt paralysed. She was no doubt still suffering from shock. And to make matters worse, Jake had eyes just for her. He called her all sorts of names, threatened her with horrible things, and then demanded to know where Billy was hiding. He was going to kill him, he said. The photographer and his assistant tried to step in, and for their bravado, they were attacked."

Thoughts spun around Riley's head.

"So it was Gwen who killed Billy," she whispered, knowing it already, but still feeling uneasy about it. Then something inside her shifted. She felt the slip; the pressure in her head returned.

Liam looked at her strangely, and Riley found it hard to breathe.

She turned to Sarah, whose eyes glistened with unshed tears.

Sarah nodded. "Yes, she killed Billy."

Riley reeled. The sense of loss suddenly overwhelmed her,

making her double over. "No, no, no!" she said, vigorously shaking her head, sobs convulsing her body. They weren't hers, though. The screams tearing her skull open were someone else's.

A strong arm went around her, holding her together while she felt like she was being split open. She put her hands to her temples, trying to shake away Gwen's grief. Gwen was in her head.

She focused on the fingers pressing into her shoulder. Liam pulled her closer until her cheek lay on his chest and she focused on his warmth, the smell of his cologne, until she felt the pain dissolve, until Gwen's sobbing became a whisper again.

"Is she okay?"

The voices in the room slowly came into focus.

Riley swallowed and gently pushed herself away from Liam, wiping her eyes with her hand.

"I'm so sorry," she said.

Liam dropped his arm from around her. "It was her again, wasn't it?"

So he believed her. The realisation came with a wave of relief. She nodded and bit her lip.

His eyes studied her, concern written all over his face.

"It was who?" Sarah's voice trembled.

Riley turned to her. The blood had drained from the old woman's face.

"It was her, wasn't it?" She held her hands to her chest.

Riley and Liam said nothing. They didn't need to.

"Gwen?" Sarah whispered.

Riley nodded, and Sarah's eyes filled with tears.

"She loved Billy," Riley whispered. Tears ran unrestrained

down her face again.

"Yes. Yes, she did," Sarah said softly.

"She thinks Jake killed him."

"That's what she told herself. It was easier…" Sarah's voice trailed off.

Liar, the voice screamed in her head again. *Liar! Liar! He did it. He did it! He killed Billy! Murderer!* The words flew at her, attacking her from within.

"No, no!" Riley said, her hands at her temples. "She doesn't believe it. How could she have killed her soulmate?"

A look of fear passed from Sarah to Liam.

"Riley…" Liam reached for her and she jumped up.

"I'm not crazy! I didn't do it!" she yelled at them. It was her voice, but not her words. Though she knew it, she couldn't stop it.

"I didn't kill him, I didn't!" she yelled first at Sarah and then at Liam.

Sarah's hand flew to her mouth in horror. "Gwen?"

"Riley!" Liam was beside her, his hands on her shoulders again. "Riley, it's okay." He tried to tug her back down to the seat beside him, his hold on her strong.

"It's not me," Riley said between sobs.

Liam pulled her against his chest again, hugging her tight, and it helped. Gwen's grip lessened when he held her.

"It's her. It's Gwen. She doesn't believe you," Riley cried into his chest.

"Riley, we should leave."

"No!" both Riley and Sarah cried out at the same time.

"Of course she doesn't believe us," Sarah said. "The story's not over. Gwen created for herself a whole other story; she needs to hear the truth. If she's really with us, she needs to hear the truth."

Riley's breathing slowly returned to normal, the voice in her mind slinking back to the shadows.

"I think we've heard enough." Liam said. "Riley, we need to leave."

"Please, Liam. I'm sorry. I know this is your family, but Sarah's right. Gwen needs to hear the truth; then maybe she'll be at peace."

She was still pressed up against him, her hands on his chest. She could feel every tremor of his body. The awareness of being so close made her self-conscious, and heat flooded her cheeks. She pushed herself away from him again and sat back down on the sofa, noting the wet spots she'd left on his shirt.

He stood there for a moment, unmoving. Then, giving in with a sigh, he plopped down beside her.

She sniffled, and Sarah leaned forward in her chair, passing a box of tissues over to her. Riley gratefully took it, embarrassed.

"I need to hear the rest," she said to both Liam and Sarah. "And I know it sounds crazy … I know *I* sound crazy," – she paused for a moment – "but I really think Gwen needs to hear it."

Sarah nodded. "I agree."

Sarah leaned back in her chair, quiet for a moment before she began the story again. "The rest of the day was a mess. Students were crying, and Gwen could hardly hold herself together."

Both Sarah's and Liam's eyes flicked her way.

"It's still me," she said, grimacing.

Liam held his open palm up on his knee, and she accepted the invitation, slipping her hand into his. As his fingers

347

wrapped around hers, her skin tingled. Gwen retreated further away.

Riley wondered what Sarah was really making of everything.

Sarah continued. "The headmistress, Ms Flemming, snuck one of the older children out the back to where the horses grazed, and had him get help from the garage down the road. The rest of them barricaded themselves in Gwen's classroom while the photographer and his assistant tried to distract the still-drunk Jake. Before long, an entourage of help arrived, a few of the men from the garage, and even Ol' Man Tom himself – Jake's father," she said.

Liam and Riley both nodded.

"The gossip was, it nearly broke Ol' Man Tom's heart to see his eldest acting in such a state, acting such a fool. He tried to get him to leave with him before law enforcement got called in, but it almost came to fisticuffs.

"I remember Ol' Man Tom," Sarah said, her eyes welling up again. "He was a good man. A good businessman and a good father. I had never seen him as much as raise his voice before, so to nearly come to arms with his own flesh and blood…" She shook her head, and Riley passed back the box of tissues.

"Jake was nothing like his father. His heart was dark, though when he wanted to, he could hide it well. He hid it from me when we courted. Otherwise, I would never have married him."

The statement sat heavy over the room. How different would things be if she hadn't?

"What happened to Gwen?" Riley asked quietly.

"Gwen…" Sarah wiped at her eyes and let out a weighty sigh.

"Well, they shooed as many kids home as possible after Jake had been sent on his way by Ol' Man Tom's entourage. Their instructions were to keep the incident on the down-low and for the men to stay with Jake until he sobered up.

"No one had any need to check out the back by the shed, so Gwen was given another day, though she didn't know it at the time. She thought she had attacked Jake, and he had survived. I can only imagine what must have been going through her mind when she arrived home.

"I had no idea of the goings on at school, of course, so my heart jumped into my throat when I saw a convoy of three cars pull up my driveway and then some of Ol' Man Tom's men dragging my husband by his arms up the steps and into the house. All the while, he was swearing and cursing, slurring and spitting, his legs kicking out at this and that, making a real fuss.

"I know how heartless it might sound, but oh, how I had wished he were dead. It felt like God had been playing a cruel trick to have me believe for a moment I was free and then have such a creature dragged back into my house.

"They shut him in the bedroom, and two of the men stood guard, holding the door until he calmed down or passed out. The entire time I didn't know what to do. Once the men left, he would kill me. And if Gwen came home, he'd kill her too.

"He must've passed out, because after a few hours, the men left, and I did what I knew I needed to do." Her eyes swivelled to Riley's. "To protect us both. Gwen and myself." She paused there, clearing her throat.

"I'm an old woman now. I'm surprised to have lived this long, and I certainly don't expect to last much longer. This is where the story turns, and I can tell you, and maybe it will help her move on. But she won't like it. Or I can leave the story here. I've already told you Gwen killed Billy—"

No, no, no, the words whispered through Riley's head, and she squeezed Liam's hand harder.

"—and you already know Jake was accused of murder. I have kept my secrets for so long; it would not be much effort to keep them until I meet my maker."

"Please," Riley said, "We want to hear the rest." She turned to Liam, hoping for his affirmation.

He frowned, worry lines etched between his brows.

"You already know some of it, don't you," Sarah said directly to Liam.

He nodded. "I think so. Some I learnt yesterday from my father; other bits I can surmise."

Riley studied his face. He had shared nothing else with her on the drive. Maybe she had overstepped. She wasn't family, she reminded herself.

"You can tell us," he said.

Chapter 44 – Sarah

As soon as the men drove away, Sarah hurried to Jake's office. They had offered to stay, and it had taken some insistence on her part to get them to leave. It had been quiet in the bedroom for a while, and they'd all assumed Jake had fallen asleep, a victim to his overindulgence – which, from the smell of him, seemed to have gone on until the morning.

The men, Harry and Albert, left reluctantly, their features painted with concern. Perhaps they knew how violent Jake was. Perhaps rumours travelled of how he treated Sarah, evidenced now by the bruise across her jaw. But they were all too loyal to Ol' Tom, and rightly so, to take it any further. What happened behind closed doors wasn't their business. So they left.

Sarah locked the door to his office from the inside and sought the rifle from where she'd left it on his desk. It was still loaded from the previous night.

Could she? If it came down to it, could she be the one to pull the trigger? Too many times she'd let him beat her, force himself upon her, and now Gwen was at his mercy too. She couldn't know how he'd react to either of them when he came to. But no more. *No more*.

The rifle shook in her arms, and a tear rolled down her cheek, staining the stock where it fell.

It was a precaution, was all. Hopefully enough to scare him – maybe even send him away. The thought sat weakly in her mind. She had never stood up to him before. Could she really trust this time would be different?

She stole a glance at the clock. The men had said many of the kids had been sent home; she wondered if Gwen would be too. She moved closer to the window. Though unable to see the drive from there, she hoped to catch the sound of bike tyres on gravel or something else to indicate Gwen was home. If, of course, she came home after the experience she'd had. Every sound set her nerves on edge. Every movement of a branch outside the window or bird in the brush, every passing vehicle, made her shoulders tense and her hands shake more.

She wanted to pray but couldn't think of what to pray for now. For Gwen to stay away or to come home? For Jake to stay passed out or to wake up? A heavy sense of foreboding filled the air. She'd never thought herself a superstitious person, yet she felt as if she were in the eye of a storm. As if, for everything bad that had already happened, the worst was yet to come.

After a while, the need to relieve herself became too strong. The latrine was not far, and she'd heard no noises coming from the bedroom. Yet. If she took the gun, she reasoned, she'd be fine. Depending upon how much he'd drunk, he might be out until the following morning. She crept to the door and had to juggle the gun in her arms to unlock it. She paused for a second, trying to quieten her breathing, all her senses on wide alert for any sign of sound or movement. The house was silent.

She crept to the bathroom where a separate room with a toilet had been added on.

After relieving herself, Sarah slowly crept back into the hallway, wincing every time a floorboard creaked under foot. She held the gun in two shaky hands, wondering if she'd ever be able to work the thing, for all her shaking, if the time came. Her blood turned cold when she heard the tentative unlocking of the front door from outside.

Oh God, it was Gwen. She should have stayed away, found friends to stay with. Even as she thought it, Sarah knew how ridiculous it sounded. This was where all her belongings were. Jake, by inheritance, was a founding father to the community. No one would believe badly of him, or admit to it, at least.

Sarah didn't realise she had the gun pointed at the door until it cautiously opened, and she saw the stricken face of Gwen.

Gwen's hand instantly flew to her mouth despite a shrill scream escaping.

"Shh!" Sarah tried to put her finger to her lip and then realised too late the direction of the gun. She quickly turned it sideways and then carefully laid it on the ground in front of her so she could gesture with her hands. Palms up, she mouthed, "Stay where you are," then pointed towards the main bedroom, hoping Gwen would understand what she was silently indicating. Gwen clasped her hand tighter over her mouth and stood frozen on the spot.

A groan came from the bedroom. Then a cuss. Sarah's heart sped up so much it pulsed in her throat. She retrieved the rifle, pulled back the cocking piece, and cushioned the butt up against her shoulder. Calming her breathing and the shaking in her hands was impossible with her mind threatening to race ahead in panic.

Sarah tried mouthing the word "Leave" to Gwen, but she was frozen.

Heavy footsteps moved closer to the bedroom door. The door so close to Gwen.

"Leave," she tried whispering again. Billy had hurt Jake's pride something terrible, and if he had allowed himself to show his dark side in front of others in order to harass Gwen, she dared not think what he might do with her in his own home.

The bedroom door was thrown open. It was not her husband who stumbled through, it was a monster.

Sarah didn't think she'd ever seen him so dishevelled. He wore the same clothes from the night before, bloodied and dirty. His normally slicked hair hung greasy across his forehead, his nose swollen, broken maybe, and his face all shades of colours. He noticed Gwen almost right away.

"Bitch," he half shouted and spat on seeing her. Lunging towards her, he went to grab her by the front of her shirt or her throat, Sarah didn't know. She reacted almost simultaneously.

"No!" Sarah yelled, "Leave her alone!" She pointed the gun and pulled the trigger, knowing too late she had closed her eyes. Another high-pitched scream from Gwen and swearing from Jake meant she'd missed her mark. Oh God, Oh God.

Jake had Gwen by the front of her shirt. He pulled her properly into the hallway, slamming the front door closed with his other hand, and then pushed her hard against the wall. Gwen's head hit against it with a sickening blow. He turned to Sarah, shock as visible on his face as anger and fear.

"You worthless, little whore," he yelled at her. He released Gwen, who slumped to the ground, and hobbled down the hall towards her.

She should run, her mind told her. The gun was worthless without more ammo, and that was in the office. Her legs wouldn't cooperate.

Behind Jake, Gwen moaned, her hand on the back of her head. She pulled her fingers away, shock painting her features as her hand came away red. She looked up then, making eye contact with Sarah, and staggered to her feet.

"Run!" Sarah screamed. "Get help!"

Gwen's mouth fell open. She did nothing for a moment, and then, to Sarah's own surprise, Gwen ran at Jake from behind. As slight as she was, catching him off guard in the state he was in sent him sprawling onto his hands and knees, almost in arm's distance of Sarah's own foot.

Jake twisted around, grabbing Gwen by the calf and, and yanked until she fell backwards, then he pulled himself on top of her, swearing and yelling, trying to hold on to her wildly flailing arms as she did her best to strike at him.

Without thinking, Sarah rushed at Jake, his back now towards her, and brought the butt of the rifle up high before using all her strength to slam it into his lower back.

Jake cried out and gave a moan. His legs gave out under him, yet he still held onto Gwen's arms as she struggled to untangle herself from him.

"Get off her," Sarah screamed, raising the rifle up high again, this time bringing it down hard on the back of his head. A nauseating crack, and his body went limp. His arms gave out, and Gwen screamed, caught beneath his body.

Gwen twisted and struggled to push him off her, screaming and crying all the time. For a moment, Sarah couldn't move. She stared down at the limp thing pinning Gwen to the ground. The monster. Her husband.

Shaking herself from her trance, she grabbed Gwen's arms and attempted to pull her out from under him. Nothing. Next, she tried rolling Jake off her, and his body fell onto his back. His eyes were closed. Blood pooled under him, making a small puddle on the floorboards.

"Is he dead?" Gwen asked, sitting on the floor, her arms wrapped around her middle, eyes wide.

"I don't know," Sarah whispered back. She focused in on his chest, watching for any sign of him breathing. It was too hard to tell.

He was unmoving, however, and there was more blood than Sarah had ever seen. She picked up the discarded rifle and gave him a poke. Nothing.

Oh, God. She had done it. Finally done what she'd always feared he would do to her.

Ended his life.

Chapter 45 – Gwen

"'May she wake in torment!' he cried with frightful
vehemence, stamping his foot and groaning in a
sudden paroxysm of ungovernable passion. 'Why,
she's a liar to the end! Where is she? Not
there—not in heaven—not perished—where? Oh!
you said you cared nothing for my sufferings! And
I pray one prayer—I repeat it till my tongue
stiffens—may you not rest as long as I am living!'"
- Wuthering Heights

"Help me," the voice said. Stricken, Gwen heard the words. They floated through her mind without fully taking root, and she continued staring at the man on the floor. The blood filled and followed the space between two floorboards.

"Gwen!" the voice said, sterner this time. "Gwen!"

Gwen's eyes seemed to move of their own accord now to the space where the voice had come. Sarah stood, the rifle still in her hands, eyes wide, face drawn. She threw the gun away from her. Its echo resounded around them, making Gwen jump.

"We need to move him," Sarah said.

Gwen's jaw dropped. She couldn't touch him, not now, not ever.

"Gwen," Sarah said, stepping closer. "We need to do something. Help me, or we'll both get life for this."

Gwen felt the words like a slap.

"Life?"

"We killed him," Sarah choked out. "Two women against one man, by simple virtue of who he is… I'm not swapping one prison for another," she said.

"No," Gwen said, shaking her head. "They saw him today, they all know what a drunk he is, a violent, horrible drunk—"

"Would you risk it?" Sarah challenged. "Would you risk your life on it?"

Gwen tried to clear her mind. Think, she told herself. She hadn't actually done anything wrong. Sure, she'd thought she'd killed him, but she hadn't. In the end, it was Sarah. She was in the clear. Oh, God. She couldn't do that. Sarah, who was so willing to cover for her when the roles were reversed.

"What do we do?" Gwen said.

"Help me." Sarah turned from the mess to the door.

Gwen had never seen her take charge in such a way. It made her uncomfortable. Who was this person?

"We'll put him in the pickup. Take him somewhere. When it's dark." She paced, wringing her hands in front of her dress. "We'll put him back in his office for the moment. Out of sight until tonight."

Gwen watched her from her position on the floor. She had shuffled as far away from the body as she could, pressing her back up against the wall, unsure if her legs would cooperate yet if she risked trying to stand. Eyes traveling back to the body, Gwen covered her mouth to keep from vomiting.

She still wasn't convinced they were doing the right thing, but what else could they do? They could rot in prison for this. Or worse. And the image of Aunt Jeanne kept jumping to mind. And the horrible doctor. Oh, Mother would cry, she was sure of it. Crocodile tears, though. Having her daughter in an asylum meant she had an excuse to flutter her eyelashes and woe-is-me to anyone who would listen. "I always knew," she would say. "I always knew something was wrong with that girl."

She wavered to her feet, and they took an arm each to drag him into the office before closing the door on him. Gwen helped Sarah scrub the blood from the floorboards, listening all the time for any sound from the office, any sound that they had messed up completely and he was still alive. Again.

When darkness fell, Sarah made them wait even longer, and Gwen counted off the tick-tocks of the clock.

Neither of them could eat. Gwen's entire body ached from fear, overwhelm, shock and even grief. Everything rolled into one.

When Sarah had suggested the river, the Willows, Gwen panicked.

No. The river was *her* spot. Hers and Billy's. Jake may have stolen their future, but he could not have their past.

Sarah hadn't understood. She said no one went down there until summer, and she knew the way well, having swum there so often as a young girl. They would take the torch but use it only when they had to. It was so secluded; she was sure they'd be safe.

359

They would let him float, float away with the river's current. He would wash up on someone's farm, but it would take time. In the meantime, they could claim he did a runner and they hadn't seen him since. As long as they kept to their story. The *both* of them.

They followed her plan, though it was not half as easy as Sarah had made it sound.

Every time her eyes fell on Jake, her skin prickled, and nausea shot up to the back of her throat. Touching him was worse, and a few times she had to rest with her head between her knees to stop from fainting. Sarah was stronger.

And he was not so easy to carry. In fact, it took everything. They were both slight in figure, and although Jake was not a large man, he was tall and they struggled with his weight. Where they could, they resorted to dragging him, carving noisy paths in the gravel. Trying to get him onto the pickup's deck was even more of a challenge. For such an emaciated looking figure, it surprised Gwen how strong Sarah really was. And determined.

They did their best to stand him up, but his body was not so pliable, and for a time, it seemed like Sarah was dancing with him as she struggled to get him onto the flatbed. In the end, they did it.

Sarah drove slowly, indeed knowing the way by heart. Gwen prayed the whole way to meet no traffic, particularly anyone who might recognise Jake's pickup. And they were lucky.

Sarah parked the vehicle in the same spot Hugh had all that time ago, and Gwen thought of Billy. What would he think of her if he was ever to find out? Her hands shook, and her legs threatened to give out, and Gwen couldn't tell whether it was because of emotion or exhaustion.

With no energy to carry him even if they could, both took an arm, and they dragged him, a jerky stop-and-pull, wheeze-and-puff, exertion. Tears freely rolled down her cheeks. Oh, how she wanted to sleep. To sleep and put the whole of the last few days behind her. The baby kept moving, kicking, as if it knew what she was doing was wrong. But she kept on with it, Sarah's determination fuelling hers. She wanted to believe Sarah; it was a good plan, an airtight plan, one that would grant them their freedom. And in a handful of years, as Sarah put it, the cause of Jake's death would mean nothing, replaced by all the freedoms they'd experienced since.

Maybe freedom for Sarah, although what freedom would she have, really? No family, no job, no income. Gwen was still ruined. She still carried his child.

It took much longer than Gwen had expected. Everything looked so different in the dark, and although the moon was out, little light filtered down through the trees. They could not bring the torch Sarah had wanted to bring. She could not find it, and Gwen had bitten her lip and said nothing on remembering having lost it during her own altercation with Jake. The one where she thought she had killed him.

Instead, they used a smaller one, its light not as bright. Taking turns to hold the thing whilst dragging a body was a feat in itself. At times, they would shine it ahead to get a bearing of their surroundings before turning it off, pocketing it, and making a slow struggle in the direction they remembered.

Eventually they arrived at their destination. The naked trees were shadowy with spindly fingers reaching towards them from across the bank. The small reflection of light from the moon made the water appear darker, threatening.

They stopped for a while, both sitting on the stones, catching their breath. They would have to go into the water with him, and all Gwen could think was, should they ask permission of the Taniwha first? How would it feel to have such a gift given to it? Would it protect them? Would Jake be welcomed as a fitting sacrifice or would the Taniwha be insulted? Gwen remembered the story Hugh told of Henry Walken who had drowned, and she looked across at Sarah, hoping to catch a sense of what she was thinking on her face. But only shadows resided there.

They sat for some time before Sarah spoke.

"Ready?" she asked.

It dawned on Gwen how she had always seen Sarah as a weak victim. A mouse of a person while she, Gwen, was stronger. Now, there was no doubting who was the stronger of the two of them. Gwen's head struggled to focus. Her body ached all over and something in her, buried deep, seemed to be slowly rising to the surface, threatening any moment to extinguish her. It came with the sensation that when – not if – she broke, the damage would be irreparable.

Sarah stood. With a firmness in her voice, she said, "We have to do it now, before the sun comes up."

And it surprised Gwen to realise a new day was almost upon them.

Sarah aimed the torch at the water before them. Black. Empty.

Using the last of their reserves, Gwen and Sarah took an arm each, and digging their feet into the gravel for traction, they pulled Jake towards the water.

The cold seeped through her shoes and the bottom of her

dress. Her skin prickled, more from fear than the chill. What beasts lurked in the murky darkness?

Taniwha, Taniwha, please don't eat me, Gwen thought.

Her feet kept slipping in the water, and every step felt herculean.

"A bit further," Sarah said, her voice choking under what Gwen thought was exertion rather than emotion.

They were both grunting now as they pulled him through the water. The river was up to Gwen's knees, and her skirt kept wrapping around her legs, making her think of eels. But of course eels would be there too. Somewhere. Maybe watching from against the bank.

Taking another step backwards, she thought she would fall, as the ground seemed to slip off a little. She caught her balance at the last moment, wondering what would happen if she were to fall. What would happen if the current increased, and she were to float away? She couldn't swim. Would Sarah come after her? This other side of Sarah, steely, cold, made Gwen suspect she wouldn't.

Finally, teeth chattering with cold, goosebumps tattooing her skin, and exhaustion making her legs nearly buckle, she could no longer move. Sarah indicated they could stop. The water was barely over Gwen's knees, but he was too heavy, his body not yet floating. Gwen suspected he would. Animals did, bloated and deformed. Jake would too. The thought made her nauseous again, and she swallowed hard.

It didn't matter. If he was found, it wouldn't be immediately. She was sure of it. It was not the time of year for swimming, and the current would move him. And the secret would stay with them.

After letting go of Jake's arm, she surreptitiously wiped her hands on her shirt.

They had done it, they really had.

As she stepped around him, she thought she felt his hand brush against her leg. Squealing, she jumped and ran the last few paces out of the water before collapsing on the shore, rocks under her hands and knees. Sobbing and heaving. Gwen didn't even care anymore. Jake had been a monster, but was she any better? She closed her eyes, not even caring for the vomit that had caught in her hair.

So little had been said between them this whole time, so it surprised Gwen to hear Sarah start rambling. Panic seemed to build by the increase of pitch in her voice.

"We need to leave," she said. "I've filled his pockets with rocks. If he's found, it'll look like he wanted this, but we need to leave. Now. Fast. And we need to cover our tracks. We can kick around the gravel as we make our way back, try to disguise any footprints."

Sarah bent down and helped Gwen to her feet. Her whole body shook. Her water-logged skirt tried pulling her to the ground. With her entire body pleading to give out, she found her feet, anyway. The plan was to keep moving; there would be time enough to sleep back home.

Gwen felt a movement in her belly and stroked it.

Sarah picked up the torch, turning it back to the track they had come down. Gwen stifled the impetus to take one more glance behind her. In her mind, she thought she'd see pale white fingers stretching towards her from the inky black water, and she covered her mouth to stop from vomiting again.

He's yours now, Taniwha, she thought, as she made the painstaking trip back to the pickup.

The murdered do haunt their murderers, she thought, and wrapped her arms around her tight against the cruelness of the night.

Chapter 46 – Riley

I t was a quiet drive home. Riley didn't know what to say.
She was exhausted. Liam must have felt the same way.
It had been a lot to take in, and a lot had happened.

Sarah had followed them to the door. It amazed Riley how
smoothly she moved, how youthful she appeared for her age,
especially considering all she had been through. And it was
for that reason Riley found she could hardly believe what
Sarah had said. If it was true, then both Gwen and Sarah
were killers of a sort, and yet she couldn't condemn either of
them for their tragic situations.

"You look like him, you know," Sarah repeated to Liam as
they were leaving. "Except your eyes."

And Riley had stolen another look at Liam's face and the
crystalline green of his irises.

She realised then why the colour of Liam's eyes had seemed
so familiar. Gwen's reflection from the mirror at the pub
flashed before her. Liam had inherited Gwen's eyes.

They said their thank yous and goodbyes, and Riley had
waited a second more, expecting Sarah to say something else,
or to embrace for maybe the one and only time, her great
nephew, or was it grandson? Instead, she closed the door,

stepping back into her solitude.

They had walked to the car in silence.

The quiet drive gave Riley time to think over all they'd been told. The story had been more horrifying than she had imagined, and part of her felt exhausted from experiencing so many emotions in one day.

As they got closer to Riccarston, Riley broke the silence.

"How much did you know?" she asked, and Liam's jaw clench slightly.

"Some. Not all. I was told whispers as a child, and mostly from Grandma Peggy. She and my father never really got along. She said he reminded her too much of her brother-in-law. My grandma was opinionated. She liked you or she didn't. She liked my mother. She liked me and my sister, but Dad… they always had a kind of tension between them. She once told me my great uncle was a murderer who had killed a local farmer, and the family had it covered up. Reputations were everything back then." The corners of his mouth turn down in distaste. "Not much has changed."

"Only he hadn't really killed anyone," Riley said.

"No, I guess he didn't."

Sarah had shared the rest of the story without emotion, just a factual retelling, and Riley felt sorry for her. She had won her freedom, yet at what cost? A long life. But a long life alone. Other than those at Rosewood, she had no one.

Sarah had sent Gwen back to work the next day. As tired and exhausted as they both were, having gotten home in the early hours of the morning, Sarah had insisted they keep up appearances. Sarah, Riley learnt, was calculating in a way she hadn't expected from reading Gwen's diary entries. Sarah had been under no illusion Jake's body would surface in time.

For the moment, they needed to distance themselves from him, and part of that was in acting normal.

From here details were brief with only so much she could glean from Gwen, who slipped in and out of lucidity once the boys found the body.

Gwen had been exhausted. She started her workday by sending a couple of boys out to collect kindling and wood for their classroom wood burner.

Before long, shouts interrupted the morning song, and the boys came screaming into the room, bringing the head-mistress out of her classroom to see the goings on.

They had found a body.

The rest Sarah had picked up from the local bobby and his entourage who showed at her house later that morning.

Billy's body was found, already a day or so old, around the side of the shed. His bike was discovered later, half hidden in the long grass by the horse paddock, unnoticed until now. With Jake's outburst and the torch found near the scene, it was easy to track back to the house.

The children were sent home, and Gwen on finding out who it was had fainted away. She was delivered home by the headmistress herself.

Gwen drifted in and out of consciousness for the best part of five days. Breaking her silence now and then to sob, but little else. She spent most of her time in her room. Broken.

Hugh and Peggy had come around, Hugh helping with the manhunt to find Jake, as Sarah had said he'd run away not long after the incident at school. Peggy had stayed with Sarah then. Neither had much to do with each other, though were bonded now by Gwen. They each took turns bedside. Peggy confided she had let it slip that Gwen was pregnant, and

Billy had heard. Sarah shared Billy's altercation with Jake. For Peggy, it was easy. Having never liked her brother-in-law, it was easy to believe he had sought revenge on Billy for humiliating and threatening him. Only Gwen and Sarah knew the truth.

Peggy shared how devastated Billy had been on learning Gwen was pregnant, and how furious she herself had been in finding out Billy was not the father. But Billy had promised to do the right thing by Gwen, and he had left their house in a state Peggy had never seen him in. It hadn't surprised her at all that he'd gone right to Jake to have it out with him. What did shock her was how he hadn't killed him on the spot.

Peggy and Sarah agreed Billy must have gone to the school to see Gwen, to tell her he knew, to make things right. Peggy believed Jake must have followed him there, or else gone to have it out with Gwen himself. No doubt existed in Peggy's mind that Jake had killed Billy, and Sarah had just as easily thrown her husband under the bus.

Gwen, the entire time, said nothing.

A local farmer found Jake's body two weeks later, caught amongst some tree debris along a bank, while searching for a missing member of his livestock.

It took even longer for the coroner's report to rule: he likely had drunk himself stupid near the bank somewhere, and with the heavy rainfall they'd had over the previous week, ended up in the river as the water rose. The river weaved throughout Te Tapu. His place of entry was never clearly determined. Rocks were found in his pockets, though not enough to point to suicide. Rumours got out anyway.

Hugh and Ol' Man Tom had been beside themselves. The town grieved for them rather than with them and did all they could to erase the incident from the town's history. Jake was not spoken of, and Sarah was left on her own. Though Ol' Tom and Peggy and Hugh had always treated her well, the rest of the community mistrusted her. For many, she was a reminder of the blight on their founder's lineage and legacy.

Gwen never recovered and never went back to teaching. Instead, Sarah took care of her best as she could, feeling she owed it to her. Peggy helped where she could too. Forging letters home when it was called for, shielding her the best they could from gossip and keeping her hidden from judgement as her belly continued to grow. Arrangements were eventually made by Peggy to visit some distant relatives down south. Gwen and Sarah were to go with her.

They were gone many months, with Hugh being the only one in Te Tapu to know the truth. Letters were sent back to Te Tapu announcing Peggy's surprise pregnancy and how she had been too sick to travel back. When they came back Peggy had a bouncing baby boy, a child she never really took to. Gwen returned looking even more emaciated than before. Her unseeing eyes were shadowed black, the bones of her cheeks protruding. Sarah never returned, having chosen to break ties and start fresh where she was.

After no more than a week of being back, and having been relocated to Peggy's and Hugh's, Gwen hanged herself.

Riley had cried when Sarah told her. Gwen felt a part of her. She'd expected Gwen's voice to be back, but all had remained silent. Maybe she had accepted it, Riley thought. Maybe hearing the complete story aloud had brought her peace.

"Do you think your dad knows Jake was his real father?" Riley asked.

Liam's eyebrows came together. He glanced at her then, as

if trying to read her mind, before turning his eyes back to the road.

"I think he does," he said. "And I think he knows Gwen was his mother. Although for how long he's known, I'm not sure."

"What do we do now?" Riley asked. The story hadn't been as cathartic as she had hoped. She still felt like a piece was missing.

"What do you mean?" Liam asked, pulling into her driveway.

"I mean, do we tell people? Do we tell Victoria, explain why it's important for people to know the truth—"

"Is it though?" Liam asked, cutting her off. He killed the engine and turned towards her in his seat.

Riley's heart fluttered. Maybe it was just that she felt she knew him better, but something about him looking at her so intensely disarmed her in a way she didn't completely hate any more.

"Think about it," Liam said. "We can tell everyone the actual history of my family, but all it does is hurt those living. My dad. Sarah. You."

"You, too," Riley said understanding what a horrible situation it would be to put Liam in. He'd be badmouthing his own family.

"You saw yourself how protective people are of bad things being said about my family. We tell them and we're just adding to it. More scandal, more gossip. And people want to believe what they want to believe. Some won't care and others will be furious that we're criticising the forefathers of Te Tapu.

"I'm sorry," Riley said. She got it. She did. Yet it seemed so unfair. Billy and Gwen had been real living people. For them to be pushed aside by history so brutally – it just felt wrong to her.

Liam reached over and gently put his hand on her knee, giving it a quick squeeze. Riley's breath caught in her throat.

"You know everything now," he said, offering a gentle smile and taking his hand back. "Now you know what you're getting into if you decide to stay."

"Why wouldn't I stay?" she asked.

A hint of pink flushed his cheeks. He raised an eyebrow and gestured out the window.

Justin was sitting on her doorstep. Riley's jaw dropped. He must have parked on the road and she hadn't noticed his car. Liam had blocked the view to her doorstep.

"Do you want me to stay?" he asked.

Closing her gaping mouth, Riley quickly found her senses. "No. No, I'll be fine," she said, noticing the hint of disappointment on Liam's face as she opened the car door and threw her bag over her shoulder. Her heart tripped, and butterflies swarmed in her stomach.

"Thank you," she said, keeping her eyes locked on Liam's for a moment, not wanting to say goodbye. In her periphery, in the side window behind Liam, she saw Justin pace.

"We'll talk again tomorrow," he said.

A giddiness welled up to replace her annoyance at seeing Justin. *Tomorrow.*

"Are you sure you don't want me to stay?"

She shook her head and closed the door, watching while Liam backed out the driveway and disappeared down the road. Then she turned to Justin. Saying nothing, she fumbled for her keys in her bag and then walked to the door.

"Riles?" he said, sounding confused by her nonreaction to

him.

"You can come in if you want," she said in greeting, unlocking the door and swinging it open.

Justin hesitated.

He wasn't the worst guy, Riley reminded herself. He cheated on her, yes, and could be a bit of an ass, but he was no Jake. *No Liam either.* The thought rose unbidden and made her blush.

She could give him a moment or two for closure if he needed it.

Justin shifted nervously from foot to foot. "I think I'm fine here, thanks."

Riley stood in the doorway facing him on the porch.

"Who was that, Riles?" he asked, and Riley was sure she detected a hint of jealously.

"His name is Liam O'Regan," she said. "A colleague." Not that she should need to clarify.

Justin stiffened and then shook it off. "I think we can still work this out."

Riley sat with it for a moment, surprised by how little she felt towards him right now. No anger. No animosity. And definitely no love. Whatever they'd had between them, for her at least, it was over.

She pulled the sleeve up on her jacket where she wore her bracelet and undid the clasp. *Whatever our souls are made of, yours and mine are the same.* And she held it out to Justin, who opened his hand before he realised what was happening. She dropped it into his palm and watched as a slew of emotions whipped across his face.

Their souls were not the same. As much as she might want that type of love, it was not, nor would it ever be, with Justin.

373

"It's over," she said, catching herself before she apologised. She wasn't sorry, not really.

His shoulders slumped, and she closed the door, slower than she should have, expecting him to argue or protest or *something*. But when the door latch clicked and no argument came from him, she knew he knew it too. Riley waited a few seconds before moving to the window next to the door. All she saw was his back as he walked away, and somehow she felt lighter than she had in ages.

Chapter 47 – Riley

A few days had passed since Riley and Liam had dug up the O'Regan family history.

True to his word, Liam had sought her out the next day; he had an idea to float past her. They met at the local tavern after school, much to the amusement of Katrina, who found excuses to check on them more than was needed, arching her eyebrow in Riley's direction when she thought Liam wasn't looking.

Liam's idea surprised Riley, but she loved it completely. They had to get Victoria's permission, of course, being on school property, but Liam was convinced if anyone would understand, she would.

And when they checked with her, she did. Somewhat, at least. Their names had mostly been lost to history, so Victoria had surmised it would be okay, particularly as few people ventured near the caretaker's shed. They had to promise to keep it a secret from Arthur though.

They chose sunset to meet at school. Riley stuck around after work, cleaning up her classroom and promising Brittany and Rob that she and Liam would meet them at the pub a little later.

The school always felt strange without people around. Eerie and charged with a different sort of energy than when the kids were there.

Though she hadn't heard Gwen's voice since talking to Sarah, Riley had tested it, anyway. Standing at her whiteboard, she picked up a marker.

The back of her neck prickled, like eyes were on her again, and she gave her shoulders a jiggle to dislodge the feeling.

Pressing the marker tip to the whiteboard, she let her hand flow across the surface.

Gwen?

She felt a sense of the ridiculous in doing so, but she took a step back and waited. She wasn't sure what she was expecting. Words to magically appear, maybe?

Footsteps coming towards her room broke the spell. Riley lunged for her eraser and swiped it across the whiteboard. Evidence gone.

"Are you ready?" a voice said behind her.

She spun around to face Liam standing in her doorway.

He leaned against the doorway. He'd been home, cleaned up, and she could smell the gentle mix of body wash and aftershave. A fluttering grew in her belly, and she willed herself to play it cool.

A smile played on his lips as his eyes locked on her.

Do not faint, she told herself, and nodded her head in answer to his question.

She grabbed Gwen's journal from her desk and followed him outside.

The sun was dipping behind the hills, spreading vibrant magentas and pinks across the sky. Riley clasped the journal to her chest and followed Liam around the back of the building to the caretaker's shed.

He walked slightly ahead of her, and she kept her eyes pinned to his back, noting the broadness of his shoulders and the narrowness of his waist and recalling what it felt like to be held by him at Sarah's.

Remembering why they were there, Riley felt a lump grow in her throat.

Liam stopped in front of the shed and Riley went and stood beside him. It was horrible to think this was the spot that in a way took three lives.

"So," Liam said. "What do you think?"

He stepped aside and let her see the wooden carving he had fixed to the side of the shed. He had told her he was going to make it himself, an apology in part from the O'Regans.

Riley moved closer and traced the smooth wood and its lines with her fingertips.

It was a round plaque, a heart in the centre, a crown on top with two hands on either side of the heart, like the traditional Irish Claddagh ring. Inside the heart were inscribed the names Billy MacKenzie and Gwen Davies, to honour them so their names wouldn't be completely forgotten.

Liam had told her the Claddagh ring design was in honour of Billy's heritage, and represented love, loyalty and friendship.

"It's beautiful," Riley said, moved to tears.

Liam gave a small smile and Riley could tell he was proud. She stepped back to stand beside him again.

"Did you want to say anything?" he asked her gently.

Oh, she did, but finding the words was so hard. She wanted to apologise for all the horrible things the two of them endured. She wanted to tell Gwen it hadn't been her fault, not really. She suspected Billy already knew. She had not heard Gwen's voice since Sarah's, and she desperately wanted to believe she was finally at peace. But Riley wanted even more than that. She wanted to wish them a whole afterlife together, since this life had been taken from them.

Instead, she opened Gwen's journal.

She turned to the page after Gwen and Billy had been to the Willows waterhole, when she first knew she whole-heartedly loved him, and read aloud the Wuthering Heights quote Gwen had written there:

"If all else perished and he remained, I should still continue to be; and if all else remained and he were annihilated, the universe would turn to a mighty stranger."

"But you can be together now, Gwen," Riley whispered, her voice choking up. Holding her book in one hand, she used the other to wipe a tear from her cheek. "He's waiting for you. I know he is." And she felt it. Really and truly, just as Liam put his arm gently around her shoulders, pulling her close and gently brushing the top of her head with his lips.

Billy MacKenzie and Gwen Davies. The whole truth had been heard now. Not by everyone, but by her and Liam, at least. And as long as she was alive, she'd make sure their names weren't forgotten.

They spent a moment, Riley and Liam, standing there as the heavens flamed into marmalade skies, then gradually faded as dusk closed in.

Liam kept his arm light around her shoulders and Riley let herself, for a moment, rest her cheek against his shoulder.

"Shall we go?" he finally asked

She nodded, and they turned to leave. Liam dropped his arm from her shoulder, and she instantly felt the loss until her hand was enclosed in his.

As they neared the car park, Riley stopped, drawing Liam to a halt too. She turned, taking one last look towards the shed. Liam followed her line of sight before turning back to her, eyebrows lifted.

He didn't see them, but she did.

The young man and woman standing hand in hand, looking at the plaque. Riley could see the woman's dress, cinched at the waist and flaring slightly at the bottom, her shoulder-length blonde hair with gentle waves, she held the man's hand, her other arm across her body gripping the same arm as if afraid to lose him. The man stood more relaxed. Long pants with suspenders, and a long-sleeved shirt rolled to his elbows, just as she'd seen him the very first day. He turned slightly, making eye contact with Riley.

With a slight tilt of the brim of his hat in acknowledgement and a whisper of a smile, he turned back to face the plaque.

Thank you. The words hung for a moment, disappearing as the sun slipped fully from sight and day became night.

Rest easy, Riley thought, before turning back to Liam to give his hand a squeeze.

THE END

Free eBook!

Thank you for reading *Unspoken Truths*. I hope you have enjoyed it.

If you would like to be updated about my other books, including a future one set in Te Tapu where Natalie and Victoria get to tell their stories, please consider joining my mailing list.

I regularly send newsletters with details on new releases, special offers and other writing news. And if you sign up to the mailing list, I'll send you a copy of my short story collection, *Between the Shadows*, for **free!**

Sign up at https://www.jobuer.com/

Enjoy this book? You can make a big difference and keep this writer writing!

Reviews are an authors' secret weapon.

Honest reviews of my books help bring them to the attention of other readers and allow me to promote them to a bigger audience. In turn, this opens many more doors for me to keep writing.

If you've enjoyed this book, I would be super grateful if you could share the love and spend a couple of minutes leaving a

review. It can be as short as you like on whatever platforms you prefer, including Goodreads.
Thank you so much!

Acknowledgements

This book was a true passion project. I was first inspired to write it back in 2015 when the image of a woman killing a man with an axe first popped into my mind. Yes, my imagination can be very dark at times. The story continued to grow and evolve over the years. The characters seemed so alive that even now I struggle to let them go, to remind myself, they are not real.

Throughout *Unspoken Truths* I have had secondary characters nagging me to write their stories. It seems Te Tapu holds many more secrets waiting to be exposed. Expect to hear from Natalie and Victoria in the future as they reveal more long unspoken truths. Make sure to follow me on social media or join my newsletter at https://www.jobuer.com/for updates on this second book.

As always, this book would never have been written without the amazing cheerleaders I have in my life:

My husband, Marty, and our family of cats, who not only keep me sane during the many hours that go into writing a book, but also put up with much less attention than they deserve when I am doing so.

My parents, Ian and Nicky, who love to brag that their daughter is an author, and share my books with everyone willing to listen.

Hannah, the best editor an author could have. Not only does she do an amazing job with helping to bring my writing to the next level, encouraging me on and sharing scenes she loves, she also goes above and beyond to fit me in when deadlines need to be tweaked.

My friends, family and colleagues, newsletter subscribers and social media followers, all those who keep me accountable to deadlines, encourage me on the tough days, and give my writing a purpose beyond myself.

My amazing ARC team who so willingly read my books, share their thoughts, and find those niggly mistakes that creep in despite numerous edits.

To all of you: thank you, thank you, thank you!

xxx

Jo

About the Author

Jo Buer is a gothic and ghost fiction writer living in New Zealand. She is a sucker for the supernatural, time travel and all things woo-woo. From an early age she came to realise that sometimes truth *is* stranger than fiction, and what we think we know isn't always true.

Jo lives in an ordinary house in an ordinary town with her muggle hubby, feline familiars, Atlas, Gaia and Zeus, and ghost-kitties, Loki, Rhea and Odin. When not doting on her cats, devouring self-help books or gorging on chocolate, she writes slightly dark, sometimes scary, often ghostly stories with a smattering of romance.

You can connect with me on:

- https://www.jobuer.com
- https://www.facebook.com/jobuerauthor
- https://www.instagram.com/jobuerauthor

Also by Jo Buer

Rest Easy Resort: A Novel
A cursed resort and unsettled ghosts will put one relationship to the ultimate test.

Hannah O'Connor wants nothing more than to enjoy her honeymoon at the newly revived Rest Easy Resort with her true-love by her side. But when the past and present become intertwined and an awakened curse threatens those around her, Hannah must decide whether her marriage is worth the cost to human life.

How much will Hannah sacrifice for the one she loves?

Rest Easy Resort **is the gripping debut novel of Jo Buer. If you like Barbara Erskine, Susanna Kearsley, and Shani Struthers, then you'll love this haunting, gothic love story.**

Buy it here: https://www.jobuer.com/or from your favourite retailer.

Voices: A Collection of Short Stories

Poignant, haunting and deliciously dark. Grab a blanket, hot drink, and maybe some tissues, and settle in for five short stories by gothic suspense author Jo Buer, including:

VOICES

Everything that dies comes back... someday.

While reconnecting with old friends, a mysterious voice and chilling song force a woman to confront her tragic past.

DEWEY DECIMALS

Tick, tick, tick. The red hand tiptoes round the face. Six o'clock. Time to begin.

A man with sinister intentions watches a librarian go about her tasks.

RABBIT SKIN

If you can't see them, then they can't see you...

A young girl tries to make sense of her grandmother's death, and her grandpa's actions thereafter.

THE WALNUT TREE

Something nags at you. Something snarls and snaps and nips at your insides, making you pause...

A teenage girl comes home from school to find that something unsettling has changed in her parents' demeanours.

RUATAPU RIVER

The river remembers us as we remember it: the canoeing, the swimming, the paddling... It even remembers the drowning.

But how much is memory, and how much is imagination.

And can intuition really precede death?

Buy it here: https://www.jobuer.com/or from your favourite retailer.

Between the Shadows: A Collection of Short Stories
A man waits in the shadows watching his lover with someone else. A young girl must say goodbye to the only friend she has - a friend no one else can see. A boy writhes in agony in his hospital bed as his sister tries to calm him with a story. A mother must learn to let go of the child she has already lost.

Between the Shadows is an eclectic collection of poignant and haunting tales about grief. If you like stories that fill the senses with ghostly interludes and meditations on life and death, then you'll love this short story collection.

Free to download at https://www.jobuer.com/

CPSIA information can be obtained
at www.ICGtesting.com
Printed in the USA
BVHW031931040921
616081BV00005B/97

9 780473 578497